NOT HIS TYPE
NOW AVAILABLE

Also Available From Genesis Press

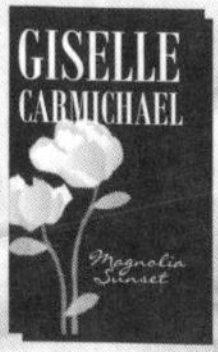

Not His Type — Chamein Canton

Broken — Dar Tomlinson

Giselle Carmichael — Magnolia Sunset

Coming Soon

Truly Inseperable - Wanda Y. Thomas
The Color Line - Lizzette G. Carter
When I'm With You - LaConnie Taylor-Jones
The Mission - Pamela Leigh Starr

GENESIS PRESS MASS MARKET BOOKS ARE DISTRIBUTED BY KENSINGTON PUBLISHING GROUP

ISBN-13: 978-1-58571-254-0
ISBN-10: 1-58571-254-X

GENESIS PRESS
$6.99 U.S.
$9.99 Can

Genesis Press is distributed by Kensington Publishing Corp

PQQ595303
Many Shades of Gray
DYANNE
DAVIS

"You're delicious," he said, biting her nipple softly.

"Do I taste better now?"

"I don't understand what you're asking me?"

"Now that you know all my secrets, do I taste better?" She grinned.

"Let me see," he said and licked her skin, nibbling along the way. "You always did taste good."

Janice flipped him over so that she was on top and began kissing his little bud of a nipple. "You taste good, too," she said softly. "Any secrets you want to divulge? Any ghosts in your closet you want to bring out?"

Simon shivered beneath her touch and for one moment he thought seriously about telling her—until he saw the brown fire in her eyes. And then all he wanted was to lie there and let her make love to him. Her hands were roaming over his body and his naked flesh quivered, readying itself. The ghosts could wait. She was kissing him, teasing little kisses that blazed a fire in his soul. He ran his fingers through her thick mane of hair, fisted his hands and took control of the kiss.

MANY SHADES OF GRAY

DYANNE DAVIS

Genesis Press, Inc.

Indigo Love Stories

An imprint of Genesis Press, Inc.
Publishing Company

Genesis Press, Inc.
P.O. Box 101
Columbus, MS 39703

All characters in this book have no existence outside the imagination of the author and have no relation whatsoever to anyone bearing the same name or names. They are not even distantly inspired by any individual known or unknown to the author and all incidents are pure invention.

ISBN-13: 978-158571-254-0
ISBN-10: 1-58571-254-X
Manufactured in the United States of America

First Edition

Visit us at www.genesis-press.com or call at 1-888-Indigo-1

DEDICATION

This book is dedicated with love to all the wonderful ladies who are part of the Dyanne Davis Fans Yahoo Group. You ladies make me smile and are the reason that I can keep enjoying what I do. Viola, Patsy, Lynda, Kim, Debby, Tracy, Alvena, Nikki, Lisa, Brenda, Mona, Patricia, Linda, Haronica, Joy, Anne Marie, Stephanie, Thelma, Stephanie, Desta, Irene, Tarra, and Abigail.. I want to thank all of you for being so active. And to the rest of you, ,each and every one of you, you're all the best!!!

Namaste

Dyanne

ACKNOWLEDGEMENTS

As always my thanks are given to God who first and foremost deserves my honor and praise for every breath I take.

I thank the readers who wait patiently or impatiently for the next book to come out. Without the readers this journey would not be nearly as joyous. It's because of you, the readers, that writers endure all the trials and tribulations that it takes before a book comes to your local bookstore.

To my sister, Jackqueline Jackson, as always I thank you for just being you. Now if you could just convince yourself to point out the way to the bookstore instead of your usual method of introducing my books to everyone, I would be most appreciative. LOL.

To Evelyn Palfrey, Your speech at RSJ in 04 concerning the dwindling independent bookstores is what inspired this story.

To Genesis Press, I would be remiss in not acknowledging the part you've played in my life. For the good times and the bad times, everything that has happened thus far I believe had to happen.

As always, I have to say Thank You to Sidney Rickman. When I turn in a manuscript, it is your word that I wait with bated breath to hear. When you say, "Well done," that is what carries me through. Thank you so much, Sidney, for all that you always do for me. You go above and beyond the call of duty and I know that.

As always, Bill and Billy are my mainstays in this life. Without them life definitely would not have been the same.

CHAPTER ONE

Okay, I'm not a heroine, I'm a flesh and blood woman and I've made a lot of dumb ass mistakes in my life. So if you're looking for someone to emulate I would suggest that you close this book and find someone else. I am not the one you're looking for.

This is not a pretty little romance where all of the characters will do what you want and you will be left with a 'feel good' feeling. I have no idea how this will play out.

It's my life we're talking about and it's real. Most days it's so damn real that I want to rewrite it. It's ugly and it's brutal but it's me. If you can handle real life then you might just be able to handle what I'm going to write.

If you're still reading, good. You're the one I'm looking for. What I will tell you will be an honest story of my life and I won't pull any punches. I'm not asking you to root for me and I'm definitely not asking for sympathy. If I were the one reading this story and learning of my bitchiness for the first time I would definitely want to slap the hell out of me and fling the book across the room.

But even bitches have a reason for being that way. Trust me. Just don't judge until you have all of the facts.

If you're still with me, I suggest we get started.

Simon laid the page back on Janice's desk and walked up the stairs to see if she was ready. He wondered what the hell her book was going to be about. He knew one thing for certain: She was definitely starting it out differently from any of the others. Another thing he knew: She had left the first page there for him to see. If she had not wanted him to read it she would have closed the door to her study, a signal that she wanted her office to remain private, or she would not have not printed it. But now he'd read it and she had him curious, as always.

Janice gazed in the mirror, surveying her appearance. Everything had to be perfect. She was about to be in the public eye. Again. And no matter how often she was, she always felt butterflies in the pit of her stomach.

As a writer she was used to the attention paid to her but this time would be different. This would be the first time that her relationship with Simon Kohl would be the main focus. It would also open the flood gates to questions regarding her meteoric rise to fame in the last two years. Had she slept her way there? And the answer to that was yes. Well, in a way.

For the past three years she'd been sleeping with the most powerful man in publishing. While he was mostly unknown to writers, agents and editors, the powers that be, the money moguls, knew exactly who Simon Kohl was. He owned more than half the publishing houses in the world and kept his anonymity by allowing those companies to operate as though he didn't exist.

He owned everything from the tree farms where the trees were harvested especially to make the paper for his printing presses to a plastic factory that distributed the tiny holders that the reporters who tried unsuccessfully to catch a glimpse of him used to carry their name badges.

And she was about to be brought full force into his world. There would no longer be the whispered rumors or innuendos. Today they would announce their engagement. After today there wouldn't be one single person left who would believe that she had a smidgen of talent. Though she'd made a name for herself long before Simon, she couldn't deny that it was Simon that had boosted her career. Not for one second could she allow herself to forget that he held the authority to easily take away what he'd given her.

A shiver ran down her back and she frowned slightly, looking at her image in the mirror. Her long hair, soft and curling, framed her honey brown face to perfection. Her deep set brown eyes tilted up a little, giving her a bit of an exotic look. And her five-foot-nine frame gave her a regal bearing. Janice tilted her head to the side, allowing what she knew to be true to seep into her pores and become a part of her armor.

She was a beautiful woman; there was no doubt about it. But she'd given up a lot to get to this point in her life. Her very large and vocal family, including siblings, uncle, aunts and cousins, thought she'd given up her heritage. As they often said, she no longer acted black, whatever the hell that meant.

There had been a time in her life when she'd worn her feelings on her sleeve and accusations such as that had cut deeply. A shiver passed through her as she thought about Tommy Strong. Look what that relationship had gotten her.

"Hey, aren't you ready yet?"

Janice's eyes slid back to the mirror to peer over her shoulder at Simon, who'd just come to stand behind her. Simon was the final proof to the black world that Janice Lace was a sell-out. He was white.

Despite what her family thought she'd not set out deliberately to become engaged to a man outside her race. That had just happened. And why shouldn't it? Simon was an extremely handsome man who'd chased her until she'd allowed him to catch her. He was a well built man in his late thirties, tall enough that she didn't have to resort to wearing flats. Simon swore he was six-three, but she thought he was just a little under. He had the thickest, softest hair she'd ever felt on a man. It always made her think of dark chocolate. His smile never failed to cause a slight hitch in her chest, though she kept that from him. He had deep dimples in each cheek and when his lips were pulled back into a smile, she could just imagine falling into those dimples. As attractive as she found him, it was his eyes that enthralled her.

He had startling gray eyes that could shoot fear into the deepest marrow of her being. Filled with lust, they almost made her believe that the two of them were right for each other. Almost. But it really didn't matter. In spite of her doubts she would stand beside him at the podium when he announced to the world that they would be getting married. And she would smile as though she'd won the top prize. It was, after all, what she'd wanted, what she'd worked her tail off to achieve.

"I'm ready," she answered finally.

"What took you so long in here?"

She turned to face him. "I wanted to look perfect for you."

"You're always perfect. Are you nervous?" He narrowed his eyes and surveyed her coolly. "Are you having second thoughts?"

"No second thoughts." She lowered her gaze. "What would make you think that?"

"The way you looked down just then and the fact that you didn't want to marry me before. It's almost as though you're somehow ashamed of me." He grinned. "That's stupid, though, isn't it?"

"Why would I be ashamed of you? Look at you. You're a handsome man, smart and funny."

"And don't forget rich," he teased. "That's the real reason that you're marrying me."

His words made her wince and she turned away, wanting to withhold the truth from him, even if she couldn't from herself. She had not told him how she felt. What good would it do to tell him that she loved him? She'd given her heart to one man and told him that she loved him. He'd left her knowing how she felt. Janice glanced at Simon. She wouldn't make the same mistake twice. Saying the words would only give him power over her, so she didn't say them. She believed that was part of the reason he stayed interested. She allowed him and the world to believe it was his money she was after. After all, she'd not bothered to talk to him until she'd known exactly who he was.

"Come on, Janice, we both know you're with me for what I can do for you. You're not in love with me."

"Are you in love with me?"

"I want to marry you."

"That wasn't the question. Are you in love with me?"

"I love having pretty things and I like the finality of marriage, knowing that I've closed the deal, so to speak. I don't like what shacking up represents—instability, no commitments. It's just a nice way of having someone available for a ready screw."

He was being deliberately crude. She knew it was because she hadn't admitted to being in love with him. Whenever the subject of love came up, Simon always behaved this way. If Janice didn't know better, she would think he did love her. But she did know better. He didn't love her; he wanted to possess her.

For the most part he did. He controlled her career completely. But apparently that wasn't enough. He'd almost demanded that she say yes to his endless proposals. Sometimes she wondered why it mattered so much to him.

She watched in the mirror as he toyed with the Rolex around his wrist. His jaw was set firmly and his brows furrowed. There was something up with him. What? she wondered.

"I read the beginning of your new book."

She wanted to turn around, to face him, read his thoughts. But she'd play it cool, behave as though what he thought didn't matter. "So what did you think?" she asked finally as she fluffed her hair around her face.

"I noticed you wrote it in first person. Is it going to be autobiographical?"

"I guess it could be." She smiled. "I'm not sure. I just wrote what came out. What do you think of the beginning?"

"I don't like giving my opinion on a book until I've read the entire thing."

"Simon."

"Okay, it's different."

"That was my intention. I'm sick to death of writing stories with an end the reader can predict from the first paragraph. I want to write about characters that are, for lack of a better word, evil and mean. I want them to do stupid things. I want them to be human. I don't want a hero and I don't want a heroine." She tilted her head just a tiny bit and smiled into the mirror. "I want the protagonist to be more like me."

"Am I going to be in it?"

"I didn't say it was going to be a completely true story. It's a work of fiction."

"In that case I'll hold off on my critique. I have a surprise for you." He came closer, turned her around and kissed her.

A flutter ripped her sense of calm and she hesitated before asking, "Where is it?"

"Surprises are not to be just lightly given. There has to be something leading up to it. You'll get it, don't worry."

His gray eyes suddenly looked cold and he moved away from her, giving her the sense that her surprise wasn't going to be pleasant.

"What's up with you?" she asked, feigning a curiosity she didn't truly feel. She'd made her deal with the devil, so to speak, and there was no going back. She'd come into this relationship with her eyes wide open. They each served a purpose for the other.

For Simon, she was exotic arm candy, his entrée into the black world, his way of proving that he was a man of the people. She almost laughed at the thought. He truly thought he was, but he would never be able to buy his way into being black, same as she could never buy her way into being white. They served as passports for each other, allowing each to travel the other's world. At any time they could each cross back over into the world they'd come from.

But for Janice there was no going back. She was in Simon's world for a reason, a reason known only to her. And she'd kept it deeply buried in her heart.

"Is there a chance that you could at least pretend to be happy when we make the announcement?" Simon asked, his voice dripping with sarcasm.

"Sure, I can pretend if you can." She squared off with him. "I don't get it. You're behaving as though you're angry with me and I have done nothing to provoke your anger, so either tell me what's going on or knock it off. I swear, you're worse than a woman having PMS."

"Why do you risk what we have?" Simon said as he sidled up next to her, fingered the double strand of expensive pearls around her throat and frowned. "Sometimes I think you forget who I am and what I can do."

"How can I? You remind me constantly."

"Is that the reason you don't love me?" he asked pointedly.

"What is all this talk of love? What's with you?"

"I'm thinking I'm too old for this charade. I want to be happy. I want a family, I want love."

"You have to love in order to be loved." Janice started to walk away but felt strong hands reach out, grabbing her and holding her in place.

"Let me go," she ordered.

"Or what?"

"Or you're going to wish that you had."

"As you wish," Simon replied, releasing her, smiling at her and shaking his head in wonder. He wished he knew what the hell it was about her cold disdain that had made him fall in love with her, kept him trying to please her, trying to make her love him.

Well, actually, he knew in his heart that she loved him even if she refused to say it. And despite her public persona she proved it in the privacy of their home. No woman touched a man the way she touched him other than in love. He thought about the times in the still of the night when he held her in his arms, caressing her, and she softly shared her dreams, telling him without the actual words that she loved him. When they made love she always kept her eyes open, and for sure he saw her love reflected there.

Now Simon was after two things: He was going to make her tell him that she loved him and he was going to discover why she had thus far been unable to do so. In the next couple of hours the game would begin.

Though in the beginning he hadn't been altogether sure that it was love he felt for Janice, it had angered him that she'd didn't admit to feeling love for him. Maybe that was the reason he'd chased her until she ended up in his bed. At first he'd wondered what would happen if they both cared. Now he wondered what would happen when they both admitted to caring.

One thing for sure, Simon didn't want Janice for an enemy and she sure as hell didn't want him for one. They would settle their differences in the marriage bed. But he wasn't marrying her until they resolved her past. He believed he'd discovered the reason why she went cold when he talked of love, why she substituted fighting for admitting her feelings for him. Well, they'd fought for over three years. It was time to end the war.

He had a test for his soon-to-be fiancée. He demanded one thing and one thing only from her and that was fidelity. Her verbal abuse and disdain he might tolerate as long as it stayed behind closed doors, and so far Janice had played her part well in public, pretending that she adored him when they both knew that wasn't the case. Loved, maybe. That he stood a shot at. Adored? No way in hell would Janice Lace ever adore any man.

At least he was hoping that part was true. He didn't want her giving to any man something that she couldn't or wouldn't give to him. In the past he had tolerated many things from her. But now it would be different. He was marrying her.

"This is supposed to be a happy occasion." He smiled inwardly as she eyed him with disdain. "You're treating me as though I'm the enemy. Anyone watching this display of temper might think it was only my money that you're interested in." He braced himself for her expected answer.

"I have my own money," she sneered.

"Money that you wouldn't have if it weren't for me."

She glared at him and he grinned. He loved getting a real response from Janice, even if it were only one of anger. God, she was beautiful when she was angry. Simon could feel himself growing hard with wanting her. He watched as her brown eyes flashed red fire. Then she suddenly looked toward his crotch and smiled.

"You always manage to get me, don't you?" To Simon's surprise she walked back to him, plastered her body to his, and slid her hand down the length of him, making him groan with need. His chest tightened and his arms went automatically around her, pulling her close. She didn't move away. Instead, she kissed him, sliding her tongue between his lips. He felt her tremble, felt the fire in her and for a moment he thought they would make love. Then she pulled away, eyed him up and down, and grinned.

"Admit it, Simon, you like our relationship just fine the way that it is."

She tossed that wild mane of hair and walked out of her bathroom, leaving him with a hard-on. And the moment faded. She'd been merely teasing him, showing him that regardless of his money, she was in control.

Simon licked his lips. He could buy women and all the sex that he wanted. He could even buy his way into a culture that wasn't his, but that he loved. And he could do that without Janice on his arm. But he didn't want to. He wanted her and God help him if it wasn't love. He wanted her and he wanted a stable family with her. He just had to make sure that her feelings for the man in her past were dead.

He took a deep breath and walked out of the bathroom. Janice wasn't a stupid woman; she wouldn't risk everything.

A little voice whispered into his brain that he should leave well enough alone but he'd never done things the easy way and he wasn't about to start now. No. One thing Simon wasn't was a coward. He allowed the sigh to escape and glanced down at his now semi-soft erection. That woman could make him hard as steel with but a touch and she could also deflate him quicker than a child could release air from a balloon.

What a life we'll have, he thought as he walked out of the bathroom and into his future. He smiled at Janice and she smiled back and again he wondered. Maybe if he said it first. He took her arm. Maybe after they were safely married he'd tell her he loved her. Maybe.

CHAPTER TWO

Janice settled comfortably in her seat, wondering what was up with her new fiancé. Simon was behaving oddly and for some reason that she couldn't put her finger on, something felt wrong with the entire reception.

The service was impeccable, as always, and the food delicious. Why shouldn't it be? They were at one of the most expensive hotels in the world. It was New York's best. Yet there was something amiss and she sure wished she could figure it out. For one thing, Simon had barely taken his eyes off her the entire time. He'd watched her as though looking for some clue. His mention of a surprise came to her mind but she had yet to see it.

"It's showtime."

As the words were whispered into her ear, the soft caress of his warm breath filled her. She looked up at the owner of the words and smiled, for the first time nervous about what she was about to do. "Are you ready?" he asked.

"I am if you are," she replied.

Simon took the podium and Janice pasted her eternal patent smile on her lips and listened, waiting for her cue to join him.

"You've all been invited here today to share in my good fortune. I have proposed to the very beautiful Janice Lace and she has graciously accepted. But what you don't know is that I am also marrying the extremely beautiful Mary Jo Adams."

Janice glared at Simon. What the hell did he think he was doing? She'd never used her Christian name in her bio. Mary Jo Adams didn't exist anymore; in fact, she knew for sure she'd never told Simon her real name.

Simon ignored the look of fire his bride-to-be was shooting his way and laughed at his little joke. "Don't worry." He put his hand up to still the rustling of people, to stop the whispering. "They are one and the same, the famed author and the small town girl."

He grinned, exuding charm, not looking directly at Janice, wondering if she would get up and march out of the room. She might when he spoke his next words, but he had to know.

"In honor of my wife-to-be I've decided to invest a great deal of money in something that is near and dear to her heart: the preservation of the small independently owned African American bookstores."

He turned back to Janice. "Darling, would you join me now?" He waited, hoping his little stunt wouldn't assure he'd have a block of ice in his bed tonight instead of the promise of sweaty hot sex that she'd indicated would be his when she'd earlier run her hand over his erection.

He watched as she rose from the chair. Her legs, long and graceful, sent a shot of adrenaline straight to his crotch, making him hard. He saw her swipe gently at her lips with the soft linen napkin, knowing she was stalling for time. Ah, if only he could be that napkin he thought for a second, and felt another quickening in his groin.

Janice sidled up to Simon and smiled even though her eyes glared at him. He laughed and kissed her right there at the podium, ignoring her rule against overt public displays of affection. Breaking off the kiss, he anchored his arm around her waist and pulled her closer than she wanted to be to him at the moment. When she squirmed, he pulled her still closer and kissed her again. "You're not going anywhere," he whispered.

"I'd now like to ask the representative for AABU, African American Bookstores United, to come up please. On behalf of my bride and myself I would like to donate one million dollars for the purpose of keeping AABU going. Please, everyone put your hands together for Mr. Tommy Strong. Tommy, would you come up here, if you would be so kind?"

He turned to Janice. "Smile pretty," he whispered, and released her in order to clap his hands. He saw the first clink in her armor, the slight tremble of her fingers as she followed suit and began clapping, but as though she'd forgotten how. Waves of anger from her washed over him but this time it didn't give him the high it usually did.

There was something lethal in her look as she eyed the man walking to the podium to receive the check. It was what he'd been waiting for. In the eyes of his bride-to-be he saw hatred for the man and Simon smiled, a genuine smile, ignoring the fact that Janice's anger also included him.

He'd make it up to her; he'd buy her some expensive piece of jewelry or send her newest book straight up to number one. He had the power to do that. Yes, that's what he would do, he thought as he saw Janice's hatred for the man approaching them intensify. He almost wished he hadn't done it. He didn't know if she would be able to pull it off and remain at the podium with him or if she would turn and leave.

Simon shook hands with the man when he approached and presented the check to him. He watched as cold fury washed over the man's face as he stared at Janice, glaring at her openly. Good, Simon thought, he hates her too.

Janice was trembling inside. She walked away from the podium feeling the frown on Simon's face. She didn't give a damn. What the hell was he trying to do and why had he chosen such a public arena to do it in? It was obvious that he'd dug deeper into her past than he had any right to do and she didn't like it.

A second later Simon joined her at the table and when he smiled at her, for the first time in public she didn't smile back. She glared at him.

"Your book will be number one by the end of the week," he whispered into her ear, trailing a finger down her cheek.

"How many times do I have to tell you to keep your hands off my career? If my book makes number one, I want it to be on my own merits. Don't you understand that?" Janice closed her eyes tightly, forcing the tears that had not emerged in over ten years to remain where they were. She hadn't known she still possessed the ability to cry and she sure as hell didn't want to do it now, not in front of Tommy, the man who'd made her shed an ocean of tears.

She fixed her gaze on the podium, wishing she had the power to make the speaker drop dead.

The boy she'd loved with her whole heart, the one to whom she'd given her virginity and her soul, had changed little in the twelve years since she'd seen him. Janice sat a little straighter to observe him as he spoke with the same air of self assurance that he'd always possessed. The same charm spilled as easily from his lips now as it had when he'd told her that he loved her. Lies, all lies, she thought and looked at Simon, feeling an overwhelming dislike for the man she'd just agreed to marry.

Simon tore his gaze away from Janice and peered intently at the man to whom he'd just bequeathed a fortune. He looked at his neat corn-rowed hair with braids that hung down to his waist. He took in the man's chiseled features, saw the expanse of his shoulders, and knew that beneath that Moroccan getup the man possessed muscles that Simon couldn't get, no matter the amount of money he paid his personal trainer.

He listened to the polished voice, to the warmth that spilled from the man, and he watched intently as he turned his attention in their direction and paused boldly in his speech, perusing Janice with the same cold hatred she'd displayed toward him. Then without missing a beat, the man continued with his speech, most of which Simon didn't hear.

Simon had badly miscalculated his move. So much steam was rising from Janice that he wondered for a moment what would happen. Then she turned her eyes on him and he knew. She was going to explode. And soon.

"I'll make it up to you, just stay for now. It won't look good for you to walk away only minutes after I've announced our engagement," he whispered as her eyes narrowed into slits. Nevertheless, she stood and walked away from him with barely a glance.

He should have left well enough alone. He'd given her the damn gun, aimed it at his own foot and told her to pull the trigger and she had. She'd left him alone, knowing that every tongue in the room would be wagging about the reason she'd left. Of course he knew that was her point. He wasn't a fool. At least he'd never been a fool until he met her. Now she had him doing things he would have sworn on his deathbed he would never do.

Simon picked up his wine glass and sipped, pretending that nothing was wrong, that he'd not just detonated a bomb and had no idea in hell how to avoid the explosion.

The thought that he should have just asked her about Tommy came months too late. He'd been so determined to find out everything there was to know about her before he married her that he'd not batted an eyelash when it had been suggested that he use investigators to fill in the blanks. He did it all the time in business, why not in the most important merger of his life? With marriage he was handing Janice the keys to half of what he owned. Damn right he was going to check things out.

Simon didn't notice that Tommy Strong had left the podium and was standing next to him until a deep and firm masculine voice said, "May I speak to you out in the lobby a moment?"

Simon looked up at the man, thinking there was something odd in his demeanor. He rose easily from his chair, not liking the feeling of the man towering over him. "Sure." He raised his hand to pat the man on the back, but Strong moved swiftly out of his reach and walked away.

What the hell? Simon wondered as he followed him out the door. He'd just given the man a check for a million dollars. He should be doing cartwheels and kissing his ass right about now. Instead, he was behaving as though Simon had offended him.

When they were in a secluded corner, Tommy Strong held out the check toward Simon. "What is this for?"

"Excuse me?" Simon attempted to laugh.

"This check, just what are you attempting to buy with it?"

"Buy?" Now it was Simon's turn to be offended. "This is a gift."

"It's an awfully large gift. What's the string?"

"It's also a tax write-off if you must know." Simon continued smiling, albeit a bit frostily. "I can spend my damn money the way I chose or I can fork it over in taxes. I chose to spend it and score a few points with my bride at the same time."

"Don't you mean bride-to-be?" Tommy muttered.

For the span of two lifetimes the men stared at each other, squaring off at least mentally if not physically.

"What the hell is this about? I don't get the hostility. I heard that African American bookstores are being forced to close down and I learned that you were orchestrating something to help them. I want to help."

"You wrote the check out in my name."

"That's because you're the one in charge."

"Why didn't you make it out to the group?"

"Because I like to know who's handling my money. Use it for the good of your people."

"My people?" Tommy glared. "What the hell do you know about *my people?* You think because you're sleeping with a black woman that it makes you black?"

Simon took a step back, visibly shaken. This he had not expected. He'd expected gratitude and maybe, well, he wouldn't think about what he'd expected, at least not now.

"What if I decide to spend this money on myself and say to hell with the bookstores? What then?"

"It has your name on it."

"Wrong answer." Tommy shook his head. "I'm not for sale, slavery is over."

That remark stung, as the man had intended. "What the hell do you mean by that?" Simon barked. "I'm only trying to help you."

"No, you're trying to buy me like you bought Mary Jo. It won't work. I'm not for sale."

Once again the two men squared off, this time the physical implication clear.

"What does my fiancée have to do with this?"

A deep laugh boomed out of Tommy's chest. "You have no idea how damn amusing this is. I wondered why the hell you would invite me to this thing then I found out. And the check, I knew the moment you handed it over what you were doing. You didn't fool anyone, least of all me. And from the way Mary Jo stormed out of the room I doubt that you fooled her either."

"You leave my fiancée to me, and for the record, her name's Janice now."

"You're the one who informed the world and reminded them just who she is. What carrot are you dangling before her? Money? Fame?" Tommy smiled. "You've won, she's marrying you, so why did you think you needed me in your pocket?"

"I did this for Janice."

"Bull, you did not do this for Mary Jo."

Simon was not used to being challenged, not like this, and definitely not by a man to whom he'd just given a fortune. He watched as Tommy ripped the check into shreds and tossed the pieces into the trash like so much useless confetti.

"Like I said, I'm not for sale and to ease your mind a bit, you needn't have bothered. In case you didn't notice, your bride-to-be has as little desire to be in my life as I want her in it. You didn't have to try and pay me to remain out of her life. I was already out."

Tommy strolled away, leaving Simon standing there, knowing for sure that he should never have dredged up Janice's past. He'd had no idea that Tommy Strong or Janice would understand why he'd done it. He'd thought his reasons for giving the money would work. Well, they hadn't. He wondered for a moment if he should go and attempt to calm the storm brewing in his suite but decided against it. Better to let her cool off before tackling that situation. He'd erred; he wouldn't do it again. He peeped into the trash. What a waste. What kind of fool threw away that kind of money?

Cold fury propelled Tommy's movements. He walked to the elevator, rode down to the lobby, and was almost out of the door before he changed his mind and headed in the direction of a house phone. He couldn't believe how easy it was to be connected.

"Was it worth it?" he asked the once familiar voice that answered the phone.

"Was what worth it?" she snarled.

Tommy wanted nothing more than to be facing her asking her this same question. He wanted to shake her until her teeth rattled and then shake her some more. Once he'd loved her with his heart and soul and she'd taken that love and stepped on it and thrown it back into his face.

"You sold yourself for money, for fame. God, you disgust me."

"Then why are you talking to me? I didn't ask you to. And while you're being so high and mighty, I didn't see you turning down that check he gave you."

"Do you have any idea how that money would help the bookstores?" he hissed at her. He could tell her he'd torn up the check but he refused to do that. Let her think what she would about him, he didn't care.

"I want to ask you one thing, Mary Jo."

"The name's Janice now."

"Like I said, Mary Jo, I have one question for you. Are you white now? Has Simon Kohl's money made you white?"

They both slammed the phones down at the same instant and Janice reached for the nearest item and flung it with all her might across the room. The expensive vase hit the wall, cracking a mirror and knocking a painting to the floor. Seven years' bad luck. What else was new? Janice didn't care. She walked away from the debris and toward the bedroom.

CHAPTER THREE

"Damn." Simon cursed and pushed phone buttons as he entered the private elevator. He'd overplayed his hand. He barked his orders into the phone. "I don't give a damn who else is scheduled. I want it done and I want it done yesterday. Do you understand? I want her on every show that airs tomorrow. Am I making myself clear?"

Simon disconnected and cursed again as he stepped off the elevator and walked toward his suite. The moment he opened the door he knew why the man he had installed in the next suite had called him. The room looked like a tornado had torn through it. He knew the tornado had a name: Janice Lace.

He walked into the bedroom, saw her packing and plunged his hands into his pockets. "What's going on?" he asked casually. "Did someone come in and attempt to attack you?" he teased.

"You've been spying on me. Why?"

"You didn't think we were getting married without me knowing every little thing there is to know, did you?"

Janice looked at the huge diamond that sat on her finger for little more than a second before snatching it off and flinging it across the room. "Forget it," she yelled.

No matter how many fights they'd had in the past three years, she'd never once even threatened to give him back jewelry. This was more serious than he wanted it to be.

"What did I do that was so bad? I thought I did a good deed. I thought it would make you happy," he lied.

"That's a crock and we both know it. Why him? Why didn't you pick someone else to invite? Anyone could have turned the check over to the AABU. Why Tommy Strong? Simon, this isn't a coincidence and don't insult me by saying that it is."

"You refused to tell me about your past."

"So you hired someone to dig into my past? That's sick, Simon." She stopped. "The party hasn't ended, why are you up here?"

"I just wanted to check on you, make sure you were okay."

Memory of the phone call from Tommy and the crash of glass flashed before her and she trembled in anger. "Are you having someone spy on me in our room also?"

He ignored her question and walked to the bed. "Where are you going?"

"I'm going home."

"Give me a few minutes to tie up some loose ends and I'll go with you."

"I'm going alone."

Simon plopped down on the bed and smiled up at her. He fingered her black silk panties which she promptly snatched away and he reclaimed. His gaze never left her face as his finger slid over the crotch of the underwear. Simon shivered, feeling himself grow hard, and he softened his voice, knowing he could have handled things differently. But he'd wanted the element of surprise when Janice saw Tommy.

"Are you coming back in the morning?" he asked.

"Are you crazy? No, I'm not coming back."

"Then you're going to miss your surprise," he lied, pretending that his test hadn't been the surprise. She stopped and glared at him. *Good,* he thought, smiling in the face of her glare. *At least I have her attention.*

"From the look of your surprises I don't want any more."

"What are you talking about? I haven't given you anything yet."

Janice stopped her packing, planted her feet firmly and put her hands on her hips. "That stunt with Tommy, are you crazy?" She shook her head in disgust.

"You thought that was your surprise?" He laughed, a soft sound that was meant to rattle her nerves. He stroked the panties again. "No baby, that wasn't your surprise. But I can see that you're angry with me. I'll go and cancel the surprise." He walked back toward the sitting room, ignoring the three phones in the bedroom. He counted to ten, picked up the receiver and began to dial.

"What's the surprise?"

Simon turned as though he hadn't known she was standing behind him. "Jay Leno, you're on his show tomorrow." He dialed the next number.

"Are you kidding?"

"Would I kid about something that would make your eyes light up?" He sure as hell hoped that it was happening. "I can call it off," he said and pushed another button.

"Simon, don't." Janice came up to him and took the phone from his hand. "Are you telling me the truth?"

"Yes baby, I'm telling you the truth."

She was breaking. He could almost see her salivate over the prospect. He watched while she toyed with the phone and he knew that although she was debating the wisdom of letting him off the hook, she would cave. The prize was big enough.

"Simon, you pull that shit on me again and you're history. Do you understand me?"

"I understand you, but tell me something. Why is it that I have the wealth and you have the power?"

"I have no power. You just can't figure out what makes me tick. The moment you do you're out of here. Right now I intrigue you. You never know what I'm going to do."

"We're getting married. How would I just take off?"

"Do you think I believe marriage will prevent that? There is such a word as divorce."

Simon was beside her before any more words left her mouth. "Do you think I would want to marry you if I didn't mean it to be for keeps? If you don't feel the same you tell me right now. I plan to marry only once."

His hand shot out and captured her wrist. "Look at me, Janice. I'm not kidding with you, not about this. You might have me by the balls on everything else, but this is not negotiable. If you don't want to stay married to me, don't say 'I do'. If you ever try to leave me after we're married you will regret it."

A tremor of fear claimed her and she hesitated just a second. "Don't threaten me, Simon." She pointed around the room. "This isn't angry. You have never seen me angry;

you wouldn't like me when I'm truly angry." She pulled away from his grasp. "Don't push me too far."

"I'd advise you to do the same." He brought her panties up to his nose and sniffed, his way of aggravating her. He smelled nothing but the newness of the material. "If you ever declare war on me I can promise you that you won't win. I'd say you'd fare much better with me for a husband than an enemy."

"I don't think you want me for an enemy either, Simon, just keep that in mind. If I have to fight dirty, I can and I will."

"If you're talking about withholding sex, I've lived through that already."

She smiled and turned to walk away and he pulled her back, brought her body up against his and kissed her neck, his hand ripping at the material of her clothing, pulling it away. He was hotter than the lava that burned beneath volcanoes. For a breath he thought she was going to push him away. Then she suddenly clasped him to her and sank her teeth into his neck, first softly, then a little harder. He trembled from the soles of his feet to the top of his head.

There was a hell of a lot more going on between him and Janice than any of the things they admitted to. The pounding in his chest testified to his true feelings for her, but he would be damned if he would be the first one to say it. Besides, he'd meant every word that he said. If she ever forced his hand, he had no doubt that he would go after her with the same vengeance as he did any enemy. He hoped for her sake that she never put his patience to a test.

As her hand curled around his hardened flesh, he groaned out loud. For now she was in control but this was different. This was the bedroom. He didn't give a damn about giving her the control in the bedroom, just as long as they were both aware that he was giving it to her, that she wasn't taking it. Control was his to give and his to take away. He groaned louder as she pushed the slacks from his waist and they fell in a puddle at his feet. *What the hell,* he thought. At this moment she owned him.

CHAPTER FOUR

Simon looked at Janice with wonder. She did it for him each and every time, and even more so when they were having make-up sex.

Her body was curled around his in a way that made his chest puff out with wonder and longing. His chest tightened even more at the sight of her sweet and sated smile. Who the hell was he fooling? He was in love with her. He had been from the moment he'd seen her across a room filled with hundreds of people. If only he could tell her that. But he couldn't; she already had too much control over him. His libido was one thing, his heart another.

When she smiled at him in the manner that she was doing now, he wanted to confess all. But he couldn't be stupid. He remembered how she'd treated him when they first met, before she'd known who he was.

He ran a finger down her jawline. "Why are we always fighting?" he asked her softly.

"Because you're always trying to control me."

There was a slight hint of annoyance in her voice and he thought not to push her. She was trailing her fingers over his body, touching him in just the way he liked being touched. He knew he should shift his focus, not concentrate on what he knew to be an explosive situation.

Still, they were getting married, and he wanted whatever the hell had frozen her heart to melt away. Something told him the ice in her came from Tommy Strong.

He didn't know if she loved the man but he did believe that because of him Janice didn't or couldn't confess she loved him. He wanted to hear her say it. He couldn't let the matter drop until she did.

He allowed his own fingers to investigate her body. Maybe, just maybe, he could have her mellow enough to answer him without bolting from the bed. His fingers were firmly nestled in her warmth, her wetness pouring over him, her heat searing him and her muscles drawing him in deeper. He heard a soft moan escape her and pushed a little deeper.

"Do you still love him?" he asked.

She nestled closer. "Love who?" she asked.

So that was the way she was going to play it, coy. No, not this time, he thought, this matter was far too important. "Tommy Strong, do you still love him?" he asked and held her tighter when she attempted to squirm away.

"For God's sake, Simon." She roughly removed his hand from her body and shoved him to the side of the bed.

"If you wanted to know if I was carrying a torch for anyone, why the hell didn't you just ask?" She glared at him and headed for the shower. He followed.

"Because you won't talk to me. You either clam up or tell me it's not any of my damn business."

"Then why the hell don't you listen?" Janice shrieked.

Simon glared back. "One minute you tell me to ask, then the next you tell me to mind my own business. How was I supposed to know anything if I didn't do this? You sure as hell weren't going to tell me."

"That's my right. What is it with you lately, all this talk about love?" She glared again. "That isn't what this is about with us. Why do you care whom I love?"

That hurt and he knew damn well that she knew it. She would have to be blind and a selfish little witch not to know it.

"I don't care who you love. I just don't want you screwing around behind my back after we're married."

"Have I ever screwed around behind your back?" she retorted. "Listen, you don't own me and my body is mine to do with as I please. I haven't been sleeping around but I have the right to sleep with whoever the hell I want to."

"Not now and definitely not after we're married."

"Then maybe we shouldn't get married."

They stood glaring at each other until Janice turned on the water for the shower and climbed inside, ignoring him and his feelings.

A moment of uncertainly claimed him and Simon yanked the shower door open. "I'm asking you straight out: Are you still in love with Tommy Strong?"

"It's been twelve years since I laid eyes on him."

"I didn't ask you how long it's been since you've seen him. I asked if you still love him."

"No," Janice screamed. "I'm not in love with him. Why do you even care?" She glared, then said as calmly as if she were saying it's raining outside, "I don't love anyone. Now close the damn door."

The pain in his chest tightened and he didn't attempt to open the door again. For God's sake, they were getting married. A person would have thought he'd committed a crime. She had to be blind, blind and stupid, to not know he cared, that he loved her. Blind, stupid and just plain bitchy.

She was right about one thing: What they had together was sick. She was constantly telling him that she didn't love him, and most of the time she behaved as if she were doing him a favor by even being with him. He hated taking it.

He stayed where he was until she got out of the shower. "How did you manage to stay so long in there without getting your hair wet?" he asked, wanting to change the topic as well as wanting to know. Whenever they showered together her hair would be as wet as her beautiful brown body.

"Because I didn't have some fool holding my head under the water."

Damn, he'd asked for that one. Still, he was determined to lighten her mood. "My hair always gets wet."

She was still glaring at him. "I don't put my head under the water when I don't want my hair wet."

"Why?"

"What is this? Why do you need to know every little thing about my life? Simon, back off, you're pissing me off."

"I seem to do that to you a lot lately." He hunched his shoulders. "Ever since you finally agreed to marry me. I wonder why that is."

"Do you think it might have anything to do with the fact that you practically ordered me to marry you? I was content with things the way that they were. You're the one who wanted to get married. I never did."

"You didn't have to agree."

"No, I didn't have to agree but I wanted that carrot you dangled before my nose and you knew that. Do you think my agent could have gotten me that kind of money on a three book proposal from anyone else?"

"Why is money so damn important to you, Janice?"

"Why is it so important to you, Simon?"

"It isn't."

"Liar, give it away if it isn't."

"I do. I give it to you." He knew the moment the words were out that he'd gone too far. Her eyes cut through him with the precision of a fine steel blade.

"I earn my money, every dime, either with my writing or in bed. I work my ass off for everything I have."

"Do you really think your writing is worth the money I'm paying you?" He wasn't backing off on that. He pointed toward the bedroom. "You're good, baby, but not that good. Do you really think you're worth my time?"

She glared at him and her voice was gravely when she spoke. "The question is do you think you're worth my time? If you don't like my writing, then I suggest you hire another writer. And if you don't like the rest," Janice did as Simon had done and pointed toward the bedroom, "then I would suggest you get someone else."

She smiled and he wished like hell he hadn't pushed. They both knew he was a liar on that score and now she'd issued an ultimatum that he wasn't going to take and instead of putting her in her place, he looked weak and ineffectual.

"Sometime your being bitchy to me is not going to be so amusing. If I were you I would pray that day never comes. I'll repeat, Janice, you don't want me for an enemy."

She smiled as cool as you please. "And you don't want me for one."

"I know you say you don't love me," Simon said over the lump in his throat, "but sometimes you behave as though you hate me. Do you hate me, Janice?"

"Sometimes I do. Why?"

"I was just wondering."

Janice cocked her head and observed Simon with a cold stare. She didn't know what was up with him and she didn't like it. For the past few months his behavior had become unpredictable. He'd nagged her so long about getting married that she'd finally screamed, 'Yes,' just to shut him up. Not the stuff romances were made from. And now he was talking about love and checking on her. She gave him a good hard look. His cold grey eyes revealed nothing, not even passion. That was the one emotion he'd been unable to hide from her.

She hated it when they fought. She felt evil, but she'd learned long ago that she had to be tough, had to not give a damn. She'd played her part so well, worn that veneer for so long that it was now a part of her soul. She couldn't afford to show she cared, not about anything or anyone other than herself. Her career was the only thing that mattered that she didn't have to pretend about.

Her family disapproved of her living in New York, blaming the city for the type of books she wrote. Her mother had told her many times that she needed to write something more uplifting. Her brothers thought she'd betrayed them personally for not portraying black men as more heroic. For some crazy reason they thought if she returned home she would change back into Mary Jo Adams. She wouldn't. To hear them tell it, she should be leading a revolution. They thought she'd sold out simply because she didn't write books that featured predominately African American characters. And when she did, they didn't like the way she portrayed the male characters. Who the hell were they to criticize her? They should have been proud of her for being willing to admit the truth. *Not all black men behaved honorably.* Instead, they acted as if she carried the plague.

No one would even accept money from her, money that they knew she had, money that she knew would buy extras. It wasn't as though they really needed her money, but it would have been fun to have been allowed to shower them with gifts. Yet they wouldn't hear of it. No, they behaved as though her money were tainted.

Her mother had told her she couldn't take money from a daughter who'd prostituted her soul to write smut. That remark had hurt, but when she'd received a million dollars advance from Simon, she'd soon gotten over that hurt. And she had a hell of a lot more to thank Simon for. He'd invested all of her money in sure things and she knew even without him she would never want for anything. Anything, that is, except companionship.

For now she had that with Simon. Why he wanted to be with her, only God knew. She wasn't even nice to him most time, though there were times she wanted to be. But she couldn't soften toward him. She couldn't afford to show him she cared or have him think her weak. If she so much as showed a crack, he would toss her out like yesterday's newspaper. For now he was the only one who wanted her. No one else could stand her and she knew it. Hell, if her fans were around her for more than five minutes at a time she would lose them. It was becoming harder and harder for her to control her temper, to be nice. She was constantly on edge, screaming on the inside, wondering what had gone wrong with her life, her plans.

And Simon had reminded her what had gone wrong. Tommy Strong had gone wrong. She'd loved him with every breath. And she hated Simon at the moment for reminding her of her loss.

Janice studied Simon, wishing she didn't always have to worry about protecting herself. "Simon, I don't like what you did."

"I know."

"Don't do it again."

"Are you going to talk to me?" He was talking softly, not promising her anything but willing to listen. "Every time that I asked you about the men in your life you never answered me. I wanted to know. I can deal with your not loving me." He paused and swallowed the lie. "But the one thing I can't take is finding out later that you're carrying a torch for another man. And the only man in your past I could find was Tommy Strong."

"What did you think I was going to do? Fall into his arms?"

"I didn't know."

She shook her head slowly and walked to him. "What I had with him was twelve years ago. It's over."

"Everyone that…every report said you were madly in love with him. No one knows what happened, no one. Even Mr. Strong wouldn't open up about your relationship."

She eyed him now with more than curiosity. It was with an anger that burnt from her core and through her. "You had someone question him about me?"

"He didn't know. He thought it was a woman interested in him."

Janice closed her eyes tight against the thought of Simon's paid investigator discussing her with the man who'd broken her heart. "What did he tell this plant that you sent in?"

"About the same as you've told me, nothing. He told her that his private affairs were just that, his private affairs. I've never seen two people more close-mouthed about a twelve-year dead relationship. If it's over and long buried, why can't either of you talk about it?"

"Maybe it's not that we can't. Maybe we just don't want to. Did you ever think about that?" She decided to try another tactic. "Simon, I've never asked you about the women in your life."

That's because you don't give a damn, he thought, but to her he said, "You never had to. My entire life has been written up in the papers. Every time I've so much as smiled at a woman the world has known."

"I don't believe everything that I read, you should know that."

"Why haven't you ever asked me if I've been in love?"

"What difference would it make? If you said yes, should I be upset or jealous that you don't love me? And if you said no, what do you think I should do then? Try and make you love me?"

Simon put his left thumb into his mouth and bit down on it as he studied Janice. Surely she couldn't be that blind or that naïve. Then again, the way they were forever snapping at each other, why should she think he gave a damn?

"Did he break your heart?"

"What difference does it make?"

"Maybe all the difference in the world, maybe none. Most of the time bitterness and anger come from unrequited love. Is that what happened between you and Mr. Strong? Was your love unrequited? Baby, did he spurn you?" He wanted to add, "The way you spurn me," but stopped.

"If you're asking if he broke up with me, you could say it was a mutual thing."

"I understand he left town."

"I didn't know that was a crime."

"Your friends all thought that was strange, as close as the two of you were."

"If they were really my friends, they wouldn't have talked to your people, now would they?"

"Did they get it right? Did he leave town and leave you?"

"He left town," Janice admitted. "But he returned and I left for good," she added.

"Did you leave before he returned or after?"

Simon really was giving her a terrible headache with all of his incessant questions. She didn't want to remember any of it. He had no right to dredge up her past. "I don't see how this is helping anything."

"I told you, I want to know what I'm up against."

"Simon, it hasn't bothered you for three years. Why now?"

"We're getting married."

"If it's making you this crazy, why do you want to go through with the marriage?"

"Honestly," he tipped her chin with his finger, "I don't know. I must be a glutton for punishment. I have women throwing themselves at me all day, every day. I don't have to put up with your abuse if I don't want to, and if I were you, Janice, I would be careful. Someday I might choose not to."

They stared at each other, this time without either of them glaring. Simon had struck a nerve. He knew that when he threatened to leave she would clam up. For all her big talk, he knew she didn't want him to leave. He served a need in her life, the same as she served one in his. And now he wanted to know what need he served for her.

Admittedly they were good in bed together, but Simon had never thought that his prowess couldn't be matched. And he wasn't crazy enough to think that Janice couldn't have any man she crooked her little finger at, and God help them, if she smiled at one, they would be a goner.

He knew there was something specific that kept her in his bed and even though he harped on the fact that he knew it was his money, Simon knew that wasn't all of it.

Sure, she enjoyed the power but he had sensed more than that for the past couple of years. She would never admit it, but he'd seen her eyes light up more than once when he unexpectedly showed up somewhere that she happened to be. He would watch her in fascination as a metamorphosis took place and she consciously distanced herself from him.

The first time she'd done it, the act had taken him by surprise. His heart had jumped for joy, knowing that she was happy that he'd shown up for a signing unannounced. But when he had been about to greet her, her brown eyes had slid over him and she'd barely spoken, as though he didn't matter.

After the third time he'd watched carefully and seen her struggling to wipe the smile from her face, to take the stars from her eyes, and she'd almost not made it. She'd smiled warmly at him and grinned before going back to behaving as though he were just another who wanted her autograph.

It was then he'd known she cared for him and then that he'd become aware that she neither wanted to care about him nor wanted him to care about her. He'd noticed her pattern on those times. Those would be the nights she'd be like a block of ice in bed, as though she had to pound it home to herself and to him that he meant less than nothing to her. The trouble with that was that he didn't believe her and because he didn't believe her, he'd fallen deeper.

For more than two years Simon had tried different ways to make Janice break, to drop the charade, but nothing worked, not jewelry, not sweet talk, not fighting. And always she presented him with the same false front she presented to the world. The thing was, he knew it was fake. When she screamed out and held him close, he knew she gave a damn.

Sometimes when he'd wake to find her hands stroking him softly, he knew she was where she wanted to be and he'd lie there pretending to sleep. When she knew he was awake, she would stop. Then he would take over and make love to her. On those mornings they would make love with such exquisite sweetness that it took his breath away. During those times it had been hard for Simon to keep his words to himself.

"I've made my choice," Simon said softly. "As evil as you are, I still want to marry you."

"Then let it drop. Either you want to marry me or you don't," she snapped and walked away from him, leaving him to wonder if things would change once they were married. Would she continue to pretend she didn't care? Or would she finally crack that hard shell and let him in? And if she didn't, would he keep pretending as well?

Simon was sure of only one thing: He didn't want to spend the rest of his life in a loveless marriage. He'd meant it when he told Janice that he never planned to divorce. He wanted a family and he wanted it with Janice. But he also wanted love.

He rubbed the bridge of his nose. "This is getting really old," he said, "and I'm tired. Let's call a truce for just a few hours. We can continue snapping at each other later." He held out his hand to her. "What do you say?"

For a long moment Janice stood looking at Simon, not wanting to fight, not wanting to give in either. She feared showing him she was weak more than she feared anything. Still, she didn't want to fight and definitely not about Tommy.

She could have ended his questions and just told him that she'd broken up with Tommy because she found that he didn't love her, at least not as much as she'd loved him. She could have told Simon that when she'd needed Tommy the most, he hadn't been there for her. And she could tell him that she'd sworn to never turn power over her heart to anyone else.

Janice sighed and stuck out her hand. "I'm also tired," she replied, forcing herself to look at Simon. She saw the pain in his gaze, something she'd seen a little more often in the past months and a tiny pin prick of conscience seized her.

"Tommy was once important in my life. He's not anymore. You didn't have to give him a million dollars as bait to find that out. What were you doing exactly, Simon, paying him to tell you all my dirty little secrets or ensuring that he would never be tempted to touch me?"

She watched as his eyes crinkled and he smiled. "I'm not sure."

"Since I haven't seen him in all these years, why would you think I'd see him in the future?"

Again he shrugged. "I don't know. I just wanted to see your eyes when you saw him."

"Did you get your answers?"

"I'm not sure. You hate him and he hates you, that much is obvious. But I don't know why after so much time your emotions would be that strong. It makes me wonder if your love was equally as strong." He held her gaze and she trembled slightly.

"Its ancient history, Simon, let it stay buried. We have a truce, let's enjoy that." She smiled, knowing the smile didn't quite reach her eyes but doing it anyway. "I think we can think of better things to do." She cocked her head a little. "Don't you?"

"Are you serious?" Simon asked, his suspicions rising but his libido rising faster. Janice had never allowed him to make love to her again after she'd taken her shower. In the shower, yes, but once she was out and had dressed, that was it until later.

Simon could feel the grin claiming his face. He'd never refused loving when Janice was in the mood, and he sure as hell wasn't about to start now. He reached for her outstretched arm and pulled her close, then frowned at the mess she'd made in the room.

"You're going to have to pay for this," he informed her. "Your mess, you take care of it."

"Don't worry, I never expected you to cover the cost." She grinned back at him. "Well, maybe I did but I don't need you to. By the way, how are my investments doing?"

"As long as I'm managing your money you don't have to worry about it. Leave that worry to me. I'll do what I need to do when I need to do it. That's my promise to you."

Janice didn't know why, but Simon's promise had sounded a bit like a threat. She decided to ignore it. She was going to be on Jay Leno. That thought alone had definitely put her in the mood to make love. Well, that and the fact that she wanted to push Tommy out of Simon's mind. She wanted to make him stop digging. She sank into the bed, accepting her fiancée's probing tongue and fingers and held him tight to her. This was her life now. This was what she wanted.

Waking from a pleasant dream Janice remembered the wonderful surprise Simon had arranged. Jay Leno. She rolled toward Simon's side of the bed, finding it empty. Then she peeped around the room looking for him, blinking when she spotted him sitting at the desk appearing deep in thought. "Good morning," she said.

"Good morning, baby."

"You okay?" she asked, getting up and heading for the shower. A quick glance in Simon's direction made Janice pause. He looked tired and worried. She watched him for a moment, then walked over to him. "What's the matter?" she asked.

Shrugging his shoulders, he gave her a half smile. "I'm worried about some of my recent moves," Simon answered. Then he held her gaze. "I'm just a little tense, no big deal." He lifted her hand to his lips and kissed it.

"Don't worry, Simon, you always come out on top."

"I hope so, this is very important to me." That was the truth. He sighed when Janice moved behind him and began massaging his shoulders. Her fingers were so gentle and loving that he trembled at her touch.

"I'm sorry, Simon, that I was so evil to you."

"Are you trying to get me to pay for your little hissy fit?"

"No, baby, you just seem so…I'm not sure…depressed, and that's not like you. Seeing you like this makes me worry about you."

Simon turned catching her hand in his. "You worry about me?"

"Of course I do, Simon."

She gave him a smile that touched his core, then turned him around and continued her massage. Every stroke of her fingers told him what she wouldn't say with words. She loved him. There were the private moments between them that had cemented their relationships. Sure they fought, but in the still of the night they talked without the barriers between them, without Janice trying to protect herself from getting hurt.

Simon gave a sigh of pleasure as Janice worked the kinks from his body. For a moment he wished it could always be like this between them when she was vulnerable. Maybe when he found out the reason for her hurt it would happen. He glanced at his watch. "It's getting late. Don't you need to get ready for the show?"

"Not just yet," Janice said, and continued kneading Simon's shoulders. "I'm not done with you. You need me." She dropped a kiss onto the crown of his head. "You're more important to me than being on Jay Leno. You're still tense," she said. "When you're relaxed then we'll worry about my getting dressed."

She was killing him. How was he ever going to relax with her sweet hands trailing heat to every cell? He took her ministrations until he couldn't stand it any more, then pulled her into his lap and kissed the smile that lingered at the corner of her lips. "Thanks," he murmured, gazing at her.

"For what? You're behaving as though this is the first time I've given you a massage."

"It's the first time you've given me one when you've been angry with me."

"I'm not angry with you any longer. Besides, you needed it." She held his gaze. "Sometimes even for me, Simon, there are more important things than fighting."

Her look spoke volumes, making him wish he could live without knowing who and what had hurt her so deeply, without hearing her say the words, *I love you.* He wished it but he wanted it desperately.

"You're right, I did need it." Lust quickly took over as heat pooled in his groin. "There's something I need even more. Do you still have time?"

"I'll make time," Janice answered, tilting her head back for Simon to kiss her throat.

Hallelujah, Simon thought, as he ravished her throat with his kisses. How the hell could he not want to hear '*I love you'* from her sweet lips? He moved upward, plundering her mouth with his tongue. Maybe it would be for the best if his bringing Tommy Strong back into her life would finally make her acknowledge her feelings. She moaned and he swallowed it. Oh hell yes, she was worth fighting for.

CHAPTER FIVE

Janice stood at the doorway leading to the set of *Déjà Vu*. Simon had gone all out and had her booked on every show that aired. She'd already been on four morning news shows and found it exhilarating even though most people had wanted to know about Simon and how much he'd influenced her rise to fame.

It wasn't as though any of the questions had come as a surprise. She'd known that would be the basis of the questions and she'd toughened her already tough skin to take it. The main thing was keeping her face out there, making it, showing Tommy Strong that she was everything she'd promised not to be, a full-blown diva bitch.

Janice almost grinned at the thought, not knowing why she'd thought of that, but knowing it had something to do with her seeing Tommy in her mind blown up into bits and pieces. It seemed that every word he'd ever spoken to her was now flooding back, every touch, every caress, every taste.

In the three years she'd been with Simon she'd never once thought of another man's hand on her body until last night and as she'd screamed out to Simon to give her more, she became aware that he knew her desire wasn't all about him. Neither of them had mentioned it. In fact, they'd both been unusually quiet the entire morning. That was one reason Janice had made love to him after massaging him.

She needed his touch to keep her grounded. She'd meant it when she'd told him he was important to her. He was. Still, in many ways she longed to keep things as they were between them. Changing things meant one thing: She would eventually get hurt.

She liked things the way that they were. Uncomplicated. She'd never thought about her marrying Simon as being a complication until last night. Now she understood that he wanted more than he'd let on. He wanted a traditional marriage, yet he knew she wasn't the person to give him that. So why was he pushing? She also didn't understand the hurt she saw creep into his eyes from time to time.

They had an understanding. They had always had an understanding. Neither of them was in the relationship for love. Still, she wondered where Simon's pain came from. Surely it couldn't be from her. He didn't love her or care enough for anything she did to hurt him.

She shivered. He'd hurt her by bringing Tommy Strong back into her life. She'd once loved Tommy Strong so fiercely that he took her soul with him when he left her. She'd forgotten all of that, forgotten how much he'd hurt her and forgotten why she'd turned stone cold. And now she feared a thaw. She didn't want it. Her life was just fine the way that it was. She didn't want to love, not Simon, not anyone. Not if it meant she would be hurt again.

Janice heard her name called and walked out onto the stage, pasting her fake smile on her lips and waving at the audience. She stopped when she glanced at the couch and saw none other than the man whom she'd been thinking of, Tommy Strong.

She stared for half a second, then sat in the seat that was offered to her. She felt Tommy's icy glare freeze her in place and she shivered.

What the hell did he have to be so hostile about? It was he who'd hurt her, he who'd not been able to withstand the first test that was given to them. It was he who in the end hadn't loved her enough and it was his disdain that had turned her blood into ice.

"We thought it would be nice if Mr. Strong stayed on the show to meet with you after receiving the million dollars to help African American bookstores that your fiancé gave him. He said he didn't get a chance to tell you how much this means to him."

For sure blood was going to pour from her ears. Janice couldn't even tell who was talking. All she saw was Tommy. She wanted to bolt and run.

She wondered if Simon had arranged this. But he'd promised. Then again, it was he who'd arranged for her to be on the show. Her thoughts were running rampant. She sat like a statue as Tommy reached out and grabbed her hand, and acted as though he were shaking it, holding it a moment longer than was decent, stroking her skin where no one could see. But she knew he was aware of the effect he'd had on her. She watched as the smirk spread across his face.

"I was wondering if I could impose on you and ask for your personal help with the African American bookstores," Tommy said, his voice as smooth and sweet as hot caramel over vanilla ice cream. He showed his teeth as he smiled. Janice couldn't help staring at him. His beautiful pearl white teeth gleamed, and he had the women on the show and the entire audience eating out of the palm of his hand. How could she possibly say no?

"Of course, whatever you need me to do," she found herself answering. She caught the flash of anger that passed over his face and trembled in spite of the warmth from the lights overhead. "I could send a box of autographed books, what ever you want."

"I want you to work closely with me, go into the stores, drum up business. We could use someone like you for the cause. You know you're African American, right?" he asked, as though making a joke. Janice was the only person beside himself who was aware that he meant every word.

She smiled coyly and held her arms up for him to examine. "Guilty as charged," she said, pouring sweetness into every tart word.

"What you write now, was this always the way that you planned to go with your career? I mean, did you ever consider doing anything else?" Tommy asked.

She glanced around at the other women and saw they were aware of something, yet didn't know what. They were hungry for blood, something to discuss on the next show, and she wasn't about to appease their appetite. She could handle herself; she'd been trained by the best.

"I'm sure every young person has dreams that they later realize were either foolish or just that, dreams. I am doing what makes me happy. I write and I tell a story."

"Is there ever any truth to your stories? I mean, has real life ever come into play?"

This time she held his gaze, refusing to back down. "It appears what you're looking for is a private interview. I think maybe the ladies would like to ask me some questions."

There, she thought. She'd put him in his place. Janice turned her head toward the women, determined not to send out any signals.

"So are you saying that you're definitely going to help me?" Tommy ignored her request and her turned head and waited. The four women of *Déjà Vu* waited also.

"Of course, Mr. Strong, I'll do whatever I can to help the community."

"I'm glad to hear that," he said, "because up until now your presence in the community had been limited to just your books. I'm sure everyone will be happy to know you haven't forgotten your roots, that you're going to work closely with me to see that the community recognizes you as one of its own."

She narrowed her eyes and not even when the hostess decided to take control back did she stop glaring at Tommy. He'd put her on the spot, just as he'd intended and at the moment she didn't know who she wanted to strangle first: Tommy for his undignified public attack or the women for losing control of the show to him.

Janice couldn't believe what was happening. She'd watched the show many times. It was unbelievable that those four women weren't peppering her with questions. What was up with them? Why had they allowed Tommy to take over their show? She glanced at Tommy, then at each woman in turn before bringing her gaze back to Tommy. It was obvious he'd made a deal with the women. She should have known.

Just because he was a gorgeous hunk of man with enough charm to get the panties off the most devout virgin with but a glance was not a reason for the women to go cuckoo.

She glared once more at Tommy, and then looked at the women. They weren't responsible for their attraction to Tommy; she shouldn't blame them. A whispered word or two and the most stubborn woman would change her tune, just as she had. But no more. Tommy Strong didn't deserve her lust and he definitely didn't deserve her ever thinking of loving him again.

When she thought she was safe and could leave the set, Tommy interrupted again, forcing her to give him her card on the air, forcing her to agree to a lunch with him the next day.

When she walked out, to her surprise Simon was waiting for her. She looked guiltily at him, feeling her cheeks warm with shame. She'd done nothing wrong, but still she felt the remorse. Janice unconsciously rubbed her palm down the side of her body. It still burned where Tommy had given her his secret caress, his signal to her when they were young that he wanted her, wanted to make love to her. She attempted to smile at Simon but saw confusion and pain cloud his eyes.

"Come on," she told him. "We don't have time to waste."

"You don't think I set that up, do you?"

"No, I don't." And she didn't think it.

"You don't have to go through with it, you don't have to help him. You can do a couple of bookstores. I'll come with you, that should be enough."

"No, it won't be enough, Simon. Did you hear him? He accused me of abandoning my roots, of not being black."

"I didn't hear him say that."

"That's because you didn't know what to listen for. I heard him. He issued a challenge. I have to follow through with it." She walked out the door, leaving Simon behind.

Have to or want to? he thought. And for the third time Simon wondered at the bad move he'd made. There was unfinished business between Janice and her ex. Should he allow it to play out or put a stop to it now before it got out of hand? Before...He hesitated, not wanting to even think it. Maybe he should stop it before she either realized she still loved the man or fell in love with him all over again.

Tommy watched Mary Jo leave with one of the world's most powerful men and for a moment he hated both of them. For twelve years he'd held firm to his hatred of her. She'd broken his heart, taken his love and stomped it as though it had meant nothing to her.

She'd not given him a chance to become a man. Sure, he'd run when she first told him she was pregnant. He'd been scared shitless, eighteen years old. How the hell was he going to take care of her and a baby? It was going to ruin everything—their college plans, their dreams of starting a powerful group dedicated to black love and black achievement.

They had plotted and planned to be what the Black Panthers had started out to be. Only their weapon would be knowledge. They would start schools across the country to teach the community all the contributions made by African Americans.

Tommy pulled his cell phone from his pocket, wondering how many people, black, white or brown, knew that it was an African American man, Henry Sampson, that many claimed invented the cell phone. Of course, there were differing reports that said Sampson didn't invent the phone, that he had invented the gamma-electrical-cell, not the phone.

Tommy didn't care. The man could have probably invented it if he wanted to, so Tommy gave him the credit each time he made a call.

He dialed the number, thinking of Mary Jo, of what they had planned. She'd abandoned that just as she'd abandoned him and she'd taken on the persona of the white world and wore it like a glove. He didn't believe one thing black remained in her. This woman who'd taken her place he didn't even like.

He thought about what she'd done. She'd aborted his child without giving him a chance to tell her he was sorry, that he'd realized that they could do anything together. Then she'd delivered the devil's blow. She'd told him that the baby might not have even been his.

Tommy had felt in his heart she was lying but it had hurt all the same and he'd been moments from slapping her.

He still remembered how she'd jutted out her chin and told him defiantly that if he hit her, she'd cut his balls off. It hadn't been her threat that had made him pull back but the knowledge that he had wanted to hit her.

He'd never ever hit a woman in his life. He detested men that did, and since that day he'd never had that overwhelming anger come over him again. He knew it was due in part to the fact that he'd never allowed himself to love anyone as much as he'd loved Mary Jo.

Tommy didn't deny that she had a right to be hurt. That much he acknowledged, but the thought that she could pull an emotional response from him toward violence frightened him. He could still picture her the day she'd ended it.

"*I think this is over, Tommy. We're not children any longer. You go your way and I'll go mine.*"

And just like that she'd walked out of his life. She didn't cry or behave as if she hadn't meant it and she hadn't answered any of his calls or letters. She'd cut him off and had forgotten him as she'd done his child, and he'd hated her every day after.

Sure, he'd made a mistake, but he'd apologized. Their ending was her doing and it rested squarely on her shoulders. He doubted if he lived for a thousand years if he would ever forgive her for the way she'd left.

CHAPTER SIX

Simon sat in the limo for the rest of Janice's quick stops. Every time she returned to the car he noticed she was more agitated. "You okay?" he asked finally. "You're looking worn out."

"I am a bit."

She tried smiling and he noticed it was forced. "Maybe we should get some lunch, or if you want, I can cancel the rest of your interviews."

"No, don't."

Janice answered too quickly, he thought. She was trying to put off spending time alone with him. He didn't like it. He wanted to ask her a thousand questions but he didn't want the answers.

"You're not hungry?"

"No," she answered, again quickly.

He looked at her and thought that probably wasn't a lie. She looked as if she would heave if she took even a bite of food.

"Are the shows making you nervous?" he asked, hoping she'd level with him, tell him without him probing that seeing Tommy Strong was more than she could handle.

"I don't know if I can go through with it," she said quietly.

"Go through with what?"

"I don't know that I want to work that closely with Tommy." She smiled. "Now you know. This is what you paid a million dollars to learn. Was it worth it?"

"I wasn't trying to hurt you, Janice."

"You sure as hell weren't trying to help me."

"I just wanted to know what you were hiding from me."

"I've always been honest with you. I have never lied to you."

"Maybe not, but I knew you were keeping things from me. We're getting married, it shouldn't be that way. You forced me to find out for myself."

"I didn't think my past was your business. I still don't."

Simon stared at her, his gray gaze thoughtful. And again she saw the flicker of pain and remembered her own pain. She didn't want to hurt Simon. Given that he'd gone to the trouble of digging around in her past and finding Tommy, it was also evident that her source had told Simon how much she'd loved Tommy. She studied him for a moment, knowing he had a right to be concerned. She didn't want her past relationship with Tommy to be a cause of concern. They'd been over long ago.

"What do you want to know about Tommy?" she asked finally.

"Tell me what he meant to you. Tell me if you still care. Tell me who ended it."

Janice sucked in her breath. She didn't want to talk about Tommy Strong, not now, not ever, but Simon deserved an answer to his questions. Besides, if she didn't answer them he would probably keep digging even further.

"At one time Tommy was my world," she whispered. "No, I don't still care about him and in answer to your last question, he ended it. He left me without a word. I felt abandoned. I needed him and he wasn't there for me." *In a way it was true. Tommy's leaving town and abandoning her was what had ended it for them.*

Simon looked hard at her. "Why was that so hard for you to tell me?"

She shrugged, thinking maybe it was time to say out loud what had happened, to tell the man she was going to marry why she'd reacted so violently to Tommy. Still, it was hard. She had no wish for anyone to know of her weakness, either past or present.

"It hurt." She began. "I was a fool and I didn't relish reliving it. I had promised myself that I would never tell anyone, ever."

"So why did you tell me?"

"I'm not sure." *I wish I could tell you all of it,* she thought. But she couldn't. She only felt safe enough to go so far. The rest would have to wait. Maybe forever.

Simon was staring at her so she closed her eyes, wishing that she could feel safe enough to tell Simon that he was the only one she wanted to share her past or future with. Wishing as she took a deep breath and shuddered that she didn't truly believe Simon would stop loving her the moment she admitted her feelings for him. It wasn't Simon's fault that Tommy had taught her not to trust a man who claimed in either words or deeds to love her.

Simon didn't know what to make of it. He watched her while her eyes were closed, deciding not to question her. She'd told him more than she ever had. He'd let it go for now. Still, the pain in her voice was fresh and he knew it had something to do with her seeing Tommy Strong again.

Damn. He cursed under his breath, wishing he'd never dug into her past. As he'd originally thought, there was unfinished business between Janice and Tommy Strong. Simon could only hope that when it was over, he would be the one she ended up with. He leaned his head into her, stroked her left cheek with his hand and prayed like hell that the knot in his gut would go away.

Acute awareness snaked through Tommy's body. For the past twelve years he'd thought of women as treacherous, conniving skanks, something he'd never wanted to do. All his childhood dreams had focused on elevating the African American woman to her rightful status as queen. He was still able to talk the game but he couldn't walk the walk.

He'd never fooled himself about the reason. He'd always known it was because of Mary Jo Adams. She'd hurt him and because of that hurt Tommy was distrustful of women and their words of love. When she'd abandoned him she'd also abandoned all of the plans that they'd had to bring pride into the black community. Mary Jo had taken it a step further by portraying her black male characters in a stereotypical negative way.

He'd watched her career for the last seven years. He'd read every word she'd ever written, something in him hoping that he'd see something of the girl he'd loved. But he hadn't. Instead of doing something that the black community could be proud of, she'd sold out completely. If she just happened to include black male characters in her books, they were drug dealers, gang bangers and thugs, cons or other negative characters. But the one portrayal that hurt the most was that the black man didn't give a damn about his babies. That he knew was a direct slam on him and it was a lie.

When he saw her on the news, she was always on the arm on any man who wasn't black. Her nose was so far up in the air that if it rained when she was out, he knew she would be in danger of drowning.

He hated knowing that four years of his life had been wasted sharing his dreams and love with a woman who'd wanted neither. Seeing her finally face to face, he wanted answers. He wanted her to tell him if everything had been a lie. He no longer cared that she'd not wanted him; he just wanted to know if anything about her had been real. So far, he didn't think so.

He hated that seeing Janice made him remember the sweetness of her body. They had both been virgins when they first made love and it had taken them awhile to get the rhythm, but after they had, it was as though God had made them for each other.

In her arms he'd gone from being a boy to a man. And in the years since he'd seen her, he'd searched fruitlessly for that same sweetness. Apparently she'd not had the same problem.

Tommy couldn't believe she was really going to marry Simon Kohl. He wondered if she knew that the man had tried to buy him off. Tommy still wasn't sure what he'd expected. He just knew in his gut the man wanted to buy something Tommy wasn't willing to sell.

Well, with any luck he should get some of his answers. He'd put Mary Jo on the spot. She had no choice but to work with him. If there was one black cell left in her body, he was determined to find it. It might be too late for the two of them to work together to bring enlightenment or to revive the Panthers, but it sure as hell wasn't too late to change her back.

He shivered, wondering why it was important to him to have Mary Jo change back to what he'd thought she was. Then he knew. He didn't want it all to have been a lie. He had loved her. Even when he'd failed her, he'd loved her. She should have waited for him. She should have known he'd return and for that he didn't believe he could ever forgive her or forget her.

Pain filled him and he knew there was one more reason. He wanted to make her tell him that she'd lied, that the baby had been his. He felt it in his heart, but he needed to put a period after it. Only one person in the world could tell him what he needed to know. And that was Mary Jo.

CHAPTER SEVEN

The pile of clothes lying on their bed was beginning to resemble a small mountain. Simon stood there observing her, the amusement fading after he realized the reason for her distress.

"I don't see why you're having so much trouble finding something to wear for a business lunch."

"I want to send the right message."

He picked up the most recently discarded pants and blouse and held them up. "What's the right message?"

She leaned out of the huge walk-in closet and frowned at him.

"Did you go to so much trouble for our first date?" he couldn't help asking.

Janice walked out of the closet, a burnt orange sweater making her golden skin glow. He sucked in the whistle. He didn't want her looking this good for another man. But it wasn't the clothes that worried him, it was the glow in her face. She was excited, more excited than he'd ever seen her and it hurt that her excitement had not a damn thing to do with him.

"I don't want you following me," she ordered and moved to her mirror to apply makeup that she didn't need.

"I don't follow you."

"Then I don't want you having me followed."

"I was thinking that I would like to help. I'm sure that there are things that I can do."

"You have work to do, you don't have to come with me."

"You forget I don't have to do anything; there is no one who can make me come into the office. I'm my own boss. What's wrong? You don't want me with you?"

"Why don't you tell me what's wrong? Why are you acting so possessive? You don't own me, Simon."

He turned from her and winced wondering why lately 'you don't own me' were the only words she appeared to know. For God's sake, she was a writer; she should be able to think of something. Those words had the power to destroy him. He didn't want to own Janice, he wanted to marry her.

"Are you telling me that there is nothing I can do to help?" He walked up behind her. "I don't want him upsetting you."

"And I don't want you fighting my battles. I am not looking for a white knight, Simon."

"Is that the problem after three years, you don't want me with you because I'm white?"

"Grow up, Simon, do you think I give a damn about that?"

"Maybe you're worried that Tommy Strong will accuse you of selling out. Maybe that's the real reason you don't want me there."

Janice struck a pose, her hands on her hips, her lips pursed in concentration. "Why would you worry about Tommy? I'm sure that the million dollars you gave him will do what you intended. He's too indebted to you. If you think he's going to rekindle something, think again. He hates me as much as I hate him. You saw the way he glared at me. Money is more important at this stage of the game than him trying to get into my pants. Don't worry."

She walked to Simon and kissed him playfully, surprised when he crushed her to him and held her for a long moment. "Simon, what's going on?" She looked at him. "You've been behaving strangely for months now. Are you ill?"

"If I were, would you care?" he asked, releasing her at last.

"Of course I'd care."

"Why?" he asked. "Why would you care?"

"Because contrary to public opinion I'm not completely cold. I can care."

"Tell me something. Why in three years if you care have I never met your family? Are you afraid they wouldn't approve of me?"

Janice laughed. "They'd approve of you, they would love you. It's me and what I write that they don't approve of."

"Then introduce me to them, set it up."

"Are you asking me to prove something to you?"

"I'm asking you to introduce me to your family as the man you're going to marry."

She stared at him, hating the change that had come over him. They had said they would avoid all the usual relationship pitfalls. They had more of a merger, she'd always thought, but now he was behaving strangely, as though, she shivered, as though they were in love and he was jealous. "Simon, if you want you can come with me," she offered.

"Are you giving me an either/or choice? Either I come with you to Tommy's lunch or I meet your family?"

"You can do both." She frowned slightly, dabbed on a bit of lipstick, put her hair in a ponytail and walked away.

Simon stared after her, not liking the way he was feeling. He hadn't been indecisive in twenty years. He'd always known what he wanted and had gone after it, and that included Janice Lace. He'd wanted her from the moment he'd first laid eyes on her. She, however, had not wanted anything to do with him. She'd looked him up and down, smiled coolly and walked away from him the same as she'd done now. It was only after she'd learned who he was that she'd taken the time to give him a second glance.

He'd approached her and asked if that made a difference. She hadn't hesitated when she raised her eyes and smiled and told him, 'Of course.'

He'd laughed at her brutal honesty, at her refusal to pretend and he'd set about to woo her, get her to change her mind, though she kept reminding him that she wasn't into commitments. He'd proclaimed it also. In the beginning he'd thought he meant it until he woke one morning with her in his arms and knew that he wanted her there for the rest of his life. He'd tried to tell himself that he didn't love her, that he wasn't sure. So many excuses and all of them a lie.

He'd worked hard to keep his past from her, probably as hard as she'd worked to keep hers from him. But with money, hers had been easily uncovered. If he'd found one person to tell him that Janice had dumped Tommy Strong he would have left it alone, but he hadn't. Simon knew they had never really ended it and now Simon had a funny feeling that he'd started something that wouldn't be so easy to stop.

Chills raced up and down his spine with lightening speed and he wanted, no, needed to be near Janice. He followed her into the dressing room, wanting to make love to her, lay claim to her body if not her love. She looked ravishing in the sweater, much too ravishing, he thought as he eyed her critically and lied. "That sweater makes you look fat," he stated in a matter of fact manner.

She turned and glared at him, then at her reflection in the mirror. "Are you sure?" she asked.

"I'm sure."

She turned from side to side. "I thought it looked nice."

"There is just something about it that makes you look washed out. Maybe you need some more makeup. I don't know." He hunched his shoulders and stood rooted to the spot as she began changing again, this time asking his opinion, which he freely gave. Finally she pulled a shapeless top covered with flowers over her head. A top he hated, had hated from the moment she'd bought it. He'd told her so and had always believed she'd bought it out of spite.

"That's the one," he stated. "You look professional and warm, not cold and callous. That one will be perfect." He turned and left, disappointed that she was putting so much time into looking just right for a man she claimed to hate. He couldn't even be pleased that no man with eyesight would find her attractive in that hideous outfit. Well, they could, but the blouse would definitely peg her as a woman without taste.

Janice smiled to herself as she tugged on the top, wondering if Simon really thought she was not on to his little ploy. He hated that top, and as a matter of fact so did she. She'd only bought it to put him in his place. He'd gone shopping with her and had expressed too many opinions on her choices. In the beginning it had been fun, but then he'd started acting in a high-handed manner, giving the saleswoman the things that he approved of and discarding the things that he didn't.

He'd discarded this top and Janice would have left it on the discarded pile, but she thought she saw a smirk around the corners of his mouth and she wasn't having it. So, she'd grabbed the blouse, pleased when he protested. Matter of fact, that day she'd worn the thing home and generally only wore it when she wanted to annoy Simon.

Now she would wear it for a different reason. It was ugly, and like Simon, she didn't want to have Tommy think that she was trying to impress him. She surveyed the blouse again. *This should do it*, she thought, and left the dressing room.

"I need to put in a couple of hours writing." She walked toward the door before stopping and glancing over her shoulder. "Come and get me in two hours. You know how I lose track of time."

"You still working on the same book?"

"A little, but that will be hard to sell. So, I'm working on the one I'm contracted for."

"Hard to sell? Are you kidding? You want it published, you've got it." Simon narrowed his eyes and waited.

"Stop trying to manipulate my career. Two hours, then come to my office and get me," Janice repeated as she headed down the stairs to her office.

For two hours Janice had sat with Simon while Tommy laid out his plans. One thing was certain: It would take up more time than she had. He had more graphs and charts with market studies than she would have thought possible. It was evident he'd done his homework and now he was expecting her to do the same.

"Have you forgotten I'm a writer? I have deadlines; I can't possibly put this much time into the bookstores."

"Of course not," Tommy said in a cool voice. "I forgot you work, unlike the rest of us who are trying to help."

"Look," Simon interrupted, "she's trying."

"Really?" Tommy countered. "So far all I've heard is that she's willing to do a few book signings."

"I said I would also donate books," Janice interrupted. "You're leaving that out."

"I can help," Simon offered. "I can do some of the things you have lined up for Janice. I can go into the communities and where I go the press will follow. That will create a buzz."

Tommy turned slowly from staring at Mary Jo to gaping open-mouthed at Simon Kohl. "That's very generous of you but I was really looking for a high profile African American to do the promo, no offense."

Watching, Janice saw the little muscles that twitched in Simon's jaw and she felt anger toward Tommy for treating him that way. He'd been barely civil to him during the entire meeting and she was sick of it.

"Tell me something, Tommy. Why is Simon's money good enough for the cause but he isn't? You didn't complain about the color of his skin when you took his check, did you?"

She watched while Tommy's head snapped back to Simon with his eyes narrowed. His mouth parted as though he were going to speak but he remained silent. The two men eyed each other and she tried unsuccessfully to decipher what was passing between them, what unspoken message they had exchanged. It was Simon who finally broke the silence.

"Don't worry about it." He squeezed Janice's hand. "I understand Mr. Strong's objections. I'm sure it wasn't anything personal."

"No, it wasn't anything personal," Tommy offered, yet there was a hidden message there and Janice didn't miss it.

"Janice, you can stay. Just let me call for a car and you can take the limo." Simon smiled in Tommy's general direction. "I'll loosen things up for you with your deadline. Take all the time you need to help with the bookstores."

"Thanks for giving Mary Jo your approval and your permission. I didn't know that anyone but the writer dictated the time that was needed to write a book. It's interesting that after all these years of running a bookstore, I'm just now finding out it's the publisher pulling the strings." Tommy smiled at Simon, the smile not reaching his eyes. "Do you also do her writing for her?"

"Simon doesn't do my writing or my planning. I take care of my own schedule and I run my own life. You don't need to make arrangements for me, Simon. I can get home on my own. You take the limo."

"Yes, Simon, you take the limo. I'll bring Mary Jo home when we're done."

Both Mary Jo and Simon turned and glared at him. "Sorry," he said. "After a lifetime of knowing a person it's very hard to just adjust to calling them by another name." He smiled. "Somehow Janice Lace doesn't fit you." Tommy cocked his head to the left and squinted. "But then again, neither does Mary Jo. I think Mary Jo died about twelve years ago. Am I right?"

The question was asked politely but it was a loaded one and all three of them were aware of it. Both men wanted to see how she handled it. "Yes, Mary Jo died twelve years ago," Janice answered Tommy, "but that's because she grew up."

"And became Janice Lace." Tommy smiled.

"And became Janice Lace," she admitted.

"So you went from a determined young woman wanting to be a positive role model for African Americans to a woman who with the power of her voice, could use words to change things for the better, to write about good things that African Americans do...to being what? What do you do? A hatchet job on us. Now it's hard to tell that you yourself are black. On second though, it might be easier to package Simon Kohl off to the community, pretend that he's black. At least they are aware of who he is."

"Janice has done a lot to be proud of." Simon defended her, his voice angry, his stance defiant.

This time Tommy wasn't polite. "Maybe Janice has, Mary Jo hasn't. Mary Jo would never have allowed any man to take over and fight her battle." He smiled sadly. "I guess you're right, Mary Jo did die."

"Janice doesn't need me to fight her battles."

"Doesn't she?" Tommy laughed.

"No, she doesn't." Janice glared at Simon. "I can handle my own battles, though I didn't know we were at war, Tommy. How can our petty fights help with any cause?"

She waited while silently he fumed. She sensed an underlying anger beneath Simon's polished veneer but she wasn't giving into it. She wasn't going to be in the middle of a testosterone posturing contest. "Simon, I'll see you at home later."

"What time do you think you'll be there? I'll wait dinner for you."

"I don't know," she said, a bit annoyed seeing the smirk on Tommy's face. "Don't wait up for me. It will probably be late before I get home."

Simon looked at her and bent his head toward hers to kiss her and she turned her face slightly, causing his kiss to fall on her cheek. She saw the quick flash of hurt in his eyes and turned away.

"Okay, Tommy," she said, "let's get started." She was aware that Simon was still standing there but there was nothing she could do about it now. The one thing she wouldn't do was have Tommy Strong think she'd changed so much that she was now a weak female. She ignored the silence and pretended that Tommy staring over her head at Simon had no significance.

"I trust you'll take good care of my fiancée, Mr. Strong. Make sure she gets home safely," Simon said, emphasizing the word fiancée. Then he walked out of the bookstore at last.

"What the hell was that all about?" Janice said as soon as the door slammed shut.

"I didn't ask for Simon Kohl's help, I asked for yours. Why don't you tell me what the deal is with you and that guy?"

"You know what the deal is. We're engaged. You were there the day he announced it."

"Tell me something, did he check out your teeth as well as everything else?"

"What the hell are you talking about?"

"I'm talking about you and that guy and his attitude toward you. He acts as if he owns you. I've done a lot of research on him."

"Why?"

"When a man hands me a million dollar check, I want to know something about him, like why. And what the hell he's trying to buy."

"He was only trying to help the bookstores stay open."

"I don't believe it," Tommy answered. "He found out about us. I may not have the resources to get the information as quickly, but I can still get it. He's been digging into your past, our past," he amended, "for months and I don't like it. I know how the guy treats people, like he owns them."

"He's not Donald Trump."

"I know he's not. He's richer and more devious. He thinks money buys everything, including people. I just don't want you hurt."

"When did you start worrying about what would hurt me and what wouldn't? You sure as hell didn't give a damn about my feelings twelve years ago," Janice snapped. She wanted badly to throw something at him. He had a nerve talking about Simon. It wasn't Simon who'd hurt her, it was Tommy.

"Do you think you know everything about Simon Kohl that you need to know?"

"If I don't it's my business, isn't it? It's my life."

"Are you sure about that? One minute you tell me you have to write, that you don't have time to help me, the next he gives you permission to do so and look, here you are, your schedule is freed up."

"Simon didn't give me permission."

"That's what it looked like from where I stood."

"He doesn't own me."

"Right."

"He doesn't."

"Whose house are you living in?"

Janice cringed and refused to answer.

"Who pays your salary?"

"I earn my money."

"Yeah, right."

Again Janice cringed. "Why are you doing this?"

"Just conversation." Tommy smiled. "Tell me who manages your money." He looked at her face and smiled again. "Don't tell me, Simon Kohl. You don't think he owns you, think again. You sold your books to him, and then you sold yourself." He picked up her hand and flicked his thumb over the sapphire and diamond ring. "You're everything you said you would never be." He hunched his shoulders. "But like you said, it's your life."

"I'm marrying him."

"Good, I could see the love between the two of you."

Janice knew she should end the conversation, stop talking with Tommy about her private life. "What are you talking about?"

"Well, I've seen you two together twice now and the first time, you looked as if you wanted to kill him. You were glaring at him so hard that the man's heart should have stopped." His lips twitched and he paused. "Of course some of your reaction might have been to seeing me again."

"I had no reaction to seeing you."

"Then that was a strange way for a woman to treat the man she's going to marry, the man she loves, within moments of having it announced to the world. And just now, for example, he attempted to kiss you goodbye and you turned your head. I'm only going by what I see. What's wrong, Mary Jo, don't you love him?"

"There are many ways to care for a person." She tossed her hair, trying not to let him rile her. She was determined that she wouldn't tell Tommy that she loved Simon. Why should she? She hadn't even admitted it to Simon.

"And you care for him, is that it?" Tommy asked, knowing that he was annoying her. "Does he care for you also?"

"Look, Tommy, how Simon and I feel about each other is not your concern."

"I agree, but if you aren't marrying the man for love, then that means it's something else, something he has that you want. Not that I'm complaining, mind you, but that would mean he bought you. Sort of makes you his slave, wouldn't it? Maybe you have helped the cause, Mary Jo. Now instead of our people being hunted and captured, we can sell ourselves into slavery for a few trinkets and our name in the papers." He smiled. "Ready to start working?"

CHAPTER EIGHT

It was well after midnight when Tommy pulled up in front of Simon Kohl's mansion and turned toward Mary Jo.

"Nice place, Janice."

"Janice?"

"That's your name now, isn't it?"

"Yes, but I thought you weren't going to use it."

"Why not? You're not Mary Jo Adams. When she returns I'll use the name. Until then, while we're working together, I'll call you Janice."

She smiled at him, a weak, uncertain smile. She knew he was saying he was disappointed in her and his concession to use the new name she'd given herself expressed his disapproval.

Somewhere inside her she didn't want that from him. As much as she still hated him she didn't want him to not respect her. His anger she could deal with, but she didn't know if she could deal with his lack of respect for who she was now, for what she had become. She couldn't think of anything to say to him, so she just smiled, feeling inadequate, not remembering having ever felt that way in Tommy's presence.

"Nice place you have here," Tommy repeated.

She almost said that it wasn't hers, but of course he was already aware of that, so she said nothing.

"Goodnight, Janice." He stared and she got out, wondering what she had been waiting for. Was it for Tommy to open the door, for him to say something nice, for him to kiss her? She shivered. She didn't know what she had waited for.

She went into the mansion and walked up the spiral staircase to her bedroom.

"You're awfully late."

"I didn't know I had a curfew," she said, turning to where Simon sat in a chair by the window. "What were you doing? Spying on me again?"

"I was waiting for you," he answered.

"Did you see anything that interested you?"

"Where have you been? I know there are no bookstores that are open this late."

"You forget Tommy has his own store. He can keep it open as long as he likes."

"Is that where you were, in Tommy Strong's bookstore?"

He'd turned from the window and was staring at her. "All of this time, is that where you were?"

"Why the third degree?"

"I didn't know that was what I was doing. I was only asking."

"And I told you, but still you're asking and you're beginning to annoy me." She walked past him, stripping off her clothes and tossing them into a chair, thinking that was a Janice act. Mary Jo would either hang up her clothes or put them in the hamper. She knew no one would take care of it for her. She turned the water on in her shower and climbed inside, letting the hot water wash away the tension she'd shouldered the entire day. When she was done, she still felt the weight of it but she couldn't hide in there forever.

She opened the door, not surprised that Simon was standing there waiting for her.

"Here," he said and handed her the towel. "I don't know if I need to tell you this again but somehow I get the feeling that I should. I will not tolerate your sleeping around."

"Have you known me to sleep around?"

"I'm not kidding, Janice."

"Neither am I."

"I don't want you sleeping with Tommy Strong."

"Then suppose you tell me who I can sleep with?"

He walked up to her, tilted her chin with his finger and warned, "You're trying my patience. Don't push me too hard or you're going to force me to push back."

"You don't own me, Simon." Again she noticed that strange quirk of his jaw and a flash of something in his eyes.

He lifted her finger with her engagement ring. "We're getting married."

"That doesn't mean that you own me."

"It does mean that I have the right to expect you not to embarrass me, not to go screwing around. How the hell do you think it looks when you're climbing out of this guy's truck at all hours of the night?"

He had almost said what he wanted, but now wasn't the time. Janice was more combative than usual. He couldn't let her know now how much it mattered to him. He'd have to make her believe that it was because of his reputation.

"Come to bed," he said and held out his hand. "I've missed you."

"I'm tired," she answered and walked away. He sucked in his breath as she dropped the towel and headed for the bed, not bothering with a gown or even one of his shirts that she sometimes liked to wear. Simon knew her plan. She was going to torture him, lie there naked in bed with him growing harder by the second, and she was going to turn over and go to sleep. Yes, he was well aware of her tactic. She'd done it before, anytime she'd gotten angry and wanted to teach him a lesson.

Tonight he wasn't in the mood to be reprimanded for asking what he had a right to ask. He went to her drawer, retrieved the first thing he saw and tossed it at her. "I suggest you put that on, because if you decide you're going to sleep in the buff I'm going to make love to you."

"You mean rape me?" She threw the gown to the floor.

"Call it what you will, but I'm not kidding." He retrieved the the garment and held it out to her. "You've got five seconds." He waited while she debated the matter and for once seemed to know that he meant business. She yanked the garment over her head.

"What's wrong with you, Simon? You're acting crazy."

He climbed into the bed beside her and turned his back to her. Yes, he was acting crazy, like a man possessed, a man afraid of losing something he valued. He had yet to know what it was about the woman in his bed that turned him into someone he didn't like. He only knew that she did and he was tired of putting up with it.

As hungry as he was for her body, he didn't want to touch her, not after she'd been in the company of her former lover for hours, not after she'd taken hours getting dressed for Tommy in front of him, as though he didn't matter, as though they weren't engaged, as though they had not been in each other lives for three years. As though she didn't care.

Simon shuddered and turned, surprised to find Janice staring at him. His resolve vanished and he crushed her to him, kissing her deeply. He saw fear slide into her eyes and her fear slid into his soul and froze him. He stopped instantly. He couldn't believe what he'd almost done. He released her and stared at her until he saw the fear replaced by confusion. He didn't blame her; he was confused as hell himself.

The thought occurred to him to move to another room but that would be admitting defeat, that he couldn't lie next to her in bed and not have her. He had to prove to both of them that he could.

Besides, he didn't like that momentary look of fear in her eyes and if he left her now, only God knew what she would make of that. She'd probably think he had planned to rape her. He moved his body as close to the edge of the bed as he could get, knowing that she was still awake. After about an hour of silence he said to her, "I'm not going to pounce on you. You don't have to stand guard."

"Simon, what's wrong? Why don't you just tell me?"

"I'm just tired, baby."

"Are you sure that's all?"

"I'm sure," he said, moving to lie on his back, opening his arms for her, wondering if she would come to him. She did. He sighed and closed his arms around her. "Go to sleep, baby," he said. He kissed her forehead and promptly fell asleep with her in his arms.

When he woke Janice was still in his arms, awake and staring at him, a puzzled look on her face.

"Have you been awake all night?"

"Off and on." She smiled.

"Why, is something wrong?" He ignored the flutter in his chest and waited.

"Nothing happened with Tommy," she began and looked more directly at him. "Nothing's going to happen with him."

"Why are you telling me? You said it wasn't any of my business."

Janice smiled. "Simon, I'm not taking the bait this morning. I've been thinking about it and I guess you did have a reason to be upset. I could have called and told you I was going to be out so late."

"It would have been the considerate thing to do." He watched as she rubbed her chin and studied him before speaking again.

"I'm not very considerate of you or your feelings am I?"

"As much as I'd love to say it's not true I'm afraid I'll have to be truthful. No, you're not very considerate of me. Sometimes I get the feeling you don't even like me."

"That's not true."

"I hope not."

"Simon, I'm not very good at this mushy stuff. Call me crazy, but I like fighting. I like fighting with you. I thought you did too. I thought that was us, our thing, that neither of us felt the need to mess things up with all the crap other people bring into their lives."

Simon lifted his body on one elbow and stared curiously at her. "What kind of crap are you talking about?"

"You know, always kissing in public, getting jealous if you see the other person smile at someone else."

"Since you don't do any of those things, I suppose you're talking about me." He closed his eyes. "I can understand why you like our fighting," he said as he opened his eyes again. "It always nets another piece of jewelry for you, but what do I get?" he teased. "You've never bought me jewelry."

"Would you like for me to?"

"No, I can buy my own."

"Then what would you like?" she asked, her voice dropping low as the lust in Simon's eyes filled her and she trembled at the intensity.

"I want you," he moaned as he slipped the gown from her body and lifting her, pulled it away with one swift movement. "Our love-hate relationship is beginning to make me dizzy. But I'm not ready for it to end." He looked down at her in awe and wonder. He definitely wasn't ready for it to end.

Simon couldn't believe his good fortune. One minute she was hot, the next cold, and now she was hot, hot and ready for him. He lay over her, sucking her nipples into his mouth, loving the feel of her golden caramel body. She was as smooth as silk, and softer than anything he'd ever touched. And deep inside he knew she hid a secret hurt.

How he wanted to be the one to share her pain. But she wouldn't open up to him. She'd told him about Tommy's leaving her and he'd heard the pain in her voice but sensed an even deeper hurt and he wanted to be the one to comfort her.

Simon feared Tommy Strong. He feared Tommy would banish her pain and regain her love. He didn't want that to happen, but he had no idea how in hell to prevent it.

Tommy was his doing, he'd brought him back into her life, but somehow he knew as much pain as he would probably feel, it would be for the best.

Whatever secret torture Janice was hiding she had to let go of before she could finally give him what he wanted. Until she told him that she felt for him what he felt for her, he would be incomplete.

He slid into her body, finding her wet, hot and ready. His flesh trembled with need. He rode her as though it were the first time, or his last. He reveled in the way he felt buried inside her, the way her body seized him, clutching him, wrapping him in her heat. She belonged to him whether she wanted to believe it or not. And he belonged to her.

He came with a guttural groan a second after he felt her writhing beneath him, clutching him in her need, her lust, and her fulfillment. He lay on her for a few long moments. "Did we just make up?" he asked, a smile in his voice.

"I'd say so," she answered.

"I guess that means I need to go shopping later." He smiled and looked down, wanting to make her smile. "Want to come with me?"

"Simon, you don't have to buy me anything. In fact, I don't want you to," Janice answered and he noticed the slight chill in her voice. Damn. What had happened in just a few seconds to turn her from a raging inferno into a block of ice?

"I don't understand," he tried again. "I always buy you something when we fight. You always like it. You've never complained before."

"I'm not complaining, Simon, I'm just saying it's not necessary. You don't have to buy me," she said.

He rolled off her and flung his hand over his face. Only a fool wouldn't know that that remark had come from somewhere, and he had the strong impression it had come from one Mr. Tommy Strong. The man was a fast worker, he'd give him that.

"I've never tried to buy you. I like buying you nice things. I like the way your eyes light up." He laughed softly. "I like the way your greedy little fingers rip the wrapping paper to shreds. I like buying you gifts."

"But if you give me something now, it makes it seem like you're either paying for sex or you're buying me."

Simon was slowly losing patience; still, they were at a nice place. At the moment they weren't fighting and even though Janice had said she liked fighting with him, he'd found he didn't like it so much. He'd much rather sit and stare at her or make love to her than fight with her.

"Okay, how about a day of pampering for both of us? We'll take a long hot shower or a bubble bath and then we'll climb back into bed and have our breakfast brought up and we'll stay here all day. I'll cancel all of my appointments and we'll just stay in bed and make plans for our future."

Janice wanted what Simon was offering her. She didn't want to do the things she'd promised she'd do. She didn't need to spend the day with Tommy again. It was too soon, much too soon. Still, she'd given her word.

"I wish I could...but...I...I told Tommy I would be there early." She saw a flash of pain, then a look of anger come into his eyes and again she wondered what was going on. He'd never acted like this before.

She took a good long look at the man she was going to marry and a shiver of recognition began somewhere inside her and wormed its way through to her brain and made her aware.

Simon Kohl was in love with her. This wasn't what she expected. A small gasp of surprise came out before she could stop it. The thought of his truly loving her would possibly have made her happy a few days ago. Now all she could think about was the fact that her loving Tommy had not been enough. He'd failed her when she needed him most. Her chest constricted with fear. Janice was afraid for Simon to love her, afraid that once he admitted it, he would stop, that he would leave her, just as Tommy had.

"Simon," she almost moaned. "I like us the way that we are. Don't change it please."

"We could have so much more," he answered.

"Don't, Simon. I don't know how to give what you're asking. I thought you understood that. I thought we were together because we each filled a need for the other. I thought what we had was…" She shrugged. "I thought it was uncomplicated."

"My feelings for you make things complicated?"

"Yes," she answered.

"We're getting married."

"I know, but still…" She closed her eyes. "I told Tommy I would work with him again today."

"Is working with Tommy more important to you than spending time with me?" There, he'd said it. He'd not intended to, but what the hell? Might as well get it out in the open between them.

Janice got out of the bed, went to her purse and got out Tommy's business card. She'd looked at the thing so many times that she knew the number by heart. But something told her it wouldn't be wise to dial his number without making a show that she didn't know it. She came back to the bed, aware that Simon's eyes had never left her body. She slid between the covers.

She looked at the card and dialed the number, expecting a machine to pick up. She wasn't prepared for the strong masculine voice on the other end of the line.

She felt a strange sensation in the pit of her stomach and an even stronger one on the back of her neck. That one she knew the cause of. It was her fiancé's razor sharp gaze burning her with the precision of a laser. She was on trial.

"Tommy, I'm sorry, I'm going to have to bail on you today."

"Did Mr. Kohl disapprove of the late hour?" Tommy replied.

"Look, I said I'm sorry, just rearrange the store appearances. We can fit them in later."

"Don't you think you'd better ask your fiancé for permission? I don't want to make plans for you to visit bookstores and have you not show up. But then, what can I expect? You've never given back anything to the community. What made me think you would start now? Go ahead, ask the master when you can come, and try telling me again he doesn't own you."

Janice knew what he was doing yet her mouth felt as dry as cotton. She also knew as loud as Tommy was talking that Simon could hear every word. She saw his eyes narrow and she opened her mouth, but he didn't give her a chance to say a word.

"Why do you have to make excuses to him? Why can't you just tell him that you've chosen to spend the day with me?" Simon growled angrily.

She knew he was asking as a request but with Tommy's words still burning in her ears it felt more like a command, more like he believed he had a right to control her, more like he owned her.

For a moment she wavered. Then Simon looked away from her and she snapped out of it.

"Look, I said I would make up the stores we're not visiting today. Don't try using guilt on me, Tommy, it's not going to work. I stayed out much too long with you last night. That was inconsiderate of me and yes, if you must know, I'm spending the day with my fiancé. Just so we're clear on this, it's my choice."

The phone slammed in her ear and she smiled. Tommy had almost pulled her back into his clutches. She was surprised at the ease of his manipulation.

Her victory didn't last long. She looked up and saw that Simon had gotten out of the bed and was staring down at her.

"Is that where all that nonsense about me trying to buy you came from?"

"Tommy knew me when I was young. We were going to do so many things to change the world. Tommy has worked very hard at uncovering families in the United States and across the world with ties to slavery. You've been hearing about that." Janice hunched her shoulders.

"I'm afraid Tommy gets carried away and sees a slave master in the face of every non-black person that he meets. He's probably more dedicated than most." She smiled an apology. "I don't know why he keeps trying to annoy me by saying things about you. I mean, the generous donation you gave him, that money would really help his work."

Simon fought to keep his voice steady. "I thought he was heading up the campaign to save the bookstores."

"He is. That's his passion. But the history, that's his life."

"It seems like the two of you have stopped hating each other."

Janice looked closely to see where this was going before she answered. "I didn't get all of this from him. I got it from the people that work with him and the other bookstore owners that he took me to. As for the hate between us, I'd say it's still alive and well."

"Are you sure you want to work with him? I could find other ways for you to help the bookstores."

"No, Simon, thanks," she said, wondering at his sudden change of mood. "This will be good for my career. Maybe it's something I need to do." She laughed. "If not, I'll write about it. Anyway, I'm not going to give Tommy a chance to say he knew I would fail, that I wouldn't follow through."

"Does his opinion matter?"

She studied him. His color was gray and she noticed the little twitch in his face. Something was definitely going on. She thought she'd put her finger on it but there was something more. "Simon, do you want to tell me what's going on with you? You've been acting so strange now for months."

He smiled but it didn't go farther than his lips. "Nothing's wrong. I guess I'm getting wedding day jitters."

Janice laughed with relief. That made sense. Getting married was enough to make a person nervous. "We don't even have a date set; you have a long time to get nervous."

"A long time?" He stopped and stared. "Why a long time?"

"Do you have any idea how long it takes to plan a wedding?"

"Yeah, give me a couple of hours and I'll have it all arranged."

"Oh, that's right, I forgot. Well, it still takes time to invite people, to pick out a dress, flowers, get a church, a banquet facility, and we have to decide whom to invite."

"I don't want it to take forever. I want us to get married soon and I don't want a lot of people, family only. I get tired of the press in every aspect of my life. I don't want the buzz."

"But you made a public announcement."

"That's because I'm proud to be marrying you, but I don't want the world involved in our wedding." Simon paused and studied her. "Is a big wedding something you always fantasized about? If it is—"

"No, Simon, small will work for me also."

There was no need to tell him that yes, once upon a time in a life far away, when she'd been a little girl named Mary Jo Adams, she'd dreamed of a big wedding. But all those dreams had been shattered. She felt a tremor steal over her and Tommy's face popped into her mind for some reason. She thought of the picture he made sitting behind the wheel of his Explorer. The truck was so much like the man, big, strong and black.

Janice's gaze slid to Simon's face and she eyed him guiltily. She felt shame for her thoughts burning into her. She'd never tried to make Simon Kohl into something he was not, and she'd not given a care about the color of his skin. If Tommy Strong had not reentered her life with a bang, she was sure she wouldn't have thought about it now.

Damn Tommy, she thought angrily. He'd always possessed the ability to have her thinking about him constantly. That was going to change.

"Janice, are you thinking about Mr. Strong? You've got this funny look on your face."

"I thought we were going to spend the day in bed together. Please, for one day let's not fight," Janice pleaded.

"I can't believe you don't want to fight."

"Believe it, I don't, not today. I want to not answer the phone, not turn on the computer. I don't want anything to do with work for either of us. So call your secretary and let him know."

"Do you want to set a date today, maybe plan a visit to your parents?"

"We can do that, but not today, maybe tomorrow. I just want a carefree day."

"To make love?" he asked.

"To make love," she answered.

"To love me?" Simon tried, pushing farther than he'd ever pushed before.

"Don't ruin things, Simon."

She closed her eyes and a stab of pain pierced him. *Ruin things? Talk of love would be ruining things?* He closed his eyes also. "I've never pushed you," he said at last.

"I know," she answered. *And I'm grateful for that,* she thought. "That's why I'm with you, Simon, you've never pushed me. You've never asked me for what I can't give."

"Why not?" he asked. "How do you know? You never allow yourself to try. The moment you feel something for me you shut it off like a valve to a hot water tank. Tell me, how did you become so adept at turning off your emotions?"

"Simon," she pleaded.

"What? I'm curious, I'm not picking a fight."

"It feels like it."

"You're trying to get me to change the subject." He smiled. "Don't worry, baby. I'm still not going to press you. Just remember that most people find the things they're looking for have been right there in front of them the entire time."

"What are you saying, Simon?"

"I'm saying don't go looking, I'm serious about that."

"Simon."

He swallowed. "I can't forgive infidelity on either of our part. I've never been unfaithful to you and all I ask is that you do the same."

"I haven't been."

"I mean even in your thoughts. I don't want you dreaming of anyone else when I'm in bed with you."

Janice frowned, wondering where that had come from. She'd known Simon Kohl for over three years and as far as she knew he wasn't a mindreader.

Before she could protest, even before she could frame an answer, he lifted her in his arms and carried her to the shower.

He did as he promised and made love to her the entire day. At one point she looked at him and saw his need and passion mixed with his emotions and she'd wondered how long he'd loved her, and how it had happened. Then she wished she had known before Tommy came back into her life and reminded her of her reasons for not trusting a man's love, for not letting Simon know that she loved him. All the trust she'd had had died the day she'd lain on the table submitting her body to an abortion, doing something that could never be undone.

Since then Janice had secretly done penance, enduring her family's disappointment in her career and lack of a steady relationship. She'd deliberately put up barriers when her boyfriends wanted to get closer, when they told her they loved her. They couldn't accept that she could make love with abandon yet not love the man who gave her the pleasure.

In the end her relationships always ended with her being accused of being cold. She wasn't cold, she just didn't see the need for involvement. It wasn't necessary in her life.

She'd thought Simon was the perfect lover. She'd checked him out and found he'd never been in love. He'd agreed that love wasn't on his mind, that he wouldn't expect it from her. And that she wasn't to expect it from him.

They'd shaken hands on it then made love with wild abandon. Janice had thought it was settled. She was Simon's caramel arm candy. She made him feel comfortable when they frequented black night clubs and he was hers.

She never questioned his preference for anything black, from the culture to the food and to the women. She thought that like many white people he had some hidden guilt he was trying to atone for. She didn't care. He was a good lover and he didn't love her.

He was perfect. Besides, the added bonus was that she didn't have to worry about money because Simon had personally invested her money. She had only to watch it grow.

If she ever decided to give up her career, she would have more than enough to take care of herself. And regardless what anyone thought about her marrying Simon, she would always know that it wasn't because of his money and he would know it. She had her own.

But this, his falling in love with her, him wanting her to love him, this wasn't supposed to happen. She clung to Simon, wishing with all her heart that she could let go of the past enough to trust him with her love. If only that were possible she could give them both what they wanted.

She quivered in his arms and held him even closer, wishing for the impossible.

Simon made love to Janice the entire day, only stopping to replenish his energy. It was liberating, making love to her, loving her and having her know that he loved her. True, she didn't want to have him love her and she refused to let him say it, but he'd made sure he said it with the way he touched her, with his tongue, his hands and his body. He'd tasted every inch of her, made her scream out for him over and over again.

And he saw a crack, microscopic but there. He intended to hammer away at that crack until he splintered the ice around her heart. As he thought that, she screamed out again and he wondered what would happen when she allowed herself to love him.

He was going for that. She was his and Tommy Strong would not be the one to make her say those words. He was a winner and he would win the love of his bride.

Simon glanced down at her as she gave in to release and he smiled at her. For him it was a done deal. She would love him. He'd see to that.

He made love to her from the bottom of her feet to the top of her head and every inch in between. He loved her until she was more than tired, worn out. She kissed his face, laughing and begging him to stop.

But he didn't. He wanted her to know that it was him loving her. He wanted to make sure that the next time she saw Tommy Strong it would be Simon Kohl on her mind. It would be him she felt caressing her deep inside. He gave her what she wanted, not demanding anything in return but for her to accept him and enjoy their being together.

Simon glanced in Janice's direction. She'd been sitting there for five minutes staring at the evening newspaper in front of her. "What's wrong?" he asked.

"Nothing," she answered.

His heart thudded hard in his chest and his breath caught at the pain etched on her face. "Baby, what's wrong," he said, moving over to her and taking the paper to read what had her upset.

"This review? Is that it?" He waited, puzzled, not wanting to admit to himself that he'd thought it was something in the paper about him that had put the pain in her eyes, glad that it wasn't. "Sweetheart, you're a professional, this happens and you know it. You're going to get bad reviews no matter how great your book is."

"I know that."

"Your book's number one."

"I know that also."

"Then what's the matter?"

"I'm human."

She'd said the words so softly that they tore away at his insides more than tears would have. His lady didn't like admitting to weaknesses. "Baby, I'll take care of this...I'll make sure—"

"No, Simon, like you said, I'm a professional. I'm in the public eye, people are entitled to their opinions and they're even entitled to take potshots. I have to suck it up."

Tears pooled in her eyes but didn't fall. Simon crushed her to him, rubbing her back. He felt her tremble, then grip him tighter. Then he felt the first crack in her emotional armor. She was right. She was human, she bled like he did. As much as he didn't like to see his baby hurting he was thrilled that he was the one who was comforting her. If he could he would go out and get every single person who'd ever said a mean thing about her and he would...Her lips lifted for his kiss and he entered her mouth, feeling the shiver of want trail down his spine into his groin.

Two little words, '*I'm human*' had melted away Janice's stoic resolve and liquefied Simon's heart. One day soon he was hoping the erosion of her emotions would allow her to see how very much he loved her, to admit how very much she loved him also. *I'm only human also,* he thought as he comforted her and himself with kisses. He attempted to take her pain away with his tongue.

"Simon, thank you," she said when he pulled away to catch his breath. He gazed into her eyes and saw all the things she couldn't hide. He smiled as he pulled her back into his arms to love her properly. It was in moments like this when her shield was down that he knew he mattered to her. It was moments like this that he prayed the gamble would pay off in the end, not only would Janice Lace marry him, but that she would love him in the still of the night and the quiet of the morning, in public, and in private. This was the promise he saw in her eyes. This was what made it all worthwhile. Simon had never been a fool going after the unattainable. What his soul desired was in his arms and moaning his name.

CHAPTER NINE

Tommy turned off the computer. The Internet site had yielded nothing that he didn't already know. But he didn't give up easily. He was determined to trace Simon Kohl all the way back to Adam and Eve if necessary. If Simon was going to marry Mary Jo, Tommy wanted to know everything there was to know about the man.

Janice Lace, a voice whispered in his mind and he cursed. She was not Janice Lace, no matter what he'd told her. She was Mary Jo Adams and he was determined to make her remember that.

The question as to why ran through his mind and he ignored it. It had nothing to do with old feelings. She was a black queen, and what he was about to do he would do for any of them.

He ignored the fact that the anger he'd carried in his heart for the past twelve years had flared anew from the moment he saw her and was now a raging fire.

"Hello," Tommy said to the voice on the other end of the phone. "I got someone I want you to check out, Simon Kohl."

"Do you know who the man is, what he can do, has done for the black community?" the voice asked him.

"Yes, I know who he is. He's too clean."

"Why him? He's always poured a lot of money into the black community," the voice answered.

"And that alone makes me wonder what he's hiding. The man thinks he's black."

"This wouldn't have anything to do with the fact that the man just announced his engagement to your old girlfriend, would it?"

Tommy gritted his teeth in anger. He was tried of people sticking their nose into his business. And they wouldn't be if Simon Kohl hadn't pulled him into his mess with that sham of a banquet. The only thing the man had wanted to do was buy Tommy's absence from Mary Jo's life. He should have kept him out of it. Until he saw her Tommy had no plans on ever contacting her. Now…well, Simon Kohl had started it.

"Tommy, you do know that we don't do this for personal reasons. So if that is the only thing you have going against the man, we're not going to get involved. That is not what we do."

"I'm not after revenge."

"Can you assure me of that?"

"Why would I be? I don't want Mary Jo."

"Who?"

"Janice Lace. I don't want her, I haven't thought about her in years," Tommy lied. "Why would I care about a woman I dumped so long ago that I'd almost forgotten her name?"

Tommy closed his eyes, knowing no part of anything he'd said was true.

"Give me some proof that Simon Kohl should be investigated."

"It's just a feeling," Tommy answered. "We've checked people out for less. What's the deal?"

"He's a powerful man."

"So what? We've exposed powerful men before and big business."

"He helps."

"I didn't think our heritage could be bought with money."

"Sometimes it's a little like one hand washing the other."

"If that's the case, then we're not doing the job I thought we were. Maybe it's our organization that should be exposed."

"Listen, Tommy, I didn't say that we wouldn't search information on the man. I just want to make sure it's not some personal vendetta."

"It's not," Tommy assured him, "but if it happens to help someone who used to be an old friend, would that be so bad?"

"No, it wouldn't be bad at all."

Tommy gave the man all the information he'd managed to dig up and told him just where he'd searched so he wouldn't have to bother turning over the same ground again.

He turned at the sound of Mary Jo's voice drifting to the back of the shop where he was.

"Later, man," he said and ended the call. "Janice," he yelled, "I'm back here." He felt a strange warmth creep over him and he rushed to assure himself that it had nothing to do with Mary Jo Adam, AKA Janice Lace, being less than five feet from him.

He knew eventually they would have to revisit the ghosts of their past, only now wasn't the time. Neither of them was ready for it; they'd hurt each other. He'd cursed himself a million times through the years for having run out on her. And he'd cursed her a million times for not believing that he loved her enough to come back. If only she'd had a little more faith in him, but she hadn't. She'd let what she wanted and her own fears deprive him of being a father to his child.

True, it was a child he hadn't wanted but he had come back to take over his responsibility like a man and she'd deprived him of that. He'd never been able to forgive her for that. She'd even taken the thought that together they had created a new life and crushed it, telling him that it hadn't been his. Tommy shook with the memory as he stared at the woman standing before him.

She was beautiful and polished self-assured and talented. And as cold as ice. He sensed no genuine warmth coming from her and he wondered for a moment what Simon found in her. It was as though she were dead inside.

She could fool the people who didn't know her but he'd known her intimately for four years, her body, mind and spirit, and he knew she was faking 'the woman with no emotion' persona she presented to the public. Every breath she drew was a lie. The only thing approaching genuine emotion had been the first day she'd seen him. Her hatred had been real enough. Since then, she'd managed to cover that up and show him the same artificial faces she'd shown her public. Before he was done with her he intended to crack that facade, melt the ice she'd encased her emotions in. Before they were through he would uncover her buried emotions. He would have the truth.

Simon Kohl called the one man he trusted with his life, more than his life, the one man he trusted with his past and his future, to come into his office.

"Harold, are you sure no one will ever find out about my family?"

"I'm sure, Simon. Why, what's the problem?"

"A problem I created. I made a wrong move and now I'm being called on it."

"Care to enlighten me on what the devil you're talking about?"

Simon didn't want to tell the man who was more like a father to him than his own had ever been. He knew Harold wouldn't approve of the methods he'd chosen to dig into his bride-to-be's past. He would have told Simon that it was none of his business. He would have said that she had as much right to her past as he did to his. Of course he knew all of this but still he'd felt the need to know and that need had overridden every decent emotion in his body.

"I just want you to make sure no one can get their hands on any of the information."

"Have they ever?"

"No, but I have the feeling this man will not rest until he digs up some dirt on me."

"Who is this man?"

"Tommy Strong."

"The man you gave the million dollar check to?"

"The man I tried to give the million dollar check to. He ripped it up."

"Oh."

"Oh what?" Simon asked. "What do you think you know, old man?"

"More than you want me to know. Your money couldn't buy the man and now you've made an enemy out of him. Is that the gist of it?"

Simon cringed at how easily Harold read him, how easily he had always read him.

"Why don't you tell her the truth? If she loves you she won't hold what happened in your family against you."

"That's the problem, Harold, old man; she doesn't want to love me."

"Then why are you doing all of this? Dump her and find a woman who does."

"It's not that easy."

"Please, I have to hear this one. Tell me why not."

"Because I love her."

For a long moment Harold was silent. "I thought you told me the two of you had an understanding."

"That was in the beginning."

"Funny, you never mentioned that you'd had a change of heart," Harold said.

"I didn't know that I needed to," Simon said, letting the sarcasm drag the words out, letting Harold know that it was Simon who was the boss and not the other way around.

Despite his love for the man, sometimes he was forced to put Harold in his place.

"When did this happen?" Harold asked.

"The timing doesn't matter." Simon smiled to himself, knowing he'd loved her almost from the beginning. It had just taken him a while to admit it to himself. That was one of the reasons that he'd been willing to give Janice time to come around, to recognize her love for him as he'd recognized his for her.

"Do you plan to have her sign a prenuptial?"

"Hell no," Simon shouted.

"That's suicide, man. How can you even think of marrying a woman without some type of protection? She can take half of everything you own."

"She doesn't have to take half of everything. I'm going to give her half of everything that I own."

"Are you thinking with your head?"

"I'm not sure, but it is what I'm going to do. Look I didn't call for us to debate my marriage. Just make sure my secret stays a secret."

"Don't worry, I'll take care of things on my end. It's not your secret I'm worried about, it's your senses. You seem to have taken leave of them and I'm afraid there's not very much I can do to help you if you don't allow me. I have told you since you were a child that what happened in your family was not your fault. You can't make up for it now, but God knows you've tried. Are you sure that your marrying this woman isn't another form of seeking absolution? You've been looking for it your entire life."

Simon closed his eyes tightly and growled low in his throat. Harold was lucky that he loved and respected him or he would be out on his ass and Harold damn well knew it.

"I'm going to tell you this one last time and I want you to listen, because I do not plan on ever repeating it to you again. Janice Lace is not my means of absolution. Yes, she's black; yes, I feel guilt; yes, I wish I could change the things my family did to black people but as far as my relationship with my fiancée is concerned, I love her with my whole heart, my body, my mind and my spirit. I want to make that clear. All that I have I give freely to her."

"Then that will have to be good enough for me," Harold said, his voice showing the resignation that he felt. Even Harold knew that there was a cutoff point for Simon's patience with him, and he would not push the man farther on the subject.

Simon slid his expensive loafers to the end of his desk and sighed. He wanted to be alone with his thoughts. He turned toward Harold and smiled. "Thanks for coming in. I'll talk to you later," he said, politely, indicating that it was time for Harold to leave his office.

He rubbed his eyes. Janice had promised not to stay all night with Tommy. They had plans and he was holding her to them. He didn't give a damn if he had to drag her kicking and screaming from the bookstore, he was determined that his fiancée would remain just that, his fiancée.

CHAPTER TEN

Janice stood for a moment on the threshold separating the back room of Tommy's store from the public arena. She felt strange, as though by crossing the barrier she would somehow be going back in time. It was a crazy feeling and she knew it, yet a faint memory was pulling at her and she didn't know if she wanted to take the step.

"Why are you just standing there?" Tommy was staring at her with a strange expression on his face. "Have you been standing there long? Did you hear me on the phone?" Then he shook his head and smiled. "I'm sorry, I didn't hear you come in."

Janice wondered about his questions. Was he worried about her having overheard something?

"Janice, are you coming in? We have a lot of work to do today."

She looked out at the open store and wondered what it was that made her hesitate. Then she crossed the threshold and followed Tommy.

She glanced around, saw the pile of papers spread out across the coffee table. She caught the scent of raspberry cinnamon coffee and started. He remembered. She had not had that since…It had been a long time. She bit down softly on her bottom lip, wondering why he'd remembered and why he'd made it.

She sat and began sifting through the papers, barely able to contain her composure. She lifted her eyes to him as he poured two mugs of coffee, put in the cream and sugar, then reached into the small fridge. She knew immediately what he was going for. He put a large dollop of whipped cream in one mug and sprinkled cinnamon over it and just like that Janice could feel herself slipping into the life of Mary Jo.

She reached for the cup, not making any mention of what he'd done, not saying more than thank you.

Tommy smiled to himself, barely able to stop the look of satisfaction from showing in his eyes. Did she really think that after four years of loving her he'd simply forgotten the things that made her mouth water?

Tommy wouldn't carry the thought any farther. He didn't want to look at her and imagine the smell of her sex, the feel of her nipples as he bit down softly. No, he didn't want to think of the way the juices flowed from her body to cover his fingers, his tongue, his burning flesh. Tommy had no need to remember those things, because as he turned back to look at her he realized that on a certain level those things had not changed.

What had changed was their faith in each other. That had been shattered. He watched as she sipped the coffee, saw her lick the whipped cream from her lips and got an instant erection.

For the past twelve years Tommy had not allowed lust to rule his life and he would not do it now. "How's the coffee?" he asked, moving away from her. He had to have normal conversation, anything to cool the fire burning in his loins.

"It's great," she answered.

He knew she was being deliberately vague, not a mention of the flavor, or the whipped cream and cinnamon sprinkles, though he knew she enjoyed it. He'd seen the pleasure wash over her at the taste.

If he hadn't been staring at her with that cocky quirk of his brow, Janice would have moaned aloud with her pleasure. In a way, the coffee competed with sex for her. It always had. She'd thought that Tommy had invented a secret aphrodisiac.

Later she'd realized that the coffee had always come either after or before they made love. It was their youthful passion that had been the catalyst, not the coffee. Still, the brew had been special to her, which was why she'd not allowed herself to drink it in a decade.

Now sitting here drinking it with Tommy, she felt her face flame as her eyes fell on the bulge at his crotch. She couldn't tear her gaze away. Thoughts of Simon weren't enough to make the flow of memories cease. It was only when the cup was empty that the feelings lessened.

"Want some more?" Tommy asked and she looked into the bottom of the cup, almost surprised that there was nothing left, even more surprised that Tommy had known.

"No thanks," she said. She didn't dare. "One cup was more than enough for me. I had coffee with Simon, before I left," she said, deliberately bringing her fiancé back into her life, back into her thoughts. Still, she felt a tremor as Tommy's hand brushed hers as he took the cup away.

"Good, then we can get down to business," Tommy said with a slight quiver in his voice.

"Just what are we going to do?" Her voice sounded strange to her ears. At least she'd torn her gaze away from Tommy's most intimate secrets, though those particular secrets were very well known to her. She blushed at her wanton thoughts, even though they had nothing to do with love or wanting but were simply a bit of déjà vu, nothing more.

"I was thinking you could write an article for *Black Train of Thought*, and maybe do an interview with *Black Rose.*" Tommy stopped at the puzzled look that crossed Mary Jo's face. "What's wrong?" he asked. Anger of what he knew the problem was pushed at him. She didn't have any idea whatsoever of what he was talking about.

Janice was embarrassed. "I don't mind doing the article or the interview. Just give me some background information."

"Just what kind of information?" He was going to make her sweat, make her say out loud that she had no knowledge of two of the most successful black publications to be launched in the past year.

He watched as she looked away, her look embarrassed. Well, she should be. Tommy was angrier than he'd been in a long time. Damn, he'd thought the change was just on the outside. Now he saw it was all the way through. She wasn't just an Oreo; she had nothing black left of her. She wasn't his Mary Jo. She was Janice Lace; he'd been kidding himself.

"Don't tell me you've never heard of these magazines?"

"Tommy, you don't have to speak to me as if I'm a moron. I can't possibly know of everything that's published."

"Have you heard of *Romantic Times*?"

"Of course."

"Then why can't you keep up with what's happening in the black world? You're black, Janice Lace. Regardless of what name you want to call yourself, you're still black. Remember that."

"Do you want my help or are you planning on picking apart everything that I don't know?"

As he looked at her with disgust, a genuine feeling of loss ripped through him. All the planning they'd done to have it come down to this. How was it possible? "Are you serious, you really haven't heard of them, Mary Jo? They've written articles about you. Didn't you know it?"

"No." She shook her head. "What did they do, rake me over the coals?"

"No, they praised your talents."

"I've been busy, Tommy. A lot of things have happened to me. My not knowing was not deliberate."

"What have you been doing, living as an ostrich? I don't see how all these months you could not have known."

"How long have they been out?"

"*Black Train of Thought* for nine months. *Black Rose* for six."

"That's not a long time."

"Long enough."

"Tommy, can't you let that go? I don't need your indignation. I just need to be briefed about them. I don't want to seem ignorant when I give the interview."

"But you are."

Janice recoiled from his words and for the first time in a decade the sting of tears burned her eyes and she sucked in her breath to keep them in. Still, her eyes pooled and she turned away.

She knew Tommy hated her but she'd never expected his cruelty to tear away at the carefully built facade she'd created. She stood and shivered, wishing she could fight with Tommy as she fought with Simon. She'd never been able to.

Tommy felt like a heel. He stood silently for a moment, the pool of tears in Janice's eyes getting to him. He'd made her cry. He'd not intended that. Sure, he was angry with her but he didn't want her to cry. He wanted her to fight back, something she'd always seemed to have a problem doing with him. He'd seen her go toe to toe with many people but never with him. He'd always wondered if he intimated her.

Intimidation wasn't what he was after now. He walked toward her, slid his arms around her waist and pulled her body against his. He heard the soft sobs in her throat and pressed his face against the back of her head, smelling the fragrance of her shampoo, smelling her, and his flesh quickened in his pants, his erection straining, telling him that it remembered the feel of her. His hands moved over her body, their statement clear. They also remembered.

"I'm sorry," he whispered softly. "I didn't mean to come down on you so hard. I didn't mean to make you cry." He attempted to turn her to face him but she wouldn't budge. "Mary Jo, he pleaded, "look at me."

"Call me Janice," she said.

Tommy pressed her more firmly to him. "Okay, I'll call you Janice. Now will you look at me?"

She turned to face him, her eyes downcast, not believing that she'd actually cried. She hadn't known that she remembered how. She sniffled.

"Would you like more coffee?" Tommy asked, tilting her chin with his finger to look into her eyes. She didn't answer and he smiled. "I'm sorry."

"For what?" she asked. "Tell me, Tommy, what it is that you're really sorry for?" She held his gaze now, her question loaded, knowing that he knew what she was asking. Had he ever told her that he was sorry that he'd left her or that she'd had to go thorough everything alone? She couldn't remember. But she clearly remembered his anger. Now she wanted to know why he was sorry. She waited.

"I'm sorry for now," he said, "for making you cry. I had no right to do that." He stared at her, knowing what she wanted, unable to give it. He couldn't tell her how sorry he was that he'd left her. His anger at her lack of faith in him wouldn't permit it. She'd always looked up to him, asked him before she made any decisions. Even now he couldn't believe a decision so major, so important to both of their lives, she would have made alone. "I'm sorry for now, Janice. There was no cause for me to do what I did."

Another tear slid down her cheek, then another, and he gathered her into his arms, feeling the soft roundness of her curves, feeling her skin smooth as silk as his arms tightened around her. And he pulled her ever closer, not caring that she felt his hardness. He pulled away just a little, wanting to see her face, the urge to kiss her trying to overcome his good sense. He'd not had these feeling for anyone for more years than he cared to remember.

Something had happened to him while drinking the coffee. He'd made a trip into the past. He shouldn't have done it. Now he was on fire with lust. He looked down into her brown eyes and saw the memories swirling there and just when he was about to taste her, melodic notes from her purse made him pause. And then it was too late.

She opened the bag and took out the phone. Tommy watched as the memories of the past receded from his own Mary Jo and a guilty look took its place. The mask fell into position. She was Janice Lace again.

"Hello," Janice said, answering the phone and moving farther from Tommy, trying to still her rapidly beating heart, knowing that it would be obvious to Simon that something was wrong.

He wasted no time in asking. "What's wrong?"

"Nothing," she answered.

"Don't give me nothing. I hear it in your voice." There was a brief pause, then Simon asked, "Have you been crying?"

"Don't be silly." She tried to laugh. "Why would I be crying?"

But she didn't fool him, something had happened, someone had made her cry. A lump formed in Simon's throat and he choked on the feeling of fullness. He'd never wanted to make Janice cry, but still it hurt that someone other than him had brought something out in her other than anger.

Maybe he'd been wrong. Maybe she didn't love him. She certainly had never cried over anything he'd ever done or said. Then again, where she was concerned it was always he who felt like crying when she viciously attacked him with verbal barbs. He now felt betrayed, betrayed and scared, scared that if Tommy Strong had made her cry, he might also make her love again.

"Janice, who's there with you?"

She moved the phone away. Her body was shaking so hard that she couldn't talk to Simon. She should have never answered the phone. She clicked the off button and looked at Tommy.

What the hell? Simon stared at the buzzing phone in his hand and shook his head. He couldn't have just been hung up on. Anger flared, then was quickly doused. Janice had never hung up on him, and she'd never cried. Something was wrong. He pushed the redial button and waited. She wasn't answering.

"Aren't you going to answer that?" Tommy asked.

"What am I supposed to tell him? Believe me, when it goes to voicemail Simon will leave a message." She almost laughed thinking of the message he would leave. "Don't worry, Tommy. Simon knows something is wrong. I haven't cried in…" She stopped, telling him how long it had been would be handing him the power to hurt her.

Tommy didn't need to know that since him there were a lot of things she hadn't done. "I don't do a lot of crying," she finished, biting her lips. "I just need a couple of minutes, then I'll be able to call him back. Do you think you could pour me another cup of coffee?"

She walked away toward the bathroom to splash cold water on her face, not bothering to wait for Tommy's answer. She cupped her hand under the cold running water, splashed her face, and dipped her hand once again under the faucet, filling it with the liquid and bringing it to her lips to sip. Then she breathed in deeply, calming herself.

With a deep sigh she blew out the breath and pulled her phone out and called Simon.

"What the hell is going on?" he screamed. "I'm on my way there."

"No, Simon," she said, panicked. "No, don't do that."

"Then you tell me what happened. Why were you crying? Why did you hang up on me?"

"There are so many things I should know," she said, "things that I've neglected."

"What are you talking about?"

"Did you know in the past few months two black magazines were launched?"

"Of course," he said, "*Black Train of Thought* and *Black Rose.*"

"Oh," she said softly. "I didn't know it before today."

"Janice, why would not knowing that make you cry?"

"You knew it. I'm black and I should know it. Did you know they've run stories on me?" she whispered.

Simon held the phone to his ear, his chest hurting. He wanted to be the one comforting her. He imagined that Tommy had but he wouldn't ask that. "I'll be there in thirty minutes."

"No, please, if you come..." She caught herself. "Things are bad enough right now."

"Bad enough? You're supposed to be helping the bookstores. You're not there to be abused. Did Mr. Strong say something to you? Is he the one that made you cry?" *Damn*, Simon thought. He'd not meant to ask.

"We were fighting."

"That's not enough to make you cry, we fight all the time."

"It was pretty personal, an assault on my character, on my blackness," she admitted.

"Our fights are personal."

"Yes, but it's generally me doing the assaulting, not you. You just fight back. I'm sorry for being so mean to you, Simon."

Now she was scaring him. She rarely apologized and never to him. He didn't want Tommy Strong to change the way she dealt with him. At least he could depend on her disdain. At least then he knew it was them, the two of them, not a third party.

"I'm on my way," he said again.

"No."

"Why?"

"How do you think that will make me look for you to run here to fight my battles?"

"I don't care how it will look. You weren't supposed to be going into battle. You're not talking me out of coming."

"Simon, I'm alright. I don't want you to come."

That was the whole thing and he was painfully aware of it. She didn't want him emotionally involved in her life, never mind that they were getting married. She wanted to keep everything between them...what was her word for it? He thought for a moment. She wanted to keep things between them uncomplicated. Well, they weren't uncomplicated, they were as complicated as hell. He loved her and he would be damned if he allowed Tommy Strong to hurt her.

"I'm coming."

"Simon, I'll make you a deal. Don't come and tonight we'll sit down and set a date for our wedding." She waited.

Simon sighed. She'd pulled out the heavy artillery; she definitely knew where to hit him. "Why don't you want me to come?" he asked.

"I want to complete the job I started."

"But it's not something that will be finished in a couple of days. This project will take months. If you can't handle a few days, what's going to happen as time goes on? Why are you willing to put yourself through that?"

"I gave my word."

That was a very interesting remark, very telling. She'd given her word to a man who meant nothing to her, a man she hadn't seen for a decade. After two days alone in his company he was sensing a change.

"Would you give me your word about something?" he asked.

"What?"

"Will you give me your word that tonight we'll set a date?"

"Yes."

"And that you'll knock off early so that we can have a romantic dinner, just the two of us."

"Yes, I give you my word."

He could hear the smile in her voice and he smiled in return. But still he wondered why she was so willing to give in just to keep him away.

"Janice, when I call you again, don't ignore me and send my calls to your voicemail, answer your phone."

"I will," she answered. "I'll see you at five," she said and hung up, not waiting for him to say goodbye.

"Yeah," he said to the air. "I'll see you at five." He couldn't believe it, he'd not even had a moment to tell her off about hanging up on him. Well, maybe he should just be happy with his small victory. She was willing to set a date; he'd take that for now.

Simon picked up the phone in the limo, watched as his chauffeur answered, then gave his new instructions. He would go to his office and work, attempt to keep his mind off what was happening with Janice and Tommy Strong. He'd resist the temptation to barge over there and play caveman.

He dialed the phone once again and this time he ordered back copies for the last three years of every black publication that was known. If Janice wanted to know about African American culture he'd help her. He had the means and he had the will.

CHAPTER ELEVEN

Janice felt as if a steamer had run over her body. She hated to walk out and confront Tommy, but she didn't have a choice. She could hear him pacing. Bracing herself, she opened the door and stared straight into Tommy's eyes.

"You okay?" he asked.

"I'm okay."

"You were in there for a long time."

"I know. I had to talk to Simon."

"I know, I heard."

She looked at him, aghast, but he smiled and her heart lurched, an unexpected thing.

"I wasn't actually listening to your conversation. I just heard you talking and figured you weren't talking to yourself, at least I was hoping that you weren't. I poured you more coffee," he offered.

"Thanks," Janice answered, squeezing past him and heading toward the back room. "I've been a little stressed lately. I have a deadline on my next book and I should really be home working on it. Plus," she smiled, "I'm getting married and I need to set a date and get ready for all the craziness that goes with it."

She walked past him, wishing she weren't so aware of him as a man. The sheer magnetism he'd always had had become more potent with maturity. She shouldn't be thinking these thoughts. She didn't want to think these thoughts. Still, she thought them, and for the first time since he'd reentered her life she was happy that he had.

Janice drank the still hot coffee, her mind set on work and nothing else. She had an inkling about why she was willing to work so hard and put her writing to the side.

She'd never cared what anyone had thought about her lack of involvement in the black community, not even her family, but Tommy's disgust with her had made a tiny hole in her armor and she intended to prove to him that she wasn't as bad as he thought. Maybe he'd look at her with the same pride he once had. She leafed through a magazine he'd evidently gotten for her, wishing she didn't care what he thought of her. But it was too late for wishing that. She did care.

Janice perused the charts, amazed at the steady decline in the black economic power structure. Shame for her lack of awareness burned through her as she picked up a discarded magazine, pausing at the article that mentioned her. She looked at the date; it was over two years old. She wondered how he'd found it so easily.

"I just had it," he answered her unasked question, "no big deal."

He was lying, her heart told her that. She drank the coffee, staring at him for a long moment. For a split second he was the young boy she'd loved madly. She flipped the page over, saw a picture of a happy family complete with baby, and just like that, the happy memory faded and the remembered pain returned.

Janice swiped her tongue across her top lip, worrying the same spot over and over, not liking the way she was feeling. After all, she'd not felt anything for a decade. This was strange. She looked up and saw the way that Tommy was staring at her and realized that her unconscious action was having an effect on him.

"Why are so many bookstores closing at this particular time?" Janice asked, determined to bring both of their minds back to the problem at hand.

"Technology, lack of support, black authors going to larger companies that don't cater primarily to the independent bookstores but to the large chains."

Janice frowned a little. "Tommy, you had me thinking that I single-handedly destroyed the stores."

"I never said that."

"No, but you implied it. You have said more than once that my lack of support played a big part in this."

"And I stand by that," Tommy admitted, coming to sit across from her.

She watched as the passion of his words pushed aside the burning sexual passion she'd seen in his eyes earlier. They were now on safer ground. They were where she needed to be. Janice had no desire to revisit old graves.

"Tommy, I don't control technology or big business."

"But you could bring more readers into the neighborhoods, do more signings at the smaller stores, and create a buzz."

"I said that I would."

"Too bad it's almost a decade too late." Tommy looked in Mary Jo's direction, wanting to continue hating her, not wanting to recall the sweetness of her body.

His gaze traveled to her lips and he felt another surge of passion and wondered how on earth he'd ever believed he could work with her and not remember.

"Internet sales are killing us," he said, suddenly deciding to let her off the hook. "Publishers are now doing their own sales directly to the public via Internet, so we're getting cut out."

"This is about the dollars?"

"This is about tradition. Do you have any idea what the bookstores really mean to the black community? Do you know how many years you couldn't find a book by an African American or by anyone for that matter who might be considered different or that the government termed subversive? It was the small independent black bookstores that got those books and pushed them, that allowed groups to gather and talk about the books. And believe it or not, this method helped the sales. It was the bookstores that supported the writers and now it's the writers' turn to support the bookstores."

"If I never knew any of this, how can you blame me? I had no knowledge that when I started writing I had to make sure where my books were placed. I didn't do anything in my career to hurt anyone. I was just trying to make a living."

"That's a lie," Tommy sneered. "As often as the two of us planned this out, don't insult me and say you didn't know."

"Those were childhood dreams, Tommy. We wanted to make a difference but we didn't have figures to back us up. We didn't really know everything there was to know."

"You knew more than most."

"I knew what you told me, Tommy. You were the rebel, I was just your foot soldier. I was there to cheer you on. You made the plans and assumed I would carry them out."

"What are you talking about?"

"I'm talking about what we're skirting around. You think I'm a traitor because I wrote and then sold my work to the highest bidder. And I want to know why you are angry about that."

"Because—"

"I'll tell you why," Janice said, interrupting him, "because even after all this time it ticks you off that I wasn't your puppet, that I was doing something different from the life you'd planned out for me. My role in that whole thing was not to be a writer but to be what, Tommy? Part owner of a bookstore with you? I don't think it was even that. I have a good memory and what I remember is that you were going to do all the booking of authors. You were going to do poetry readings, you were going to all sorts of conventions. And I would do the books, manage the store and raise our kids. Wasn't that the plan you had, Tommy?"

"You were happy when I made it."

"I was a kid and I was in love."

"And are you in love now?"

For a moment Janice stared at him, wondering whether he was talking about himself or Simon. "How I feel now is none of your concern."

"It may not be my concern, but you sure as hell don't act as if you can't wait to see the guy, to have him touch you. Tell me you don't remember how I made you feel, how my touch burned you. Tell me that and I'll call you a liar."

Janice rose from her chair. "Tell me you don't remember the same things and I'll call you a liar." They stood no more than an inch apart, their eyes blazing, and as they both had known it would, it happened.

Tommy grabbed Janice, roughly pushing his body against hers as though he hated her and kissed her, shoving his tongue forcefully in her mouth. She struggled against him until something happened and she stilled and trembled in his arms and he pulled slightly away, still holding her.

"I'm sorry about that."

Janice fought the urge to swipe her fingers across her lips. What the hell was she doing? She didn't want Tommy anymore. Simon would kill her if he ever found out. She began to shake as though she were chilled. Oh God, she thought as the memories of her past warred with her future with Simon. They were just that, memories, but still they had the power to destroy.

"Janice, I'm sorry. I had no right to do that. I didn't plan it, I just couldn't stop myself."

"I know," she said at last, wrapping her arms around her body. "It was bound to happen, Tommy." She pointed toward the coffee. "The two of us planning, I think we just picked up for a moment where we left off." She pushed away from him. "But we're not kids anymore, Tommy. I'm engaged to a wonderful man and I'm getting married."

"Tell me that you feel in his arms what you felt in mine."

"I'll tell you that Simon satisfies me and that when we're making love I've only thought of him. So if you're thinking that I thought of you, I want you to know that I haven't thought of you, not one time."

"Any man can satisfy a woman with just a little skill and a bit of practice. But that doesn't mean that the feelings are the same." He cocked his head. "I'll be honest with you and tell you that no woman has ever felt right in my arms since you. I've enjoyed making love and I've had women who were way more experienced than you would ever want to be. And they've really rocked my world, but there was always something missing, Mary Jo. When the act was over, when all was said and done, I was never fulfilled. That's what I'm asking you. Does Simon Kohl fulfill you?"

She backed away. "I'm not discussing my fiancé with you, Tommy. He's not you and he's not my first. Why would I compare him or any man to that?"

"Because you should," he said, walking back up to her, running his finger down the side of her arms, watching her tremble. "Because if he doesn't make you feel that," he said, looking meaningfully at her, "do you really want to spend the rest of your life in his bed?"

Janice backed away again. "That's dead, Tommy. Do you really think that all you have to do is touch me and I'm going to fall all over you?"

"You used to."

"That was twelve years ago, that was before you hurt…"

Anger flared in Tommy. "Before what? Go on and say it. Before I hurt you? You're kidding, lady, you destroyed me. What the hell are you talking about? You're not the one with the right to be angry, I am. If anyone is justified in hating someone it should be me. You seem to have a faulty memory. You, Mary Jo Adams, you broke my heart. You took from me everything that I had to give and you threw it into my face, you." He was growling at her, the threat of really losing his temper washing over him.

"Tommy, hold it down, man. What the hell's going on in here?"

Tommy and Janice's eyes both shifted toward Neal, the man who'd come to interrupt their fight. Both knew it must have gotten pretty loud to bring him from the counter and the customers.

"You okay, Ms. Lace?" Neal asked.

"I'm okay." Janice attempted a smile but lost. "Thanks, Neal, I'm okay and call me Janice."

"Her name's Mary Jo," Tommy blurted, his eyes blazing as he looked toward Neal, then glared at Janice.

"Keep it down, man," Neal said to Tommy and closed the door.

"I didn't come here to fight with you, Tommy. I came to help."

"You came because I challenged you on national television and you didn't know how to get out of it."

"I came because I wanted to help with the bookstores. I mean, if Simon can help with a million dollars, I thought I could help."

"I didn't take his money."

Janice stared at him. "What are you talking about?"

"The check, I ripped it up."

"Does Simon know that?"

"Does Simon know that?" Tommy mimicked, anger in his voice making him tremble, making her move back.

Janice swallowed down the lump. "He didn't tell me. I wonder why."

She stared as Tommy shook his head. "Why should he? You have your head buried so far up his butt that you wouldn't know or care. He tells you to jump and you ask how high. When did you turn into such a…I don't know what the hell you are."

"I'm not what you think. That's what I was with you. That's not what I am with Simon."

"What are you with Simon Kohl? I know you're not hot or loving. What are you with him? You wouldn't even allow the man to kiss you in public. I know you can't possibly make him wet with wanting you. You're a cold fish around him."

"You have no idea how I am when I'm in bed with him."

"I'd be willing to bet you're a cold fish, a hooker playing a part."

The color flooded her face and her mouth hung open. She stared at Tommy, not being able to find an answer. She sat down and began to go through the market research as though nothing had happened.

"I didn't mean that," he said as he stood rooted in his spot. "I didn't mean that," he said again and came and knelt by her chair. "Really, I'm sorry. I shouldn't have said that. I didn't mean it."

Janice closed her eyes and for the second time in one day she chocked back tears.

"You know, Tommy, I haven't cried in a dozen years. I know we need to talk about our past, although I'm not sure why. We both seem to have different recollections of it. You've apparently been hating me for a decade and I've been hating you."

She glanced up at him. "But I don't think this is the time or the place to rehash. I came to work. If you care anything at all about trying to save the bookstores, then forget our personal history and let's get to work."

She ignored him still kneeling at her side, ignored the pain he could still produce in her, and pretended that he wasn't there. What was more pretending? She'd been doing it for years.

"I'm sorry for attacking you," Tommy repeated for the third time, still kneeling at her side, and he meant it. "I thought I could handle being around you and not lashing out at you. I didn't mean to kiss you either but I guess I've known that I would from the first time you agreed to help me. I don't know if I wanted to reclaim something I lost, or make you remember. But you seemed so different to me that day at the banquet, so cold and stiff and artificial."

"Is this still an apology?"

He smiled. "You're right. I'm not very good at this. I always wondered how I would behave if our paths crossed. Now I know." He smiled again and got up, holding his hand out to her, "Can we be friends?"

"I'd like that, Tommy," Janice answered, taking his offered hand.

"When this is over I think we need to talk. Are you agreeable?"

"Yeah, I'm agreeable. We have unfinished business between us but I hope when we talk we can do it without the anger. I never liked fighting with you, you always won." Then she smiled.

"Maybe that's why I spend so much time fighting with Simon." She tilted her head to the right. "The two of you are so different. He doesn't really care about winning the argument. I think he just fights with me because I want to."

"That's strange," Tommy said, peering at her. "You enjoy fighting with the man you're going to marry? I don't understand that."

"Tommy, we'll save analyzing me for another time, okay?" She took a look around the room, wondering herself why she fought so much with Simon. She knew in part it was her desire to keep him at a distance, only he was now attempting to break down all of her barriers. She knew he wanted her raw, but she couldn't allow that. Sitting there talking to Tommy, knowing that he'd always held the power to hurt her, that he still could, gave her clarity.

Janice was beginning to figure it out. She didn't want to give Simon the kind of power over her that Tommy had always had. And now more than ever she knew she'd been right not to want that.

"Wouldn't money to publicize the plight of the bookstores help, Tommy?" she asked, steering the conversation back into safer waters.

"Of course it would."

"Then why on earth would you tear up the check? Why didn't you use it to help?"

"Because he was trying to buy me."

"How was he trying to buy you?"

"He wanted to make sure with that money that I didn't touch you. Don't you understand that?"

"Tommy, that makes no sense. I hadn't seen you in a decade."

"I didn't say that it made sense. I said I knew what he was doing. A man in love doesn't necessarily make sense. He sometimes does the wrong thing, the total opposite of what he should do. Sometimes it's the fear that gets to him."

"What would Simon have to be afraid of?"

"Suppose you answer that one for me. He's the man you chose. If he went to so much trouble to hunt me down and try to pay me off, then he has to be afraid of something. I'll take a gamble that it has to do with you. I guess he wanted to ensure that the kiss I gave you earlier wouldn't happen."

"Are you saying if you had kept the check that you wouldn't have kissed me?"

"I'm saying that Simon Kohl was more than likely hoping that it wouldn't happen. I would probably have kissed you even if he had given me every dime he had. I wanted to see if you still tasted as sweet as you did in the past."

And did I? She wanted to ask but didn't dare.

"You did," he said in response to the question in her eyes. "You still taste like golden brown sugar. Only difference, I sensed a lot more fire."

Janice could feel the blush on her face. "Let's get back to business, Tommy. I have money, I can give you a check."

"For a million dollars?"

"I'm not Simon Kohl."

"But you're sleeping with him."

"I'm engaged to him."

"Still?"

"His money is his. And the answer to the question you're dying to ask me is, no, I'm not marrying Simon for his money. I have my own."

"Then why are you?"

"Why do you keep insisting on getting off the subject?"

"Sorry, how much are you going to write that check for?"

"How about ten thousand?"

"What happened to all those million dollar contracts I keep reading about you getting?"

"Simon manages my money for me. I keep only a little in my checking account."

"You don't have a savings?"

"Why are you being so nosy?"

"I'm just wondering if you were dumb enough to turn over all of your money to one man. Like you said, you were the one who was good with figures. Why aren't you running your own affairs? Why do you trust Simon Kohl to handle your money? Aren't you worried in the least that one man managing your life has total control over you?"

"Even if I were, that one man is Simon Kohl. Do you really think he has a need to steal my money? Please. How do you think I got those million dollar contracts? He paid me. Why would he have to steal it back? That's crazy."

"I thought you said he didn't buy you."

"I said he didn't own me. I worked for my money." Janice could feel her blood boiling and stopped. They'd already had this round. "Tommy, if I write you a check are you going to tear mine up also?"

For a long moment he stared at her, his right hand resting on his chin, his left hand tapping the coffee table. "Was it mine?" He saw the puzzled look on her face. "Was it mine?"

"I thought we were going to stick to the bookstores."

"I guess I can't. This has been weighing on my mind for twelve years. I didn't believe you, yet I've hated you for a decade because I didn't know for sure. I think we need to talk now. At least answer that one question, was it mine?"

"Yes, Tommy, it was yours. How could you have doubted that?"

"Because of the look on your face when you told me. You looked as though you hated me. You had never looked at me like that."

"Tommy, I couldn't believe how you acted." Red-hot fury claimed her, causing her to wrap her arms around her body in order to contain it. She'd known it was going to come to this and she'd dreaded it just as she'd dreaded it that night so long ago. Tommy still didn't seem to understand what she'd been upset about.

"Tommy, you left me."

"You knew I would come back."

"How did I know that?" Her voice dropped and she was talking so softly that he leaned in to hear her. "I never thought you would leave me."

"But I came back."

"But you left me."

"You should have known I would come back for you."

Tears spilled from her eyes. "Tommy, don't you understand just how scared I was? The one person that I thought would always be there for me took off. You didn't call or anything, you just abandoned me. You left me all alone and you knew what my parents would have done if they had found out. They would have been so disappointed."

"But they would have stood behind you. All these years and your mother has been asking me what happened. She still wonders. I'm surprised that you never told anyone, especially your parents. I know they would have stood behind you."

"I didn't want them to stand behind me. I wanted you to stand beside me and you didn't. Yes, I know when all was said and done they would have helped me with the baby, but, Tommy, at that time I couldn't go on without you in my life. I didn't want to be an unwed mother or a single parent. I didn't want to be another statistic. Don't you understand that?"

Tommy was trying to hear her, but all he could see was that she had not had enough faith in him, in his love for her and she'd not bothered to give him a chance to come to his senses. "You should have waited."

"And you shouldn't have left me. What if you never came back?"

"But I did."

Janice sighed. "Tommy, we're never going to see things differently. I did what I thought was best for me at the time. I didn't have you to count on. What was I supposed to do? Maybe you should have told me that if I ever got pregnant you would leave me. All you ever told me was how much you loved me, how much you wanted to marry me, to have a dozen babies with me. I still remember worrying about that the first time we made love. I was afraid, but you assured me that you would never leave me that you would always be there for me. You weren't, Tommy."

"Do you hate me, Mary Jo?"

"I have for so long that I don't know how to answer that. I don't think I know how not to hate you."

"I tried to make it up to you. I came back. We could have gone on from there, but you acted like I wasn't important to you, that you didn't want me in your life. That was one of the reasons I wondered when you told me the baby wasn't mine. Seven days before you'd loved me like crazy. Seven days later you hated me. I didn't want to believe you, but what was I supposed to think?"

"You were supposed to think my feelings had something to do with my pregnancy. Maybe my hormones were off because of the pregnancy, I don't know. All I know is that when the procedure was over a part of me was gone that I could never get back. You did nothing to ease the pain of that loss or to make me feel that there had ever been anything between us but sex and lies."

Tommy tapped the table again. "I guess I asked for all of that, didn't I?"

"Yes, I guess you did."

"Before that did you love me?" he said, going to her. "Tell me that it wasn't all a lie."

"It wasn't a lie," Janice said softly, getting up to stand before him. "My loving you was never a lie." She saw the look in his eyes and knew he needed to be comforted as much as she. He held out his arms and she went into them as easily, as if they'd never been separated by the past, and when he tilted her chin up to kiss her she didn't resist.

The kiss was soft and gentle and sweet. It was the remnants of their forgotten youth. It meant nothing more than comfort to her. She allowed herself the familiarity of his arms for a few seconds more before she wiped her eyes and moved away. She smiled. "I don't know if Simon would think that was as innocent as it was, if he'd seen us."

"I don't imagine that he would."

"But we know there wasn't anything sexual in that kiss, don't we, Tommy?" Janice asked even more softly, her voice barely more than a whisper.

"Yes, we know that it was nothing sexual," Tommy answered, plopping down in his chair. Nothing sexual—like hell. He was so hard that he was gritting his teeth as he willed himself not to touch her. He surveyed her and saw her nipples pushed against the material of her bra and top. He'd bet they were every bit as hard as the erection he was sporting. Nothing sexual? What a crock.

CHAPTER TWELVE

With his erection finally under control Tommy put away the huge graph he'd been using for cover. Working with Mary Jo was either the best idea he'd ever had or the worst. For over ten minutes they'd each worked in silence.

"I arranged for a couple of signings next week." Tommy looked in her direction. "We've pretty much got New York covered. I was thinking we could drive to Pennsylvania and New Jersey in the next day or so. There are three stores in Washington D.C. that are doing pretty good. We can hit those also. I've got a shitload of market research to take with us."

Mary Jo wasn't answering him. She was chewing on her fingernail and staring at the files he'd given her with a glazed expression. He would make bet that their kiss was as much on her mind as it was on his. He wasn't against staring at her all day, but they still needed to get some work done. "Mary Jo, do you have your day planner with you?"

"No, just give me the schedule and I'll fill it in when I get home." Janice reached across the table, jerking her hand away at the touch of Tommy's fingers to hers. He'd started a heat deep within her core and the thaw was coming. She glanced at him, at the smirk on his face and laughed. What an arrogant fool. He thought it was himself she was hot for. He had no idea.

"I didn't mean anything, I wasn't trying to do—"

"I know. Listen, I need to get home by five." Janice stopped him, not wanting his touch to mean what it did for both their sakes. "I promised Simon that tonight we would set a date for the wedding. We're going to have a romantic dinner."

She didn't know what she'd expected, but Tommy didn't answer her, just stared at her as though he didn't know her. But that in itself didn't surprise her. They didn't know each other, not anymore. She had her doubts that they ever had. Her reaction to him could be easily explained away. He was her first, and after reliving past history, old feelings had surfaced.

"When do you want me to do the magazine interviews? Was that with *Black Rose* or *Black Train of Thought?* I know you asked me to write an article for one of them, but I don't remember which one. Will you make the arrangements? Do you think I should contact them…I'm not sure…just tell me how you want to handle this. Whichever magazine you wanted to interview me they could just phone or…or…email me with questions?" She was rambling but couldn't seem to stop.

"I'm not going to attack you."

"I didn't think that you were."

"So why are you so nervous?"

"Tommy, stop!" She began to tremble. "I can't do this all day."

"I haven't done anything; I just asked why you're nervous."

"Can't you just answer my question? How do you want me to do the interview?"

"I'll take you to see Gerald from *Black Rose*, when we go out walking later to pass out fliers of your upcoming signing. He can take your picture and get what information he needs from you."

"Good." She was doing her best to control her breathing. At least it was getting a little easier since he wasn't standing so close.

"Did you hear that Martha August's bookstore is also closing?"

"No, I didn't," Janice answered, not bothering to tell Tommy that she had no idea who Martha August was. "Is it too late to help her?"

"Yes. Her lease is up and the landlord wants to triple the rent for her to stay."

"Wow!"

"Yeah, wow. She was barely making enough as it was to keep the store open, but there would be no way she could pay the new rent and make a living."

"Tommy, it sounds like what I said, economics."

"Some are, some aren't. I think it's a conspiracy to drive the black business owners out of business."

Janice smiled for the first time in hours, feeling lighter. "You always thought everything was a conspiracy. You even thought that snow being white was a conspiracy." She laughed and to her delight he laughed with her.

"Did anyone go to the owner of the property and try to get him or her to maybe extend the lease?"

"Of course we did, what do you think? We've been doing this for a number of years. He wants her out. He's going to rent the space to a large chain, get the money he wants, and another specialty store closes. A meeting place for black people will no longer be. That's why I think this isn't an accident."

"What about your store, Tommy? Are you in danger of closing?"

"I'm doing okay."

"What does okay mean?"

"It means I can pay my employees, and my bills. Can I charter a private plane and fly all over the world? Hell no, but for at least a year my lease is firm."

"Do you handle specialty books as well?"

"Of course."

"Do you have any of my titles?"

"I stock all African American books."

"You've done a good job, Tommy. It looks like you stayed true to your dreams. Do you mind if I take a look around your store?"

"What is it really?" Tommy laughed. "Do you need a few minutes to get away from me?"

She smiled. "Matter of fact, I do. But I also haven't gotten a chance to look in your store."

Janice walked into the store and took a deep breath. The past had crowded in on her in a way she'd not expected. She'd thought she had erected enough barriers to ward off any attacks. Even her mother's constant questioning and trying to make her angry had not made a dent. The one person she'd never counted on fighting was Tommy. Tommy had always been able to wear down her defenses. The more she thought about it, the more aware she became that she had indeed needed a break from him.

The smell of potpourri and scented candles in the store captivated Janice's senses. That too had been part of their plans. She would be lying to herself if she didn't admit that she was touched that he'd included her ideas in bringing his dreams to life. She gazed at the coffee shop to her right. It had a brisk business. Tommy would survive. He was giving his customers what they wanted. He'd applied a basic rule of marketing, diversify.

Tommy had done well for himself and despite everything else she was proud of him and of his success. She stopped under a poster of Langston Hughes and fingered the books. Her smile faded. How sad it would be if years from now Langston Hughes' work was not available.

She moved farther into the poetry section, reaching hungrily for several books by Gwendolyn Brooks and Maya Angelou. She ran her fingers lovingly over the binders of the books, for the first time in years missing the plans she'd made so long ago with Tommy. The pain of what she'd given away gnawed at her. She'd purposefully pushed away her rich heritage out of anger at one man. Now she wanted it back.

Janice took her time looking at the books. She couldn't prevent the audible gasp at a first edition of *The Color Purple*. Seeing the names Booker T. Washington, Dorothy West, James Baldwin, W. E. B. Duboise, and Zora Neale Hurston was like being in a candy store. Tommy had not been merely bragging. He probably did have books by every African American writer who had ever lived.

Janice spent over an hour picking out books, her earlier emotions forgotten, Tommy forgotten, as she sifted through the books. She took an armload to the counter, handed them to Neal, then reached for her purse.

"No, whatever you want you take," Tommy's voice sounded from behind her.

"No, Tommy. I have over five hundred dollars' worth of books here."

"And I'm giving them to you."

"Tommy, I can't. I came to help, not to take books from you."

"You're not taking them, I'm giving them to you. I want to." His gaze caught hers. "Please let me, it's the least that I can do and I want to."

He smiled then, and she could feel her soul thaw a little more.

"Consider this my apology."

Janice couldn't stop the smile from spreading over her face, nor could she stop the sudden flood of heat that washed over her, pooling between her legs and creating an ache, a longing for a memory. She couldn't look up at Neal and she didn't dare look behind her to where Tommy was standing.

She glanced at the ring that sat on her finger and thought of Simon, wanting to feel grounded. No, she didn't have with him what she'd had with Tommy but some of it was because she wouldn't allow it. Simon wanted more but she'd closed herself off. She wouldn't and couldn't blame Simon for not having that connection.

In the end it didn't matter. She did owe him something. She felt cold suddenly and wanted to bolt from the store. She wanted her life to live over again and that was impossible. No matter how much she wished that things had gone differently, they hadn't.

"Do you accept my apology, Mary Jo, for being so rude to you today? Do you think we can be friends?"

He was standing alongside her, his voice soft, warm and gentle and filling her ear in whispered tones. She heard the longing and knew he was remembering as well and more than likely also yearning for what might have been.

"I meant it when I said I would love it if we could be friends," she answered at last and finally turned toward him. He was the eighteen-year-old she'd loved and his eyes held the same things they'd always had, hope and yearning. Janice shook herself. She thought she saw love too, but that love had never been real. She couldn't let herself be seduced by that look now.

For the next few hours Janice worked with Tommy with a lighter air. She walked a thousand blocks, it seemed, stopping in any store that would allow them to come in and do an impromptu signing of bookmarks. She met with customers and signed books new and old, that Tommy had brought with him for prizes. The only thing the person had to do to win a book was answer a question Tommy had written about the book and have the right number.

The longer they stayed out, the more word spread. The business owners were thrilled. Instead of being a nuisance as she'd expected, they had brought in more business to each place they stopped at. She wondered how Tommy had managed to pull this together so quickly, the bookmarks, the questions, the prizes. She'd not even known he was going to do it. He was committed, she would give him that.

Janice had almost forgotten how passionate he could be but she listened as he told every single customer that came into the stores of the importance of supporting the businesses in the community, the importance of protecting the meeting places. And she didn't know if they bought from the stores out of pity or shame but not a one left without buying something and not a one left without talking to her for a minute.

In the beginning the customers had trailed past her trying not to make eye contact, trying to pretend that she wasn't there. They didn't know her, didn't want to know her, but Tommy wouldn't have that. He'd literally drag them over to her, telling them of her success and she'd feel mixed emotions, shame that he was basically forcing people to come to her and joy that he was proud of her despite the hatred he'd displayed earlier. He had not forgotten her and that made her heart quiver.

Janice became aware of a fluttering on her right hip and gasped, wondering that her thoughts had just become reality. Her heart had fluttered and now her phone was vibrating. She almost laughed out loud as she realized what it was. Pulling the phone from her pocket she pressed talk.

"I wanted to check in with you." Simon's voice sounded worried and she smiled. Of course he'd be worried. She'd behaved like a woman he didn't know, someone from out of space.

"Don't worry, I'm doing fine. I've been doing a lot of walking, canvassing the neighborhood."

"Really? I didn't know that you were passing out fliers today."

"Neither did I. Tommy got it together."

"Hmm, if I had known I would have swung by. I could have brought people to pass out fliers."

Janice didn't answer. She was suddenly happy that Simon hadn't known, glad that she hadn't told him. She wouldn't have wanted him to stop by. A lot of things had happened today that needed to happen. She'd needed to cry, and she'd needed to talk with Tommy. They had not settled everything between them, but they had made a start. And they would make more. They didn't hate each other anymore. And for that she was grateful.

"I wanted to know if you want seafood or Italian tonight. I'm going to make reservations. What's good for you, six-thirty or seven?"

"Either," Janice answered.

"You're still going to be home at five?"

"I'll be there."

"Okay, I have a couple more things to do, and a meeting. I'll meet you back at the house at five. See you then."

"See you," Janice said and looked at the phone before hanging up. As she'd known he would be doing, Tommy was looking at her.

"I told you I would have to leave. I promised Simon that I would be home by five."

"I arranged a surprise for you. You said you wanted to meet a few of the black writers that were in the area. There are several here in town. They're coming over to my shop but it might make you late."

"Who's coming?"

"I believe Donna, Gwen, Edwina, Seressia, Barbara, Lisa. They are planning on swinging by. They're involved with saving the bookstores, have been for quite some time."

Janice didn't need to ask the last names. Tommy had been preaching to her of these women since she'd started helping. "Do you think Wayne is in the area?"

"I believe so," Tommy answered, and she laughed out loud. "I can't leave without saying hi."

"Better call your boyfriend tell him you're going to be a little late."

She should but she wouldn't. There was no way Simon was going to understand and he'd think she had dissed him. "I'll call," she said to Tommy. "Don't worry about it."

Tommy had seen the way Mary Jo's eyes lit up when he told her of the writers that were coming. He'd just told her a lie, but now that he knew how much she wanted to meet them, he was determined to make it happen. He'd move heaven and earth if he could. He'd trade. Okay, he'd didn't have anything to trade, but he would definitely do everything in his power to make it happen. "Listen, will you be cool passing out fliers alone for awhile?" He grinned at her. "I have to go back to the shop, nature calls." He took off the moment that she said yes. There was no time to lose.

After a dozen calls and promising everything that he could, Tommy was pretty sure that by at least five-thirty some writers would be there. But if at least one didn't get there at five he knew he didn't stand much of a chance of keeping Mary Jo past that time. And now he wanted her to stay. As they ate a late lunch together he wanted her to stay even more.

When it was almost five he knew he had no choice but to pack it in and head back to his store. Mary Jo had made him proud. She was tired, he could tell. He'd neglected to tell her not to wear heels. Yet she was still smiling at every person who stopped to take a bookmark and that smile was taking him back to the time when she'd loved him. He felt the warmth of her smile when he suggested they call it quits. For twelve years he'd missed that warmth.

Neal grinned at them as they entered the store and brought a chair for Mary Jo. For a moment Tommy felt a possessive jealousy. He should be the one getting a chair for her. When she sighed in pleasure, he laughed, knowing she didn't care who gave her the chair. Mary Jo just wanted to rest.

For a few minutes the three of them chatted. At ten past five he saw her eyeing the clock and cursed softly, wishing he'd thought to make the calls sooner.

"Want to go over the plans for next week?" Tommy asked. When she turned in his direction he knew she was aware of what he was doing.

"No, Tommy, I need to go. I'm already late, I promised Simon that I would be home. He's going to be going crazy in a few minutes." She walked toward the back to retrieve her belongings, taking only a moment. When she returned she walked right dab into Wayne. Janice stopped and grinned. "That's the way to make an introduction," she said and shook his hand. The little bell sounded over the door and one after the other of the familiar names strolled in. Janice felt her heart swell. It was as though her soul were being filled with something that she wasn't aware that she needed. She had never thought much about where she did her signings or the conventions that she attended. But this influx of talented black writers, this was something that she wanted, needed, and she was glad that Tommy had made up things to get her to stay. She wouldn't have missed it for the world.

An hour later the smell of pizza was wafting across the room as an impromptu party erupted. Janice stood back and watched as the group of writers mixed with the customers, giving them pizza and drinks.

"Welcome back to being black, Mary Jo. Did you miss it?" Tommy whispered into her ear.

Until today Janice had not known just how much she had missed her heritage. "Yes, I missed it," she admitted.

When her phone vibrated she almost didn't answer. She knew exactly who was calling her and groaned at the knowledge.

There was nowhere to talk in private. Writers and readers were hogging every spare inch of space. "Hello," she answered, almost having to shout to be heard.

"Where the hell are you?" Simon shouted back. "You're supposed to be home. It sounds like you're at a party."

Several people were staring in her direction and her embarrassment soared. She didn't want to explain, didn't want to see the knowing smirk on Tommy's face that said she was owned by Simon. She walked outside. "I can't leave yet," she said to Simon.

"You gave your word."

"I know but I can't leave."

"Does anyone have a gun on you?"

"You're acting childish."

"I'm asking you a question and I expect an answer. I want you home. Now!" he shouted. And just like that she hung up and turned the phone off, walked back inside and shoved it into her purse that was behind the counter. She didn't want to be shouted at. Tommy was wrong; Simon Kohl didn't own her.

CHAPTER THIRTEEN

Simon looked at the dead phone in his hand, not believing that she'd hung up on him. *Hell no,* he thought to himself, this was not happening. He dialed repeatedly and each time Janice's voicemail kicked in, causing him to swear louder.

Enough of being the nice guy. He'd tried everything he thought would work. If she thought he was going to just roll over and beg, she had another thought coming. He'd warned her; now he'd just have to show her he meant business.

Simon hated driving in Manhattan traffic, especially at this time of day, but he didn't want his chauffeur hearing what would undoubtedly be the fight of the century. There were some things that he wished to keep private.

When he found a place to park at last, and walked into Tommy's bookstore, pissed wasn't the word for what he was feeling. He was enraged.

The moment he stepped inside the door the sounds of people having a good time greeted him. Then he heard the tinkling laughter and frowned. He knew the sound but there was something different about it, a clarity, a sheer joy that he'd heard only a few times in the past few years.

His eyes zeroed in on her like a laser and she lifted her eyes. She wasn't glad to see him. That was evident, not only by the expression in her eyes but also by the pinched look around her mouth.

He followed her line of vision as she looked around the room, wondering who she was searching for. Her gaze landed on Tommy and so did his. Then she glanced back in his direction and this time there was a pleading expression on her face. Simon frowned again, wondering exactly what she was pleading for.

"Simon, how are you?"

He turned, saw Donna and Deatri, and pasted a smile on his face. Then he began circulating around the room, shaking hands, chatting, glaring every few seconds at his fiancée who was not making a move toward him. He watched Tommy Strong go over to her, whisper something and stand with her. Simon's blood boiled.

As he glared directly at Janice, her look changed from one of pleading to mild irritation, to open defiance. And still she didn't come to greet him. He made his way toward her instead, chatting as he moved, feeling the temperature of the room change with his every breath. He could feel the eyes on him as he stopped in front of Janice. For a long moment he said nothing. Then he leaned in to whisper into her ear. "You're trying my patience," he murmured. "You gave me your word." Then he pulled back and stared at her.

"Would you like some pizza?" Tommy asked. Simon wanted to strangle him. This was partly his doing. Of course Janice had her own mind and she could have done as she'd promised, but he knew that Tommy's hand had helped mix the brew.

"No thanks," he said to Tommy, making his voice cold. He looked meaningfully at his watch. "I have," he stopped and looked at Janice, "*we* have dinner reservations." He watched as she dropped the slice of pizza she'd been munching on back onto the paper plate.

"There's plenty of food," Tommy insisted. Both Janice and Simon stared at him but he didn't back off. He looked directly at Simon and said, "It's a rare occasion to have so many black writers together in one place. Something really important is happening here, don't you agree? Everyone's pitching in to help."

Simon wasn't going to be baited. Of course he thought what they were trying to accomplish was a good thing. He'd given the man a million dollars to help, money he'd refused to accept, and his fiancée was helping by meeting all of Tommy's crazy demands. So yes, he agreed it was important.

But he wouldn't be foolish enough to offer his help again. He looked around the room and saw the quick way everyone turned away. They had been staring at them and he could just imagine what was going through their minds.

"We're setting our wedding date tonight," Simon said as his glance slid over to Janice. "That's pretty important, too, don't you think?"

"Would you like a glass of wine?" Janice interrupted and handed him her glass, which he took holding her gaze, challenging her to side with Tommy.

"No thanks, I'm driving," he said and handed the glass back.

"You're driving?" she asked. "You hate driving."

"It doesn't mean I won't do it when I have to, when there's a need."

"There really wasn't a need."

"I beg to differ. Since I know how important giving your word is to you, I assumed when you broke it that there was something wrong, a major catastrophe." He shrugged. "I thought perhaps you were being held hostage." He glared at her. "I guess I was wrong."

"I didn't do this deliberately." At her words he tilted his head so slowly that her breath caught and she blinked. She'd pushed too far. A feeling of panic filled her, robbing her of her senses. Janice glanced quickly around the room at the black faces watching her, at Tommy with his smirk, daring her to prove that she wasn't owned by Simon.

Janice brought her gaze to Simon. He was fuming. Until recently she'd only worried about him finding out how much she loved him and having control over her. Now she stood to lose his love before she even told him her feelings about being in a room with so much black talent. They were a connection that she wanted desperately. At the moment it didn't look as if she could have both.

It was Simon's move. She waited for him to make a decision. He looked away for a moment. When he looked back at her, disappointment showed clearly on his face. For the first time since he'd come in the door she knew the entire day had been wrong. She'd been so caught up in her past that she was neglecting her present and her future.

"Is there a problem, Simon? I thought Janice was here with your permission."

This time Janice glared at Tommy. He was being snide and sticking his nose in something that was none of his business. She knew exactly what he was trying to remind her of—that he believed she was owned by Simon. She wanted to warn him but knew it was unwise. She watched as Simon turned in Tommy's direction.

"There *is* a problem," Simon answered. "I'm trying to have a private conversation with my fiancée and you don't appear to know the meaning of the word *private*." He turned slightly toward Janice. "I would suggest that you stop behaving as if I were a fool."

"Simon, don't do anything," Janice continued and touched his arm. His muscles were corded beneath his expensive tailor made suit. He was angry and he had a right to be. She'd not expected him to come to the bookstore after her or make a scene. That would have been the last thing she would have expected.

He was really angry and spoiling for a fight. She felt a twinge of regret, knowing that she'd put him in this position, that she'd made him a promise and had broken it.

She touched her hand again to his arm. She thought at first that he would brush her away but he didn't. He tilted his head even more to the side and traced a finger down her neck. But she thought he was envisioning strangling her, not making love to her.

She unsuccessfully fought the shiver that invaded her body and licked her lips, not daring to tear her gaze from Simon, knowing that Tommy was standing too close to her, that at any moment one of them would push things to a head. She wanted to tell Tommy to stop but knew his behavior was also due in part to the feelings they'd shared through the day. Something had been resurrected and she knew Tommy was feeling as if he had a right, as if he were the man in her life.

She moved a step closer to Simon, deliberately away from Tommy. She heard a low growl and didn't know if it was emanating from Tommy or Simon. Glancing around the room, she saw several people looking in their direction. There was no denying the animosity between the two men. The room didn't lend itself to privacy and even if it had, their combative stances alone would have alerted even the most casual observer.

As she watched, the mood of everyone shifted swiftly. The gaiety was now forced and the tension emanating from the men standing near her, one in front, one to the side, grew so thick as to almost be visible.

She tugged on Simon's sleeve to pull his gaze from Tommy's, wondering what had really happened between the two men.

"You want to leave?" she asked.

He glanced at his watch and smiled.

She licked her lips. "Are you sure you don't want pizza?" she asked, staring straight into his eyes. She wasn't sure what his expression meant, but she sure as hell knew he didn't want pizza. She was doing her best to have a normal conversation, trying to pretend that everything was rosy.

"I'm sure, he answered, "but if this was what you meant when you said you wanted Italian for dinner, you go right ahead." He gave her a half smile and moved away. "I want to have a word with Wayne," he said.

Simon kept the smile on his lips despite the fact that he was boiling inside. How dare she think that this in any way was a romantic dinner for two? Eat pizza? How the hell could he think of eating anything? He would choke.

His right hand was fisted in his trousers. Simon wanted to punch out Tommy and strangle her. But he wouldn't. If he made a scene he would only embarrass himself and Janice. But for one blessed moment he hadn't cared. The pleading look in her eyes had only angered him. She apparently could give her word and keep it to a man who should mean nothing to her, but her word meant less than nothing to the man she was going to marry.

"Simon, how are you?" Wayne asked, sticking his hand out. "It's been a long time."

"Too long," Simon answered, grateful that he now had a reason to bring his balled fist out of his pants.

"Don't you want something to drink?"

"Maybe a cola," Simon said, attempting to smile as he reached for a paper cup filled with ice. He filled it and took a sip as he continued talking to Wayne, deliberately keeping his back turned to Janice. If he had to look at her standing next to Tommy Strong as though he were her savior, he would not be able to continue the simple act of civility. If she wanted to behave as if he weren't important to her, then he'd return the favor. He smiled as Barbara and Lisa joined them, aware that he was talking and laughing a little too loudly.

The sound of Simon's laughter rang false in Janice's ears. He was highly upset and had every right to be. Still, she wanted to stay, and she didn't want him there. It didn't matter that he belonged; he knew most of the people whereas she'd just met them.

She couldn't help resenting Simon for knowing a group of black writers when she didn't. Maybe if Tommy had not pounced on her ignorance of African American publications she wouldn't be feeling so territorial. But he had and she did. She wanted this gathering of talent, this energy, to be for her.

There was no way to tell Simon how she was feeling, that being in the same room with so many black writers filled her with pride, that as much as Simon wanted to be a part of this he wasn't.

Janice glanced at Tommy and caught him watching her, as he'd done all day. She knew what he was thinking, that she wasn't behaving like a woman in love. That, she'd never claimed to be. She made her way up to Simon. "Excuse me," she said to Wayne. "Simon and I can't stay long, we have plans. Simon, are you ready to leave?"

He looked at her and she felt the chill.

"Not just yet," he answered and turned back to talk with Wayne, his refusal telling her that he was giving as good as he got.

She stood there, her face flaming. Then she caught sight of Tommy and realized he had seen the snub. Her face flamed even hotter. Janice held his gaze for a moment longer, then turned back toward Simon. He stared at her, then over Wayne's head to where Tommy stood.

"Wayne, it was nice seeing you again. I guess my fiancée is right. We do need to leave," Simon explained.

Janice watched while he shook hands with the man, said goodbye to a few more people, then waited as she paused at the counter to retrieve her books. He carried them to the car. held the door for her, then got in on the driver's side.

"What the hell did you think you were doing?" he barked the moment he was seated. "You gave me your word."

"Things happened."

"I know things happen but there is a new invention called a phone. You have one, I know, I've talked with you on it. You could have called. You could have asked me if I minded, you could have invited me to join you," Simon said, trying hard to keep the hurt from his voice. "Tell me something, Janice. Are you that embarrassed to be seen with me when you're around a group of black people? It never seems to bother you otherwise."

"When have we ever been around just a group of black people?" she asked. "In three years it's never happened."

"And that is my fault? You've never wanted to go to events that were billed as African American functions. I know I've asked you."

He stopped, counted in his head to ten, then started over again. "You are not starting a fight with me over something so stupid. You're the one who's never once wanted me to meet anyone from your past, not a friend, not your family. I've gotten nothing from you in three years, so don't you dare."

"How did my family get brought into this?"

Simon glared at her. "What the hell's going on? I saw the way you looked at Tommy Strong, is something going on with the two of you?"

"No."

"Then why are you more worried about his feelings than mine? Would you please tell me that?"

"I'm not," Janice protested."You shouldn't have come looking for me. I'm not a child, I know when to come home."

"You arrogant little witch," Simon snapped and before he could stop himself, he grabbed her by the shoulders.

"I have warned you not to keep trying me, but you refuse to listen. Tell me why." He licked his lips and sighed, letting go of some of the anger. Still, he held her. "I want you to listen to me and listen good," he began. "If you think you can marry me and have it all in a neat little bundle, think again. There is no such thing as an uncomplicated relationship. You're a fiction writer, for God's sake. Can't you tell the difference? The way you're acting this moment, do you want me to tell you what you remind me of?"

Only he didn't wait for her to answer before he began again. "You're behaving like one of those women that you tell me you read about in books—the ones who are too stupid to live."

"Did you just call me stupid?" Janice asked, anger fueling her also. She tried to shove his hands from her body.

"Yes. If you think you can treat me this way and not pay the consequences..."

"What are the consequences, Simon? Why don't you tell me?"

His eyes closed and Simon fought with the demons that were now controlling him and lost. He kissed her, hard, brutal and demanding, not waiting for her to grant him entrance into her mouth. "I'm not a kid," he said when he finally let her go. "You play with fire you're going to get burned."

"What's wrong with you? You're acting like a madman. You can't just treat me any way you please," Janice said indignantly.

"And you can't treat me any way you please," he answered her.

"What do you think I did to you?"

"For starters, get rid of that sarcastic tone. Did you think I was blind? I saw the way you kept looking at Tommy. What was that about? You were behaving as though you needed his approval to come near me."

"I don't need Tommy's approval and I don't need yours. I'm my own person, Simon. If you don't like it why don't you drop me off at a hotel and let's end this now."

"I'll drop you off when we get home and if you want to leave, you go. I'm not going to try and stop you."

"I'm relieved to hear that, since you have no right to stop me. You may be rich, Simon, but there are laws to govern you also. You don't own me. I'm not your slave." She saw the muscle twitch in his temple, saw the pain that crossed his face and she stopped.

"Tell me something," Simon said quietly. "Why all of a sudden whenever we fight do you say I don't own you? I've never behaved as if I did."

"I don't want you thinking that you do," Janice hissed.

"That wasn't the answer to the question. Why do you think that? Why do you even say it? Have I behaved in that manner toward you?"

"Simon, it's not as easy for me to be with you as you might think."

He cocked his head to the side, frowning, and waited.

"I know what people think," Janice said, her voice no longer hostile but quiet, pleading for understanding.

"What do they think?" he asked.

"That I'm with you because of your money."

"That's partly true," Simon said, ignoring the denial on her face. "But if I don't give a damn about it, why should you?"

"I'm not with you because of your money, Simon."

He raised a brow. "If you're not that's news to me and to everyone who ever asked you about our relationship. You think I haven't heard what you said to people, how you explain us? You shout it out for the whole damn world to hear and now you give me some lame ass excuse that you're concerned that people think you're with me because of my money. Bull! Think of another reason."

"I'm not with you because of your money," Janice repeated, this time more insistently.

"Then why don't you tell me why you are." He was hoping that she'd say love but wasn't about to place bets on it.

"We each have our reasons."

"I know mine. I want to know yours. Tell me, Janice Lace, why are you with me? Why the hell did you agree to marry me? Why did you say you would set a date, then behave as if it was no more to you than a hair appointment? I'm damn well more than that. If not, then maybe we are making a mistake."

"I don't know why I'm with you," Janice finally said, so softly that he had to strain to hear her.

He sucked in his breath. This he'd not expected. "You can't think of one reason for marrying me?" he asked, holding her gaze.

"You asked me." She looked out the window. "You demanded it."

He couldn't believe it, not her words and not her manner. He knew why she was marrying him even if she refused to acknowledge it. She loved him. But he didn't know how long he'd be able to take this. He was not going to be reduced to a wimp for anyone, not even Janice Lace. He started driving while he thought of what to do next. The next move would have to be drastic, something to show her that he meant business.

"All of this and you think I treat you like a slave," he said, not looking in her direction, not speaking to her as he drove back to the mansion.

Simon popped the trunk, got out the mountain of books and carried them in. Janice had already gotten out and walked into the house. She needed to be taught a lesson. He was a man and there was just so much nonsense he was willing to take before he started fighting dirty. He'd reached his limit. No more. He was now willing to fight dirty.

Simon stopped in the foyer to give instructions to his assistant to pack his bags. He pushed the buzzer for the chauffeur, then placed a call to Harold to give him further instructions, filling him in quickly.

"Harold, if Janice calls, if she asks for me, tell her the jet is fueled and ready," Simon muttered, ready to end the conversation.

"What games are you playing, Simon? If the two of you had a fight why don't you just stay and work it out like a normal couple? How the hell is flying halfway around the world going to solve anything?"

"I've heard absence makes the heart grow fonder. I'm ready to check out that theory."

"But if she doesn't ask for you? What if she doesn't care that you're gone—"

"Look, let's move on," Simon said, interrupting the man from saying more. "Have you heard any more on that other matter?"

"As a matter of fact you were right. An investigation has been launched into your family's history."

"Damn," Simon muttered angrily. "He started it."

"At this point it's an unofficial investigation. But I did manage to get the name of the man who asked for it."

"Spit it out," Simon almost yelled. "Do you think I want the suspense? Just tell me."

"Tommy Strong, as you thought all along."

"Have you taken care of things?"

"Of course. No one will uncover a thing. You have my word on that."

"You'd better make sure or your word will not be the only thing that I require." Simon allowed his unspoken threat of firing Harold to lie between them for a moment. "Harold, I don't mean to treat you like this, but this is important."

"I know that," Harold answered, his voice offended. "I've always known how important this matter was to you. Simon, please, may I say something?" He asked for permission rather than just giving Simon advice, as he usually did.

Simon hated that he'd talked so brusquely to the man. Still, he was the boss and he had to let Harold know just how serious he was. "Go ahead," he said.

"Try telling her, tell Janice, before she finds out."

"I thought you said that would never happen."

"Never say never. It won't happen on my watch as long as I'm alive. But I don't want to be the last barrier of defense for you. I want you to bring this out and live with it. Then it won't have the power to hurt you so much. People will understand and they will forgive. You've been a generous benefactor and people will shove anything away as long as it's backed by the color green. Tell Janice if you're going to marry her. For God's sake, tell her."

"Do you want to know what she's been asking me lately?" Simon dropped his voice, the pain in his chest burning him like hot coals. "She's been asking me if I thought I owned her, telling me that she wasn't my slave. She's the one who owns me. Tell me she hasn't treated me like her slave for the past three years. I've gone along with her nonsense because I love her, because at any moment I thought there was a chance she'd come to her senses and stop talking crazy. And your advice to me is to tell her. Do you really think I'm going to tell her now?"

"Do you think she knows?"

"No, but I do think our friend has been putting ideas into her head."

"Simon, maybe if you gave him—"

"Please don't say more money. The fool tore up a check for a million dollars and you can bet by now he's told Janice. Who do you think will look like the good guy in her eyes, and who the villain?"

"She's marrying you."

"That doesn't matter, we're not married yet. Besides, she has a past with him, and I can't get her to open up about it."

"Is that why you brought him back into the picture, into her life?"

"I just wanted to make sure what she felt for him was dead."

"And is it?"

"I don't know. It seemed so initially, but it looks now as if something has been awakened."

"And you think now is a good time to leave her alone?"

"Are you saying I can't trust my fiancée?"

"I'm saying you're asking for trouble leaving her alone with a man who's out to destroy you, a man with whom she had a long term relationship."

"I don't believe she'll cheat on me, I trust her. I know she loves me, regardless of what she says, and I know she knows just how important fidelity is to me."

"What if you're wrong?"

"If I am, now's the time to find out, only I don't think I am." Simon was suddenly tired. "Listen, I don't want to talk about this anymore. I just want you to know if Janice calls anytime, day or night, make sure she knows I left a way for her to come to me."

"When are you coming back?"

"That depends."

"On what?"

"On who gives first."

"I don't understand."

"Sure you do," Simon teased. "If my beautiful fiancée does as I want and gives in, she will come to me and who knows if I will ever come back. But if she doesn't, then when I can't stand being without her I will return home."

"Good luck." Harold offered.

"Thanks, I have a feeling I'm going to need it."

CHAPTER FOURTEEN

Amazed, Janice sat at the end of the bed eying the more than two dozen boxes stacked neatly along one wall, all addressed to her. She pulled one African American oriented magazine after another from the boxes, knowing that Simon had made this happen.

She curled on the bed, wondering where he was, why he hadn't followed her up the stairs to finish the fight. She wanted to tell him that she was sorry but she didn't know if she would. Simon wanted something from her that she no longer wanted to give. He wanted one hundred percent of her. She was willing to give him seventy-five. She feared she'd lose herself if she gave more.

She'd loved Tommy so much that when he'd abandoned her she'd lost her soul and herself in the process. She could not give Simon that power over her. She knew he loved her and she loved him. Janice wanted to have what they'd agreed on three years before: an uncomplicated relationship. It was Simon who worried her. When she admitted that she loved him, how long would it take before he stopped loving her, before he also broke her heart? Janice flipped the magazine on the bed angrily. *Simon was the one who'd changed everything,* she thought. She'd stuck to the original plans.

Damn, she thought as she leaned over and picked up another magazine. What a mess. Though she hadn't told

Simon she loved him she knew he already knew. The only thing standing between them was her unwillingness to confess her love for fear of being hurt again.

Simon came quietly into the bedroom and stood watching as Janice rifled through the boxes. *God, how he loved her.*

He knew he was about to gamble with his future, but he had hope. She brought her eyes upward. He waited, maybe for a thank you, maybe for an apology. When she remained silent, he began to move around the room.

Her eyes followed him and he sighed, wanting to do something to make her crack, make her act as though she were alive, as though she gave a damn. He opened a drawer and slammed it with so much force that he thought it would splinter. Then he turned to face her. He wished for a moment that his assistant had had to go to his bedroom to pack his bag; then Janice would know just how serious he was. But the majority of his clothes were in a downstairs bedroom since she used every spare inch of space for her clothing.

"This won't happen again," he said quietly, refusing to yell. "I will not come last on your list. I don't care if you think I'm trying to own you. I'm warning you." He saw her eyes change from the soft misty brown, saw when she began glaring but he didn't give a damn. He was going to continue.

"This game we've been playing, the two of us." He used his fingers to make a see-sawing motion between the two of them. "It's over. I'm not going to continue substituting fighting for the things that I want."

She opened her mouth and he held up a hand. "Don't say anything or I might say something I'll regret."

Simon was surprised that Janice did as he demanded and didn't talk. He saw her eyes go to the books. He didn't want her gratitude, not for something that was easily accomplished with one phone call.

He pointed at the magazines. "Don't let that be an influence on your feelings. It wasn't done to make you feel something that you don't."

With that he went into the bathroom just to give her time to say something that might stop him from leaving. But she didn't. She watched as he left their room and his heart broke thinking that even if she knew what he was about to do she still might not do anything, that she would let him walk out.

Three hours later when he was in the sky flying away from her, he realized that Janice didn't know that he had left town, let alone the country. Since she'd not bothered to come down, she'd not seen his bags loaded into the limo. He wondered how many days it would be before she noticed that he'd left his cell phone on the vanity in the bathroom. How many days would it take before she noticed he wasn't in the bed?

Simon closed his eyes and sighed, not knowing what he was going to do if things didn't work out the way that he wanted.

There was one thing he wouldn't tolerate and he'd meant it from the moment he'd first uttered it. He would not stand for infidelity. He'd grown up with it. Both of his parents had engaged in it, all of his parents' friends had. And many of their relatives had had battles with illegitimate children. Luckily his father and mother had not brought any illegitimate children into the world.

Simon had vowed that he would never bring children into the world until he was married and that he'd never stray from his marriage bed. He meant it and he hoped to God that Janice had meant it when she agreed to it. As much as it would hurt him, if she slept with Tommy Strong or anyone else, he would leave her and he wouldn't look back. It would hurt like hell, but he would do it.

Janice waited in bed for Simon to return. She'd thought his leaving in a huff was a bluff. When she heard the limo drive off, she thought he would return shortly. She was surprised when the limo returned without him and hour after hour ticked by. Simon had never stayed away without telling her. When she found his cell phone in the bathroom, relief flooded her body. He was trying to make her beg, she was sure of it.

As much as she didn't want Simon to have the upper hand, her curiosity finally got the better of her and she went downstairs looking for him. She wanted to ask the staff where Simon was but felt embarrassed that they would have that knowledge when she didn't. Left with no other choice, she finally crawled back into bed, only to toss and turn because of her worry about Simon.

Janice was angry with Simon for making her worry and angry with herself for not somehow knowing that he was planning on leaving. If anything happened to him…What if his idea wasn't to make her beg? What if he was abandoning her just like…Shivering, she blinked away the thought, refusing to allow her mind to take that turn. She couldn't remember ever worrying about Simon. She'd never had to. She thought of the pain she'd caused him, how angry he'd been when they arrived home, and she hoped that he was not doing anything foolish.

Then the one thought that had been lingering at the back of her mind pushed its way forward with a mighty whoosh. Panic filled her at the thought that he might be with another woman. She'd never thought of herself as jealous or possessive, but she didn't want Simon with another woman no matter their relationship.

She'd foolishly allowed her past to intrude on her present. She regretted that she'd allowed Tommy's kiss. She'd made Simon a promise and even if it was only a kiss, he wouldn't like it. It was heavy on her conscience as she finally drifted off to sleep.

The next day Janice ignored Tommy's pleas that she needed to stay longer, that they had more work to do. At four P.M. she called a taxi and left. She was home before five but Simon wasn't. She ignored the calls to dinner and went to bed wondering again where he was.

After a week of this she was angry. She knew that Simon staying away was deliberate. He was probably trying to teach her a lesson, one of the consequences he'd mentioned. Well, he could go to hell, she thought angrily as she climbed into the empty bed alone.

This was the second time that a man had abandoned her. She'd asked for an uncomplicated relationship so that she wouldn't hurt. Only she wasn't supposed to care either, but she did. She had no idea what to do about the situation.

After nine days Janice couldn't take the not knowing anymore. She missed Simon in bed beside her, she missed him there for her to fight with and she missed the making up. They had never ended a fight without making love. Even though she'd been the one to call for no emotions, she was drowning in them. If her missing him was one of the consequences, then Simon was right. She'd played with fire and she'd gotten burned.

Before she could talk herself out of it Janice picked up the phone and dialed Harold. If anyone knew where Simon was he would.

"Harold, I just wanted to check on my stocks." she began when he answered her call.

"Oh, they're doing nicely," he answered her, his voice friendly but not giving away anything.

"So how are you?" she asked, stalling.

"I'm fine and you?" he asked politely.

"I'm fine."

"Was there anything else?"

She couldn't keep him on the line without a reason, and she couldn't bring herself to ask where Simon was. She had the feeling that Harold didn't fully approve of their relationship.

"No, Harold, that's all I wanted," she lied.

She lay across the bed caressing Simon's pillow. The fight rolled through her mind and she tried unsuccessfully to make Simon's leaving his fault, but it wasn't and she knew it. She tried hard to remember his words to her and didn't know if he'd told her he was leaving her. She should have listened more closely.

Dialing the phone again she did what she had to do. "Harold," she said the moment the phone was answered. "I know this might sound strange to you but I'm afraid that I don't know where Simon is. He's been gone for nine days," she said quietly.

Harold laughed. Janice wasn't sure she'd ever heard him laugh.

"I was wondering which of you would crack first," Harold laughed again. "Oh, never mind. Janice, did you ever think of just phoning Simon? His cell phone will work anywhere, you know."

"Simon and I had a fight more than a week ago. He left his phone at home and I don't know how to get in touch with him. Do you have a number where I can reach him?"

"You can go to him if you'd like. He left instructions that if you called me that I was to tell you the jet was fueled and ready. Should I make arrangements for you?"

Stunned, Janice didn't know what to say.

"Janice, would you like for me to alert the pilot?"

"No thank you, Harold. For right now I just want to talk to Simon."

Wasting no time in dialing the number once Harold had given it to her, she held her breath and released it in relief when Simon answered.

"Simon, I miss you," she said.

"It took you nine days to miss me?"

"No, it took me nine days before I wanted to admit to you how much I miss you. Please come home."

"Why Janice? Give me one good reason why I should."

"I need you," she replied.

Simon sighed. She hadn't said she loved him but needing him was pretty damn close.

"When are you coming home?" Janice asked, her voice soft and unsure, her words faltering.

"I don't know." And he didn't despite the fact that she'd made the first move. She'd called and still he didn't know what he was going to do. "I'll talk to you later," he said, disconnecting the call.

"Janice, this isn't a job, this is a commitment. You can't punch out every day at four. Sometimes you need to stay longer."

She was tired of Tommy's picking at her nerves the way a child picked at a scab. For ten days he'd needled her and she was annoyed with it.

"Look, Tommy, I have a life. We've been all over New Jersey, New York and Pennsylvania. I've done everything you've asked. I've stood on so many street corners that people have wondered if I was begging or hooking. And I've walked more miles than I have in my entire life."

"And I was right there with you. So were many others."

"I have a fiancé who requires my time."

"Right," he answered. "Tell me, where has your fiancé been? It's been almost two weeks since I've heard you mention him. And he hasn't called you once. Don't think I haven't noticed that you haven't called him." Tommy smiled. "But I have noticed that you don't dare leave here a minute after four." He laughed aloud. "And you don't think Simon Kohl owns you."

Janice wanted to slap the cocky grin from his face but she resisted the temptation. She knew he was baiting her, trying to get her to stay, and she wondered for a moment why she didn't. She had stayed the day she was to set a date for her wedding and now that Simon had taken off without a word to her she was doing what she'd promised. Only he didn't know it; he wasn't home.

"Tommy, I'll see you tomorrow," Janice answered instead and left.

On the ride home she thought over the mistakes she'd made in the last few weeks and hoped for a chance to rectify as many of them as she could. She might not be able to say the words 'I love you,' but she could start showing Simon that she did, if he ever returned.

She said a prayer and opened the door to the mansion. It was getting harder each day to not know if Simon were ever coming back. She started to walk up the stairs, heard a voice and ran back down.

"Simon!" Shocked relief washed over her as she stood staring at him. She wanted to run to him, in fact started to, then caught herself and stopped. He was staring at her with a strange look on his face. She wondered if he was still angry, where he'd been. Most importantly, did he still love her?

Simon smiled slightly, relieved to be home and find that his fiancée was not spending her nights with Tommy. He stood by the bookcase in the library, his heart thudding in his chest. He knew Janice had been getting home before five everyday. Though his staff loved her, they were aware who paid their salaries.

He saw the look in her eyes—the sheer joy. He had seen her start to run to him, then catch herself and stop. But she had been unable to make the joy of seeing him leave her eyes. *Please come to me,* he thought while he looked at her. *I'm home.*

"Hi," she said and turned away.

"Hello yourself," he answered, not going near her, though he inhaled her scent deep into his lungs. He wanted her so badly that he ached with the wanting, but he would not be the one to give in, not this time. He knew she had questions and he would not provide the answers unless she asked.

She didn't.

"You're home early, aren't you?"

"I've been trying to come home early," Janice answered.

It seemed forever that they stood there, each waiting for the other to crack. The mutual longing took over as they became increasingly aware of each other. The air crackled with their heat, with their energy, and with their need.

"Simon, I'm glad you're home."

"Baby," Simon whispered. He opened his arms, saw her eyes light with golden brown fire and planted himself solidly.

Janice didn't want to give him power over her but when he opened his arms to her she found herself running to him. Tears spilled down her cheeks and she couldn't stop those either. She wrapped her arms around Simon so tightly that that she heard him laughing, pleading with her that he couldn't breathe.

"Why did you leave me?" she cried, "I thought you weren't coming back. I was going crazy with worry." The words had come unbidden out of her mouth. What the hell was happening to her? She couldn't seem to stop herself. "I missed you," she sobbed, surprising Simon as well as herself.

"Why did you wait so long to call?" Simon asked, kissing her lips, her eyes, and her ears. "Why didn't you pick up the phone?"

Janice trembled in his arms. His hands were all over her, trailing liquid fire.

"Why didn't you?" she asked. "You were the one who abandoned me, I didn't abandon you."

"Abandon you?" Damn, in his anger he'd forgotten about Tommy and what Tommy had put her through. He should have remembered that. He hated to think that somewhere in his soul maybe he had. At least consciously he hadn't, though he would admit that his leaving was in part to teach her a lesson.

"Baby, forgive me. I should have thought of that. Is that what you thought?" Simon asked. "But you should have known, I would have never…" He held her tighter. That was exactly what he'd been going for when he'd left. Nothing else he'd done so far with Janice had worked. "I'm sorry to have put you through that. I didn't want to make you worry," he lied. "I just wanted to make you…oh hell, I'm sorry. I guess I did want to make you worry enough to know that you would miss me."

"It worked. I missed you."

"Don't you know I'd never leave you for good?"

"That wasn't what you've been saying. You've been threatening me since…" She stopped not wanting to mention Tommy's name. "You told me there were going to be consequences. You even said if you thought I cheated on you that you would leave me."

"Have you cheated on me?"

"No, Simon."

"Baby, the only way this relationship will ever end will be if you walk away from me." Then he took her. His tongue plundered the inside of her mouth, ravishing her, sending chills skittering through him and her. He pulled her even closer, heard the air whoosh out of her lungs and couldn't loosen his hold; instead he swept her up in his arms and headed for the stairs.

"What about dinner? Aren't you hungry?" Janice asked.

He laughed. "Do you really think food is what's on my mind?" He hadn't known how quickly he could move upstairs carrying Janice's weight. He saw several of his staff as he rushed forward. They looked away but not before he saw the smiles on their faces.

"Show me how much you missed me, baby," he said, tossing her on the bed, ripping at her blouse, throwing it on the floor. He felt her hands pulling at his belt, loosening it. He kicked off his shoes, bent to take hers off, then stopped and kissed her. He wanted the clothes off her, off him. He was so hungry for her body that he didn't know if he could wait. When her breasts were bare he fell on her, feasting as though he were starving, and he was. He was starving for her, for her body, for her love.

Somewhere at the back of his mind was the knowledge that Janice had never displayed such emotion, not in three years. She had battled to not come to him and she'd lost. For that he was grateful. Still, some inkling of dismay pulled at him, taking away some of his pleasure. Another man had wrought the emotion from her that he'd wanted to unearth. Sure, he was now benefiting, but...but...hell, he thought and gave up thinking as he heard her moan.

"Simon," she moaned, pulling his hair, tugging a little harder than she'd intended. "Don't you ever do that again."

She had not even touched him, but he could have come right then if he weren't so conscious of her needs. She finally did and he almost lost it then and there. He slid his fingers deep inside her and found her ready. She clenched her muscles around his fingers, pulling him in deeper.

He found her spot, did what he knew would bring her to the edge and quickly. "No," she said, "not yet," but his body was trembling with the tremendous effort it was taking to not enter her. She pulled away, not wanting to come, and he almost laughed. She was so determined to keep her control, even in the act of making love. Even though she wanted the release, she wanted to orchestrate things, be the conductor.

"I want you inside me," she moaned.

Simon caved. Why the hell would he try to resist? He looked down and she was looking at him with the sexiest smile on her face. "I'm so glad you're home," she whispered, and he entered her, plunging deep into her, riding her with all the fever he held in his body. He felt his passion for her swelling, reaching a crescendo and he moaned, riding her harder, going deeper, wanting to touch her very soul with his thrusts.

Simon was trembling in his need from the built up passion of the past ten days. He poured everything into loving her, taking her moans of pleasure into his mouth and pouring his heat into her. He filled her and she filled him, his body and his soul. He felt his release rising from the bottom of his being and growled his pleasure, feeling her give in at last to her passion. They clung together in the aftermath, holding on to each other with an intensity that produced aftershocks of desire.

Janice was shivering, overcome with emotion. She'd lost control, something she'd sworn not to do. For three years she'd done her best to keep a part of herself separate from Simon. All that time she'd relied on her mantra and in the end it hadn't worked.

Even now in his arms the refrain pinged in her mind. *I shouldn't depend on Simon. I shouldn't depend on anyone but myself.* But something had happened when he'd held out his arms. She'd tried to not run into them but she had and she'd told him things she wished she hadn't. Now he knew how much she cared; now he could hurt her, damn him.

Damn him for leaving her. If he hadn't, she would not have missed him so much that to not touch him would have been pure torture. She felt the beating of his heart against her skin, heard his satisfied growl in her ear. She bit him, first softly, then as she thought of his leaving her, harder, relishing the feel of causing him physical pain.

"Ouch," Simon said and put his finger on her lips. "Baby, that hurt."

"Did it?" she asked.

"Did it? You know that it did, you meant it to hurt." He rolled over to look down at her and saw fear in her eyes. "Baby, what's wrong?"

Janice closed her eyes, knowing he was reading her emotions in them. She didn't want him to. She felt a tear slide beneath her closed lids and cursed silently, wondering what was happening to her. She hadn't cried in over twelve years now and at the drop of a hat she was bawling.

"Baby, you're crying," Simon whispered, wiping the tear away. "What's wrong?"

She only gritted her teeth together and closed her eyes tighter; her body shuddered with her new emotion.

"You were serious, weren't you? You really thought I had left you for good?" He kissed her cheeks. "Open your eyes, Janice, look at me."

She didn't. She couldn't. If she did, that would be the end of her. He would know, she would know, and there would be no going back, no pretending to either of them that she didn't love him.

"Open your eyes and look at me," Simon repeated sternly. "I want you to see me when I tell you this." He nipped at her lip, biting a little harder when she didn't comply, and a little harder still until her lids fluttered and she opened her eyes.

"I'm not Tommy," Simon began.

She felt the tremble begin at the top of her head and travel downward. "Why did you leave me?" she asked.

"I didn't leave you," he said, narrowing his eyes. "I'll never leave you, not like that…not without telling you."

"You didn't tell me." Janice felt as though she'd been in this position before, only one of the main players had changed.

"You refused to talk to me. You wouldn't even look at me. If you had not wanted me to leave all you had to do was talk to me, tell me why you were allowing Tommy to come between us. If you wanted me home all you had to do was call."

"You left your cell at home. I took that to mean you didn't want to talk to me."

"I didn't want to make it easy for you to talk to me. But you knew Harold would know how to reach me." He tilted her chin so that he was gazing into her eyes. "Baby, you were aware the staff would know how to reach me. Admit it."

"I didn't want to ask them. Why should you have left them with that information and not told me?"

He looked at her thoughtfully for a nanosecond. "You're right, but what about Harold? You could have called him." He frowned. "You did call him. Why did it take you so long?"

"You were so angry when you left our bedroom and went downstairs. I didn't know you were leaving. Then when I figured out that you had...I didn't know if...I didn't know if you were coming back. I thought that you had—"

"Listen to me. Don't compare me with anyone else." He looked at her. "I wanted to give you some time to come to your senses. I wanted you to know that I meant what I'd said about fidelity on both of our parts. I was pissed big time. You disrespected me and our relationship. I wanted to teach you a lesson. Looks like I went about it all wrong. Like I said, infidelity is the only thing that would tear us apart. I have no plans on being unfaithful to you. Are you planning to cheat on me?"

"No, never."

Simon smiled at her. "Then we're good. Trust me, baby, I would never abandon you."

"Leaving without telling me is abandoning me." Janice couldn't believe it. She was appearing weak and vulnerable and as much as she didn't want that, she wanted even less for Simon not to be a part of her life.

"So, you think I abandoned you without a word?" he asked, looking at her with a hint of a smile around his mouth. He pushed the button on the intercom behind the bed.

"Would you get the package for Ms. Lace that I left for her and bring it to our room."

"Simon, we're not dressed," Janice reminded him as she burrowed under the covers.

"Do you think I'm going to let him come in here? I never want anyone to see you like this but me," he said and allowed his eyes to roam over her flesh. She turned as the knock sounded on their door.

"Just leave it," Simon called out. "Thank you." He bounced from the bed not bothering with a robe; he knew he would have no need for clothes. The moment she was sufficiently satisfied that he was telling her the truth he was determined to drive that point home in other ways. He felt his flesh rising at the thought and he smiled. *Crazy woman, how the hell did she think I would ever abandon her?*

He opened the door, retrieved the package, brought it back to the bed, and presented it to Janice with a flourish and a smile. "Here is the proof of my innocence." He smiled broadly. "If you had asked the staff about my whereabouts, they would have given it to you."

The package was sealed so tightly that Janice knew it hadn't been opened.Simon handed her a pair of scissors from the drawer and waited. She looked at him, then at the package, wondering what was in it. Her heart fluttered in her chest.

She took out a picture of the front page of the newspaper dated ten days before, along with a note. She glanced at Simon, then began reading.

"*I think we need some time apart. I know that I do. That number you pulled with Tommy was foul and totally disrespectful. I have no plans on putting up with that ever again. Maybe you need to not have me in your life for a time in order to admit that you need me and yes, that you love me. If you don't come to your senses, then maybe I'm wrong. Maybe you don't love me after all. By the way, my staff located the back issues of* Black Rose *and* Black Train of Thought. *I hope you enjoy them. Also, congratulations on making the front page of the paper. I may be upset with you but I'm also very proud of you. Just so you know, I had nothing to do with the mention in the paper. If you want to call me, Harold has the number. If you want to come to me call Harold and he will get the jet ready for you. If you don't call or come to me I'll assume that you can live without me. Simon.*

Janice's heart fluttered again. This was nothing like when Tommy left. Simon had made sure she knew she could come to him. As angry as he'd been he had thought of her. She barely glanced at the magazines in her hands. Her eyes skimmed over the newspaper and she blinked away the sudden tears.

"That wasn't the reason I didn't call. It's not that I ever wanted to live without you, but you were so angry when you came to the bookstore."

"I had reason to be angry."

"I know," she answered, "you did. But, Simon, you were playing dirty. You took my worst fear and used it against me."

"A little, you're right. But I was desperate and desperate times..." Simon nudged her ear with his nose. "Why do you think I left the paper with the magazine and the note? You're so darn paranoid that I knew that without proof you wouldn't believe I had left this for you the night I left." He tapped the paper. "Look at the date."

She already had. "I guess maybe I shouldn't have been so stubborn about calling Harold. You did sort of let me know by leaving this. But, Simon, next time just try telling me."

"I don't plan on there ever being a next time. I missed you far too much to ever want to be apart from you again."

"I missed you too. I really did. I'm sorry for making you feel as though I didn't care. But you don't have to worry; Tommy's not a problem for us."

"What you had with Tommy was nothing more than puppy love." He paused and laughed. "Okay, maybe it was real but it was what young people feel. It wasn't a mature love. Regardless, he was crazy to ever leave you. Don't lump me with him, baby. I'm not Tommy; I'm not going to hurt you. I love you and you can depend on that always. I'll be here for you no matter what. I love you," he said. He saw her attempt to pull away and pulled her back, tilting her chin upwards. "Are you listening to me?"

"I am."

"Then tell me you know how much I love you, tell me how much you love me."

"I do."

"Tell me," Simon insisted. "Saying the words is not going to stop my loving you. I just want to hear you say them."

She pulled his face down to hers, kissed him and grinned. "I'm so glad to have you home."

"I'm glad to be home, baby," he answered, kissing her back, not forgetting that she hadn't told him that she loved him. He sighed heavily. "You told me before I left that I had demanded that you marry me. Now I want to ask you, no demands, do you want to marry me?"

"Simon Kohl, I want to marry you. You're the man that I want, not Tommy Strong." She tilted her head, "I know what you thought. You were wrong. You're the man I want in my life."

"Now tell me that you love me," he smiled, trying again.

"Simon, I have a hard time saying it, but I do. Know that I do. Besides, the way those words are bandied about I don't put much stock in them. Can't we just move past the need for words, for now?" she purred, touching him in his most intimate area. "Why don't we go downstairs and get a bite to eat."

Simon grinned from ear to ear as he reached for her. "Woman, you are truly evil. Look at me." He looked at his erection. "Do you really think I'm in any condition to go anywhere?"

"I know where you can go where that won't be a problem."

He watched as she fell back on the mattress, opening up her arms for him, knowing that he wouldn't resist the delectable treat she was presenting. He knew she'd not said what he wanted to hear but he would let it go for now. He wanted her in his arms. They'd wasted enough time. He wrapped his arms around her and held her tightly for a long moment before he pulled back in order to kiss her. He felt her shiver, felt her fire and delved deeper, tasting her juices.

"Are you sure you're not hungry?" she asked, laughing.

"I'm starving," he answered, "and there is only one thing that can satisfy my appetite."

Simon swooped down on her and Janice trembled from her head to her toes. He ran his hands up and down her torso, his look melting her. He laved her flesh, suckling her as if he were indeed starving. And all the while his hands were probing, testing. And she moaned as his fingers brushed against her. She felt the juices from her body rushing out of her and felt herself going under, her orgasm fast approaching.

She heard Simon telling her that he loved her and with his words she went under completely, crashing, barely able to breath, choking out his name in surrender.

Janice trembled in his arms, waiting for him to join her, feeling the changes in his body, hearing him growl, feeling him driving even deeper and feeling his release as he roared.

"I love you," he moaned softly into her neck but she didn't answer. She held him as close as possible, hoping he would know how she felt, hoping she wouldn't have to say it. And she hoped that the day would come when she could.

Hours later, neither of them could do much more than make promises. They were tired and deliciously achy. The need for actual food had finally pushed in on them and Simon called for a tray while Janice showered.

They ate dinner in relative quiet. She smiled at him every now and then, touching him between mouthfuls of food. He couldn't resist smiling back. He watched as she got up from the table, and was in the same position when she returned. He looked in her hand and wondered what she had.

She came to him, kissed his shoulder, his neck and his ears, then blew breath along the back of his hairline and he felt an instant erection. "I thought you were tired," he teased, reaching for her hand that was caressing his shoulder.

She came around to face him, her face lit by an inner glow. The warm brown fire that filled her eyes filled his soul. He looked in the hand she was holding toward him and saw the calendar. He looked at her, not saying a word, pretending not to understand.

"What month looks good?" she asked.

"For what?" he asked, still not wanting to make it easy for her, knowing this was her way of making amends. He needed more.

"For our wedding," she answered. "I thought we should set a date."

Simon pulled her into his lap. This was part of what he needed. Now he was almost glad that they'd fought. "Is this what you want?" he asked.

"It's what I want."

"Am I who you want?" he pressed.

"Simon, I want to marry you," she answered.

"I asked if I'm the man that you want."

She moved in his lap, pressing her body against him, leaning her head against his. She stroked his cheek with her tongue and her hand went down and groped him and he felt the movement before he pushed her way.

"Not this time." He shook his head. "Am I the man that you want?"

"I answered that question already."

"That was when we were making up."

"Are we done making up?"

"We've taken the edge off." He couldn't help smiling. "And that's permitting me to think clearly. I know that we need to talk."

"Simon, come on, please, let's not fight."

He laughed aloud. "I don't believe it, you, the queen of fights, don't want to fight." He chuckled. "Don't worry baby, I don't want to fight either. But we have to get some things straight between us."

Janice sighed. "Okay, what?"

"First, about my leaving, I meant it. I would never abandon you. I hate to keep repeating myself but I want to make this perfectly clear to you. I'm getting tired of paying for Tommy's sins. I'm sure I don't know everything that happened with the two of you but I'm not him and I refuse to continue in this relationship and allow you to walk all over me. What I told you before I left I meant. We're not doing this dance between us anymore. Now back to my original question. Before we pick a date, am I the man that you want for the rest of your life? I plan to do this only once. You marry me and that's it," he said seriously, "I will not leave you and you will not leave me. Till death do us part."

"You're the man that I want," Janice admitted, not looking directly at him. She knew if she didn't admit to at least that much she would lose him. Her throat tightened. She didn't want to lose Simon from her life.

"Can you look at me and say it as though you mean it?" Simon said, pulling her closer.

"I meant it," she said.

"Look at me, and tell me again," he ordered, his voice not leaving any room for kidding.

"Simon," she whispered. "You know that you're the one that I want. Haven't I shown you that?"

He looked backwards at the bed. "You mean that? No, baby, that's not showing me."

She lifted her brow.

"That was showing me you needed me, wanted me, maybe even missed me and believe me, I love it. But that's not showing me that you love me."

"What do you want from me?"

"I want you to share your soul with me."

CHAPTER FIFTEEN

Janice shivered. Simon wanted her soul. She'd known it would lead to this. What had happened to the man that she fought with, the one that she could depend on to fight with her, the one who didn't have the look in his eyes that Simon did, as if his entire life was riding on her answer?

She wanted only to see his passion, his lust; she didn't want to see his love. And it had gotten so that lately love was always in his eyes. A part of her wanted to grab onto that love and beg him to never stop loving her. But she remembered how fragile love was, how easily it could change. And she never wanted to hurt that way again.

"Simon, what happened, what changed you?"

"You did."

"How?"

"I don't know."

"I liked the way we were together."

"So did I, but I'm not getting any younger. Neither are you," he said pointedly. "I want more in my life. I want that one special person. I want to know that I can depend on you, that no matter what happens, no matter what secrets we share, we can weather the storm, that we will be there for each other. And I can't count on that if you aren't willing to share your soul with me."

"There won't be any going back from that, Simon, and life doesn't offer any guarantees. If I do as you ask, open myself up to you, expose my soul, bare it all, can you guarantee me that I won't regret it?"

He swallowed. "No, I can't guarantee it. But I'd like to think that we can build a future where we can work past any obstacles."

"What if I promise you that I will try?"

Simon swallowed. He thought of Harold telling him to tell Janice his secret. But now was not the time; it might never be the right time to tell her.

"Did you tell Tommy that you loved him?"

"What?" Janice asked.

"When you were with Tommy, did you tell him that you loved him?"

"That was such a long time ago."

"Did you tell him?" Simon persisted. "I want you to give to me what you gave to him. No," he stopped and shook his head. "I want more than you gave him. I want more than you've ever given any man. I want all of you."

"Do you want me to tell you simply because I told Tommy? Look where that relationship ended. You want my soul, you said. What do I get in exchange, Simon?"

"You get all of me. You get my soul."

"Simon, I'm not playing games with you, I promise. I'm only trying to protect myself from being hurt. When I give you my soul, I give you the power to hurt me. I know how I've been treating you, Simon. I didn't want to love you because then you would be able to hurt me. But I knew you wanted more and that alone made me want to run away."

She swallowed and blinked, trying to blot out her pain. He wanted her soul. She'd see how much he could really take.

"When I thought you might not come back," Janice whispered, "it hurt. I didn't like it. No one has been able to make me hurt in a long time."

"Don't you trust me?" Simon asked.

She wanted to tell him yes, but she couldn't say it because she didn't trust him not to hurt her. He was human and humans were flawed. She was flawed.

She wondered how he'd ever started loving her in the first place when she'd purposefully treated him like shit. Now he wanted her to join him, to step out on a branch that was already creaky and without a safety net. She needed her net.

"Simon, give me time," she pleaded.

"Is it so hard for you to tell me that you love me?" he asked, a wry smile on his face, his hope in his eyes. "I can tell you."

"One river at a time. That's all that I can cross."

He looked at her, stunned. A flash of pain filled his eyes and he turned from her. Janice moved with him, laid her head against his back and pressed her hand to his chest. "I've never planned a wedding," she said, hoping that somehow he would interpret it the way she meant it, that she was committed to marrying him. She would not cheat on him. What more could he ask?

To hear the words, 'I love you.' The words pounded at her and she pushed them away. She was willing to share the rest of her life with him. Surely that weighed more than words.

"Can we set a date?" she asked, teasing him, pulling on his hair, noticing how long it was, knowing that he hadn't cut it since he'd been gone. "I like your hair long," she said, tugging on it gently, swaying her hips, grating her front to his rear. "I can't wait to marry you," she tried again.

Simon turned to look at her, saw the pleading in her eyes, the worry, the unspoken words. She loved him. God, how he wanted to hear her say it. He held her in his arms. "I'll make you a deal. I'll do as you ask for *now*. But I will eventually want to hear you tell me."

"What's the deal?" she asked, smiling.

He knew she thought she'd gotten her way. She had no idea that what he was about to propose would be equally difficult.

"I want to meet your family." He saw her start to protest and narrowed his eyes. "Take it or leave it."

She should have known. "When do you want to meet them?"

"No time like the present."

Janice stared at him. Surely he didn't mean he wanted them to fly somewhere tonight. "Now?"

Simon laughed, picked up the phone and handed it to her. "Call your parents."

Now what the heck could she do? "Shouldn't we at least have the date?" she asked.

"I have it. We're getting married in six weeks, on your birthday. September first. Dial," he said.

She sighed. Nothing to do but make the call. Janice waited while the phone rang, praying it wouldn't be her mother who answered. But it was. Janice blew out her breath. "Mom, hi."

"Mary Jo."

Janice cringed at the way her mother said her name, making it a reprimand for her having changed it.

"I have some news, Mom."

"You mean that you're getting married? I heard it on the newscast and I saw you on that talk show."

Janice waited a moment, counting, knowing what was coming.

"It's nice that you remembered you had a family and called to tell us. I thought I'd have to read the entire thing in the paper."

"I didn't call to fight. I called to introduce you to Simon."

"By phone?" her mother screamed. "You can't even come home to introduce him?"

Janice glared at Simon and let out an overly-exaggerated sigh. "This is what you wanted," she quipped as she handed him the phone and attempted to move away. He pulled her back into the shelter of his arms and smiled down at her.

"Mrs. Adams, how are you? I'm Simon Kohl, I'm sorry that we haven't met formally or spoken sooner but…"

"Yeah, I understand. My daughter didn't want you to meet us."

Simon laughed easily. "Nothing so dramatic. She's really been busy."

"Too busy to come home for a visit, Mr. Kohl? Too busy to pick up the phone?"

He glanced down at Janice and saw the look in her eyes. She wanted to run away. For a moment he wished that he'd not forced this but it was the right thing to do. They were getting married; her family should be involved.

"Maybe that was my fault. I've kept her pretty busy. When you're trying to spotlight an author, you have to strike while there's momentum. Between writing and doing promotions you wouldn't believe how little I get to see of her."

"Well, it seems she's been having a lot of time to spend on television and radio lately. I saw her on that talk show with Tommy."

Simon heard the woman hesitate, then laugh a little.

"You do know Tommy, don't you, Mr. Kohl?"

"I know him, Mrs. Adams. Janice has been working with him."

"Did you know that I didn't name my daughter Janice Lace? I named her Mary Jo. Guess she's too good for that name."

"Lots of writers use a pseudonym to protect their privacy."

"From their family? No one wanted anything from her."

"That wasn't what I meant. I do apologize for keeping your daughter so busy and I would like to make up for that. I would like to bring your entire family here for a visit so that we can all get to know each other."

Janice pushed away from Simon with so much force that she toppled backward. "No," she said in a loud whisper, "not here."

Simon shrugged; he was stuck. "I can put you up in the best hotel in town, the penthouse if you like, and you can live like royalty."

"You want us to visit to get to know you?"

"Yes," Simon said, "yes, I do."

"Then why do you want to put us away from you in a hotel? I hear you live in a mansion. Why can't we stay there? How many bedrooms do you have in that place?"

Simon grinned as he shrugged his shoulders again to let Janice know he didn't have a choice. "Ten," he answered honestly.

"Are they all taken?"

Simon saw the look of panic that came over Janice and he hesitated. "No, all of the rooms aren't filled but we're having work done. It would be more comfortable for you at a hotel or I could rent a house for you, if you'd like."

"Is Mary Jo's standing in front of you shaking her head no?" the woman asked.

Simon couldn't help it. He burst out laughing. The woman was nothing like her daughter.

"Don't lie, Mr. Kohl, or you and I will not have a chance in hell of getting along."

"I wish I could answer that question for you but you must understand I'm about to get married. I've waited my entire life to do this. I'm not going to ruin it now by shooting off my mouth."

Laughter greeted Simon and he was delighted that he had not angered Janice's mother. He looked across the room to where Janice was scowling at him and wished that he could say the same for his fiancée.

"If you let us stay at your place I promise I'll behave," the woman coaxed.

This time it was Simon who laughed. "I'll let you know. I'm looking forward to meeting you."

"And me you. Now may I speak to my daughter?"

Simon walked to Janice and hugged her, kissed her cheek, then handed her the phone. "Be nice," he whispered. "I'll make it worth your while."

Janice took the phone. "Yes, Mom."

"I like him."

"So do I."

"Why didn't you ever introduce us before?"

"There was no need. Simon and I weren't committed." Simon tilted her chin until she was looking directly at him. "It's different now, Mom. We're committed and we're getting married on my birthday." Janice couldn't help grinning as Simon kissed her lightly on the lips.

"Mom, you're not talking. Aren't you going to say anything?"

"Congratulations. If that man can put up with your cold ways, he's bound to make you a wonderful husband."

Her mother hung up before she could think of a retort. "She likes you," she said. "Me, well, not so much, but you won her over. You should be happy."

"I would be more happy if you told me the deal with your family."

"Can't you let anything go? You're becoming..." She thought about it and smiled, though not amused. "You're becoming demanding. Is this what you're going to be like after I say 'I do'?"

For an answer Simon smirked.

"What do you think getting married means?"

"A hell of a lot more than our co-habiting," he answered.

"What, for instance?"

He laughed then, a huge belly laugh. "Please, I want kids. I want babies, lots of babies, and I don't want them until I'm married."

"How did you ever get to be so old-fashioned? Simon, you're an enigma. Here you are, one of the richest, most powerful men in the world. You can have anything and anyone that you want and what do you want? A baby," she said and smiled, this time amused.

"Not just any baby," he corrected. "I want babies with my wife. I want a family with you."

"Why me, Simon? With so many women wanting you, why did you choose me? Anyone taking bets would have thought it a sure thing that our relationship would end on the battleground, not in church."

"That's anyone looking on the surface." Simon stopped smiling and became serious. "Maybe that's what you've been doing, looking at the surface. I have to look deeper. I make my living by knowing people, by knowing what they think, how they really feel, what they're going to do. I need to be two steps ahead of them. I can't afford to make mistakes."

"So you think you're two steps ahead of me?"

"If you have to ask me such a silly question as why I want you, then yes, I'm a lot more than two steps ahead of you. I love you because you love me."

He saw her look of panic. "What do you think is going to happen because I said the words? Do you think the world is going to collapse? I know what happened with Tommy turned you off love, but you were young and so was he. And even if you hadn't been, not every man is Tommy."

"You know all of this because it's your business to know? Simon, you're a fake."

He could feel the blood drain from his face. "What do you mean?" he asked softly.

"Your so-called insight needed to make a living. It's all bull. You don't have to make a living, Simon. You were born into money, tons and tons of it. You could make bad decision after bad decision and you would still be rich."

For a moment he allowed the quick relief to wash over him. Janice didn't know about his family. But he couldn't enjoy that fact because the crux of the problem was his cursed family fortune and at some point she'd have to know.

"I work very hard at what I do," he admonished. "I don't just lie around on my butt living off money that I didn't earn. I've made my way since I was a kid."

"A rich kid," Janice amended.

"I have always worked for my money."

"That doesn't matter. You didn't have to."

"Is that really what you think of me, that I had this privileged life because I was born into a wealthy family?"

Simon stared over her head, closing his eyes and swallowing. "You know none of us have a choice in the family we're born into. And money is not always a blessing.

Sometimes it can be a curse. I've never wanted to be known for my family's fortune. I've always been driven to make my own and I have." He added, "I'm very proud of everything that I've accomplished."

"And you don't think your family's fortune opened doors for you?"

"I'd rather believe I did it all on my own."

"Why?"

"Maybe I'm not proud of the way my family made its money."

Janice noticed the sudden sadness that permeated Simon's voice and wondered why. "We're not responsible for what happened before we were born. We can't take the burden of generations that came before and put that on our shoulders. I was just teasing you, Simon."

"You were asking me a question, and then you made an assumption. I always want to be honest with you, as honest as you'll let me. I want to share everything with you." He smiled and tilted his head to look at her.

"I want to tell you my every secret, my every thought. And I want you to love me in spite of my secrets. But you won't even say you love me. So how can you prepare yourself to know my every thought? How do I stand a chance of telling all?"

She simply smiled at him.

"You're evil, woman. Do you know that?" He smiled more broadly this time. "Do you hold out purposefully to torture me?"

"You're the expert on people, at least that was your boast, Simon," she laughed. "Besides being an enigma, you're a sweet, gentle man."

He grabbed her and pulled her to him so quickly and so hard that the air left her lungs with a whoosh. He kissed her then, not soft, but hard and demanding. He felt her attempt to pull away but tangled his hands in her hair and held on. He used his tongue to attack her barriers. He felt her tremble, felt her moan and continued with his oral assault. When he released her, her eyes were glazed over with lust and passion and she was swaying.

"Don't underestimate me," he warned.

CHAPTER SIXTEEN

Underestimate Simon. She wouldn't do that in a million years, Janice thought as she woke slowly, moaning as she moved. She was deliciously sore. Simon's legs were still tangled with hers and his hand was trapped between her thighs. She couldn't believe they'd fallen asleep like that.

During the night something had changed in their relationship, something she couldn't put her finger on. She felt Simon move against her, his fingers going inside her, and she smiled. He was faking, he was awake. And then she had a glimmer of the change. Somehow in the hours they'd made love, Simon Kohl had taken almost complete possession of her.

The only thing she'd withheld from him were the three little words he'd fought to hear. He had no idea how close she'd come to screaming the words out.

"I'm sore," she said, attempting to shove his hand away from her heat.

"I know just the cure," he answered, moving his hand over her until she was aroused. She glanced at the clock. "Simon, I want to but I don't have time. I told Tommy I would be in at eight today."

"Fuck Tommy."

"I don't want to," Janice quipped, thinking to make him smile.

Simon, caught by surprise, suddenly pulled his hand away. "What did you just say?" he asked.

"I was only answering your question. You told me to... Well, you know what you said and I said I didn't want to." She groaned and tried to roll away.

He pulled her back.

"Don't turn away from me."

"You can't order me around."

"We're getting married." He kissed her deeply. "We're getting married. Get used to the idea of my input."

She groaned.

"What?"

"Is there now a leash around my neck?"

"You're putting Tommy before me again and I will not come last in your life. Is that clear?"

"How is my keeping my commitments making you last in my life?"

"You're worried about keeping your commitments to Tommy, but it's me you should worry about keeping your commitments to. We've done things your way," he said, his voice getting louder. "Now we do things my way. I love you and I don't think that my saying that should make you uncomfortable. I wouldn't be marrying you if I didn't love you."

She looked at him. It hit her again that something in her had changed.

"Call Tommy and tell him you're not coming today. In fact, tell him you're not coming tomorrow."

"No, I will not."

"You will."

"I won't, I gave my word."

"Fine," he said and got up from the bed, strolled over to the desk and picked up her personal directory. Janice watched in amazement as he picked up the phone. She didn't believe he would do it; he was bluffing.

"Mr. Strong, this is Simon Kohl. I'm calling to tell you that Janice will not be able to keep the appointments she made with you." He glanced over to the bed where she sat watching him in shock. "She's going to be busy for the next week."

"Why didn't she call me herself?" Tommy asked.

"She doesn't have to, I did."

"She's scheduled to do a signing today."

"Then I suggest you cancel it."

"If she starts backing out on signings she's going to lose fans, and if she loses fans she'll lose sales, and then you won't make any money."

Simon laughed. "Do you really think I'm worried about money or her sales? Check the bestseller list. Her book's number one."

"You bought her the number one slot."

"Why not?"

"Maybe she'd like to earn it."

"Maybe she'd just like to be number one, which she is." Simon hung up the phone and looked at Janice, narrowing his eyes. "Now baby, this is my game." As he walked toward her, she moved away on the bed, but it didn't matter. Last night he'd staked his claim and he wasn't going back to letting her control things. He'd done that for three years and what had it gotten him?

"Simon, who the hell do you think you are? You can't just cancel my appointments."

"I already did," he said, bending and scooping her up into his arms. She was squirming to get away, hitting him, and he growled low, "You'd better stop that right this minute or I'll drop you on the floor."

She settled down and he smiled. "That's better," he said, taking her into the bathroom. He filled the massive tub while he held her, then plopped her into the warm water.

"Just what do you think you're doing?" she finally asked.

"Staking my claim."

"What am I, a piece of property? You have a lot of nerve."

"All's fair in love and war."

"So we're at war?" Janice asked.

"I've tried the love route but you seem to think I'm a doormat. So yes, I guess you could say this is war and it's a war I intend to win. You're going to be my wife, the mother of my children. We're going to be a family and it's about time I set some ground rules for you. I've warned you that I am not as gentle as you think. Let's see how much you like fighting when I don't let you win."

He laughed as she squinted, knowing that the edge was being taken off of her anger.

"You let me win."

"That's right, my evil love, I let you win. You want to play in my league, then get ready. I don't lose and I'm not about to start now."

He poured body wash on the sponge and began rubbing her back. "Hold still," he said softly as she tried to move away. "I'm going to bathe you. You said you were sore. When I'm done you'll feel better." He laughed at her expression. "I promise, now hold still."

Janice couldn't help noticing that his voice was not harsh, but in fact filled with, she couldn't believe it, passion. She glanced over the rim of the tub and saw his erection. *Yeah right*, she thought. Like heck he was in charge.

"You think the evidence of my wanting you puts me at a disadvantage?" Simon asked. "Think again. I've worked against a handicap all my life." He smiled at her and began washing her breasts in circular motions. His eyes moved over her as desire pooled in his belly. He wanted her with an intensity born of love, but he would wait. He would prove to her that he couldn't be controlled by his lust. Still, he wanted to throw down the sponge and use his tongue to finish her bath but from the look in her eyes that was what she was expecting. She propped her leg on the rim of the tub, giving him a full view of her secrets, and half closed her eyes, looking sexy and sultry. He grinned.

"You are evil," he said and averted his gaze though his arousal intensified. He didn't try to hide the fact. Hell, he was naked and couldn't hide it if he tried. He just continued bathing her as she laughed at him. When he went to her thighs her laughter slowed, then stopped.

Gotcha, he thought but didn't say a word. He did drop the sponge and put more body wash in the palm of his hands. "The sponge is too rough for such a delicate area," he said as he rubbed the liquid soap over the curls nestled between her thighs.

He dipped his hand in the water and put one finger into her and moved it around until he felt her muscles tightening. Then he slapped playfully at her.

"This is a bath, you hussy, not play time." She was panting. She was so hot and so was he. And God, how he wanted her.

"Simon, stop teasing me," she whispered. "You know you want to."

"Of course I want to, but baby, this is war."

"Couldn't we call a truce?"

"I don't think so."

He inserted another finger, then rotated them and felt her shiver. But he wasn't done with her. "Give me your foot," he said, moving his hand from her treasure to massage her foot, kneading the heel and working his way around to rub her toes. She was teasing him by touching herself and moaning.

She was definitely playing to win but then so was he. He let her go abruptly, then headed for the shower, turned the water on full blast and jumped under the cold stream. He was so hot from wanting Janice he barely shivered. He should never have let them go so far in the first place. He could kick himself for going along with all of her silly rules for so long, but hell, he'd wanted her so damn badly that if she'd told him to cover himself with honey and dance down Broadway with a hive of hungry bees in pursuit he would probably have done it.

Simon heard the splash of water and paused. If Janice dared come into the shower the war would be over. He would win the skirmish. But there was no way he could withstand an assault of either her hand or her mouth at the moment. He leaned against the cold tiles made colder by the falling water and held his breath, waiting.

Janice thought about going into the shower after him. She thought about tasting him and could almost feel his heaviness in her mouth. She had the urge to taste him from head to toe, then start all over again. With a doubt he would yield to her hands, her mouth, and her teeth. But then what? They would make love and he would still think in his smugness that he'd won.

No, she had to remain focused and talk to him about making her decisions for her. Maybe with clothes on and a table filled with food before them, she'd at least have a chance to restate her position.

She wrapped a towel around her body and picked up the extension that connected her with the house staff.

"We'll be down for breakfast in thirty minutes."

Simon's head popped out of the shower. "You ordered breakfast?"

"Yes."

"Why downstairs? Why not up here?"

"Because we need to talk."

"And we can only do that downstairs?"

"Downstairs lends itself to a more serious conversation."

"Do you concede defeat?" Simon asked, staring intently at her.

"Are you kidding? I thought we could both use some replenishing."

"Speak for yourself," Simon said as his hand darted out and he grabbed for the end of her towel, spinning her toward him. She landed naked against his nakedness, warm dry flesh against wet cold flesh and the feeling was so erotic she trembled. Janice closed her eyes and nibbled at his lips, kissing him, enjoying having him home. Ten days was ten days too long. "I really did miss you."

"I can tell. Maybe I should leave more often."

"Not without telling me." She bit down harder on his lip, then licked the area. "You only get one time to leave me, Simon, no more."

"I'll remember, but like I already told you, baby, I'm not going anywhere."

"Good," she answered, moving away. "Let's have breakfast; we really do need to talk."

Janice marched out of the bathroom. Knowing Simon was watching the wiggle of her behind as she walked away, she added an extra jiggle and turned to catch him watching.

"Evil," he grinned. "You are pure evil."

Two cups of coffee and a sampling of everything on the table and Janice was ready to talk business. "We have a lot of things to discuss," she began, "and not all of them pleasant."

He smirked. "I can imagine what the unpleasant topic will entail. 'Simon, you can't run my life, you can't tell me who to see, what to do, you can't cancel my appointments, you can't tell me I can't see Tommy." He laughed at the shocked look on her face. "Come on, baby, don't you think I knew how you would react to what I did? Next subject."

"Next subject? We haven't discussed this one yet."

"It's finished. I don't want you spending so much time with the man. Period, final, end of discussion."

"End of discussion." Janice laughed, and speared a strawberry and watched as the juices squirted out.

"Are you imagining that's me and that it's my blood spilling out?"

"How did you ever guess?" she asked.

"Because you have a vicious streak. When you're crossed, you go for the jugular."

"If you know that, why do you always tempt me?"

"I love the fire in your eyes when you're angry and I like living dangerously."

"I think your little stunt with Tommy was despicable. Do you have any idea what kind of explaining I will have to do when I see him?" *Oops, I said the wrong thing.* She watched as his gray eyes narrowed and turned icy.

"You need to explain my behavior to Mr. Strong?"

"Of course," she answered. "That caveman routine was cute, but come on, do you really think I would go along with that nonsense if I didn't want to?"

Simon studied her. She was baiting him. Round two, but he wasn't going to give in easily. "What do you have planned now that you're free?"

"You have plans?"

"We could go for a drive, pack a lunch, have a picnic somewhere, just the two of us and then," he smiled even wider, "maybe make love under a tree."

"Forget the tree. We can make love out in the open, on the grass."

"If we get caught we'd get arrested for public lewdness."

"Your lawyers would have us out in seconds."

"Yes, but think of the publicity. Bad press can kill you."

"I'll have to remember that." Janice smiled. "About my book, thanks, Simon, but I really don't want you doing things to make my book number one. I want to do that on my own."

He looked thoughtfully at her. "Your writing's very important to you, isn't it?"

"Of course, you know that."

Simon lifted the china cup to his lips and took a sip of the coffee. "Am I important to you, to your life? If I couldn't help your career, would you care?"

"The only way you'd ever know the answer to your question would be for you to get out of the publishing business. Stop pushing my career, Simon. I love the things that you do for me but maybe you should stop."

"I love making you happy."

"But you have to ask yourself if the price is too high."

"It wouldn't be if you'd just tell me what I want to hear."

"You already know the answer, Simon."

"Would it really kill you to tell me?"

Janice smiled slightly, looking serious. "I've given you everything that I can. You know how I feel about you and to answer your earlier question, yes, Simon, you're very important to me. I'm glad that you're in my life but I can't help wondering if my saying those three little words would be the end of us. You're used to making people bend at your command. Maybe it's the challenge, the fact that I won't, that intrigues you."

Simon blinked and stared at Janice. She really didn't believe totally in his love and therefore was afraid to tell him that she loved him. He was beginning to understand.

"You think if you tell me that you love me I'm going to stop loving you? Love doesn't stop that easily."

She didn't answer.

"Listen to me. Love doesn't stop that easily, not real love."

"What if I'm just another pretty thing for you?"

Simon pushed his chair back, sighing as he allowed his gaze to land on the woman he loved. He stood and walked toward her. "I love you with all my being, Janice. You have to trust me, trust me not to hurt you. Please don't keep making me pay for things I didn't do. I'll never hurt you."

"I want to trust you, Simon, I really do." She rose to meet him. "And in most things I do. But look around you. How many people say that they love someone today and tomorrow they're sleeping with someone else and saying they love them?"

"Do you think I slept with someone else while I was gone?"

"No, but—"

"No buts, not about that. I've told you that I believe in total fidelity. That's supremely important to me. I've never cheated on you and I hope you've never cheated on me." He raised a brow.

"I've never cheated on you, Simon," Janice said softly, meeting his gaze, determined to keep the memory of the kiss she'd shared with Tommy from her eyes.

"Then why won't you trust me and trust us?"

"Because you ask too much. You said you wanted my soul. What would that leave me with? I would be your puppet."

"As I am yours."

"But I don't want to be a puppet. Total surrender to me is like...like...like...it's like slavery!" she blurted out. "I can't do it."

"Is that really how you feel?" he asked, his voice heavy. He reached out to touch her cheek, running a long slender finger down the side of her face. She caught it, kissed it and gazed into his eyes.

"Yes, Simon, that's how I feel." She looked down, then back at him. "The thought of not having you in my life sends me into a panic. I want you to be in my life. I could live without you but I wouldn't want to."

He gave in, pulling her into his arms. "I know that little speech was supposed to make me feel better, but I could have done without you saying you could live without me. You are definitely rough on a man's ego."

"In that case I'll have to soothe that bruised ego, won't I?" She pressed her body against his, drawing him into a kiss. This she could do. She could show him with her body what she couldn't tell him with words. "Give me just a couple of hours to get this scene down that's been floating around in my head, and I'll be more than ready to join you for that picnic under the tree.

"And the lovemaking under the trees?"

"Especially the lovemaking." She grinned, kissed him and headed to her office to write.

"Leave me alone," Tommy shouted at Neal for the fourth time. "God, I hate that man! Who does he think he is?"

"He thinks he's the man she's going to marry, Tommy. You have no right to hate him just as you had no right to tear up a check that he meant to help the cause."

"This is not about money."

"No, maybe not, but a million dollars would have gone a hell of a long way toward saving the bookstores."

"He was trying to buy me," Tommy yelled. "Don't you understand that?"

"So what? For a million dollars he could have bought me. So what if he wanted to make sure you kept your hands off his woman? I don't blame him. And I don't blame him for finally telling your ass off. You've tied her up for three weeks and you've got the sister feeling so guilty that she's listening to every word you say as though you're the Messiah. I'm surprised that even she allowed you to take over her life like that.

"Damn, man, she's a writer. When is she supposed to write? You've kept her so busy that I know she hasn't had time to even write a thank you card. I know she couldn't have been taking care of her man, not as tired as she was every day when she left here. That shit you pulled on her that day you got that little impromptu party started, man, that wasn't cool. First you had her crying, and then you kissed her."

Tommy looked up, stunned; Neal had never told him he'd seen that. "Were you spying on me?" Tommy asked, snarling.

"I wasn't spying but the way you were yelling at her I was keeping an eye on things."

"What, you thought I was going to hit her?"

"How would I know? You were angry. I've never seen or heard you like that and the look on her face, she was terrified of you."

"You're crazy, she's never been afraid of me."

"She was that day. It was in her eyes."

"If she was afraid, why would she let me kiss her?"

"Who knows? Maybe she was too afraid not to."

Tommy glared at the thought that Mary Jo could have been afraid of him. Why would she—A memory flickered of the one time he'd wanted to. He blinked rapidly and kept it at bay. "I wasn't going to hit her. I've never hit her."

"You shouldn't have been yelling at her like that."

"I agree," Tommy said, this time sobered and ashamed of his past actions. "Still, why couldn't she call herself?"

"Maybe her fiancé has noticed that around you she loses her will. It's like she can't say no to you, like you're the puppet master and you're pulling her strings. I just don't think you have a right to hate the dude. If she was your woman, you wouldn't like her hanging out every day with an ex, now would you?"

"No, guess I wouldn't," Tommy said, knowing that part of the reason he'd jammed the days with things for her to do was to keep her near him and away from Simon Kohl. It hadn't started out like that, but it had quickly turned into that as being near her forced the memories of what they'd had to spring up like sweet grass covering a field. He'd been unable to control his jealousy.

"Still, what the hell am I going to do about the signing? I promised Sandra I'd have her there. She has people coming."

"Give Donna and Andrea a call. They're in town. If you can get them to go, you can take a bunch of the signed copies that Ms. Lace left in the store."

"That's not her signing them in person."

"No, but for now it's the best you can do. Besides, Donna and Andrea are heavy hitters. The people won't be disappointed for long."

No, Tommy thought, they wouldn't, but he would.

CHAPTER SEVENTEEN

Seven days and seven nights of passion. Simon wondered how their honeymoon would ever top it. Who in the world would have believed he would enjoy a week in Branson, Missouri, but Janice had wanted to go and he'd conceded. She'd been right. For once they weren't pursued by the press.

If he'd known how much of a buzz he'd create when he made the public announcement of their upcoming nuptials maybe he would have done it quietly, as she'd wanted. Still, he was making a point. He wanted everyone to know that Janice Lace or Mary Jo Adams belonged to him and he belonged to her.

Her hair was tousled on the pillows. He tugged at a few strands and she swatted at him in her sleep. He smiled as he looked at her creamy brown skin. It was flawless. He wondered why she would ever wear makeup. For the entire week she hadn't worn any, not even lipstick. That, she'd tried initially but he'd kept kissing it off, so she'd laughed and said forget it.

"Wake up, sleepy head, I'm lonely," he whispered in her ear as he ran his hands up the side of her body. Longing swelled in his chest, threatening to consume him. Very soon he would test her. Harold was correct; she had a right to know all of his secrets and he would tell her. After they were married.

"Wake up, baby," he whispered again.

"Why?" she moaned sleepily.

And he grinned.

Two hours later they were sprawled across the bed, exhausted, sated and happy, not wanting to leave their own special paradise.

"This entire week has been the most fun I can remember having in a long time," Simon said.

Janice stared at him in amazement. "We always have fun."

"Not like this," he insisted. "Not an entire week, with no fighting, no baiting each other, no appointments, just the two of us. I wish it could always be like this."

She knew what he meant. Once they returned home, their hectic life would return. Besides that, she had a deadline for her book and she had not written a word since they'd decided to just take off.

"God, I hate to go home," he said softly. "I wish we could just stay here forever."

"We could," Janice laughed.

"Real life, baby," he said wistfully, "real life awaits us at home."

Real life hit with a bang. Simon had a stack of urgent messages to return, all from Harold. It was the first time in his life that Simon had never told Harold where he was going. He hadn't wanted anyone or anything spoiling the week.

Janice had her own pile. Her lips twitching, she smiled up at Simon. "Honey, we're home."

He laughed and kissed her. "I guess we should both return some of these calls." He turned to walk toward his office but Janice put her hand on his arm to stop him. "Why don't we forget waiting and just go down to city hall and get married today?"

"Are you serious?"

"What's the matter, you're getting cold feet now?" She stared at him, issuing a challenge.

"You're serious." He gave her his full attention. Flipping the mail back into his basket, he smiled and asked, "What about your family?"

"I think it's better this way: We get married, they come, they go home and we go off on our honeymoon."

"Oh baby, I forgot I promised your mother that we would have her here before the wedding, so she could get to know me."

"Tell her we changed our plans."

"Do you really want to start off our marriage with your family hating me?"

"Join the club. Besides, we're in a good place right now. I think we should do it." She stood before him, her hands planted on her hips. "We should do it before something happens to change things."

Simon kissed her, breathing in her essence. "Don't worry, baby, nothing's going to happen." He drew her into his arms."It's up to us to either keep the spirit of what we found on our vacation or go back to our old routine of fighting. I'm giving up fighting. What about you?"

"I don't want to fight either," Janice finally admitted.

"So, do you want to make the arrangements for your family to come or shall I?"

"Just remember that I warned you about my family. This was your idea. You make the arrangements. I have to work on my book."

Something was happening to her. Janice could feel it deep inside. Her heart felt freer than she could ever remember. It was as though she was coming into the light after a long period of darkness.

Janice passed the mirror on her way to her study. She saw the grin on her face and stopped, not believing at first that the face was hers. She was happy. Damn, she was really happy; there was no pretense. Simon made her happy.

And for the first time in twelve years the desire to make another person happy filled her. She wanted to make Simon happy. She wanted to give him what he wanted: her total trust, her love and most importantly, the words.

She stood still for a long moment thinking about it. The thought of giving her all to Simon, to anyone, still left her petrified, but she wanted to try. He deserved so much more than she'd given him over the years. After all, she trusted Simon totally with her money; maybe it was time she trusted him with her heart. She grinned again. She knew just how to start.

"Tommy, hi, sorry that I had to bail on you." Janice waited, determined not to let Tommy's opinion change her mind. If he didn't like Simon calling him and canceling her schedule, he certainly wouldn't like what she was about to tell him now.

"Tommy," she laughed, "come on, stop pouting."

"I'm not pouting," he answered. "You really messed things up for me," he lied. "I have a reputation and if I don't come through with the things I promise then my word is no good."

"I know and I apologize for that."

"Why didn't you call?"

"No reason."

"Don't lie to me."

"It was no big deal." Janice sighed. "Don't make more out of it than it was."

"How can you stand letting Simon Kohl run your life? You were never like that before."

Now she was getting annoyed. She'd wanted to try to keep this conversation friendly but Tommy was determined to make it personal. "Tommy, you complain about Simon running my life but when we were together you seemed to do a pretty good job of doing it." She heard him sputtering his objections on the other end of the phone.

"You were not like that with me; you were a fighter."

"With everyone else, Tommy, not you. Tell me one time you remember our fighting."

"I remember one time," Tommy answered immediately.

Janice winced and closed her eyes to stop the pain of the memories. "Don't do this to me, Tommy. That's not fair. You've never once tried to understand how I felt."

Her stomach clenched and she swallowed. This wasn't what the call was about. "Other than that time, Tommy, I never fought with you. You controlled me, my thoughts, my wants, my dreams. I don't know now if my plans were things that I wanted or things you told me that I wanted."

"Are you saying you don't want to save the bookstores?"

"I'm not saying that. I'm saying I don't know if any of the plans we had then were my plans. Look at me now, I'm a writer, not a revolutionary. Maybe that's what I always wanted to be."

"You were never interested in writing. You started that to take a dig at me."

"You think that's why I started writing?"

"Yes," Tommy answered without a pause. "Look at the things you write about: men who can't be trusted, women in pain. You don't think I knew all of your books were aimed at me? I knew they were."

"Then why did you bother reading them?" For that he had no answer. "Maybe in the beginning I did write things to get over you, to not hurt so much, but that's not what I'm doing now, Tommy."

"Of course not," he almost shouted. "There isn't a black man anywhere in your books, let alone a strong black man. If you're going to write, the least you could do is show the African American male in a positive light."

"I'm not out to change society. I'm writing books about and for women."

"Yeah, right. You could do so much good if you wrote stories showing black men how to step up to the plate, or stories that champion black men who take care of their families, who don't leave their women when the going gets rough."

"Besides my father and my brothers, where would I find such a man, Tommy?"

"You're talking to one," he snarled.

"You weren't that man when I needed one."

The phone slammed in her ear and she looked at it. She hadn't taken care of the reason for the call. She dialed again.

"Neal, would you ask Tommy to give you the schedule he's worked out? If you'll fax it to me, I'll see if it's doable." She gave him her fax number and waited. The fax beeped at the same instant that the phone rang on her desk.

"You need to look at what I've planned and get back to me."

"Yes," Janice answered. She'd known Tommy would call back.

"Do you have it?"

"It's coming through now."

"What's been wrong with the way things have being going?"

"I've not bothered to ask Simon his plans. I neglected to see if your plans conflicted with his."

"Are you telling me that some fancy dinner or an award ceremony compares with saving the bookstores?"

"I'm telling you that I'm getting married in six weeks and my husband's schedule will influence my own."

"Where the hell did you disappear to, Mary Jo? You're acting like you're his slave."

"I'm not his slave, Tommy. I'm going to be his wife and he deserves my consideration. We both know why you keep using that analogy; you're trying to rile me up. It's not going to work. Just a minute," she said and retrieved the papers from the fax machine. "I have the schedule."

"And?" Tommy barked.

"And I have to check it out with Simon and get back to you."

"This isn't about Simon. Do you think he gives a damn if every black bookstore in the country closes down? He's not black, Mary Jo. You are. Or did you forget it?"

"I don't see how I could, Tommy, but I can tell you that Simon has done more for the black community than you'll ever know. And he cares, Tommy, you're wrong about that. And he doesn't care because of me. He cared long before he ever met me."

"Why?"

"Because he's a decent man."

"I find that most decent white men working hard to help black people have a reason, some guilt some baggage. What about Simon Kohl? This entire country got rich off the backs of our people. You don't think Simon Kohl money's tainted?"

"Do you have any proof of that?"

"No."

"Then you're reaching for straws. Don't try to sully Simon's reputation because you don't like him. Another thing, Tommy, you should have taken that check he gave you and used it to help the bookstores. The fact that you tore it up tells me you haven't changed that much. You're still arrogant, determined to do things your own way."

"You know, I should just forget about you, stop trying to help you find your way back to being Mary Jo. I use to think that I knew you, knew what was important to you. What the hell happened to you, Mary Jo?"

"You happened, Tommy." This time he didn't hang up and neither did she. "I'll go over this with Simon and I'll let you know what things work with our schedule."

"Why don't you just forget it. The bookstores can get along just fine without you."

"If that is the case why did you ask for my help? Why did you get me on national television and make such a big deal out of it?" Janice's voice was rising and she caught herself and stopped. Simon's study was at the other end of the mansion but still she didn't want him to hear. She didn't want anyone to hear her.

"It's your choice, Tommy, but you're not going to make me feel guilty. This is my life and I'm going to do what I please. Like I said, I'll call you back later. Bye," she said and placed the phone on the cradle.

Janice clenched her teeth and flung her arms around her trembling body. Tommy was not going to get to her. She'd given him too much power once in her life. She was not going to do it again.

Disgusted, she turned on her computer and attempted to write. She found herself writing about Tommy, things she didn't know she still felt. When she heard a soft knock on the door, she deleted it.

"Ms. Lace, Mr. Kohl wanted me to tell you that he's going to work for another couple of hours returning phone calls. He wanted to know if you would be able to take a break then. He'd like to take you out for lunch."

Janice smiled. "Why didn't he just buzz me?" she said, pointing to the intercom.

"He didn't want to disturb you."

"Tell him I'll be able to take a break in two hours and I'd love to go to lunch."

As the door closed, Janice looked at the schedule in her hand. She had hoped that she and Tommy could be friends; they'd both agreed that they'd like that, but their past kept coming back. He couldn't forgive her and she couldn't forgive him.

One day they would have to bring everything out into the open. *Maybe a fight to the death,* Janice thought. She laughed, then sobered immediately. Death was what had caused the hole in her heart. Because of the abortion she'd stopped trusting. It was her reason for hating Tommy and his reason for hating her.

Simon was doing his best to keep his temper. He'd been going back and forth with Harold for two hours. One week, that was all the time he'd asked for to try and have a normal life. Yet in that one week utter chaos had erupted and Harold had barely contained things. To say Simon was livid was an understatement.

"Harold, are you telling me that an official investigation by the group has been launched into my past?"

"Well, it's not government initiated."

"Do you think this is funny?" Simon snarled. "I thought you said this would never happen on your watch."

"I said no information would be found. I didn't say people wouldn't come looking. Hell, what with everything that's going on you knew they would."

Harold was a bit annoyed himself. "You should have left it alone. You never had to involve the man. You threw money at him thinking he wouldn't know what you were doing. Well, he did. He was insulted and rightly so. I don't blame him."

Harold griped the phone tightly, wishing for a moment it was the throat of his surrogate son.

"Simon, it was you who made the man into an enemy. Now you're looking for someone to blame. Don't blame me. I warned you to tell Janice. I even tried to get you not to go digging into her past, but did you listen? Hell no! You're as stubborn and arrogant as your father. Fire me if that will make you feel better, I don't care."

The heated anger from Harold stopped Simon. Harold rarely lost his temper and generally not with him. The comparison to his father meant that Harold was fed up.

"I'm sorry," Simon said and sighed. "You have no idea what a good time we had. It was what I've always known it could be. It was perfect."

"Then tell her."

"I will," Simon said tiredly. "I'm waiting for the right moment."

"There is no right moment," Harold admonished him. "You just have to tell her before Tommy Strong does and turns her against you."

Simon continued talking as though he hadn't heard Harold. "We finally set a date. We're getting married in six weeks; she's going to be my wife. Her family's coming for a visit in just a week. I want them to have a chance to know me, know that I'm not my grandfather or my great-grandfather. I want them to meet me before they judge me. Then I'll tell the whole damn world."

"You only need to tell the woman you're going to marry." Harold spoke softer now. He'd never liked being harsh to Simon. Simon felt more like a son to him than an employer. In fact, Harold had been stand in for Simon's real father when he had been too busy or just plain didn't give a damn.

He'd been there when Simon had accidentally found out about his family history and he'd been the one to console the boy and assure him that things long dead had nothing to do with him, that it was what he made of his life that was important. And he'd done everything in his power over the years to bury the truth so deeply that it would take someone more determined to hurt Simon than Harold was to protect him to find it.

Harold hadn't thought such a person existed, but he now believed Tommy Strong to be a strong contender. If only Simon had listened to him and not to his cronies who'd all had a shot or two more than they'd needed of brandy. They'd goaded Simon, telling him he wasn't much of a businessman if he'd marry a woman without knowing everything there was to know about her. They'd pestered him until it had gotten under his skin and he had to know.

Some of it Harold understood. Janice didn't mind telling anyone who had ears to hear that she didn't believe in love. Hell, he'd heard her on more than one occasion say that she would never have given Simon the time of day if he weren't rich. Of course Simon was right to doubt her; he'd be a fool not to.

But Harold had seen the way the woman's eyes would light up when she'd see Simon, the way she'd touch her fingers to his face, the gentle way she'd smile at him when his back was turned.

Several times Harold's gaze had caught hers when he'd found her looking at Simon. Each time she'd turned away, but not before a guilty look crossed her face, then annoyance, as though she didn't want to love Simon. Harold knew that she did, despite their fights. If he had thought for a moment that one word of what the woman said publicly about love or Simon were true, he would have wasted no time in warning Simon.

For the future happiness of his surrogate son, he would have risked Simon's wrath and his dismissal. But he knew deep within his being that Janice Lace was the right woman for his Simon. He didn't doubt that she'd been deeply hurt by Tommy Strong. That, he assumed, was the reason she was afraid of loving Simon.

"Harold, where are you, old man?" Simon asked playfully.

"What?"

"You were daydreaming," Simon said. "I've been talking to you and you haven't heard a word I said."

"You're right, I've been thinking, doing a little wool gathering. I'm sorry I compared you to your father."

Simon swallowed and waited for the *but,* the one telling him that he'd been acting like a jackass.

"Your father wasn't a bad man, maybe just a bad father. He didn't like the family legacy any more than you and he chose to hide it too. Only he did most of his hiding by living the good life, booze, women, cars and planes."

Both men stopped for a moment, thinking of Simon's parents dying in a plane crash, a small plane piloted by his father.

"Do you think they were ever happy?" Simon asked.

"Yes, your father was happy the day he married your mother and he was happy the day you were born."

"What happened to them? I wish I could have seen them happy together."

"The family legacy. Your mother found out and it tore them apart."

"She hated him because of it?"

"No, but he thought she did. She hated that he hadn't trusted her enough to be honest with her. He did what he always did. He ran to other women and she tried to compete. I think for a time she still loved him but...well, maybe it's just wishful thinking."

"Harold, is that story true or are you trying to manipulate me into telling Janice?"

"Both," Harold answered and chuckled. "I wish you luck, son." Then he hung up the phone, more determined than ever that Tommy Strong would not find information to hurt Simon.

"Tommy, we can't keep investigating the man when there is no evidence that he's done anything. We've searched his family history; we can't find anything. He's clean."

"I don't think so." Tommy answered. "There has to be something. I can feel it in my gut. The man tries too hard; he's trying to make up for something."

"Look, we can't keep going on your gut. Six more months of this and we're out. You're not using the organization to go after someone that you have a grudge against. If we don't find anything in that time and you still want him investigated, you're going to have to go it alone. We're not using the manpower or the money to do it if there's nothing there."

"How much were you paid?"

"Excuse me."

"How much were you paid?" Tommy asked angrily. "Did Simon Kohl pay you off?"

"Go to hell, Tommy."

The phone slammed in his ear and Tommy saw Neal watching him. He knew what the man was thinking, that he was losing it. He'd been losing it ever since the day Mary Jo Adams had sashayed back into his life.

CHAPTER EIGHTEEN

Gray skies and fat drops of rain heralded the arrival of Janice's family. She groaned, wishing there was some way she could get past the visit. She looked toward Simon, who grinned at her.

"It's going to be okay. I promise."

"You don't know my mother. She's been picking a fight with me for years."

"Sound like anyone you know? Listen, I'm going to go and help with the luggage."

"Why? The chauffeur will bring it in."

"I'm trying to score points with your mom," Simon answered, rushing out into the rain.

For some reason his action gave her mixed emotions. For all his money Simon was very much a gentleman; her mother would love him. It hit her then how much she really wanted her family to approve of him.

True, she'd vowed that she didn't care what they thought, but she didn't want them to hurt his feelings.

It wasn't the color of Simon's skin that would bother her mother. She could care less about that. Besides, their family was its own little United Nations. No, the one thing she hadn't told Simon was that her father was a deacon of the church and her mother would be condemning them both to hell from the moment she stepped through the front door until the moment she left. Well, he'd asked for it, she thought.

"Nice place."

Janice's stomach twisted in knots at the sound of her mother's voice. *Nice place indeed. It was a mansion.*

"Mary Jo, there you are." Her mother stood back observing her from head to toe. "I suppose you didn't come out to the car because you didn't want to wet your hair."

Janice ignored the remark and went to kiss her mother. "Hi, Mom."

"Is that the best you can do? I swear, I hugged that chauffeur tighter than that."

Janice laughed at her mother. Maybe Simon was right. Maybe she'd actually gotten the tendency to argue from her mother.

"You're not wasting any time are you, Mom?"

"Have I ever?"

"Not that I can remember," Janice said, hugging her tighter. Then she saw her father coming in in front of Simon. Smiling, she went to her father and kissed his cheeks, feeling a tightening in her chest. She didn't realize how much she'd actually missed them. In fact she'd thought she hadn't.

"Where's everyone else?" Janice asked, looking for at least one sibling.

"I thought it best just your father and I visit the first time out."

Janice held her mother's gaze for a moment, then nodded. "I guess you've both met Simon," she said, and glanced at Simon.

"Yes, we have," her mother answered for both her and her father. "He's a real gentleman and doesn't mind a little rain."

Simon started laughing and soon they were all laughing, including Janice.

And for the first time in years she enjoyed them. That was until dinner was over and as she'd known would happen, her mother started. For real.

"I'm happy to see you finally in love and getting married," she said, looking at Janice.

Janice didn't answer. She glanced at Simon and smiled.

"You are in love, aren't you?" her mother insisted.

"I'm getting married, Mom. Doesn't that answer your question?"

"No, it doesn't answer my question. I had assumed that if you were finally getting married you had to be in love. I've been wanting that for you."

God, why couldn't her mother stop? And why couldn't she just say yes? If she admitted to her mother that she loved Simon, her mother would stop.

"Do you love Simon?" her mother asked again, not letting up.

"Why are you being so nosy?"

"Mary Jo," her father cautioned. "Don't talk to your mother like that."

Janice rolled her eyes. She should have known. They were back where they always began, back in her childhood. Did they conveniently forget that she was almost thirty years old? She would be the day she married. That was one of the reasons Simon had chosen that date for them to get married. He was going to be her birthday gift. She'd laughed when he said it.

"What's the big deal?" her father said, frowning. "Your mother asked a simple question. If you're not marrying this man for love, maybe you should not be marrying him. Now answer the question."

Did every man in the world think they were put on earth to control her? She stood, looked her father in the eye and lied. "Simon and I don't believe in love." She hoped that would shock both of them enough to make them mind their own business. "That's not why we're getting married. We're adults, we're not looking for the mush." She shrugged her shoulders. She barely glanced at Simon, not wanting to see the pain that would be on his face. "Goodnight," she said. Not waiting for anyone to answer her, Janice ran up the stairs.

"I thought you said you were going to be good," Simon said softly. He waited for Janice's mother to turn to face him.

"Are you in love with Mary Jo, Mr. Kohl?"

"Yes, Mrs. Adams, I am."

The couple exchanged looks. Then her mother looked at Simon again. "That's obvious, you can't keep your eyes or your hands off her."

"Was it my loving her that you were worried about?" Simon observed the woman as he talked to her. She didn't appear to have any problems with him being white, neither did the father, but still he wondered why the woman had suddenly and deliberately gone for the one topic that Janice hated to talk about.

He watched as the woman turned toward her husband. When silent communication flashed between the couple, he wondered whether he and Janice would ever achieve that. Would there ever come a time when she would trust him with her innermost thoughts. A deep yearning filled his chest and he wished for that bond with Janice more than anything.

"We weren't worried about you, Mr. Kohl."

"Call me Simon. I'm going to be your son-in-law." Simon smiled. "If you weren't worried about me, that means you were worried about Janice."

"Mary Jo."

"Mary Jo," Simon mimicked, deciding to go with the flow. He wanted to learn as much about the woman he loved as possible. Now if he didn't alienate her parents, he might finally get real information.

Carol Adams smiled slowly and shrugged her shoulders. "It's just that I've been waiting an awfully long time to hear my little girl say she was in love. She hasn't been since..." She held back a sob.

Simon sat quietly waiting, something alerting him that this was what he wanted, what he'd spent thousands of dollars on and still hadn't found.

"Mary Jo doesn't like to tell people how she feels about them."

"I know," Simon said quietly and caught another look that passed between the couple.

"You're hurting from that, aren't you?" Carol Adam asked quietly.

Simon smiled but didn't answer.

"You don't have to say it. We've been waiting years to hear her tell us again too." The woman shrugged her shoulders again. "I guess that's why I try and pick fights with her even though I know I'm going about it in the wrong way. It only turns her off, makes her more standoffish, makes her not come home, not call."

She tilted her face to look at Simon. "I was surprised that she called a week or so ago. I know it was your doing. Why do you want us here?"

Simon smiled. "I want a family. I want lots of kids. My parents are gone. I want grandparents; you two are going to be that. So I wanted to get to know you. I don't want our kids to not have that. Everybody needs someone they can count on."

"Can you count on Mary Jo?" Carol asked.

"She loves me," Simon said licking his lips. "Listen, I'm not a fool. I wouldn't be marrying her if I didn't know that." Again a look passed between the couple. "Don't," he said, "don't pity me. She loves me."

"Wouldn't you like to hear her tell you that?"

"You said you've been trying for years."

"Have you told Mary Jo that you love her?"

He bit his lips softly, narrowing his eyes and looking toward the door Janice had run through. "Yes, even though she didn't want me to." He grinned. "Was there ever a time that she didn't mind saying or hearing the words?" He snapped his head back around, knowing the couple was going to communicate silently again.

Carol shrugged her shoulders. "When she was young."

"What happened?" Simon asked, his throat closing up, his voice strangely brittle. Hell, what was he doing? He'd always known. There was no doubt in his mind that she'd had no problem telling Tommy Strong that she loved him.

"What did he do to her?" he asked.

"I wish I knew. It was like one day she went to bed this happy girl who would stand toe to toe with the devil and fight to the death. The only person she never fought with was Tommy. I always wished that she would, that she wouldn't just let him lead her around."

An uneasy feeling developed in the pit of his stomach and Simon wished he'd never asked. "She never told you what happened?"

"No. All I know is that one day she was Mary Jo, the next she was this Janice Lace person, as different from my baby as day from night. I didn't know her. In the beginning it was kind of nice that she'd mellowed, that she wasn't fighting everyone on everything. Then I saw that she wasn't just learning to control her temper. It was like my baby had died. Ever since I've been trying to revive her, but nothing I do or say has made a dent."

"So you fight with her to make her fight back?"

"Yes, but she won't. She doesn't fight anymore."

"That's not quite true," Simon said softly, then laughed. "That's what we do most of the time. You don't have to worry about her following me around like she adores me." The last Simon said a bit wistfully.

"Yeah, but I kind of wish she did. I wish she wasn't so afraid to show her emotions."

"Did you ever ask Tommy?" Simon asked. The words burned in his throat and he closed his eyes briefly, blinked, then looked straight at the woman.

"Yes, Tommy always said he didn't know. Actually we've seen him more in the past few years than we have our daughter. He always sends us her books when they come out."

"She doesn't send them to you?"

"Yes, she sends them."

"So why does Tommy send them?"

"I guess he just wants us to have them and maybe he thinks Mary Jo won't send them. I'm not sure. Maybe it's his way of still feeling close to Mary Jo."

"Do you think he still loves her?"

"I don't know. Most of the time he won't talk about her."

"When did she change her name?" Simon asked.

"Right after she went through that breakup. She sent us a note saying, 'I've changed my name legally. It's now Janice Lace.' "

Her father cringed and shook his head. "We named her after my mother. It was a slap in the face when she did that."

"Is that why you disapproved of her writing?"

"We never disapproved of her writing; she just thought we did. We read her books. Yes, there was a lot of sex in them, more than we would have liked to know that she knew about, but we're not dumb about sex. I mean, look how long we've been married." She looked at her husband. "And we have had a satisfying relationship, haven't we, honey?"

Joe laughed and his eyes sparked. "The best."

"So why did she think you hated her books?"

"I'm a deacon."

"Oh," Simon said, beginning to understand."When you started reading her books, did you ever tell her that you didn't disapprove?"

"No."

Simon shook his head.

"I know, I just wanted to get her back to the way she used to be. She wouldn't even fight back to defend her work. It was as if she no longer cared. Her soul and her spirit were dead and what we got was a shell. I'm sick to death of having a daughter who's a shell."

Janice's mother sighed, then Janice's father, then Simon. They all laughed.

"I was hoping that you'd done what I couldn't."

"I've tried," Simon admitted.

"How, what did you do?"

Simon smiled. He wasn't about to answer that question.

"Maybe that's the problem. I think you've asked too nicely. I think you should demand for her to tell you that she loves you."

"Didn't you try commanding her?"

"Yeah, I guess I did," her mother admitted.

"How did that turn out?" Simon said, standing. "Did she yield to your demands?" he asked with a knowing look. "Good night, I'll see you in the morning."

Simon started up the stairs only to be stopped by Carol's voice.

"Are you planning on sleeping with my daughter while we're here? Can't you wait until we're gone?"

Simon was amused. "How long are you staying?"

"Are you wishing now you hadn't invited us?"

"No, but I am rethinking that whole hotel thing," Simon said and ran up the stairs two at a time, laughing.

He pushed the door open and stood for a moment looking at Janice on the divan, pretending to be reading, pretending that she didn't know he was in the room.

"Hey, you okay?" he asked.

She finally turned her head toward him and his heart caught in his throat. God, how he loved her.

"Why did you stay down there so long?"

Simon narrowed his eyes and stared at her. She was behaving oddly, almost as if she were jealous of the time he'd spent with her parents. But that was crazy. She was never jealous of the women who threw themselves at him.

"It would have been rude if both of us had left them alone." He decided to change the subject. "Your mother doesn't want me sleeping with you." He smiled as she rolled her eyes. "What?" he asked.

"It figures. She thinks I'm a sinner bound for hell anyway."

"I don't think so," Simon said, still watching her closely.

"You're taking her side now. I thought you said I could trust you to be there for me."

His gaze narrowed. "But honey this isn't..." He saw the expression on her face and stopped. For some reason, this was important to her, and he wasn't going to belittle it. He walked farther into the room, came and knelt by the divan, his arms going around her as he pulled her close.

"If you want me to be angry at your mother I will." He felt her shift. Then her hand went into his hair and she began caressing him. He pulled back and stared so long into her eyes that she trembled. Still he stared.

"Can't you tell me what happened with Tommy, baby?" Wrong question. She closed off, pushed him away, and walked toward the bed. He followed. He took her face in his hands and stared at her, shaking his head slowly.

"You really have no idea how much you mean to me, do you? I thought this was all an act, that you were just afraid. I thought you had to be blind not to know how I feel. Now I see it's not an act, you really don't know." Simon kissed her eyelids, her nose, a butterfly soft kiss on her lips, then walked away.

"Where are you going?" Janice had to stop him. She was trembling inside. The thought of Simon walking away from her again was unbearable. She'd just been through hell and back thinking he'd abandoned her. She couldn't go through it again.

"Your mother doesn't want me sleeping with you. I decided to sleep in a guest room."

"Simon, don't leave."

He stared at her.

"Please," she pleaded, "don't leave me."

He shook his head and licked his lips. "I think maybe I should."

"I had an abortion."

Simon's heart stopped; surely she wasn't telling him that she'd aborted his child. He felt the blood drain from his face and his hand fisted at his side.

"When?" he asked.

"Twelve years ago."

"What...?" He blinked, not understanding at first. He'd been so shocked that he hadn't really heard the date. When he did, it was as though someone plunged a samurai sword through his body. Pregnancy was something he had thought he would share with her, something she'd never shared with another man. The pain consumed him and disappointment rose in him. Then he saw the pain in her face and hurt so much for her that he allowed his own pain to fade away.

"I know how much you wanted to share something with me that neither of us had ever shared with anyone else. I'm sorry, Simon, I wish I could give you that."

So did he, but he wouldn't say that to her, not now. He wrapped her in his arms, felt her quiver, heard her sob and he held her even closer. Damn Tommy Strong.

"I didn't lie to you when I said we both called it quits. We did. It's true that in the end I was the one who walked away from him, but I had a reason for saying he was the one who ended things." Janice sighed, knowing that he wasn't going to press her but that she was still about to divulge information to Simon that she had not told another living soul. It was time she told him.

"When I was eighteen I became pregnant. I told Tommy and he took off. He didn't tell me where he was going or if he were ever coming back. I had never been so scared or felt so alone in my entire life.

"I couldn't tell my parents. For one thing they would have been so disappointed in me. I had told them repeatedly that Tommy and I were not having sex and they believed me. And they would have forced me to have the baby. I didn't know if I could handle that without him so I went to the bank, took money out of my account and had an abortion three days after Tommy left.

"I was awake during the entire procedure. It hurt like hell but I refused to cry. I can't tell you all the guilt I felt. Everything went through my mind—my beliefs about taking a life, my morals, my sincere desire for a baby. My abject shame over anyone finding out that I'd slept with Tommy, that he'd left me, kept me silent. When the procedure was over so was my love for Tommy.

"He returned two days later with a ring and told me, not asked, mind you, that we would get married. I told him that he didn't have to worry about changing his plans or mine, that I had made my own choices, that I was no longer pregnant and he could go on with his life."

She paused and sighed again. "We had a big fight. He didn't believe me, didn't believe I would or could have an abortion. He said I could have done that only if I hated him and I told him that I did." Janice stopped talking. "I didn't lie, I did hate him."

"I can see why you hated him. Why did he hate you?" Simon interrupted.

"He wouldn't let it go. He said I had no right to do what I'd done, that he was the father and he had rights also.

He started talking crazy, about suing me and suing the doctor, so I told him I wasn't even sure if the baby was his. He tried to make me say I was lying. He was so angry. It was as though I had trampled on his manhood. He didn't tell me that he would have loved the baby, that he loved me. He just kept talking about his rights. He didn't have rights to my body; he couldn't tell me what to do.

"He called me a selfish bitch and at that moment I knew he was right. And I didn't mind. In fact I rather liked it. I liked it so much that I decided a bitch was what I wanted to be. And that's what I've been. That's what I've been to you for three years, a bitch," Janice said softly. "You didn't deserve a bitch in your life, Simon."

"What made you tell me?" Simon asked.

"Because I do know."

"What do you know, baby?"

"I know that I'm important to you."

A surge of joy filled him and he began kissing her but she stopped him.

"And you're very important to me." She stared deeply into his eyes. "You're very important to me, Simon." Janice repeated. "I love you."

Simon blinked. He couldn't have heard right. "Say that again," he asked softly. "I think I'm hearing things." It felt as if he'd waited a lifetime to hear those words.

"I love you." Janice smiled shyly, looked down, then back up into his eyes. "I love you. I'm marrying you because I love you and you're very important to me."

He crushed her to him and spun around with her in his arms. And then he kissed her as if it were the last time that he would taste her, holding her so tightly that he knew he should loosen his hold. "Thank you, baby."

Now he understood what his leaving her without a word had done to her, and he knew why she'd told him tonight. She'd thought he was going to leave her again.

"I wasn't going to leave," he said in her ear. "I was only going to sleep in another room."

"I didn't want you sleeping in another room. I wanted you here with me. I wanted you to know."

"How does it feel?"

"Scary." she admitted. "Like I just handed you a loaded gun pointed at my heart."

"I'm not going to hurt you, baby. I'm going to love you and I'm going to prove to you that you were right to trust me with your heart."

He felt her tremble and a trace of doubt came into her eyes. "I'm going to prove it," he restated. He kissed her earlobes, his hands going underneath her top to rub her beautiful brown skin.

"You're so soft," he moaned, desire filling him, "and you're so sweet." He undressed her, held her in his arms and moaned, "You're what I've wanted always and when we're done tonight you're not going to doubt either of us." And he began loving every inch of her, filling the tiny cervices of his heart with her love; places that had been empty his entire life. He'd waited a lifetime for her love and now he finally felt complete.

Janice gave in to the heat, the searing, burning heat. It felt as if the room was moving and she'd gotten caught in a whirlwind, and was spinning faster and faster. This was different from anything she'd ever known. He was inside her, filling her, and she was shaking, crying, knowing that this was right, knowing that she'd thought she would never experience this. She was still fearful as she realized that Simon was claiming more than her body.

He was doing as he'd always said he wanted to do. He was claiming her soul. He was claiming all of her and she knew that when they were done she could never pretend again. She felt herself falling into a void as her climax approached, something that had never happened. "Simon," she screamed, "I'm falling."

"Don't worry, baby, let go. I'll be there to catch you."

She felt his thrust and she clung to him. "I love you," she moaned and gave up her fight to stay afloat. She fell backwards into the abyss, trusting Simon to be there to catch her.

"Simon," she moaned and screamed out again.

"I'm here, baby," he said.

When she reached her destination he was there. She was in his arms and she knew she'd been branded. She belonged to him and he belonged to her. "I love you, baby," he repeated over and over.

She felt the heat of his tears. "I know. I love you too."

This was it. This was the culmination of a lifetime of dreams and hopes, something he'd never thought he would have. As much as he'd loved Janice, as great as their physical coupling was, it had never been like this. This was the first time in three years that she'd given him everything. She'd given him her heart and soul and he'd given her his. He felt her trembling in his arms. He didn't blame her, he was trembling also. He stroked her hair. Maybe they would be able to break his family curse after all.

"Any regrets?" he asked.

"Only that I waited so long."

"We can make up for lost time."

Janice laughed. "You know, it seems like we've been doing an awfully of making up lately. I'm beginning to wonder if you didn't set some of this stuff up just so we could make up."

"If I had thought about it I would have."

They lay together in blissful silence, both knowing that the changes that had taken place in the bed would challenge them in their daily lives.

"So what are you going to tell my mom in the morning?"

"I'll lie." Simon laughed. "I'll tell her that we stayed up all night talking."

"I wouldn't mind staying up all night, but not to talk." Janice's voice had turned soft and sultry and filled with emotions. She couldn't stop smiling. Nor could she stop Simon from looking at her the way that he was, as though she were someone very special. But it didn't matter because she didn't want him to.

CHAPTER NINETEEN

The Statute of Liberty beckoned as she'd always been meant to do, a symbol of hope. Janice grinned at her mother before turning her gaze toward Simon who was a short ways off with her father, probably having a private chat, just as she was supposed to be doing.

Her mother started the conversation "This has been a good trip. I'm glad that we came and I'm glad that we got to meet Simon. We like him."

Janice was listening and at the same time smiling at Simon. "I'm glad, Mom."

"Something's changed, you're acting different." Carol's eyes raked over her daughter. Then she knew. "You told Simon that you loved him, didn't you?"

This time Janice brought her eyes to her mother and continued smiling. "Yes, I told him. Why not? I do. I love him, Mom."

Her mother grabbed her in a hug as Janice had known she would do and Janice hugged her back.

"Why has it taken you so long? What happened with Tommy?"

"Nothing I want to talk about, Mom. It's been over for a long time."

"I have my suspicions."

"I know."

"Are they correct?"

"Mom, just let it go. I don't want to rehash old history."

"But Simon—"

"I haven't held anything back from him."

"Then why won't you tell me?"

"I don't want to," Janice said, amused, "and I'm not going to."

Her mother kissed her cheek. "So you've got a bit of fire back in you. Now you want to fight with me."

"You make it sound as if I was always looking for fights and that something was wrong when I didn't."

"That's because it's true. You fought in the womb and you fought from the day you came out. You used to drive me crazy. But when you stopped fighting, that drove me even crazier." Carol looked toward Simon. "I'm glad he was able to do what I couldn't."

Janice studied her mother. "I hope you're not blaming yourself for things I've done. I made my own choices." She hugged her mother. "I'm thinking that she wants us to start over." Janice pointed her finger at Lady Liberty. "And so would I."

"You're really not going to tell me what happened, are you?"

"No, Mom, I'm not."

"Not even with Simon? What did that man finally say to you to get you to admit that you love him? He said he'd been trying for a long time."

"That's between me and Simon."

Her mother grinned. "I bet Simon will tell me. He's trying to make points."

"You noticed, huh?"

"Oh yes, I noticed. So all I have to do is cozy up to him."

Janice smiled, knowing that there was nothing on earth that would make Simon divulge the truth of her confession to her mother. In that she trusted him explicitly. The secret torment she'd carried for so long had felt like a boulder pressing down on her. Simon had relieved her of that.

"Simon won't tell you a thing, Mom. I'm not worried about him."

"What did you do, exchange a secret for a secret?"

Janice blinked, then shook her head a little and stared at the mother. "What are you talking about?"

"Everybody has skeletons in their closest. I just figured he opened his closet for you."

Janice smiled a bit uneasily. Her mother was right, everyone did have secrets. She'd never wondered what Simon's secret was. She'd been too busy protecting her own.

"Don't worry about it, baby."

"I'm not worried."

"Of course you are. I can see your mind whirling right now, wondering what it is that Simon is hiding from you. The most important thing is that he loves you. That, the man couldn't hide in a million years."

Janice glanced once more toward Simon as they hugged. She wondered about Simon's skeletons and blamed her mother for creating the question. Could her mother have done it deliberately? Most likely she'd said it because she hadn't shared anything with her about Tommy. Regardless of the reason, Janice was determined to avoid negative thoughts.

"You know, I hate to come this far and not see Tommy."

There it was. Janice had known it. This whole thing had something to do with Tommy.

"But Simon asked you here to get to know him, not to visit the competition." Janice was just a bit annoyed that her mother would think of visiting Tommy. "Mom, Tommy and Simon don't—"

"I know," her mother laughed, interrupting her. "They don't get along. Tell me when two men who loved the same woman have ever gotten alone."

"Tommy doesn't love me anymore."

Her mother laughed and Janice looked at her, puzzled. "Are you saying that he still does?"

"Would it make a difference in how you feel about Simon?"

"Of course not," Janice answered quickly.

"Then why did you ask?" her mother retorted.

Touché, they were back at it again. "I was just asking."

"Don't even think about it. It won't do you a bit of good to wonder what if. You're not wondering what if, are you, baby?"

Her mother's eyes held a look Janice couldn't read. *You're not going to get me that easily,* she thought.

"No, I'm not wondering what if. Like I said, Tommy and I are ancient history. You said you liked Simon. The way you're behaving, it seems like you're rooting for Tommy."

"I'm rooting for the man your heart wants."

"And who do you think that is?"

"I wouldn't know. It's been a long time since I could read you. But I know that this man here," she looked in Simon's direction, "loves you and I know that he's done something for you that none of us were able to do in a dozen years, including Tommy. I'm not going to lie and tell you that I don't have a fondness for that boy. I always did. He was in our home more than he was in his own and I still go to church with his entire family. Yes, I had always thought one day the two of you might find your way back together. But I'm not trying to put stumbling blocks in your path. It's just that Tommy's mother knew I was coming here and so did Tommy. How do you think it would look if I came all this way and didn't see him?"

Janice did understand. She could see all the church ladies' tongues wagging now if her mother didn't look up the child of an old friend and church member. She groaned inwardly. "Simon has planned out almost every minute of your stay. I know I should have stopped him, but he was having so much fun," Janice said weakly.

She was wondering how Simon would feel and caught herself. She was worrying about him. She laughed. What a difference a few days made. What a difference saying those three little words had made in everything.

"Don't worry, I won't hurt his feelings." Carol smiled.

"I didn't say anything."

"You didn't have to. It's there plain as day on your face."

"Can you really see it that clearly?" Janice asked, frowning slightly. She wasn't thrilled about being an open book. It was one thing to tell Simon that she loved him and another thing entirely to be an open book to him.

While her thoughts were on Simon, it was as though her energy reached out to him. He turned from talking with her father to smile at her. She felt her heart melt a little more.

Damn Simon, she thought. When he was done with her she would have absolutely no armor left.

Unable to tear her eyes away as he began walking toward her, she said to her mother, "I'm scared. I hope this is the right move."

"It is," her mother assured her. "You love him and he loves you. Don't worry about the rest. If you worry all the time about being hurt you're going to miss the happy times. If the hurt comes, you'll deal with it then."

Janice would have answered her mother but at that moment her father and Simon joined them. As Simon's eyes slid over her body, he grinned, then looked at her with so much love and lust that she could have melted right there. She grinned up at him, knowing that he was going to slide his arms around her waist. He gave her a kiss on the forehead, so soft, so loving, that she trembled, knowing what would be coming later.

"Mary Jo, you are in public," her mother chastised.

"I know," she said, grinning.

"So that's where you got that particular hang-up from," Simon whispered in her ear. She nodded her head in acquiescence.

Simon forced himself not to intrude on Joe and Carol Adams' dinner plans with Tommy Strong. He didn't want them to want to spend time with Tommy. He'd invited them to New York to meet him, to get to know him. Hell, they already knew Tommy. They'd known him most of his life. They had a history.

He felt Janice touching him, her fingers moving in a circular, soothing motion. He met her eyes. She knew what he was feeling.

Simon smiled immediately, letting go of the jealousy and instead wallowing in her love, amazed that in a matter of days they were developing into one of those couples he'd always envied, the ones who knew the other's thoughts without words. From the moment Janice had said she loved him, a thrilling change had occurred.

"Simon, I hope you understand," Carol said. "It's just good manners that we see Tommy."

"I understand," Simon lied.

"Well, I don't," Joe piped in. "Besides, what did you expect Simon to say? He can't very well object, now can he? Simon is going to be our son-in-law. He footed the bill for this entire trip. You could just call Tommy and say hi. You know these two don't get along. It's like pouring salt in a wound."

"Joe, would you be quiet?" Carol came back, glaring at her husband.

"No, I won't be quiet. You're going to see Tommy to see what dirt he has on Simon."

Simon stared at the couple, his mouth slightly open. He didn't know whether to laugh at the way they fought so openly and honestly or to worry about the dirt Carol might find.

"Joe Adams, would you please behave?"

"Sure, I'll behave, but I want Simon to know what he's getting himself into. Mary Jo's just like her mother, Simon, unforgiving." He laughed as his wife hit out at him. "Just remember that."

Simon watched the couple for a few moments and then turned toward Janice. "Is that true?" he asked. "Are you unforgiving?" He knew the day would come when he would ask for her forgiveness.

"Just don't do anything that requires forgiving." she said.

She looked at him with a smile that made his heart melt. Her words, though, were anything but reassuring.

❧

As much as Carol hated to admit it, her husband was right. She had come to Tommy's for a specific purpose.

"Tommy, how are you and Mary Jo getting along these days? She hasn't said a lot about the two of you working together, but I sensed from Simon that there is a bit of hostility between you two. What's going on?" Carol pulled her chair in closer and gave Tommy a don't-lie-to-me look and knew that he wouldn't. He was more than likely waiting for a chance to slam the man Mary Jo was going to marry.

"She lets him run her life."

"Not from where I sit. We've been staying with them and he does nothing of the sort."

"Then it's an act for you," Tommy said with authority.

"Why don't you like him, aside from the obvious?"

"He tried to buy me for a million dollars. He gave me a check and said it was to help the bookstores, but told me I could do what I wanted with the money. I knew what he was trying to do."

"What did you do with the money?"

"I tore the check up."

"Could you do that? It wasn't meant for you."

"It was made out to me and he said I could do what I wanted with it so I tore it up."

"Hmm. What about Mary Jo? Anything happening between the two of you?"

"You mean more than our fighting? We've been trying to become friends again but I don't know if we can." He hunched his shoulder. "Too much history."

"She said the same," Carol said coyly, "only she said you were ancient history, hardly worth a mention." Carol ignored her husband's menacing look. She saw the anger rise in Tommy and a tingle of excitement shot through her. Tommy was angry, angrier than she'd ever seen him. Maybe now she'd get some answers.

Tommy saw the flicker behind Carol's brown eyes and knew she was baiting him. The woman had tried for years to get him to tell her why he and Mary Jo had broken up. He closed his eyes and fisted his hands, commanding his body to breathe normally.

"She's right." he answered finally. "Mary Jo and I are ancient history."

"Then why are you worried about Simon?"

"Because he's not what he seems. He's too good to be true."

"Are you sure it's not because he loves Mary Jo?"

Tommy looked from Carol to Joe Adams. Then he took a drink of liquor and stared into the bottom of the glass before he placed the glass on the table with a thud. He was done answering questions.

CHAPTER TWENTY

If he had known how nice it would be to have Janice's parents gone for a few hours and the house to themselves, Simon would have called Tommy and made the reservations himself. Almost since the moment they'd been gone, he had been making love to the woman he adored.

"You're delicious," he said, biting her nipple softly.

"Do I taste better now?"

"I don't understand what you're asking me."

"Now that you know all of my secrets, do I taste better?" She grinned.

"Let me see," he said and licked her skin, nibbling along the way. "You always did taste good."

Janice flipped him over so that she was on top and began kissing his little bud of a nipple. "You taste good too," she said softly. "Any secrets you want to divulge, any ghosts in your closet that you want to bring out?"

Simon shivered beneath her touch and for one moment he thought seriously about telling her until he saw the brown fire in her eyes. And then all he wanted was to lie there and let her make love to him. Her hands were roaming over his body and his naked flesh quivered, readying itself. The ghosts could wait. She was kissing him, teasing little kisses that blazed a fire in his soul. He ran his fingers through her thick mane of hair, fisted his hands and took control of the kiss.

The characters were misbehaving and the writing was going slowly. Janice couldn't seem to get into the rhythm of the book. She'd been having that problem for a few weeks now. It was more a matter of not wanting to plant her butt in the chair and write than it was writer's block. She was working more on a book that would never be published than on the one that she had to turn in. But she knew the reason. Simon believed the book was about them. She had to admit that maybe some of it was.

Lately so much of her attention had been taken over by Tommy and the bookstores that naturally her writing had gone lacking. And since she'd told Simon that she loved him he'd become equally demanding. She had to admit, though, that she was more than happy to oblige almost all of his demands.

However, she still wanted to spend time helping the bookstores. Now she understood why Tommy had told her the only thing black about her was her skin and realized that her books could have had a significant impact on the African American community if she had chosen to write about positive characters.

Somewhere she'd always known there was something deliberate in her writing and now she recognized the truth. She was punishing Tommy. But in doing so she'd disconnected herself from her culture. That she intended to change. She glanced at her watch and saved her work, turning off the computer. She had to meet Tommy. He was driving her to New Jersey.

"Hi," Janice said, trying hard to ignore the frown on Tommy's face as she slid into his black SUV and snapped her seatbelt. When he continued staring at her, she rolled her eyes and turned away.

"Is it going to be one of those days where you don't talk to me, Tommy?" she finally asked, unable to bear his silence and knowing that he was staring at the back of her head.

"Usually you want me to shut up, so I decided to do it before you asked me." Tommy sighed deeply, wishing that being around Mary Jo could provoke more than anger and lust. He wasn't sure what he would do if she left Simon, but he knew he wanted her to leave him. *Like she left me.* The thought slammed into him and he looked away.

"You keep saying you want us to be friends but we do nothing but fight."

"I've been trying to protect you." He sighed again. "It's hard when you're fighting me at every turn."

"I'm fighting you because you keep trying to turn me against Simon. We're getting married." Janice looked at him, deciding to plunge right in. "We're getting married on September first, on my birthday."

"That's only a few weeks. Am I invited?"

"Why, Tommy? You want to be the one to stand up and object?" She saw his slow smile, the twinkle in his eyes and it made her miss what they'd had—the innocence of youth.

"I guess you know me. I wouldn't mind kicking it with you but I guess we won't ever do that again…will we?" he asked a bit wistfully. "I'm not trying to cock block, Mary Jo. I just don't trust the guy."

"I trust him."

"You've gone so far over to the other side that I doubt your judgment is clear on this." He was ready for the glare she shot him. He didn't care. The Mary Jo that he had known and loved wouldn't have even been with the man in the first place. He sighed, missing the old Mary Jo. "Are you deliberately closing your eyes?"

"I'm looking at the fact that I love him."

"Why?"

"Because he loves me."

"That's not a reason. I loved you but you didn't love me."

Janice looked out the tinted window of the SUV. "I loved you, Tommy. Don't play games with me," she said softly. "You know I loved you."

"Just not enough." he murmured equally as softly.

She wasn't going to go down memory lane with him again. She was feeling too good at the moment and somehow talking with Tommy always seemed to change her mood, make her feel weepy, full of sorrow, make her doubt her choices, fill her with guilt.

Janice sighed. Tommy was the voice of her conscience. His yardstick for measuring her was the same one she'd once used for herself.

"What made you change so drastically, Mary Jo?"

If she had thought it would do any good to tell him again that he'd been the sole reason for her change, she would have. "Tommy, what is it that you really want. Is it for me to hate Simon?"

"When we were together you would have."

"Tommy, hating people wasn't what we were about or if it was I didn't know it. I thought we made plans to uplift our people. I never knew we planned to accomplish that by hating other people."

"When we were together you wouldn't have given Simon Kohl a second glance."

"When we were together, Tommy, I didn't give anyone a second glance. I was in love with you." She rubbed her teeth across her top lip. "Now I'm in love with Simon. He's there for me, no matter what I do to him or how often I try to push him away."

"Doesn't it seem odd to you that he didn't tell you that he loved you until I came back into the picture?"

"Maybe the timing is a bit of a coincidence. Still, for over three years Simon has done nothing but try to make me happy."

"By assuring you the number one spot?"

Her stomach clenched at the knowledge of just how far Simon was willing to go to prove his love for her. Yes, she'd wanted to be number one, but she'd wanted to do that on her own. "I'm not saying his methods aren't questionable," she defended, "but he's only trying to make me happy."

"Yeah, by buying you."

"That wasn't what he was doing when he found all the back issues that he could of *Black Train of Thought* and

Black Rose. He did that to make me happy." She could tell that particular piece of information pissed Tommy off and that she'd just slid down another notch on his yardstick.

"It never bothered you that for three years he never told you that he loved you?"

"No. I didn't want him to."

"Why not?"

"I could only think of all the times you'd told me that you loved me." She sighed and closed her eyes. "I am marrying Simon so let's change the subject."

"What if I bring you proof that he's hiding something from you?"

"Why don't you stop digging into his past, Tommy? Stop trying to hurt Simon and stop trying to hurt me."

"I can't stop." He changed lanes and concentrated on his driving. Tommy had hoped that the trip to New Jersey would be a catalyst for change.

It seemed he was wrong.

CHAPTER TWENTY-ONE

"So you're finally getting what you want," Harold said. "I'm happy for you."

"You don't look very happy." Simon laughed. "You look downright worried."

"I guess I am, a little."

"Are you worried that Janice doesn't love me?"

"No, I'm not worried about that. In fact in the past weeks I'd say she acts like a different woman."

Simon pursed his lips, frowning in concentration. "Tell me, Harold, why does that sound like a bad thing coming from you?"

"It's just, well, I've known her for some time now and I've never known her to behave so carefree, so happy. The way she looks at you now, there is such trust in her eyes, so much love. And I know that it wouldn't be there if she knew, and that worries me. I still think you should have told her."

"I thought about it, I really did," Simon mused. "But since you think the investigation has died down, why should I bring up this nastiness to my bride? You said yourself I wasn't to blame and, Harold, she loves me, she really loves me."

"I know, but still...oh well...I'm glad you're happy," Harold said, giving up. "I really hope you two can make it work. If not you stand to lose a lot."

"There you go talking money again."

"I have to talk money. You not only didn't sign a prenup, but you gave her half of everything that you own."

"She doesn't know that."

"She will eventually."

"What do you think she's going to do, leave me when finds out?"

"I just don't think it's the best move you could have made."

"Listen, if she leaves me, she can have it all. It's not the money that's important to me; it's her and the family we're going to have. Without her nothing is important. The money only means I can buy her things that will make her happy."

Harold laughed. "It looks like your married life has already started. She's taken the mansion and banished you out here to the guest house."

"Women! Can you believe it?" Simon laughed. "I've been out here for three days because she doesn't want me to see her in her gown before the wedding and her mother thinks we shouldn't be sleeping together." He laughed again. "Harold, old man, I have to tell you, its been the longest three days of my life and tonight I plan to make up for those three days. Mrs. Kohl will be mine forever and no one will be able to take her from me."

"You look beautiful," her mother said in a whispery soft voice that still carried the remnants of her tears.

"Thanks, Mom," Janice said. "You know this isn't what I thought my wedding day would be like."

"What do you mean?" her mother asked, studying her.

"I didn't know I would be this happy when I agreed to marry Simon, that I would know without a doubt that this was the right thing for me to do."

"Are you that sure?"

"I'm that sure. I don't know how I ever thought before that Simon and I were with each other just for convenience."

"You must have been blind."

"Yeah, I must have been," Janice agreed, turning to admire her reflection in the mirror. "You know, if Simon had not invited Tommy to the announcement of his gift for black bookstores, I don't know if any of this would have happened. "

"I know you once dreamed of marrying Tommy. Did you picture yourself happy when you thought of marrying him?"

"I pictured everything that I did with Tommy as happy. I didn't know any better," Janice smiled. "Now I do."

"Are you really sure that you have no feelings left for Tommy?"

Janice let out a breath before turning to face her mother. "Somewhere inside of me there will always be feelings for Tommy, but they're mixed." She saw the worried frown begin on her mother's face and rushed to finish. "But I'm not in love with him, Mom. I think about him sometimes and what we had and I think of it fondly. But I don't want to replace Simon with Tommy if that's what you're asking me." She kissed her mother's cheek. "Don't worry, if Simon had never asked me to marry him I still would not have wanted a future with Tommy. It is because of Tommy that I realized that I no longer have to be afraid of loving someone. So in a way, we have Tommy to thank for my happiness." Janice grinned, then laughed as the thought took hold.

"I'll bet you money that Simon won't thank him."

Janice laughed. "I won't take that bet because I know he won't either. Tommy has been badmouthing Simon to anyone who'll listen."

"Don't forget, baby, just in case Tommy does come up with something, we all have skeletons in our closest."

"Do you, Mama?"

"Of course I do. So do you."

"Are you going to tell me?"

"Are you going to tell me yours?" Carol Adams laughed and hugged her daughter to her. "You look just beautiful, baby."

Simon stood under the arbor in the back yard and waited for his bride. He barely glanced at the colorful blooms that decorated the entire yard or smelled their perfume. There was one thing and one thing only that had meaning for Simon and that was his marrying Mary Jo Adams. Her parents had insisted on her using her birth name for the ceremony. In the end he'd sided with them. It had surprised the hell out of him when she'd agreed.

The music started and Janice walked out to the sound of Kelly Clarkson singing 'I Can't Believe.' His heartbeat increased and he could feel his face splitting into a grin as he stared at her. She lifted her eyes, snagged his gaze, and he grinned even wider.

He looked briefly toward Harold, who was his best man, and ignored the worried frown that furrowed his brow. Nothing would happen to mar their happiness, he wouldn't allow it.

"Hey you." Janice smiled somewhat shyly at him as her father delivered her to his side.

"Hi yourself," he answered, feeling his heart melt with love for her. Today he wasn't a ruthless business man. He was a total wuss and he didn't give a damn. He glanced around at the thirty guests assembled and grinned.

And then he kissed his bride.

He intended to just press her lips softly, but he couldn't stop himself. Once he tasted her sweetness, he had no choice but to pry her lips apart and suck on the nectar that was Janice. His heart hammered in his chest. God, how he loved her.

"Would you two cut it out and wait for the ceremony?"

He felt Janice giggle in his mouth and pulled back to laugh at her."Are you laughing at my kisses already?"

"No, darling, I'm laughing at you."

Simon grinned, wanting to strip her naked, make love to her right there. Only because he was claiming her as his bride did he have the patience to wait for the vows.

Simon searched her eyes for any sign of doubts or hesitation, and he saw none. "I love you," he whispered between the minister's words, just wanting to hear her say it back to him.

"I love you too." She grinned and owned his heart completely.

The rest of the ceremony was a blur, as was the reception. He'd suddenly turned into a possessive, jealous man and hated that his new bride was expected to mingle with the guests. Even though they were few in number it seemed that every second someone was kissing her. Simon wanted to shove them away from her, keep her to himself. But he resisted the urge.

Janice kissed another well-wisher and looked up at Simon's frowning face. She grinned and began walking toward him. Her shoe caught on a stone and she felt herself tripping forward. Trying to right herself, she did the opposite and began to fall backward. *Damn!* she thought, just what a bride needs, to fall flat not only in a pristine white wedding gown, but a one-of-a-kind one.

But she didn't fall flat.

Janice turned her head to thank her rescuer and saw Simon's grinning face. "You caught me! How? You were in front of me."

"You needed me."

"But how?"

Simon brought his shoulder up in a shrug. "I don't know. I could just picture you landing and someone snapping a picture. I couldn't let that happen. Like I said, you needed me. I will always be there when you need me, I promise." He smiled tenderly. "I love you."

"I know you mean it, Simon, and I trust you to keep your promise."

His resolve to remain patient ended. He lifted her in his arms, cursing the mounds of slippery fabric that complicated his effort.

"Simon, just where do you think you're going?" Janice asked as he started inside with her in his arms.

"You don't know?" he asked, his voice cocky and filled with lust.

"I know that we're in the middle of our wedding reception and it's rude for us to just leave."

"And would you rather not be rude to our guests or allow your husband to show you how much he wants you?"

"You know the answer. But can't you wait for a little while?"

He stopped. "I'm afraid not, darling. If you don't agree to some privacy, in five minutes I will make love to you right here on the lawn for all to see." He made a move as if to put her down and she clung to him as he'd hoped she would. "You won't miss the party, I promise." he whispered into her ear.

"If you're going to be quick, then maybe it won't be worth my time to leave."

Simon looked down into her smiling face and laughed. "That's what you think," he said, carrying her into the house, ignoring the calls and cheers, and continued with her into their bedroom.

After unbuttoning two dozen tiny buttons without actually freeing her from the dress, he was ready to rip the dress off her. He shook his head. "I don't know if I have the patience to fight any longer with this damn dress." He gave her a sly smile, pulled the mound of fabric upward, and dove under.

Taken by surprise, Janice laughed so hard that her body shook. "Simon, there's a zipper."

"Where? I didn't see one."

"You're not supposed to see one. Now come on out and let's do this the right way."

"Actually I'm having fun right where I am," Simon answered, and he was.

"I think it would be *better* if you help me take this dress off."

His flesh jerked at the word *better* and he came from beneath her dress. "Why didn't you tell me there was a zipper?"

"Because it was so much fun watching you fight with the buttons."

"You want to play with me, I see," Simon said. "Where is the zipper? I don't see anything."

"You're not supposed to, it's invisible."

"Where is it?"

She took his hand, and slid it inside the back of her dress. His fingers felt hot enough to scorch. As he slowly unzipped her, she felt his warm breath wash over her back and she shivered.

"Simon we really did it, we're married."

"I know." He answered, his voice husky and filled with need. "For awhile I didn't know if we'd make it. There seemed to be so many obstacles in our path." He slid the dress from her body.

"Tommy was never competition, Simon."

"Never?"

"Never."

"Why did it feel like it?"

She was facing him now. "We can spend our time talking about Tommy, or we can do something else," she said, and began removing his tux. "Which do you want?" Her hand moved downward and she unzipped him and reached inside.

He groaned and closed his eyes to savor the sensation. She was intentionally torturing him. He removed his own clothes, then finished undressing his bride and stared at her in awe.

"I love you, Mrs. Kohl," he said, feeling the words deeply. The knowledge of how much he loved her pierced him and a pang of regret for having lived so long without such love washed over him. He pushed it away. He had it now. The past was just that, the past.

They made love as though it were the first time, touching each other slowly, tentatively. "I promise I'm going to make you happy," Simon said as he felt her writhing beneath him, about to give in to her need.

"You already have," Janice said, clutching him to her.

"I can't believe it's over."

"Just the trip, baby, not the honeymoon," Simon said. He took a look around the plane and smiled. "We'll do it again."

"You only get one first time, Simon," Janice teased.

"I don't believe you. Every time we make love now, it's like it's the first time." He watched as her eyes widened and she smiled. He kissed her right there while his crew looked on.

An hour later the limo was depositing them at the door of the mansion. He turned toward his bride. "Welcome home, Mrs. Kohl," he said, and scooped her up into his arms.

For the next four months they lived as though they were still on their honeymoon. Simon worked minimally, doing what he needed to do from home. Janice did the same, grateful that she still had six months left on her deadline. She wasn't in the mood for writing, nor did it seem she had any time.

She'd talked to Tommy several times, ignoring his anger at her for marrying Simon, for not spending the time he thought she should for the bookstores. But she wasn't apologizing to anyone. She was doing exactly what she wanted to do, spending time with her new husband.

Janice was thinking of this when she went to her office to check for faxes. She was surprised to find Simon sitting at her desk with her day planner spread out before him.

"What are you doing?" she said as she came up to him and kissed the back of his neck.

"Just helping you out."

"How?"

"I decided to help you out with your schedule."

Janice pulled back and stared at her husband. She glanced at the black marker in his hand that he was using to cross out her appointments. "Did it occur to you to check with me before doing this?"

"I didn't think you'd mind," Simon said, looking up, slowly sensing that he'd made a wrong move. He smiled. "Are we about to have our first fight as husband and wife?"

Simon swiveled to face his wife, his look telling her that fighting was not on his mind. He had an erection. It seemed he'd had one constantly since the day they were married.

"Did I get any faxes?" Janice asked as she moved toward the empty fax machine.

She was annoyed. He could easily see this and while she didn't necessarily want to fight, Simon realized that for the first time in their short marriage, his arousal had not sent her into a fit of need. Simon scratched his chin. That wouldn't do at all.

"Who were you expecting a fax from?" he asked quietly.

"My editor."

"None from her. You did get one from Tommy." He watched her as her muscles tensed and she turned to face him.

"Do you mind if I see it?" Janice marched back toward him and now she was a bit more than annoyed.

Simon reached for the paper and handed it to her. "It's just his thoughts on what he wants you to do for the next couple of months."

Janice walked closer and peered down at her day planner. "Were you planning out my life?"

A muscle twitched in his jaw and he knew the answer to his earlier question. Yes, they were indeed about to have their first fight as husband and wife. Still, if he handled it just right, maybe he could savage something. Maybe he could still make love to her on her desk as he'd intended.

"You've been giving me Tommy's schedules for months now to see if there were conflicts with my plans for us. I don't see what the problem is now."

"The problem is that before I *gave* it to you. That's the difference. I *asked* for your input. This time you took it upon yourself to decide for me. You can't do that."

"My mistake," Simon said. "I thought I could. I thought that as your husband I had that right." He watched as Janice ran her hand around her neck. He squinted at her. "What are you doing?"

"Checking for the collar."

"Is that supposed to be funny?" he asked.

"Do I sound amused?"

Simon turned away, feeling the hard-on leave. He glanced at the desk. *Okay,* he thought, *we won't be making love on it in the foreseeable future.* Decision time: He could do what she wanted, acknowledge that he should have waited until she consulted him, or he could do what he'd wanted to do for months. He decided to do what he wanted to do.

"I don't want you working with Tommy Strong anymore."

There, he'd said it. He took a deep breath and let it out. He watched as her brown eyes filled with fire. He'd almost forgotten that look. Their truce was about to come to a bloody end. He was aware of that but he wasn't backing down.

"What are you talking about?" Janice said between clenched teeth

"I was speaking English and I know very well that you understood me. I think I've put up with this nonsense long enough. As your husband I'm telling you that I'm sick of Tommy Strong manipulating your life. He thinks he has the right to tell you and me what and when we can do something."

"And you want to take over that role, is that it?" Janice said, hands on her hips. "Listen, Tommy doesn't pull my strings and neither do you. I make my choices on what I can and can't do. I've been asking for your input."

"And I'm giving you my input. I don't want you working with him anymore. He hasn't even made a pretense of being civil to me since we got married. He's gotten more demanding of your time."

"So what? In the four months we've been home I've barely done any of the things he's wanted." Janice sighed. "Simon, where is this coming from? What have I done to make you feel this way? I know the answer to that," she continued. "Nothing. I've done absolutely nothing."

She was right; she'd done nothing. But Harold had called him just an hour before and told him that Tommy was stepping up his campaign to discredit him.

"You haven't done anything," he sighed.

"Then why are you acting like this?"

"Tell me, as a husband how am I supposed to act? Should I want you spending time with a man you've been intimate with?" he shrugged. "A man that you loved?"

"But he's not the man I love now, Simon, you are."

Simon licked his lips, then bit down. Something inside him told him to let it go but he couldn't. He didn't want to. Every time he saw Tommy Strong's name it reminded him of his mistake in bringing the man into their lives. He wanted to eradicate that mistake.

"I don't want you working with him."

"What about the bookstores?"

"I don't care." He saw her eyes narrow. "And neither did you," he added, "until Tommy told you that you should."

Janice readjusted her stance. "I was wrong about that. I should have been taking more of an interest all along."

Janice tapped her fingers on the side of her hip, breathing fast. This was crazy. She didn't want to fight with Simon. She'd tried telling him that there was no reason for him to feel insecure. She snatched her planner from the desk, ripping the page in the process.

"You have no right to touch my things. I don't come into your office and fiddle with your schedule."

"I don't have an ex blocking out all of my time."

"Neither do I."

"Then you won't mind that I made sure of that."

"I do mind."

"Why?"

Janice felt as though she were talking to a child, a pouty, adorable, sexy child, but a child. She sighed.

"Don't do that."

"What else can I do? You are making me crazy for no reason. We went to bed last night with no problems between us. I come down now and find you acting like a madman. What happened?"

He pointed toward the fax.

"There has to be more. Simon, tell me what's going on with the two of you."

"Can't I just tell you that as your husband I don't want you working with him? Can't you just respect that?"

Janice looked down at her planner, to the places where Simon had scribbled over and crossed out. "I'm willing to compromise," she offered. "We can go over this together and decide which dates I can keep and which I can't."

"I'm not asking for a compromise," Simon said, getting up from the desk and moving toward her. "I'm asking that as my wife you just do as I ask."

"Why?"

"I just want you to do it, no questions."

"Take a good look, Simon. It's me. I don't take orders. You knew how I was before you married me. I'm trying, I really am."

And he knew that she was. Just as he knew he was making no sense in what he was saying to her. He'd fought with the woman too many years to think she would just take this order from him lying down. Still, the knowledge that she would rebel didn't prevent him from saying his next words.

"What about your book? Shouldn't you be working on that?"

"I have time."

He studied her, biting his lips to keep silent.

"I'm going to the bookstore," Janice announced as though Simon hadn't said a word. "There is a meeting there today."

"Are you ignoring my request?"

"Your request sounds more like an order. Tell me why you're acting so crazy and maybe I won't go."

"If you can't do as I ask, because I ask, then go." Simon hoped that she wouldn't take him up on it. Just once he wished she wouldn't fight him.

Janice stared at her husband, wondering again what had gotten into him. A huge part of her wanted to show him that marriage had not made him her boss but she'd seen the quick flash of hurt in his eyes. She didn't want to hurt him, not anymore.

"I'll let this rest for today," she conceded. "But this isn't the end of it and I'm not going to stop helping out the bookstores. Tommy is in charge of that project. There will be times I will have to work with him. I gave my word."

She saw something else in his eyes. "We'll work on my schedule together, Simon, you and I, not just you." She shifted her weight. "I love you," she said and turned and left the room.

Simon watched his wife leave the room and go up the stairs. He'd wanted her to acquiesce to his wishes, and she had, sort of, but he'd noticed a sadness when she said she loved him.

This had to end.

And he had to end it.

Each step was heavy as he went up the stairs. Simon ignored the fact that his wife was staring at him in confusion. He went to her, gathered her in his arms and breathed in her scent mixed with the herbal fragrance of her shampoo. "I have to go out," he said as he kissed her softly. "I have to take care of some things."

He pulled back, saw the worry in her eyes and kissed her. "Don't worry, baby." He kissed her eyelids, then her lips. "When I return I promise I'll be in a better mood."

"You'll give me a reason for all of this?"

"I'm not sure but since this is our first fight," he stopped at the smirk on her face, "our first fight as husband and wife, I'll be contrite, and I'll be in the mood for some serious making up."

"We could do that now."

Simon smiled as he felt the instant erection. But for the first time since he'd laid eyes on Janice, making love to her was not uppermost in his mind.

"I have to go into the office for a couple of hours and take care of some things." He kissed her again. "And I have to do a little shopping."

"You don't have to."

"Sure I do. Now tell me which do you want, diamonds or sapphires?"

"Both," Janice teased.

"Then both you shall have." He looked down at his watch. "It's almost nine. I'll be back by three. Are you going to work on your book while I'm gone?"

"Probably."

"Probably?"

"I got my editor to give me an extension. I have six months."

"That's not a good habit to get into. You told me that, remember?"

"I know, but in the last few months my life has been a bit crazy. I haven't been able to focus on writing more than a few hours a day. Don't worry," she added as Simon's eyes narrowed. "I was planning on pulling back a little on my time with the bookstores."

"Good," Simon said as he kissed her and turned and left.

"Do it," Simon barked into the phone as he snapped his finger in the direction of his secretary. "One of your editors gave her a six month extension. I want you to make sure that's rescinded."

"Why?" the voice on the other end of the phone asked, a bit surprised.

"Because I just might feel the need to step in and run the company myself." Simon waited while he heard the man trying to adjust his breathing.

"How long do you want her to have?" the voice asked.

"She needs to have it in your office in one month."

"Can she do it?"

"We'll see, won't we?"

Simon noticed his secretary staring at him oddly. The man usually minded his own business. Simon frowned at the man, but still he continued watching him. "What?" he bellowed. "Spit it out."

"Excuse me."

"I'm not talking to you," Simon said shortly into the phone. "My secretary is staring at me like I've suddenly grown horns." Simon sighed and blinked. And then he knew why. He was behaving as though he had horns. The man was wondering why he was attempting to sabotage his wife.

"My wife has been distracted with other projects and can't refocus. She told me so this morning. She also told me about the extension. I believe that is the reason she can't get her book done. I'm doing this to help her," he explained. He saw his secretary's look of concern change to one of understanding.

He signaled the man to leave his office and continued with his call. "I don't think I have to mention how important it is that my wife doesn't know I'm behind the scenes pulling the strings. Just have a talk with her editor and stress that the manuscript must be turned in in one month."

With that Simon hung up the phone and took a look around his massive office. Wall to wall bookshelves were filled with books from all of the authors whose lives he controlled in one way or another, whether or not they knew it. Then he glanced at the mahogany bookcase that was reserved for his wife. Only her books, her covers and her pictures went into that. If he were a little bit more eccentric he would say it was a shrine. But since he didn't like the term when used on himself, he preferred to think that it was his way of displaying the talents of the woman he loved.

He glanced toward the marble fireplace at all of the awards his companies had accumulated before turning his attention toward his prized possession. He gazed at the framed oil painting and went to it.

The artist had done an excellent job of capturing his emotions on his wedding day. His love for his wife was reflected in the painting. For five months they had been happy. He'd managed to put Tommy Strong out of his mind for the most part, but now Tommy was becoming more than a pest. He was becoming a downright thorn in his side.

"Damn," Simon said aloud and reached for the control panel to open the wall concealing the numerous computers and ticker tape machines which hummed in their own soundproof environment. He checked out all of his companies, yet it didn't generate the energy in him that work usually did. For almost four years now work had become a distant second. His love life had pushed that aside. His wife was his number one priority and he wasn't going to let anything change that. He stepped back and pushed the button to conceal the machines and walked down to Harold's office.

"Harold," he called, knocking and opening the door at the same time. "How's it going?"

"I thought you weren't coming in?"

"I changed my mind," Simon answered, looking around Harold's office. Harold's office was almost as large as his and the huge mahogany desk was twice as large as Simon's. Simon looked at the sparseness of personal mementos. The only picture in Harold's office was one of Simon when he was about twelve and Harold wasn't even in it.

The man had been like a father to him and for the past year Simon had treated him little better than a servant. And all because of his own arrogance.

"You're looking tired, Simon. What's wrong?"

"Your call didn't help." He swiped his face with the back of his hand. "It looks like I painted myself into a corner."

"You can always find a way out. Your marriage is happy. Keep it that way. Tell her."

"I know I should," Simon sighed. "But now it's more difficult." He walked toward Harold's fireplace, picked up a Faberge egg and tossed it lightly in his hand, knowing Harold was more than likely holding his breath as he toyed with the expensive trinket. It had been a gift from his good friend, Simon's father. There weren't very many eggs held by private collectors. Most people wrongly thought there were more. He knew what the egg meant to Harold and after a couple of minutes he deposited it where he'd found it.

"We almost had our first fight today," Simon informed Harold. Then he turned toward the window as though he'd find the answer in the heavy paisley drapes and dark green walls.

He didn't.

"What was your fight or your almost fight about?"

"I went crazy when you called to say that Tommy Strong was still trying to dig up information on me. Isn't it enough that he's tried every tactic to turn my in-laws against me?"

"What did you do?"

Simon sighed and sat in one of the heavy leather chairs and propped his feet on the edge of the expensive desk. "I went through her planner and scratched out every day she'd put in there to work with the man. When she found me doing it, I ordered her not to work with him."

"You ordered her?" Harold laughed, then shook his head. "And you were banished from the kingdom by your new bride, I take it. We all know very well she doesn't take to orders."

"Actually I wasn't banished. I decided I had pushed my luck far enough for one day and I regained use of my few remaining brain cells and left before I did any permanent damage."

Harold studied the man who was not only his boss but his friend and surrogate son. Knowing him so well he knew without a doubt that Simon Kohl had not so easily conceded defeat. He saw the twitch at the corner of his mouth and knew he was now worrying about something he'd done. "What have you done, Simon?"

Simon smiled, slowly bringing his feet from the desk. "You think you know me so well, don't you, old man? Well, guess what? You do." He got up to clap Harold on the shoulder. "I don't want her working with Strong, and since ordering her is not going to work, I decided that I would take matters into my own hands."

"And?"

"And I ordered Peters to only give her a month to give the book to him."

"A month? But you told me she hasn't been doing much writing."

"She hasn't."

"Then how the hell do you expect her to finish it in a month?"

"I don't care if she finishes the damn book. I just don't want her with Strong. That will give me time to think of something. I'm thinking maybe we can go abroad for a year. I don't know and don't care. I just know that I don't want her near the man."

"You can't dictate to her, Simon."

"I'm her husband."

"You don't own her."

"Not you too?" Simon said. He stared at Harold. "All my life you've been telling me that the fact that my ancestors were in the slave trade had nothing to do with me. That no one would ever find out, that my grandfather had changed the family name, that my father hated knowing so much that he couldn't even bring himself to tell his wife and she was white. How the hell do you think I feel about telling my wife, who's black?"

"Simon you're not—"

"Don't," Simon said, putting his hand up to stop Harold. "Everyone keeps telling me that I don't own Janice. Tommy Strong, Janice, and now you. And you know how much that remark hurts me. But still you said it, so I have to wonder, do you think the genes of my forefathers run in my veins?"

"It was just an off-the-cuff remark. I didn't mean anything by it."

"Sometimes those are the truest statements. I don't want to own her, but I don't want her to hate me like my mother did my father. I don't want her to doubt me and I'm running out of options."

"So you're going to Europe to hide?"

Simon stared. "I just want to give my marriage a fighting chance." He thought of his words, then smiled thinly. "Let me rephrase that. I don't want the fighting, I'm sick to death of the fighting."

"You can run the businesses from anywhere. That's not a problem. Matter of fact, in the last week the employees have not been as happy as they usually are. You've been pretty hard on everyone, including all the publishers. You used to allow them freedom to do as they pleased. Now you're pushing yourself down their throat and making demands. People are more loyal when they're treated like friends."

"I'm trying to protect my marriage. Don't you understand that?"

"I understand that you don't have to work so hard at it. Janice loves you."

"I know she loves me," Simon answered and headed for the door. "I just want to keep it that way."

"Where are you going now, home?"

"No, I think I'll pay a little visit to Mr. Strong."

"What abut Janice?"

"She's home. I told her I would be home by three to make up for my actions."

"You know, Simon, if you'd just trust her you wouldn't have to spend so much time or money making up."

"Maybe I like making up, Harold. Did you ever think of that?" He laughed softly.

CHAPTER TWENTY-TWO

Janice looked at the monitor on her computer. She'd never experienced writer's block, but if it felt anything like what she was having at the moment, then maybe this was it. All she knew for sure was that she kept staring at the same line, deleting it, replacing it and writing it again.

Her mind wasn't on her book. Her mind was on her husband. For the past two weeks he had been more possessive than ever. She had curtailed her work with Tommy, only doing neighborhood canvassing when there were other authors involved. Her seeing less of Tommy should have made her husband happy. It hadn't. Simon wasn't happy. But he wasn't telling her anything.

Janice punched the button to turn off the computer. Maybe if Simon wouldn't talk, Tommy would. She glanced at the clock. It was only noon. She would be back long before Simon returned.

Janice ignored the questions that the staff asked about her destination, telling them only that she would be home by the time her husband returned. She liked all the staff, but wasn't so naive as to not know that they reported her movements to her husband.

For a change she found a parking slot for her Jeep near Tommy's bookstore and fortified herself against the thoughts that were twirling in her mind. *I'm not going against what my husband wants. I'm not going to work with Tommy.*

"Hi, Neal." she said to the clerk as she went into the store. "Is Tommy in the back?"

"No, he's shelving books." Neal grinned. "I think he's taking all of yours off. He's pretty pissed at you."

"I've been doing all that I can. I'm married to a man Tommy doesn't like. I'm doing what I can to help. You understand that, don't you?"

"Yes, I understand, but then I'm not the one who thought he stood a chance with you."

Janice ran her tongue unconsciously over her lips, wanting to deny that she had encouraged Tommy, but remembering the kisses they'd shared and knowing that she had in some way. Wanting to have closure with Tommy, she had inadvertently added fire to the flame.

"What are you doing here? Your husband faxed me that you weren't available."

Janice looked toward Tommy, surprised that she'd not heard him come up. "I know. I wasn't available earlier." She would talk to Simon later about what he'd done.

"Then why the hell are you here? I don't really need your sporadic help. We can do this without you."

Janice touched his arms and pushed against him. "Can we talk in the back room?"

"I'm busy."

"So I see. I can help you with the books." She began removing books from cartons and walking around the store with them, knowing that Tommy's need to control things would have him at her side and making sure she was putting them where he wanted.

"You made a mistake, Mary Jo."

Janice looked at the books in her hand. "What did I do?"

"I'm not talking about the books. I'm talking about your marrying Simon Kohl. You should cut your losses and get out now before you start having babies and you're tied to him forever."

For a moment she stopped and glared at him. "Is that what a baby means to you, Tommy, that you're tied to the mother forever?"

"I didn't mean it like that."

She moved from him, wondering why the past still had the power to hurt her. Tommy had hit too close to the truth. Janice thought she was pregnant but she hadn't told her husband. She'd been waiting for the perfect moment. She hadn't even taken a home pregnancy test. It was just something she'd felt intuitively, that a life was growing inside her. She'd already made a doctor's appointment to verify what she already knew. And she wanted this time to be different. She wanted her baby to be born in love and peace and she wouldn't get either if she didn't get to the bottom of what was caught in Tommy's craw.

"Why do you keep saying that?"

"Have you ever wondered how Simon's family made their money?"

Janice knew where this was going, where things always went with Tommy. She walked away toward a stack of magazines and pulled the old copies.

"Have you?" Tommy asked, following her, not bothering with the fact that there were customers in the store.

"I don't care," Janice turned to him and said hotly.

"You don't care if Simon Kohl's family owned slaves?"

How the hell could she not care? How the hell could she tell Tommy that she didn't? "Listen, neither Simon or his father or his grandfather owned slaves."

"What about his great-great-grandfather?"

"Now what? Am I supposed to convict my husband for sins of the father?"

"Why the hell not?"

"Don't you think I've done things I'm ashamed of, Tommy?" she asked him softly, biting off each word, the anger competing with the pain. "Don't you think I have my own skeletons in my closet? I love my husband and he loves me."

"Yeah, right."

"Is that what's going on between you two? You're trying to prove his family had something to do with slavery?"

"Isn't that important?" Tommy asked, amazement in his voice. "What the hell happened to you, Mary Jo?"

"I grew up, Tommy. There are many shades of gray. No one is without sin, either those we've committed or those that have landed on us by virtue of our ancestors. I won't fault my husband for things done long before his birth and as a friend, an old friend, I ask that you stop trying to destroy him."

"I won't," Tommy said. "As long as I have breath left in me."

"And what purpose will it serve?"

"Maybe it will make you choose a side."

"I have chosen. I've chosen my husband." She looked sadly at Tommy, then the books she was holding. She handed them to him. "I have to go."

"Your leash has gotten shorter, hasn't it?" he said to her back.

But Janice didn't bother to turn and answer him. Instead, she said goodbye to Neal. "I might not be around too often," she explained. She took Neal's smile as his unspoken acceptance. She would never be able to have a friendship with Tommy and for that she was sad.

She walked out the door and into the path of a man heading for the store. She looked up and into the cold gray eyes of her husband. Her cheeks burned with guilt, then anger, as the thought that he'd followed her consumed her. Neither spoke.

Janice walked down the short steps to her Jeep and turned back. Simon was staring after her, it would have done her no good to explain; he would not have believed it. And she wasn't going to get into another fight in front of Tommy.

Not with her husband.

Not today.

Simon stood there and watched his wife walk away. She'd lied and betrayed him. She was supposed to be at home. She'd promised that she wouldn't be at Tommy's today. Hell, a lot of the work could be accomplished with phone calls and faxes. He'd never thought it was necessary for her to spend all the time that she did with the man. And it wasn't necessary for Tommy to take her personally to all of the stores. Hell, she had a car. Matter of fact she had a limo. She didn't need Tommy.

It was time to talk to Tommy, something he should have done months ago. Simon pushed the door open, went inside and looked around. He smiled at the clerk and nodded. He believed his name was Neal; he'd always treated him politely. He had to admit Tommy had a very nice store, roomy, with an old world feel.

Simon looked around, noting all of the small reading alcoves and the closed door leading to the tearoom. He turned and spotted the private reading room that Tommy rented out to groups. He was doing well, much better than most of the stores, but then of course the fact that Tommy had diversified by offering more helped. He offered open mike poetry reading nights and allowed writers to congregate there. It wasn't a matter of Tommy being a Good Samaritan. It was simply good business. He pulled out a pad and began making notes.

"What are you doing?"

Simon had known that his actions would capture Tommy's attention. He shrugged. "Just jotting down figures on what it would take to make this place a real success." Then he looked directly at Tommy. "We need to talk, Mr. Strong."

"So let's talk."

"Not here. We need a more private place."

"Like a gym, a boxing ring?"

"I didn't come to fight, not physically anyway. But I'm not averse to that. No one takes anything from me that I don't want them to have."

"Is that so?"

"Can you leave for awhile?"

"Where do you want to go?"

"There's a club a few blocks down, very quiet, very private. In fact we can have a private room and we won't be disturbed." Simon pulled his phone from his pocket and waited to see what Tommy would say.

"Make the call," Tommy said.

Sitting in the oak paneled room of the private club, Simon twirled his drink, looking into the clear crystal. He took a sip and enjoyed the slow burn. Then he brought his eyes up to meet Tommy's.

"Don't fuck with me or I'll bury you."

Tommy laughed.

"I'm not kidding; you're not going to take my wife from me."

"She's not your property, Master Kohl, neither am I. I do what I damn well please."

Simon looked down at the plush carpet, the oak chairs and the plaid recliner in the corner of the room near the window.

"I knew it was you who was putting this shit in my wife's head. It's not going to work. She loves me, she's my wife."

"Did you know your wife was with me just a few minutes before you came in?"

The twitch in Simon's jaw couldn't be helped. He was aware that Tommy was trying to insinuate that something more than talking had gone down in the bookstore.

"This is a very nice place," Tommy remarked, "lots of private room. A person could do anything they wanted to in here. Kind of like my store. I could…hmm…I could make love in my private room and no one would ever know." Tommy took a drink from his glass and waited.

"I've been thinking that since I'm in the publishing industry that maybe a low end, hole in the wall bookstore with a few out of date books and a coffee shop that sells burnt coffee and stale pastries would be the way to go. Hell, I could give the coffee away and who knows, maybe have a book giveaway once a week. I can afford it. Everyone stopping by would get a free book and free coffee. What do you think?" Simon asked, smirking at Tommy.

"I think you'd have to find the hole in the wall store first."

Simon pulled out the pad he'd used to write his earlier figures on and looked at the numbers. "I think I already have." He glared as Tommy stood and advanced on him. Before he could swing Simon stood and his left fist shot out, landing a solid punch to Tommy's abdomen. He'd meant it when he said he wasn't letting Tommy take his wife without a fight.

Janice sat in front of her computer typing. For the first time in weeks the words were flowing. She was writing about her life. Simon was right; she'd been behaving like one of those women who were too dumb to live.

She heard the door slam, heard the hurried voices of several members of the household staff and then the footsteps coming toward her study. She continued to write, not wanting to face what was coming.

Simon pushed open the door of his wife's study and looked in on her. He knew she was aware he was there. Maybe it was a good thing that she didn't acknowledge him immediately. In the seconds that he stared at her back, he forced some of the residual anger away. He'd started this problem by digging into her past and throwing Tommy in her face.

"You lied to me," he said, finally coming into the room and closing the door. He continued looking at the back of her head as she typed. He couldn't believe it; she wasn't going to face him.

Simon marched across the room, stood behind her and removed her fingers from the keyboard. He heard her sigh as she turned to face him.

"Simon, what happened?" A look of horror, then guilt, rose to her face at his bruises. The guilty look hurt Simon a hell of a lot more than Tommy's fists.

"Why did he do that?"

"Because I hit him."

"Simon?"

"Is this what you wanted, for us to fight over you?"

Janice closed her eyes and shook her head slowly. "I never wanted this to happen. I didn't go to Tommy's to work. I went there just to talk."

"I didn't ask you why you went there. I asked you not to go and you agreed."

Janice could feel the rapid beat of her heart. She could stand there and go toe to toe with Simon. That was their thing, it was them. But she didn't want to. She wanted to help her husband with whatever demons were chasing him.

"Why don't you just tell me what you've been trying so long and so hard to cover up? What is it, Simon, that you don't want me to know? Tell me, I can handle it."

"Are you sure?" he asked. It was time, hell, it was way past time. "Your friend Mr. Strong has been trying to prove that my family actively participated in the slave trade."

He looked directly in her eyes, not touching her, not wanting to feel her pull away. He didn't want to see the look of revulsion that would undoubtedly come into her eyes when he told her but he wanted to see the truth, so he held her gaze.

"I know that, Simon."

"How long have you known he was investigating me?"

"Tommy told me today when I went there to talk to him."

Simon swallowed hard. "Did he say if he'd managed to get any proof?"

"No, Simon. He's on a fishing expedition. Since we were young he's always had this idea that all white people participated in slavery. We used to argue about it. It never mattered that facts proved his theory wrong. That's part of Tommy," she shrugged.

"Is that what you told him today?"

"That and a few other things. I asked him to stop trying to hurt you. I told him that you had not had anything personally to do with things that happened in the past and that I wouldn't blame you for things you weren't responsible for."

"Did you mean it?"

"Of course I meant it."

"Knowing what you know, that Tommy Strong wants to destroy me and my reputation and being in the public eye, you're aware this will also damage you. Are you sorry that you married me?"

"What would make you ask me something like that?"

"Knowing how this will make you look to the African American community, you're saying you'd stand by me?" he asked, surprised.

"Why wouldn't I? I love you."

"You haven't asked me if it's true."

"I get the feeling that I know the answer to that." She sighed heavily and looked down.

"And?"

"You didn't have to go through all of this. You didn't have to." She shook her head and stopped, frowning at him. "Simon, right now I'm feeling such anger at you." She saw the pain in his eyes and shook her head again.

"But not about what your ancestors did. You had nothing to do with that. Do you think I would really blame you for something done by your ancestors?"

"Most black people do."

"I'm not most black people. I'm your wife. I'm the woman carrying your child." She waited.

"You're what? You're pregnant?"

"I think so. I haven't taken a test yet but I'm pretty sure that I am."

Simon felt a tingle shoot through his entire body and he closed his eyes, overcome by his emotions. "Are you going to stay with me?"

"You really are a silly man, aren't you?" Janice said, at last caving in and throwing her arms around her husband. "For an entire year you've done everything wrong and in spite of it all we're here right now. Tommy was never the threat you thought he was and neither was this secret he was holding over you."

"You aren't angry?"

"Of course I'm angry. I'm angry that you thought you had to hide this from me, that you allowed Tommy to use this against you. And I'm angry that you didn't have more trust in me, in my love for you, in us, Simon. Do I like knowing this about your ancestors? No. Do I hold you responsible? No. Does it affect my love for you? Hell no!"

"Tommy—"

"I'll tell you once more, Tommy is not a threat to what we have."

"But he was a threat, wasn't he?"

"Not really."

"Never?"

"I'll tell you that the first few days I worked with Tommy we relived some memories. The book wasn't closed on us, Simon. As for leaving you for Tommy, that thought never entered my mind." She touched her fingers to his cheeks and kissed his bruises. "You didn't have to fight for me. You have me."

She kissed his lips softly. "You should have told me long ago. I gave you so many opportunities."

"I didn't want to keep this from you but look what I had to go through to get you to love me. I didn't want to take a chance on losing that."

"You didn't have a right to keep something from me that would affect both of our lives." At the sound of her own words, Janice heard Tommy's voice more than a dozen years in the past telling her the exact same thing.

"Simon, I think we need to talk. I've told you about my past. Suppose you tell me about yours. Why have you carried this burden for so long?"

She hugged him to her, caressing his shoulders, his back. "You don't have to carry it anymore. I remember you saying that you wanted us to be able to share any secrets and go on. Your secret is not going to destroy us."

Simon crushed her to him. *Maybe not this one.* Harold was right. He should have leveled with Janice. Then none of the things he'd put into play would have happened. But it was too late to reverse them.

"Are we really going to have a baby?" he asked instead.

"Yes. Yes, we're going to have a baby."

"What do we do? Go to the doctor? Get one of those little kits? Do you have one?"

She answered him and smiled. "I have a dozen and I have a doctor's appointment next week."

"What are we waiting for? Let's find out."

He started up the stairs behind her but she put out her hand. "Give me a couple of minutes, then come up."

"Why?"

"Simon, I don't need you with me in the bathroom." She laughed and ran up the rest of the stairs.

He looked after her for a second, then disappeared into her study and closed the door.

"Harold, I told her," Simon began the moment the phone was answered on the other end.

"What did she say?"

"She doesn't blame me." Simon heard the sigh of relief and interrupted. "Don't get relieved so quickly. I've done something much worse, something that she might have a harder time forgiving."

"What?" Harold asked, his voice tense. "Simon, what have you done?"

"I told you we had a fight this morning. I went to Tommy's to set things straight with him, but I met Janice leaving his store. We had a fight."

"You and Janice?"

"No, Tommy and I."

"An actual fist fight?"

"Yes."

"And?"

"And after it was over I made some calls. Right now bookstores are being closed across the country. The leases are being pulled. I don't know if I can stop it."

"Just call the same people and cancel the plans."

"I don't have time right now." He took his ear from the phone. "I'm coming, honey," he answered. "I have to go to my wife. Harold, you have to take care of this. Make the calls, stop it. If you can't..." Simon cursed softly. "If you can't—"

"Yeah, I know. Make it so you're not connected. Damn it, Simon, you should have listened to me."

"I know that but I don't have time to debate with you. I'm about to find out if I'm going to be a father." He hung up the phone and ran up the stairs two at a time, praying Harold would be able to repair the damage that he'd done.

The moment he stepped into his bedroom Simon was filled with excitement. He hadn't expected to find Janice waiting nervously, but holding out something and telling him the news.

"What is it?" he asked. "Are we having a baby?"

"I didn't look. I waited for you."

He took her hand and together they entered the bathroom as cautiously as if they expected an incendiary device to blow up. He stood a step behind his wife as she picked up the first test strip and waited for her reaction. Joy radiated from every pore as she passed the plastic handle over to him for his inspection. Then like two children they went from one of the pregnancy tests strips that Janice had lining the counters in the bathroom to the next. When they saw the positive signs in all of the test kits Simon grabbed her up in a bear hug and spun her around as she screamed.

"You meant it when you said you'd bought a dozen kits. I thought you were only kidding."

"I wanted to be sure."

"Thank you baby," he said. *Thank you God,* he murmured in his head. *Thank you.*

"Simon, no more secrets, okay? No more. We don't need them. We're finally going to be a family. I can't believe it," Janice said. "I can't believe it." Tears filled her eyes and slid down her face. "I love you," she said. "You're everything I ever wanted. I trust you with my life and my heart."

He kissed her with all the love and longing that was in his soul. Inwardly he was cursing his stupidity. He had everything he'd always wanted but because of his temper and his arrogance he now stood to lose it.

"Congratulations," Harold said and kissed Janice's cheek. Then he hugged Simon close. "We need to talk," he whispered.

Simon pulled away and held the chair out for Janice. "Harold, sit down. You're the first person we're sharing our news with. That's why we invited you to dinner. This isn't about work." Simon cautioned him with his eyes. "We don't need any stress right now. When we leave the restaurant I have the jet waiting. We're going to pop in and surprise Janice's parents."

"Simon, I need to talk with you for a few minutes before you leave. I'm sure your beautiful wife won't mind."

"No, but I do," Simon said and smiled at Janice. "I mind. Business can wait." Simon knew what Harold wanted to tell him. Things had not been so easy to halt. But at the moment he didn't want to know what had been happening in the two days since he'd placed the calls. He just wanted to take Janice to her parents and celebrate.

"Those stocks that you wanted me to buy; I couldn't get what you wanted. I'm sorry."

Simon sighed, blew out his breath and looked in disappointment at his second in command. "You're determined to ruin this celebration, aren't you?" he said and shook his head. "Eat your lobster, Harold. Everything will work out in the end."

"I don't think so," Harold replied quietly as he began eating.

Simon heard him but ignored the words. He would not take this moment from his wife or himself. He'd waited too long for it.

CHAPTER TWENTY-THREE

Simon looked at the two-story brick house and smiled. "Why don't we buy your parents a new home?"

"They wouldn't accept it," Janice answered. "But thanks for thinking of them; they love you already. You don't have to try so hard."

"You think they're going to be happy?" he asked, suddenly nervous.

"Of course they're going to be happy; they're going to be grandparents."

"But they already are."

"Yes, but this is our first baby. Besides, it doesn't matter with grandparents. They always get excited about a new baby each and every time. Don't worry, Simon, they're going to be thrilled.

"Are you going to tell them about my past?"

"I don't see a need for them to know."

"Are you ashamed?"

Janice stopped and surveyed her husband. "You really are worried about that, aren't you? Baby, there is no reason to be. Even if they hated you I would still love you."

"You think knowing would change how they feel about me?"

"Not one bit. They love you."

The door opened at that moment. Before she could do any more thinking about it, everyone was all over them, hugging and kissing her—two brothers, her sister, and the horde of nieces and nephews. They had only called her parents a few hours earlier and asked them to get everyone over, that they had a surprise.

"Now for our surprise," Janice said. Simon was glowing and had his arm around Janice as they stood together in the center of the room.

"You're going to have a baby," Carol burst out, unable to contain herself any longer. She ran to hug Simon.

"Yes," he said. "We're going to have a baby." For the next few minutes Simon was swamped with well wishes and with love. A family. Finally he had a family. When they at last went to bed, Simon turned toward Janice in the double bed."I think we should get one of these."

"What?"

"A smaller bed. I like being close to you." He sat up and looked around the purple room. He saw posters of a young Mary Jo dressed in a purple and white cheerleader outfit.

"This is your old bedroom?" he asked, looking down at her.

"Yes, can you believe they have kept all of this junk?"

"I can believe it. I plan on keeping everything connected with our son."

"What if it's a girl?"

"Then I will keep every memento of hers with the exception of cheerleader outfits. She won't have any because I won't let her wear those skimpy skirts."

"So you don't like what I had on?"

"I like it on you, just not for my daughter." He looked at the white wicker chair with the purple cushion. Then he took another look at the walls. "This room has been freshly painted."

"They always keep it like this just in case."

Simon smiled down at her. "Just in case you ever wanted to come home."

"Yes."

"I don't think you're going to need this room anymore, do you?"

"No, I don't think so."

"Then tell them that they can repaint it."

"Does it make you nervous, them having this room for me?"

"A bit, but I also like it. Tell me something. If you like purple so much, why don't we have anything in our bedroom that's purple?"

"Mary Jo liked purple."

"Well, I love Mary Jo and I love Janice, so I'm going to love whatever color the two of you come up with. Want to redecorate?"

"I would, but my deadline was pushed up to a month. That's the reason I told you we could only stay a day or so. I have to work at least twelve hours a day writing this book until I'm done. I won't have time to redecorate or anything else. I'm not going to have much time for you either. Is that okay with you?"

Simon had forgotten about changing her deadline and felt a stab of guilt. "Do you want me to call and have that changed?"

"Don't do that, Simon, please. I'd rather do what I have to do in my career. I know how much behind the scenes help you've already given me. Please just let me do this on my own. Actually I'm kind of glad the deadline was advanced. It shows that your money and influence didn't help. I'm being treated like everyone else. I like the feeling."

Simon lay back down and pulled her into his arms. He kissed her forehead. "Go to sleep, baby. We'll leave tomorrow night so you can get some rest before you have to start writing."

Damn, he thought, *like hell my money and influence had nothing to do with her changed schedule. I'll make it up to her,* he thought and pulled her even closer. He'd make sure that the moment the book was released it would go straight to number one on *The New York Times* list. And *that's another secret I'll have to keep from her.* he thought and groaned. He was raking up a hell of a lot of karmic debt. This time at least he was trying to do it for the right reason.

"We wish we could stay," Simon said to his father-in-law, "but Mary Jo has to work on her new book. She has only a month and we need her to get some rest before she starts. She needs a good night's sleep."

Simon tilted the can of Miller's up to his lips, doing what everyone else was doing. Carol had asked if he wanted a glass and had brightened when he'd said no.

"I really have enjoyed myself." He smiled. "We couldn't wait to tell you." He glanced over at Janice, his gaze lingering on her. *What the hell am I doing?* She'd forgiven him. Why didn't he just tell her what he'd done?

At that moment Janice turned and smiled at him and he had his answer. She looked at him with love and with pride and that was the reason he didn't want to tell her. She wouldn't be proud of what he'd done. She couldn't be.

Janice had been working for three and a half weeks without a break. She didn't know if she hated the book and the characters she'd created or if she loved them. She'd hardly spent more than an hour or so a night in her husband's arms and it wasn't because of his schedule but hers. Another day or so and she could send the book in. Only now she was so tired from writing her eyeballs hurt. She wanted to finish the book and go shopping for maternity clothes and baby furniture. Although she needed neither yet, she wanted to go, but she didn't have the time.

The buzzer on her timer sounded and she reread the last line she'd written, saved her work and turned off the computer. She'd made an agreement with Simon that she would not work past seven-thirty. In fact, she'd promised and this time she was keeping all promises she made to him.

She'd faxed Tommy weeks before and told him of her schedule change, informing him that her book was due in a month and that she was pregnant. She'd almost ended it there but when she thought of Tommy hitting Simon she'd added, "*After what happened, I think it best that you get another high profile African American author. I can't do it any more.*"

Simon looked at the clock. "Look, I have to go. Janice and I have an agreement that at seven-thirty it's our time together. I'll be in the office early tomorrow."

"How have you managed to keep all of this from her? It's been all over the news and in the papers. What have you done, locked her in a cave?"

Simon started to laugh until he realized that Harold was partially serious. "Don't worry," he reassured him. "This is all Janice's doing. Whenever she works, she doesn't like outside stimuli, nothing that could affect her stories. She unplugs the phone, the fax, and she doesn't read the paper or watch the news. Her not knowing wasn't my doing."

"And you didn't think you should tell her?"

"Listen, when she finishes each day she's tired. I'm not going to give her any more stress. That's not what she wants from me."

"Bull, Simon. You're only making your hole deeper. God, when it happens, you are going to have a hard fall."

"Are you hoping that's what will happen to me?"

"I'm just warning you that you'd better get ready, because she's not going to stay hidden in a cave forever. You're manipulating her life and that's not right. It was one thing when you went digging into her past. I didn't agree with it but in a way I understood it. I mean, a man with your money needs to make sure what he's getting into."

"That's not why I did it."

"I know, but everything that's happened so far, you set in motion. You're the one who brought Tommy Strong into your life. If you had not invaded her privacy, none of this would have occurred."

"But good came out of that, Harold. It forced Janice to realize that she loved me."

"That's the operative word, isn't it, *forced*?"

Harold was clicking his tongue and it was driving Simon crazy. "I had to know."

"Why did you go behind her back and interfere in her career?"

"You know why I did that. I didn't want her working with Tommy."

"She's going to be pissed when she finds out how you've been manipulating her. And the bookstores, she's been working so hard to save them, and you've gone and destroyed them."

"I'm trying to make up for that. I'm in negotiations with Eric Warren to buy the rights back from him."

"He's a rotten bastard. He's not going to sell them back to you. He thinks you see gold in them and he's not budging. Couldn't you have picked someone else to do your dirty work? Why didn't you just have me do it?"

"Would you have?"

"If you had ordered me to do it."

"And what would you have thought about my ordering you?"

"I would have lost all my respect for you but I would have done it."

"And now, Harold, have you lost all respect for me?"

"I think you're going about everything all wrong. You've always wanted a family, a wife to love you, kids. Now you have it, you have it all and you're throwing it all away. You've been trying so hard to not live your father's life but you're repeating every mistake he ever made. It wasn't the family secret that destroyed your parents' marriage. I've told you that a million times. It was his deceit, his arrogance, his mistrust of your mother, him trying to manipulate things behind the scenes."

"My parents slept around."

"Do you think that happened in the beginning?" Harold shook his head slowly. "That took awhile, a lot of years, a lot of hurt. They both hacked away at that marriage until they had nothing left but you. Is that what you want, Simon?"

"You know that's not what I want. This whole thing got out of control. If Janice had just listened to me when I asked her not to go to Tommy's..."

"You're trying to place some of the blame for this mess on your wife?"

"God, I don't know." Simone ran his fingers through his hair. "Don't worry, Harold, I know this is all my doing. Eric is being so damn stubborn. I've offered him ten times what he paid for those damn stores. And that was another mistake. Now he knows they have to be important."

"What's he doing now?"

"He's trying to buy up more independent stores and I'm trying to stop him. It's a real mess. I'm spending too much time on this."

"Messes sometimes take awhile to clean up. Are you heading directly home?"

"I have to make a stop before I get home."

"More jewelry? You've been to the jeweler every day this month."

Simon paused and studied Harold. "Correct me if I'm wrong, but am I spending my money or yours?"

"You're going about this the wrong way. That's all that I meant by my observation."

"I would be buying jewelry for my wife anyway, so you don't know what you're talking about."

Simon was tired of snapping at Harold. He loved Harold but lately he seemed to have appointed himself to be Simon's conscience, and that Simon didn't need. Every time he saw his wife his own guilt screamed out at him.

Since she was doing nothing but working, Simon had decided he might as well put in time at the office. He hated the idea of not snuggling with her in the early morning. At least he got to have lunch with her. When she worked, generally she didn't care about food. She didn't care about anything but the characters in her book. Now it was different, she cared about having a healthy baby and she cared about him. She had a standing request for the staff to interrupt her for lunch. There was no emergency that was going to keep Simon from leaving the office to go home and have lunch with his wife. That time was special for both of them.

He remembered how it used to be when she'd tried to hide how happy she was to see him. Now she didn't. Whenever he interrupted her she never acted annoyed. She would give him a huge smile, get up from her computer for a hug and a kiss and a few minutes of conversation. But eventually she would kiss him and usher him back out the door.

And every time it happened he wanted to call her publisher and tell him to give her more time. But he knew Janice would be suspicious. She would know without a doubt that he'd meddled and he was trying his best not to interfere any more than he already had.

Simon handed the sapphire and diamond bracelet to the clerk, who was beaming. Why shouldn't he be? That was another thing Harold was right about. Every day for a month he'd either had something sent to the mansion or he stopped in the store himself. Over two million dollars in jewels. He looked at the glass cases and the remaining items, thinking the entire store would not be enough to get him out of the mess he'd gotten himself into if Janice discovered what he'd done.

"You're late."

"Just a little. I got you something," Simon said, bringing the bag from behind his back and smiling. She wasn't reaching for the bag and he wondered why.

"Something wrong, baby?"

"Why are you bringing me so many presents?"

"I always give you presents," he answered defensively. "What are you complaining about?"

"I'm not complaining." Janice smiled, shrugging her shoulder. "I guess I'm just tired and maybe a bit cranky."

"Are you almost done?"

"Almost. I will be in a couple of days." She moved so that her back was to her husband, knowing that he would massage her shoulders.

"Don't you want your present?" Simon asked, moving to rub her shoulders.

"Maybe later. Right now I'm on present overload."

A lump formed in his throat. He'd thought the jewels made her happy. They didn't. "If you could have anything in the world that you wished for, what would it be?" he asked as he kneaded her kinked muscles.

"I have it."

"What exactly do you have?"

"You," Janice answered without missing a beat. "I thought I was happy with the way things were before. I really did, our fights, everything, not caring, not trusting. This is so much better," she said, grabbing his hand and bringing it to her lips. "I wouldn't trade what we have for anything."

"How about the bookstores? Are you missing helping?"

"I am, but I know that the work I've done has helped and I know that Tommy is not going to see the stores close. He's passionate about that and regardless of everything else, he can be pretty amazing."

"Pretty amazing?" Simon rubbed his teeth across his lips. "You sound as though you're proud of him."

"Honey, you don't have anything to be worried about. Haven't I proven that to you? It's you I love."

Simon wondered for a moment about that. Yes, she'd married him and yes, she was having his baby and yes, she wasn't seeing Tommy anymore, but that was because he had pulled strings and had practically imprisoned her in the mansion. Sure, she'd set the ground rules and had shut herself in her office typing all day, but it was because of his manipulations that she'd done it. He sighed.

"Simon, do you still doubt me?"

"I want to make you happy so much that I guess it worries me when I bring you home a gift and you won't open it." Simon smiled, trying to lighten the moment.

"Give it to me."

For a moment he wondered at her statement but she was smiling. It was he who was sensitive over her choice of words. He handed her the package, cursing Harold silently. If it had not been for him, he would not be thinking these thoughts.

"I was wondering when you're done with your book if you would like to come with me to Italy? I have some business there and if you're going to be done in a couple of days I could arrange it."

"I didn't know you had to go to Italy."

"Well, I've been putting it off. I didn't want to leave you alone."

Janice smiled up at him. "I'm not worried anymore about your abandoning me, not when you tell me where you're going and when you're coming home."

"Don't you want to go with me? Have you grown tired of me already?" He looked away.

"Is something wrong?"

"I'm beginning to feel neglected. I know you have to hide yourself away like this when you write but I miss you. I just want some time alone with you."

"You're going to Italy for business. I don't want to sit around in a hotel room all day."

"I promise we'll get to see and do whatever you want. Don't worry."

Simon realized that he was still manipulating things. Janice would be done with her book in a couple of days, and she would find out what was going on, what he'd done. He needed more time. A couple of weeks.

He watched her unwrap the box and smile at the bracelet. "It's beautiful," she said.

"I thought you would like it."

"I do and I like the identical one you bought me a year ago."

Simon's mouth opened and he blinked. "I already bought you that bracelet?"

"Yes, and it's time to stop buying jewelry. At least for a while," she amended. "I would like to do some shopping, but for the baby, not for me."

"Then I'll buy—"

"No, Simon, I want us to shop together. I want us to pick out the crib and everything else together. I've been waiting to finish this book. I've had my heart set on turning one of the bedrooms into a nursery. I guess that's why I didn't seem so excited about going to Italy. It's not because of you; it's just that I wanted to make baby plans. I've been shutting myself away so that that could happen, that's all."

"We'll do it as soon as we come home, okay?" Simon pulled her into his arms. Another thing to feel guilty about. His wife had been working like a demon in order to shop for the baby, their baby, and he was still manipulating, taking that pleasure away from her. But that he could make up for. They could buy all Italian furniture for the baby and have it shipped home. That would make her happy. The bracelet sure hadn't done it. If he was repeating his gifts to her, he was definitely overdoing it. He was also going to have a talk with the jeweler. The damn man should have told him that he'd already bought that piece.

The End. Janice typed the words on the bottom of her manuscript, printed it and shoved it into the envelope. For the first time in a month she re-plugged her phone and called Michelle, her agent.

"Okay, I'm sticking this in the mail and then I'm going to Italy with Simon for a couple of weeks. Hopefully nothing will come up. I don't think I have the energy right now to do edits."

"It should be fine. I don't know what happened, why out of the blue they moved up your deadline, but I guess it must have been an important reason."

"Don't worry about it. We both know that there could be a dozen reasons why they did or there could be none. I'm glad. It gives me more time before the baby is born. I've been goofing off for the past few months anyway. This made me stretch my brain having to produce and it just goes to show that no matter what or who I'm married to, I have rules to follow just like everyone else."

Michelle laughed and Janice wondered about that. There had been something, some little clue in Michelle's words, but she wasn't going to go looking for trouble. She didn't want to think that her own agent would think that she'd gotten preferential treatment because of Simon. It was true that she had, but still, she didn't want her agent thinking it. She wanted Michelle to believe in her talent, not her husband's money.

For the first time in a month she was finished with work before noon and now she felt like celebrating. She wanted to see what she'd missed in the month she'd been in exile.

She punched in the number for Simon's office. "I'm done," she began. "I have it in an envelope and ready to mail. I called Michelle to tell her. She sounded a bit odd, like there was something happening, some reason for my deadline being pulled up. What do you think?"

"About what?"

"I don't know. You know how paranoid writers can be. Do you think for some reason the publisher doesn't think I can deliver? Maybe my last book didn't do well."

"Baby, your last book was number one. What are you talking about?"

"I don't know. Forget it. Listen, I was thinking about going shopping since I've finished so early. I feel like celebrating."

"Wait for me. I'll come home and we'll celebrate together."

God, his world was caving in on him. Something would have to give or he would be buried alive under the avalanche of his lies.

❧

The two weeks in Italy were reminiscent of their honeymoon. Simon treasured each day, yet in the pit of his stomach he was aware that his house of cards would soon cave in on him. The moment they landed back in New York Simon felt the pressure. The fact that Harold was waiting for them at the mansion would have been a tip off, even if the acid churning inside of him hadn't been.

They barely had time to enter before Harold rushed toward them, gave Janice a kiss on the cheek and Simon an urgent look. "Let me talk to Harold a moment, baby," Simon said, frowning in Harold's direction. "I see business is already taking over our lives." He kissed his wife and stood for a moment watching her ascend the stairs before turning tiredly toward Harold. "Is it really that important?" he asked.

"Simon, Tommy Strong has been to the mansion. I understand from your staff that he's been trying to reach Janice. He's called and left messages for her. I'm surprised she hasn't gotten any of them. Doesn't she check her voicemail?"

Simon was silent.

"I suppose you told her not to."

"She has a new number. I told her that we were both getting new phones, that we had to protect the baby, that people would attempt to harm her or the baby because of me."

"God," Harold hissed, disgusted.

"Don't you think I know what I've done? I'm fighting for my life here. I'm thinking of moving to Italy."

"What about your in-laws? They will want to see their daughter and the baby."

"Hell, I'll bring them all over." Simon walked toward his own study. "Let it rest, Harold, I'm going to play the hand I've dealt."

Janice peeled off her clothes and headed for the shower, a bit annoyed that the moment they returned home Harold had been waiting for them with urgent business for Simon. She thought of their pact to let work wait until the morning. She glanced at the phone beside the shower and decided that if he could take care of business so could she.

"Michelle, I just wanted to let you know that I'm back." Janice waited for some word from her agent but heard a lot of throat clearing instead. "What's up," she asked, hoping to prompt a response.

"I've had several people contact me about getting a message to you. They didn't believe that I didn't know how to reach you."

That sinking feeling Janice had in the pit of her stomach was now turning into a gaping hole. She felt a burning sensation and covered her abdomen with her hand. Whether it was to protect her baby or to stop the pain she wasn't sure. She only knew she'd done it reflectively.

"Is it my book? Do I have to do major edits?" Janice asked, hoping in a way that was it. If so, the funny feeling that something was going on with her husband would go away. She could pretend that all the calls in Italy from Harold had meant nothing, that Simon's angry voice yelling at someone on the phone had had nothing to do with her. But she'd seen the way he looked at her when she'd come into the room.

She was well acquainted with guilt and something was making Simon feel guilty. Suddenly she thought of all the jewelry he'd heaped on her, and the feeling that he'd given it to her to soothe his conscience hit her in the face.

Janice tried to keep her doubts out of her voice. "Michelle, is it my book?"

"No, the editor loved it and she said there were no major flaws. There were only a couple of changes she wanted. You mixed up a time line and she wanted you to bring in one of the secondary characters a little sooner. But she said as soon as I talked to you she would fax it over and you can make the changes."

Michelle was hesitating about something. "What is it if it isn't my book?"

"AABU. They lost twenty stores across the country and there are a lot more slated to go. Someone has been buying up the leases and no one knows why. I heard there's a huge rally tonight that a lot of the African American authors that are in the New York area are planning to attend. They're trying to make a last ditch effort to save the bookstores."

There it was. A horrendous ringing began in her head. "Why are people contacting you?"

"They've tried reaching you. Your fax number was changed, so was your phone. You were holed up for a month unavailable while you wrote the book and then you went off to Italy."

"So what does that mean?"

"People are wondering if you know something about what's going on."

"Why would I know anything about it?" Janice snapped. "I've been working with Tommy Strong for months to save the stores. Why didn't anyone ask him? Why are they asking me?"

"Because Tommy said he couldn't reach you. He even went to the mansion and well...let's say...Janice, have you really not heard about any of this?"

"Any of what?"

"The bookstores, the bad press you've been getting, the innuendos about your husband."

Again Michelle paused. Janice could feel her blood boiling. "What about Simon? Every time something goes wrong are people going to blame him?"

"Listen, I'm just passing information along to you."

"Give me the information on the rally," Janice asked while reaching for a pen.

Once the information had been given, Michelle let out a breath. "Welcome home. If you give me your fax number I'll fax over copies of everything I've received."

"I'll call back."

How could Janice admit to her agent that her fax number had been changed without her permission? Sure, Simon had told her he'd done it for security reasons but was that true? Still, the idea that Simon would have been blamed for any of this was a mystery. Then she remembered the fight with Tommy. Surely Simon wouldn't be that vindictive.

Hearing Simon's voice, she walked toward the library. "Simon, I need to talk to you," she said and waited. His hand stilled on the phone and he clicked off without saying goodbye. That only served to make her chest constrict even more.

"What is it?" he asked tiredly.

"I spoke with Michelle. The bookstores are in trouble. Someone's buying up the leases. There's going to be a rally tonight. I'm going to go and help out."

"No!"

"No?"

"You agreed. I don't want you around Tommy Strong."

"Simon, grow up. This isn't about Tommy. This is about my helping to save a piece of my own heritage."

"Bull, you didn't give a damn about your heritage until Tommy Strong came back into your life."

This was crazy. Janice closed her eyes. Something was so wrong that she should have known it without talking to Michelle. And in fact she had known it for weeks.

"I'm going to the rally and I'm going to help," she stated defiantly.

"You're pregnant; you have no business getting stressed."

"My going to a rally to save the bookstores is not going to cause stress to the baby."

"I forbid it," he said through clenched teeth.

"You for-what it?" Janice said, steamed. "Who the hell do you think you are? You can't dictate to me." She walked to her husband and stood with her hands splayed on her hips. "Simon, I'm asking and I want you to tell me the truth. Did you buy up those leases on the bookstores?"

"No." Simon returned his wife's glare. What was one more lie? At least this latest lie was for a good reason. He didn't want to see the possible hatred that would be in his wife's eyes. And secondly, he'd turned over the buying of the leases to Eric to try and keep his name out of it.

"Did you know that someone was?"

"Yes, I did, and I've been trying to buy them back." At least that much was true. He turned from her to glance at some papers on his desk. He'd seen the suspicion in her eyes and heard it in her voice. He turned back to face her. "But I haven't had any luck so your going to a rally is not going to help. I don't want you to go."

"Simon, what is the number for the fax machine in my office?" Janice stared at her husband, watching while he narrowed his eyes and his gray gaze became steel.

"I don't know. Have it sent to my office."

He walked toward his office and she stood for a moment watching him. He'd made her decision. She ran back up the stairs, retrieved her purse, and ran out the door, ignoring Simon calling to her.

What have you done? Janice thought for over an hour as she drove into Manhattan and parked two blocks away from Tommy's store. *What have you done?* she said to herself again when she walked inside and saw the place filled to overflowing with black writers. Tommy glared at her as she came through the door. The reception this time was anything but friendly; it was downright cold.

"What's been happening?" Janice asked the moment she was in the room. For the longest time she thought no one was going to answer her. Deatri looked away. Wayne shook his head and Gwen looked disappointed. They were all blaming her for something. That much was obvious.

"Someone is doing a major takeover of real estate, someone with some serious cash and clout. They're buying up property left and right and every day another independent bookstore has been told they will not have their lease renewed. Now it's not even a matter of them having their rent raised; it's an all-out war. And there aren't that many people with that much cash and an axe to grind."

Donna was apparently speaking for the group. Janice looked around at all of them, her heart in her throat. But she had to know, she had to ask. "You all think Simon had something to do with this?"

No one spoke and Janice could feel the bones in her body turning into liquid. She wanted to fall down on anything and not get up.

"Simon didn't have anything to do with this," she protested. "Why would he? He knew I was helping."

"And he has an axe to grind," Donna said slowly.

"No one has been able to reach you for the last two months. Why?" Wayne asked.

"I had a book due."

"I thought your deadline was months from now."

"It was changed. I had to write the damn book. I had nothing." She looked around the room. "Surely you all understand that. What's so sinister about it? I had a deadline change. Are you going to blame that on my husband as well?"

Again no one spoke and she knew they were all thinking the same thing, that he could have easily had her deadline changed. Hell, he owned most of the major publishing companies.

"Making a call and having your deadline changed would be an easy thing for the boss of the company to do." Tommy looked directly at her.

"Simon didn't have anything to do with changing my deadline," she said, defending her husband.

"Let's get real here, Mary Jo. No one here really cares about whether or not your deadline was changed. We're talking about the bookstores and finding out who has enough money and clout to bring them all down so quickly."

As Janice looked around the room she suddenly knew why she was getting the cold shoulder. And they were right. It would have taken only a call or two from Simon and just like that the bookstores would come tumbling down like dominoes. But her heart refused to allow her to think that. Simon wouldn't go that far to keep her from Tommy. Would he?

"I don't believe any of this," she said to the group. "I trust my husband. He wouldn't do anything like this." She thought of the steady stream of gifts and glared in Tommy's direction. "His fight with you was personal. Why are you getting everyone involved in this? Don't try and make them hate Simon because you do."

"I've only stated the obvious. Mary Jo, you're not stupid. Come on, how could anyone not hear one bit of news for two months?"

"That's how I work. I cut out all association with the outside world."

"When did you finish your book?"

"A couple of weeks ago, a day before I left for Italy."

"Had you planned the trip?"

"Simon had business there and he wanted me to join him."

"What about your changing your number, no one being able to reach you?"

"We did that for security reasons, because of the baby." She looked around the room again. "I'm pregnant. We were just trying to protect our baby. Look." She attempted a laugh. "I know that this might look bad but it's not what it looks like. Come on, we can turn things around. I can help. Simon will give us what money we need. What do we do first?"

"We don't need Simon's money and we don't need you, Mary Jo. We don't want your help," Tommy said softly.

The tears quickly filled her eyes. If Tommy had glared or yelled she would have felt better, but he was looking at her as though he pitied her and that made it all the more real. "Do you all feel the same? You don't want me to help?" No one answered so she turned and walked out of the bookstore.

"You're going to owe Simon a big ass apology," Janice flung over her shoulder as she left, knowing that they wouldn't, but hoping anyway that she would be wrong.

The walk back to her car was far too long. Her chest hurt, and so did her head. She didn't want to know. She'd given Simon what she'd given no one in more than a dozen years. She should have known what was going to happen. Saying 'I love you' always led to trouble.

"You have a fax," Simon said the moment she was in the door.

Janice took the paper and looked at it. "Major edits. I just talked to Michelle. She said the editor had no problems with the book."

"Looks like your agent was wrong."

For a long moment Janice stared at Simon as the disappointment swelled in her chest. "Neither my editor or my agent has my new fax number. I don't even know it."

"It was sent on mine."

"Stop. You did this. Why, Simon?" Janice closed her eyes and shook her head. "Has this been fun for you? They all hate me, Simon, all of them, Wayne, Donna, Gwen, all of them, even Neal."

"So what?"

Janice blinked back tears. She knew what she had to do. She pushed the call button for the staff and called for luggage.

"Where the hell do you think you're going?" Simon said, coming up behind her.

"For now, to a hotel."

"You're not going anywhere. You're my wife."

"And that doesn't come with a leash. I need to think."

"You will do your thinking here." Simon felt desperate. If he could keep her in the house he stood a chance. If she left, if she went to Tommy, he might lose her forever.

Simon grasped at straws. "You can't go, you're pregnant."

"You seem to think being pregnant is a disease. I can do what I please, Simon."

"You're not leaving."

"How are you planning to stop me?"

Simon caught her arm and pulled her to him. "We made promises to each other. I'm not going to allow you to break them. I'm not going to have you running to him."

Janice sighed. "Why does everything that happens boil down to Tommy? I'm not married to Tommy. I'm married to you."

"But you wouldn't be married to me if Tommy hadn't run away like a little punk."Janice recoiled as though slapped. "I can't believe you're deliberately trying to hurt me. Why are you throwing in my face what I told you?" She moved from him.

"You're not leaving me." Simon knew the words he should be saying were 'I'm sorry.' If she would just give him a little more time.

"This isn't the way to settle an argument," Simon growled, running his fingers roughly through his hair. "You need to stay here and work this out. I'm not asking you, I'm telling you. You're not leaving this house. "

"I have to get away from you, Simon. If I don't I might forget that I love you." She turned and looked at him. "I might actually start hating you."

Simon stood there looking after her as she went upstairs. What the hell could he do? He couldn't very well restrain her. His gaze locked on the vases of flowers on various tables. He picked them up, one by one, raising them high above his head and smashing them with all of his might to the floor.

"Leave it," he yelled as several members of his staff rushed out, saw the mess and attempted to pick up.

Within minutes Janice was coming back down the stairs, a bag in her hand. She was going through with it. She was leaving him. He wanted to plead with her not to leave. If he had thought it would do any good he would have fallen on his knees to appeal to her, but he knew it wouldn't make a dent. His begging her had never worked. So he glared at her and she smiled at him as if she pitied him.

"Is this really what you want to do, Simon? You're going to act like a child now? You're throwing a temper tantrum, breaking all your toys. Go ahead, you're rich, you can always buy more." She proceeded farther down, stopped, and looked at him. "And, Simon, don't think jewelry or your money will fix things this time." She had the latest bracelet in her purse and she was taking it back. She didn't want it.

Simon was furious even though he didn't have a right to be. He was losing his wife and he was left with nothing to do but grasp at straws. "You're taking his word over mine."

"I don't need to ask him. Look at you, and look what you've done. I defended you; I didn't want it to be true."

"I don't believe you. You've had me on probation waiting for me to screw up so you could run back to him. I warned you what would happen if you did. I wasn't kidding."

Now Janice was angry. "Simon, would you get this through your thick skull? I'm not leaving you for Tommy. I'm leaving because right now I can't stand the sight of you. Get over this obsession you have with Tommy."

"When you get over your obsession with him maybe I will."

For a moment Janice stood, mouth agape, staring at her husband. He really did believe what he was saying and so far nothing she'd done had proven otherwise. She glanced at the bag she'd now lowered to the floor and knew the fact that she was leaving wasn't helping. But she had to get away for a couple of days before they both said things they would be unable to take back, before the point of no return.

"You're not fooling me. I know," Simon said pointedly.

"What do you know?" Janice turned from the door, truly puzzled.

"I know you kissed Tommy. The day that you were crying, I know you kissed him."

She could only stare before wondering if he had spies on her at all times. Maybe Neal had told him, but she didn't think so.

The look on his wife's face told him what he needed to know. It was true. She had kissed the man.

"Who told you, Simon?"

"He told me, your lover, the man you're leaving me for. He told me. He wanted me to know."

"Did you ask yourself why he wanted you to know, Simon?" She walked across the threshold and out the door. Her husband hadn't bothered to ask Tommy why he was hell-bent on destroying their relationship, but she would. This was all about a hell of a lot more than the bookstores or even Tommy trying to prove Simon's family was involved in slave trade. She knew that now. It was as she'd thought from the first day she'd worked with Tommy: His agenda was not as altruistic as he wanted everyone to believe. It was personal.

The scented bubbles were just as fragrant as those at home, the bed almost as comfortable, but seven months after being married Janice had never expected to be in a hotel room alone because she'd left her husband. She tried to ignore the tears streaming down her face.

Fighting used to be their thing. She didn't want it to be anymore. Besides all of the angry words, she'd seen the fear and the pain on Simon's face. Still, she hadn't deserved the words he'd said to her. She had done lots of things to him before they were married, but in the seven months she'd been Mrs. Kohl, she had done nothing except love him.

She wondered about his insecurity and wished she'd told him about the kiss but it was too late. Tommy had beat her to it. She had to talk to Tommy, figure out why he was trying to use her to hurt her husband. Or was he trying to use Simon to hurt her? She was sure of only one thing: Tommy was behind their trouble. Janice intended to get some answers but not tonight. Tonight she was too angry at Simon to think clearly. Tonight she might do things she didn't want to out of spite, and then her marriage would truly be over.

CHAPTER TWENTY-FOUR

Simon sat on the stairs all night, wondering what the hell had happened to him. He looked at the broken glass littering the stairs and vestibule and he cringed. He'd behaved like a madman. He'd said things to his wife that he shouldn't have. He'd seen the hurt in her eyes and still he'd been unable to stop himself. She was leaving him and he'd driven her to it. He should have never dug into his wife's past; he should have listened to Harold.

He rubbed his hands over his stubbled cheek. *What am I going to do*, he wondered. How am I going to make this right? He'd had everything he'd wanted his entire life and he'd destroyed it with his jealousy and suspicions. Simon thought of what Harold had told him, how his father had destroyed his marriage. But he and his father were different. His father had not had another man competing with him for the love of his wife.

Janice finished off every bite of breakfast she'd ordered from room service, surprised that she'd been able to eat. She'd assumed that the thought of food would make her ill.

Remembering her husband's words still did. She was going to do as she'd said and stay away for a couple of days, give him some time to get rid of some of the craziness. And she was going to see Tommy.

At ten-thirty Janice was dressed and ready to do two things: see Tommy and return the sapphire and diamond bracelet. She slipped the jeweler's box into her bag, deciding to tackle the hardest problem first. Tommy.

She prayed the entire way down on the elevator and continued praying as the doorman hailed her a cap. The talk was long overdue. She should have gotten everything out in the open with him months ago, definitely before she married Simon.

"Why did you tell him?" she said to Tommy the moment she went into the store.

"I thought he had a right to know."

"When did you tell him?"

"The day he came in here wanting us to have a private talk." He rubbed his jaw where Simon had hit him. "So I told him."

"You didn't tell him because you thought he should know. You told him to hurt him. You're using me to hurt my husband. Why?"

Tommy clamped his hand around Mary Jo's wrist and pulled her toward the private room. "Don't come in here," he growled at Neal.

Janice looked over her shoulder. She'd not known that Neal was there. She hadn't seen him and she wondered now if he'd heard them.

"Don't worry about him," Tommy snarled.

She followed along behind him, not having much choice since he was still gripping her wrist. Once inside he let her go, then locked the door.

"You want to talk, let's talk," Tommy said angrily.

"I want to know what the hell is going on with you, Tommy."

"Don't pretend to be so innocent. You know good and well what this is about."

"Tommy, I don't. Clue me in, please because this is getting crazy."

"It's about us, Mary Jo. Fate brought you back into my life. We were almost where we should be, it was right. And you ignored your feelings for me and married Simon instead. How did you think I would react to all of this?"

"It can't be about me, you could have found me long before now. You're acting as though we're a couple and I cheated on you or something."

"What about when we were together?"

"I didn't. I never did."

"How do I know that? Maybe it's true that the baby you aborted wasn't mine. That would make you a cheat." He looked at her in disgust, his glare centering on her swollen belly.

"My baby?" Janice asked softly. Her hands covering her abdomen, she moved backwards. "Why are you hating my baby?"

"Why didn't you abort this one?"

Janice closed her eyes and felt the sting of tears. "Is that what this is about? Is this the reason for your going after my husband?"

"It wasn't in the beginning. Now it just adds to the reasons that I hate him. Simon Kohl has given me enough reasons for hating him. From the moment he dug into my past I knew something was going on. People talk even when they're paid not to. They talked and every single person that his spies questioned about me told me the questions that were being asked, about you, about us, about our relationship, wanting to know who'd ended it."

"I don't like that Simon paid people to dig into our past any more than you do, but, Tommy, that isn't enough to explain everything that's happened this year. I'm sorry for Simon bringing you into this."

"He didn't bring me into this, you did."

"What do you mean, I did?"

"I saw you with him. There was no love there. You didn't even want the guy to kiss you. Then I felt the heat between us and I knew you still loved me."

Janice closed her eyes, then opened them. "I guess I did give you that impression. When I saw you I remembered how much I had loved you and how you had been the center of my life. For a moment I wished that I could go back and see if we could make it work but I was engaged to Simon."

"But you didn't love him."

"I did love him. I still love him."

"You're a liar, you didn't love the man."

"Tommy, I did. I didn't want to, that was the difference. I didn't want to trust him. You had hurt me so badly that I swore I would never love anyone again, that I would never give another person that power to hurt me. But I loved him, Tommy."

"I guess you loved him more than you loved me."

Janice looked down at her abdomen that she was still protecting. "Because of our baby?" she asked.

"You got rid of mine."

"You can't blame Simon for that. Simon and I are married."

"If you had waited for me to come back we would be married now. We would have had our baby, but you didn't give us a chance."

"We went through that. You left me all alone. I didn't do it to spite you, Tommy. I was scared. If you hadn't abandoned me, left me all alone, not even calling me…If you had told me you loved me, that things would work out…I wouldn't have felt so alone. If you had been there for me, Tommy, I would never have even thought about not having the baby. But I was all alone, too afraid to tell my parents. I didn't know what else to do. I would have wanted that baby as much as I want this one."

"But we'll never know, will we? You took that from me."

"Tommy, stop it. You're talking crazy. All of this is ancient history. If you have something else against me let's settle it so that you can stop trying to destroy my husband."

Tommy sneered. "That's the reason you're really here, isn't it? Not to make things right with me but to make sure your husband's reputation isn't damaged. My God, you really have changed. You know he's the one trying to buy up the bookstores and you're still defending him."

"Whatever Simon has done, you pushed him to it."

"Is this for real?" He grabbed her shoulders and shook her. "Are you really so money hungry that no matter what he did you'll forgive it?"

"Simon doesn't need my forgiveness on that." She paused. She'd almost told Tommy that Simon had admitted it to her. She knew in Tommy's hands it would hurt her husband and as angry as she was with Simon she wasn't giving Tommy any more ammunition to use against him.

"Even if I had left, why didn't you keep my baby?"

"Now we're back to that. This is old news, Tommy. Do you really think I wanted to do what I did? I didn't know what else to do. How many times do I have to say it? My God! I'm sick of repeating myself. I was alone. And I was scared."

"Now you're not scared?"

"Now I'm not alone," she answered, glaring at him, seeing the look in Tommy's eyes and backing up. He really was losing it and her trying to reason with him was fruitless.

"What do you think is going to happen to you now? Your name is mud with the African American community. You're a traitor, Mary Jo, a sellout. Your husband has made you that and still you stay with him, come here to me to defend him. You saw how everyone felt last night when you tried to defend him. What did you do, go home and listen to the garbage your husband told you about him not having anything to do with the bookstores?"

"As a matter of fact, I went home and confronted Simon."

"And you forgave him?" Tommy sneered.

"No, I packed a bag and left." She saw the hope that sprang into Tommy's eyes. "To give us both time to cool off. I'm not leaving my husband for good. I'm staying in a hotel for a day or two. Tomorrow I'm going home or at least in the next few days."

"Then why the hell do you keep coming back to me?"

"I'm not coming back to you, Tommy. I'm here to ask you to stop…to stop trying to hurt Simon."

"He's going to hurt you, Mary Jo."

"He already has," she said sadly. "But I'm going to forgive him the same way he forgave me for three years. Tommy, I don't understand why you're so worried about Simon hurting me. You didn't worry all the times that you did it. You think when you hurt my husband it's not hurting me?"

"Janice, what if my suspicions are correct. What if his ancestors owned slaves?"

"And if they did, Tommy, that has no bearing on Simon. He didn't do it. Let it go, please, I'm begging you."

"He wants to be black, to make up for what his family did."

Janice took yet another step away from Tommy. He was scaring her, saying crazy things out of desperation. His eyes were bulging and he was flinging his arms frantically about. Despite his desperate ploys she held out hope that she could make him see reason if she talked to him in a calm, rational voice. "I know that," Janice answered without thinking and caught the glint in Tommy's eye and rephrased herself. "I know that Simon loves black culture. There's nothing wrong with that."

"He wouldn't be trying so hard if he wasn't guilty."

"He has nothing to feel guilty for. He's done so much for the African American community that I don't understand why you're trying to crucify him."

"What he's done for the community doesn't make up for what he's done to the bookstores. And if I'm right and his family owned slaves, then that makes him just as guilty in my book."

"Even if it's true you can't fault him for what his family did. That's not Simon."

"How can you so easily shove this all aside?"

"Because I don't hold him responsible for the deeds of his ancestors."

"There has to be some dirt on the guy. No one makes that kind of money without getting dirty. How the hell do you think he got to be so rich?"

"He was born into wealth, Tommy. Even if the things you say are true, Simon has done everything he could think of to change things, things he didn't have to do because the past was not his fault."

"Not even what he did to the bookstores?"

She glared at Tommy, determined not to admit that Simon had anything to do with the stores closing. "That may be his sin, Tommy, not slave trading."

"That not true. You're his slave. He bought and paid for you."

Janice decided to ignore the cruel remarks. "Why did you tell him that we kissed?"

"Because we did. I thought he should know, I'd want to know."

"You did this to help him then?"

Tommy laughed. "I did it to let him know that no matter what he does he can never erase the fact that I had you first, that I was the first man to put a baby in your womb. And I told him that I intended to have you again."

"You...you...I don't believe you did that."

"Why? I wasn't lying. We've both known since the day of that banquet that we were going to pick up where we left off. I have no doubt we're going to eventually sleep together." He laughed again. "Your husband's really worried about that. I saw how he looked when I told him."

"That made you happy, Tommy?"

"Somewhat."

"It shouldn't. You don't know anything about Simon. He's a good man."

"If you came here to extol his virtues you came to the wrong place. Tell me something, Mary Jo. You knew what I was going to say about this, you had to. Why did you come? If this act of pretending to care about your husband is to save face, don't worry about it. You've taken the first step by moving out. Make it permanent."

"I came here because I remembered how much I loved you for four years of my life. I came because until the day you walked back into my life I had not allowed myself to feel anything, not even anger." She felt the quaking begin in her limbs and trembled as it spiraled through her.

"I wanted you to know that you don't have to attack Simon because of your anger with me. That's why I came. Seeing you again after all those years made me open myself to the truth, that I love Simon, that I had loved him all along. For that, I'm grateful to you. I wanted us to get past this. I'm sorry that I didn't wait to see if you would come back."

She sighed, knowing that she was sorry she'd not given him more time, but not sorry that her life had taken a different turn, that she was now in love with Simon. And she was, regardless of what Tommy thought.

"About our baby: I had a hard time making that decision, Tommy. Please don't hate this baby or my husband because of it. I had pain then and have had every day of my life since for making that choice."

Tommy looked down. "I will admit that I have regretted for twelve years that you thought I didn't love you. I regret that I ran off like that. But this is about Simon. I still don't believe you love him."

"That's too bad because I do."

"Yet you're living in a hotel."

"For a day or two. Then I'm going home." She sighed again. There was no use in continuing the conversation. Tommy saw what he wanted to see and none of it was true. She reached for her purse and spilled it. Watching her belongings tumble to the floor, she felt a lurch of sadness. Janice quickly picked up as many things as she could. She needed to get away from Tommy. If she left a tube of lipstick she didn't care.

"Tommy, if you ever loved me like you say you did, please stop trying to destroy my marriage." She practically ran out of the door.

Tommy stood staring after Mary Jo, wishing he could make her understand he wasn't doing what he was doing out of anger. If he didn't believe there was something left between them he'd let go, he'd forgive her. Hell, he'd even admit to the jealousy that gnawed at him. Why shouldn't he be jealous? She was going to give to another man what she'd taken from him.

He couldn't get over the fact that she was having Simon's baby. Tommy looked up as Neal came into the room. "I thought I asked you not to bother me."

"I didn't come in while she was here but, man, maybe we should lighten up on her. She was crying when she left here. It's not good for her baby for her to be so stressed out."

Glaring would have to suffice. If Tommy spoke to Neal now, that would be the end of their friendship. He didn't give a damn about the baby Mary Jo was carrying. It wasn't his.

"There's something under the table," Neal said.

Tommy bent to retrieve the velvet jewelry box. He opened the cover and took the bracelet out and held it up for inspection.

"Wow," Neal whistled, coming closer to examine the bracelet. "That's some serious bling-bling. Is it Janice's?"

"It's Mary Jo's, yes. Before you give me that suspicious look, she dropped her purse. I didn't lift the damn thing; you saw it under the table." Tommy turned the bracelet over again and examined it, smiling as he did so. "I wonder how much I would get for this."

"Aren't you going to give it back to her?"

"Sure. I was kidding. I'll make sure to return it. Matter of fact, I think I'll leave and do it now. Do you think you can handle things here for the afternoon?"

Without waiting for an answer Tommy left the store laughing. After all, it wasn't as if Neal could very well say no. Tommy was the boss.

"What?" Simon barked into the phone. All day long he'd been in a bad temper. All day his secretary had buzzed him even though he'd told the man he didn't want to be bothered.

"There's a Mr. Tommy Strong to see you. He said he had an appointment with you."

Simon growled low in his throat. "Send him in," he said, rising from his chair, not believing the man had the gall to come to his office.

"What the hell do you want?" Simon asked.

Tommy smiled. "I came to give you something that might belong to you." He smirked and pulled a pair of panties from his jeans pocket—a pair of panties he'd stopped in a boutique to buy.

He brought the panties to his nose and sniffled. "Too bad you didn't believe me before," he said. "You could have saved yourself a lot of trouble." He sniffed the brand new panties again. "I'm sure you recognize your wife's scent." He closed his eyes for a moment, then opened them.

"You dirty filthy liar!" Simon lunged at Tommy as fury cold as a winter's snow raked over him.

"You think so?" Tommy laughed. This time he reached into his other pocket and brought his hand out, dangling the sapphire and diamond bracelet in front of Simon, stopping Simon in his tracks. "I guess you need to repair the clasp. It fell off in my bed." Tommy laughed and threw the bracelet to Simon before he turned on his heel and walked away.

It hadn't felt as good as he'd thought it would. The man had turned a ghastly shade of white and for a moment Tommy had thought he was going to have a stroke or a heart attack. He looked back and saw Simon standing in the same position he'd left him in. Simon's eyes came up and Tommy saw the pain."

Join the club, he thought as he walked away. Simon Kohl wasn't the only one hurting. If Janice couldn't realize on her own that she belonged with him, then he had no choice but to show her. He pushed away the pain in Simon Kohl's eyes. He knew all too well how it felt to have someone ram a sword through your heart.

Simon clutched the bracelet in his hand. He'd been about to slam his fist into Tommy's face for lying about his

Wife, and then he'd shown him the bracelet. There was only one way he could have gotten it and that was from Janice. He clenched and unclenched his fists, willing the pain that had gathered in his chest to go away.

Simon didn't know how long he stood in the middle of his office like that. He only knew when he moved that he was going to keep another promise he'd made to his wife. He'd warned her not to sleep with another man; he'd made it perfectly clear. She'd chosen to leave him. Disgust for her actions filled him. How could she do that while she was pregnant with his child? "*Is it yours?*" a little voice said. And Simon raked every item off his desk in one massive sweep of his arm. When several employees ran in, he screamed at them to get out and slammed the door.

He was feeling clear about what he was going to do. He made several calls, then looked again at the bracelet and made several more.

Janice turned on the news, wondering if she should call Simon, surprised that he'd not called her to apologize, to ask her to come home. No matter, she would return home tomorrow. She would make her husband understand if she had to get a hammer and pound him over the head with it. Suddenly what the news anchor was saying broke into her thoughts.

Publisher William J. Davis has acknowledged that the buzz around town is true. They are severing ties with several of their writers who have used ghostwriters. New York Times *best-selling writer Janice Lace is one of those authors.*

According to him, they will be seeking a return of the two million dollar advance for Janice Lace's last contract, due in part to missed deadlines. Janice Lace, for those of you who don't know, recently married billionaire Simon Kohl. This reporter doesn't think having to return an advance, even a two million dollar one, will send Janice Lace AKA Mrs. Kohl to the poorhouse.

Stunned wasn't the word, for Janice's reaction. She was almost paralyzed with outrage. She reached for the phone and dialed Michelle.

"Did you see the news tonight?"

"I saw it."

"What the hell's happening? What is that about? You know it's not true. I have never missed a deadline."

"I know that."

"Then why are they saying it?" When Michelle remained silent, Janice knew. "Is it true about the advance? Did they ask for the advance back?" she asked, knowing that she didn't have money sitting around in a bank. It was invested, Simon had invested it all. "Oh God, no! Simon, what have you done?" she moaned.

"What?"

Janice had almost forgotten that her agent was on the phone. "Never mind," she said. "I'll call you when I straighten this out, if I ever do." She hung up the phone and screamed in frustration.

She had one more call to make. Shaking in fury, she hit the programmed number. "Simon, what have you done?" she asked.

"Just exactly what I told you I would do. I warned you and you wouldn't listen."

"Warned me about what?" she screamed.

"I warned you not to go, not to leave me for him, not to sleep with Tommy and you didn't listen."

"I didn't go to Tommy. Simon, stop talking crazy. I'm staying at the Edwardian."

"You haven't been with Tommy?"

"No."

"Then how the hell did he get your bracelet? Magic?" Then he slammed the phone down.

Janice hopped off the bed and ran to her purse. No jeweler's case. It didn't take an Einstein to figure that it had fallen out with all of her things and she hadn't seen it. And it also wouldn't take much figuring to know that Tommy had taken it to Simon. So much for Tommy not using her to hurt her husband.

Janice sat on the bed cradling a pillow against her chest, rocking her body. She'd had good reason to leave home, at least she'd thought so at the time. Her intention had been to give them a chance to cool off, to not do anything that couldn't be undone.

Well, this couldn't be undone. Simon was gearing up for battle just when she'd lost interest in fighting.

"You've gone too far. You're destroying her career. How is she supposed to continue writing with this kind of slander."

"Too far?" Simon glared at Harold. "I've only just begun. I warned her."

"She's your wife, man. For God's sake, how can you do this?"

"Easily." Simon snapped his fingers. "That's all that it took."

"Why are you doing this?"

"She slept with Tommy Strong."

"How do you know this?"

"He came here to rub it in my face."

"Simon, how do you know it's true? Did you give her a chance to defend herself?"

"Why? She's been lying to me this entire time. She didn't admit kissing him until I cornered her. Do you think she's going to admit to sleeping with him?"

"The man hates you, he could be lying."

"He gave me proof."

Harold paled, thinking Simon had pictures or a tape showing his wife committing adultery. "He filmed her?" he asked disgustedly.

"No, he gave me her bracelet."

"Her bracelet." Harold frowned. "How the hell does jewelry prove that she slept with him?"

"She was with him," Simon yelled. "She was with him and she lied to me about it. Why did she feel compelled to lie if she wasn't guilty?"

Harold ran a hand over his face, feeling tired and old, feeling as though he was reliving a part of his life best left dead. He crossed the room and slumped into a chair. "Talk to her, give her a chance to explain. Stop what you're doing before it's too late."

"It's already too late."

Harold looked at Simon and saw Simon's father saying those exact words. He'd didn't want to see Simon self-destruct but in sixty years he still hadn't learned how to stop a man hell-bent on destruction.

"It's evident that she loves you. Anyone can see it. She's expecting your child. What are you going to do about that?"

"What if it's not mine?"

"You're traveling down a very dangerous road, Simon, one that you may not be able to turn from. What is it with the men in your family? Why this need to find a way to destroy your happiness? You've dumped one burden and picked up another. Don't you think it's time to stop?"

"I can't. And I wouldn't if I could. She left me!"

"And I don't blame her," Harold said, softly rubbing his face. "You started this mess, Simon. You went looking for trouble and you found it. You've had me fooled all of these years. I thought all you needed was a woman that you loved, a woman that loved you and everything would be better for you. Now I see it won't, you can't be happy."

"How the hell could I be happy wondering each day if that would be the day she'd stop loving me?" Simon answered, allowing the pain he felt to surface in his words. "It's over. I don't have to wonder any longer."

"You think she doesn't love you any longer?"

"How could she? If she loved me she wouldn't have left. She wouldn't have gone to him." Simon stopped, closing his eyes in pain.

"It's done, Harold. I'm doing what I told her I would do."

"Simon," Harold whispered softly, coming to stand in front of the man he had loved like a son from the moment he was born, "are you telling me that you don't love your wife?"

"I'm telling you I'm going to do what I need to do. I told her that she didn't want me for an enemy. She didn't listen."

"Simon, I'm begging you. Stop this nonsense before it's too late."

"Like I said, it's already too late, unless you have a time machine and can go back and erase the past."

"It's not the past that needs to be erased, Simon, it's the present. What you do now is on your head, not your ancestors', not Tommy Strong's and not your wife's. Just remember, what you do to her, you do to your child."

Damn Harold for always being so reasonable. Why couldn't he ever see his side of things? He'd warned Janice. Why shouldn't he carry out his threat? *Because she's your wife, moron, because she's pregnant with your baby, because you would be worse than a rotten bastard to destroy her career.* Simon listened to the voice of his conscience and sighed, knowing that destroying her career would make him worse than a rotten bastard, it would be unforgivable. A shiver ran down his spine as he thought how he'd crushed his enemies in the past.

"There's one more reason that I can't destroy her career," he said aloud. "I love her." *She is my Achilles heel, the line I can't cross,* he thought, and picked up the phone.

"Janice, are you ready to come home?" he asked.

"You're incredible. Do you know that you are totally unbelievable? You try to ruin my career and now you think I'm going to just come home."

"I was wrong in that. There will be a retraction."

"There shouldn't be a retraction because you should have never said those things. This is my career you're messing with. You've crossed the line."

"I'm admitting to crossing the line on that. But if you don't come home in the next twenty-four hours I hope you plan to pay for that suite because I'm pulling the plug on that. If you're leaving me, I won't finance it. And if that makes me a bastard, oh well. You can always come home." *I want you home*, he thought, but didn't dare say.

"You are a bastard, Simon." Janice yelled as loud as she could. "I have money. I don't need yours. Do you understand? And you'd better be telling the truth this time. I'd better see a retraction in the paper and on the news or you're going to live to regret it.

"I'd advise you not to issue any more threats. I called you to apologize."

"Funny, I didn't hear an apology, only another ultimatum."

"Come home, Janice, this isn't doing you, me, or the baby any good."

"You should have thought about that before I left," Janice answered and slammed the phone down in his ear.

For a moment Simon stared at the phone. He twisted his mouth to the side. He'd gone too far trying to damage her reputation. That much he knew and had known from the instant he'd done it. He'd also known that his call to her was only going to make her dig her heels in and remain at the hotel. But she couldn't do that, not without money. He'd meant it. He wanted her home. He picked up the phone again and dialed the hotel manager.

"Listen," he said, after giving rapid fire orders, "you will not give reports on this to Harold, is that clear?" He waited for an answer. "I want my wife home." He issued his remaining orders, then was about to hang up when another pang of conscience struck him. "If she needs me it's your job to let me know. Do you understand?"

Assurance that his orders would be followed allowed Simon to breathe easier. Janice wasn't his enemy, she was his wife. A wife he very much wanted to return home. And even if he was going for the jugular he had to make sure that she and the baby would be protected at all cost.

Sighing, Simon dialed again. "Harold," he said when the phone was answered, "I have something very important I need you to do. Janice is still at the Edwardian, she's not budging. I need you to watch out for her."

"I won't spy on her."

"I want her home, Harold. I'm not trying to hurt her."

"Then what are you doing?"

"I just want to teach her a lesson."

"Simon?"

“”If she needs anything…if she needs me, let me know.”

“Simon,” Harold called his name softly, “what is it that you really want?”

“I want you to make sure Janice is protected.”

“She needs to be protected from you.”

“I know.”

“Why don’t you stop all of this nonsense?”

“I’m trying. I had Davis give a retraction to the media saying Janice’s name was mistakenly put on the list. I called Janice and apologized. Then I told her to come home.”

“Told her?”

“Harold, for once, can’t you let go of my word choices?”

“No, you’re making mistake after mistake.”

“Just take care of my wife. Okay? Protect her at all costs, even from me.”

“Simon, you continue this and her family, your new family that you wanted so badly, will be lost to you. Let this go.”

A long sigh escaped Simon’s lips. “I’ve spent two hours on the phone doing damage control with her family. They called wanting to know what was going on, why we were separated.”

“And?”

“And I assured them when we were done with our war we would visit them again.”

“This isn’t a war. It’s a fight between a husband and wife. You need to go to her on your hands and knees and beg her to forgive you. You’re the one that’s turning this into a war. This isn't a game, Simon. You're going to destroy your life and hers if you're not careful."

"That's why you're going to look out for her, to make sure that doesn't happen. You're going to protect her."

"Who's going to protect you, Simon?"

A long moment of silence passed between then. Then it was Harold who sighed, the sound as defeated as he felt. "What are you planning on doing next?"

"I plan on getting her to come home where she belongs. She has the power to end this, Harold. She has only to come home."

Janice's supposed two days from home to give her and her husband cooling off time had slowly turned into two weeks. She couldn't believe it. In the beginning Janice fought to understand her husband's motivation. Now she was just plain angry and she intended to get back at him, only she had found no way. Her family was driving her crazy with their constant calls for updates, giving her advice on how to handle the situation. She could strangle Simon for that alone.

But she had to do something. Hiding in a hotel room was not the answer and besides, she'd run out of clothes and had been forced to call one of the upscale stores to deliver her some outfits sight unseen.

A knock sounded on the door and she went to answer, wondering who it was. The only people who'd knocked in the past two days were room service and housekeeping.

Janice was surprised to see the manager standing there looking embarrassed. She opened the door wider, permitting the man to come into the room, curious what had brought him to the penthouse.

"Mrs. Kohl, your husband called and asked me to deliver a message to you personally."

Janice felt the baby kick and a lump formed in her throat as she waited for another hammer to fall. She didn't know how much more she could take of this.

"Your husband said your bills are no longer being paid by him. He said to tell you if you want to live in a penthouse then you should pay for it."

Janice's face flamed with embarrassment. She had not thought that Simon would do this but wondered why it had not occurred to her. He had warned her. She calculated quickly the money she had in her checking account and knew it wasn't nearly enough to cover the cost. She couldn't pay the man, at least not yet. She had money, but it was just invested.

"Don't worry," she bluffed. "I can pay my own bills."

"Good." The manger smiled uneasily. "There is a bill for thirty-two thousand dollars. Would you like to write me a check for it or give me your charge card?" He coughed. "I'm sorry to have to get in the middle of this but if you choose to use a card it can't be a joint one. Your husband said to tell you that he's cut you off all of the accounts."

Tears quickly filled her eyes and spilled down her face and she wiped them away. She wasn't crying to gain the manager's sympathy but out of frustration. She didn't have thirty-two thousand in her checking or savings, nowhere near that. Three thousand was more like it.

"When do I need to pay it?"

"Tonight would be fine...but we need to make sure you can continue paying." He hesitated. "We could move you to a smaller room if that would make it easier."

"Thank you," she answered. "That won't be necessary."

Damn, she thought the moment the door was closed. She should have thought of that. But in the past few years with Simon they'd never stayed anywhere but in a penthouse suite. She should have anticipated his move. Well, she wasn't out yet; she had millions of her own in the market. She would sell.

Janice smiled for the first time in two weeks. If her husband wanted to play dirty, she would accommodate. She searched for Harold's number and called him.

"Harold, I need to sell some stocks. I need money fast."

"I need to talk to you, Janice."

She shut her eyes as she felt her spirit retreating from her body. Janice could feel the suction as it attempted to leave. *My baby*, she thought and fought to come back, not wanting to, knowing that Harold wouldn't need to talk to her unless it were bad news.

Harold was calling her name "Janice. Janice, are you okay?"

"No, I'm not okay," she answered. "Why do you need to talk to me? What has my husband done now?"

"I would prefer to talk to you in person if you don't mind. I won't take up much of your time."

"Sure, come on over. You know where I am, I assume."

"Of course," Harold answered. "Listen, it might take me a couple of hours to come. Is there anything I can get for you, anything that you need?"

"Yeah, bring me a psychic. I need someone to tell me how all of this got started and how it will end."

Harold marched down the hall to Simon's office and barged in. "Your wife called me. She wants me to cash in some stocks for her. She sounds pretty desperate."

"She should," Simon answered. "The manager told her she has to cough up the money for the bill. I'm not paying it."

"You know, Simon, I never thought the day would come when I would say these words to you, but you're being a real bastard."

"Like father like son."

"Like hell. I pulled Janice's account and saw that she's flat broke. That wasn't the case a short while ago. Before the two of you married she asked me about her funds, and I checked. They were fine. Now she's broke. What the hell have you done with her money? I know you didn't dump millions of dollars into a stock that was already crashing. You're much too shrewd for that. And you can't be angry enough to see her destitute. Where is she supposed to go?"

"If she's ready to tell me what a liar she is, she can come home," Simon said, "on her knees."

"I have never been more disappointed with you than I am at this very moment."

"Then keep watching, the show is only going to get better." Simon turned from Harold and looked out the window over the city.

"Spill it," Janice said softly. "I know you have bad news. Tell me how bad."

"You're broke."

"Broke? Broke?" She fell into a chair. "How can I be? You mean there's nothing left, nothing? I have to pay the Edwardian thirty-two thousand dollars by tonight. I have at the most three thousand dollars in my checking account. What am I supposed to do for money?"

She didn't know. Simon had never told her. Harold stared at Janice for a moment, then decided on his course of action. He smiled, knowing what he would do. It wouldn't be a betrayal to Simon. After all, he'd been ordered to protect Janice.

"When you married Simon, he transferred half of everything he owns to you. There are separate accounts that are not in his name. I can arrange for you to draw from those funds."

"Did Simon tell you to tell me that?"

"No."

"I don't want his money, Harold. I know what you thought. I know what I said, but it was never true. I never wanted him for his money."

In spite of his anger and disgust with his godson, Harold heaved a sigh of relief. Mary Jo Adams Kohl, AKA

Janice Lace, had just gone up another notch or two in his estimation.

"I'll take care of your hotel bill personally, don't worry," he offered.

"I told you I don't want to use Simon's money."

"This is my money. I'll take care of your bill."

Janice saw the rare smile that lit the man's face and grasped his hand in hers. "I'll get a regular room and I'll pay you back as soon as I straighten this mess out. I promise."

"Don't worry about it." He sucked on his lips before continuing. "Simon said to tell you that you can come home."

"Oh he did, did he? I don't think it will be quite that easy."

For a long moment the two were silent. Then Harold asked, "Do you still love him?"

"Of course I still love him," Janice answered without hesitation. "I want to kill him but I still love him. I miss him like crazy and I've been trying to figure out just what went wrong, how much is my fault, what I can fix. But it's as though I'm paralyzed. Every day I think, okay, I can do something. I can call him. Then he does something else."

Janice got up and walked around the room before going to stand in front of Harold. "I don't know what to do anymore. I don't know why he couldn't just allow me to explain what happened, how Tommy ended up with my bracelet. I know what he thinks. I would be a fool if I didn't. He thinks I slept with Tommy but I didn't. I have never cheated on Simon, not once."

She saw the look of doubt in Harold's eyes and shook her head. "I see he told you about the kiss. That I can't explain. You know I had a history with Tommy so we don't have to pretend. We were working together and remembering the past. Actually we were fighting and it just happened. We both agreed it meant nothing and I saw no reason to tell Simon. He was acting crazy enough already."

"Yes, I know." Harold smiled at her. "Listen, I don't want to invade your privacy but I am curious about one thing if you don't mind answering."

"I don't mind," Janice said.

"The bracelet Simon bought for you, how did Tommy get it?"

"I went to see him. I was going to take the bracelet back to the jeweler after I left there. I dropped my purse and the bracelet must have fallen out."

Harold was shaking his head. "Just as I figured, a reasonable explanation. Why did you go to see him in the first place?"

"I went to ask him why he was trying to hurt my husband. I asked him to stop."

"I gather he said no."

Janice couldn't believe it, but she actually laughed. "He definitely told me no."

"Why didn't you just come home then?"

"I was still angry with Simon; he was acting like a tyrant, trying to boss me around."

"Were you afraid of him?"

Taken aback for a moment Janice halted. "Are you asking if I thought he would hit me?"

"Yes, I guess I am."

"Simon wouldn't hit me."

"After everything he's done to you, you still believe that?"

"He loves me, Harold."

"The things he's done to you recently aren't the things that a person would expect from someone who loves them."

"He's so afraid and I understand that, only I don't know exactly what he's afraid of. There is something deeper going on and he's never told me."

"So what are you going to do? Are you going home?"

"You know I can't go home like this."

"Tell me something. Why aren't you fighting back? Why are you letting Simon walk all over you? Why are you acting like a doormat?"

The words were the same, only the speaker was different. In the past her mother had asked her that very thing about Tommy. She'd never fought with Tommy. Maybe she'd been afraid to lose him. Maybe that's why she wasn't fighting with Simon now. Only she was already losing him.

"Harold, Simon's a billionaire. How am I supposed to fight him?"

"You never allowed that to bother you before and if I'm not mistaken you were happier. So was Simon. Now you're both miserable. Maybe you should start fighting again."

Janice thought about what Harold was saying, the things she'd been saying to herself for the past two weeks. "We started our relationship out fighting, both of us, and neither of us ever conceded defeat. It kept us even. I know it sounds crazy but that was us, that has always been us. Now I don't have any weapons to fight him with. He's too rich and powerful for me to be able to do anything to hurt him."

"Are you looking to hurt him?"

"I don't know what I'm looking for." She smiled. "Yes, I do. I'm looking to save my marriage by any means necessary. For some crazy reason for us that includes fighting, only I can't think of a way to fight him now."

"You do have a weapon."

"What?"

Harold rubbed his chin. "That's not for me to tell you. I'm glad that the two of you don't get physical. No man should abuse his wife, especially his pregnant wife. No matter how rich, it would make a man downright uncomfortable to be accused of it. Even if nothing came of it, he would get a good dose of his own medicine."

Janice jumped from her chair with more energy than she'd had in a week. She lunged toward Harold and kissed him, hugging him so tightly that he was gasping for breath. He patted her arm. "Thank you," she said.

"For what?" he said with a sly smile. "I didn't do anything."

"Harold, if you'd like to spring a little more money for lunch I'd love it if you stayed and had lunch with me and talked with me for awhile. I haven't really talked with anyone for two weeks. I'm getting a little lonely."

"So even a crusty, stuffy old man will do for company?"

"You're neither." She headed for the phone, took his lunch order and sat back down.

"What secret is Simon holding? Why is he so obsessed with Tommy?"

"It's not Tommy he's obsessed with, it's fidelity."

"Why, Harold? I don't understand. He told me he's never had a serious relationship, that he's never been in love before me." She licked her lips, hoping he hadn't lied to her. "Did someone break his heart?"

"Yes."

"Oh," Janice mumbled, feeling the pain deep in her chest.

"It was his parents who broke his heart." Harold sighed, not knowing if telling Janice would help her to save her marriage or not, but she needed to know about the demons that drove the man they both loved.

"Simon's father married his mother and never told her of the family legacy. He tried the same thing Simon did with you, to hide it. Lies, lies and more lies until, as it always happens, the truth came out. She was hurt because she thought he didn't trust her, didn't consider her to be an equal partner. She loved him madly and he was too foolish to see it."

"What happened?"

"Because he couldn't forgive his ancestors, he assumed she couldn't. So he started sleeping around, anything to avoid confronting what he thought was his wife's disgust, her hatred. She tried repeatedly to tell him that she loved him, to show him, but he didn't believe it. After awhile she started sleeping around too.

"Eventually she became pregnant and for a short time things calmed down, but his doubts eventually got the best of him and he tried losing himself in any reckless thing he could think to do. Unlike Simon, he didn't work hard at the business. He left the running of it to me. Mostly he just remained content to spend the proceeds. And his wife dwindled right before my eyes into a pale version of the beauty she'd been. All she wanted was to make her husband love her, see her as he once had."

"Simon knew about their cheating?"

"Yes, he knew. Neither of them hid it."

"What happened to him? Did they love him?"

"Maybe in their own way. They just never bothered to show him, either of them. They were too busy trying to outdo each other. Simon was forgotten."

"Are you telling me that this is what Simon and I are doing? That we're heading down the same path."

"You are. I just hope you two don't do to your child what was done to Simon. Money is no substitute for love. Remember that."

"Harold, why weren't you ever married?" Janice wanted to get the conversation away from her own problems. Besides, she was curious. "Why didn't you ever have children of your own? Weren't you ever in love?"

For a long moment he stared at her and then she knew. Harold had been in love with Simon's mother.

"You were in love with her, weren't you?"

Now it was Harold's turn to look astonished. "She loved her husband," he answered as the pain filled his voice. "He was the only man she ever loved."

"That wasn't my question. You loved her, that's why you never married. She was your one true love. That's why you never had children of your own." All of a sudden, a buzzing filled her head as she pieced the puzzle together. "You can tell me to go to hell, but please, I hope you don't. Did the two of you have an affair?"

"One night," Harold admitted, "that was all, one night. She didn't love me. She slept with me because she was lonely and she knew that I worshipped her. She loved her husband and she regretted that she'd allowed me to touch her, even for that one night."

"But you said she fooled around."

"She did, but none of the men meant anything to her, none of them loved her. I think it made it easier on her."

"So, why did she regret sleeping with you?"

"I had always been a good friend to her, to both of them. She knew our betrayal would destroy her husband. She couldn't bring herself to break his heart no matter what he was doing. She made an earnest effort to give her marriage another try. It wasn't until a year or two after Simon's birth that she no longer cared about her affairs."

"When did she get pregnant?"

Harold's eyes narrowed. "Don't go there, Janice. I've never ventured down that path."

"Don't you see that if it were true Simon wouldn't have to bear the burden anymore? "

"Do you think that hasn't occurred to me? His parents gave him nothing when they were alive except money. The one thing he wanted more than anything was love. He got that from me. Simon trusts me. No matter how angry he may get with me, he trusts me to be honest with him."

"But..."

"No buts. Do you want to take that from him? I'm his constant. I've been his constant his entire life. His father...his father," he said, ignoring Janice's raised brow, "made me his godfather. Simon has had enough hurt to last him several lifetimes. He's lived with his parents' faults and even if he doesn't like the legacy, he knows who he is. Do you think I would ever try to take that away from him?"

"Don't you want to know?"

"What difference would it make? I couldn't love him more than I do. It would only hurt Simon. And I will never be the one to hurt him."

"But you've told me how."

He frowned at her. "If I thought for a moment that you would hurt him with this information, the things Simon has done thus far would seem like child's play."

"Another warning?" Janice asked.

"Another promise."

"Rest easy then, Harold. I love my husband. I want to save my marriage."

"Good answer," Harold said, kissing her cheek as he rose to get the door. "Now let's enjoy lunch. This is a first for us."

"It is a first." Janice sat across from the old man and marveled at his love for Simon. He'd gone an entire lifetime not finding out if Simon was his son for fear of hurting him and in mentioning spousal abuse he'd given her the weapon with which to fight. Simon understood her fighting. For some crazy reason they both reveled in it. Now she knew what to do. She was determined her marriage would not end with a whimper. If it ended, then it would end with a bang.

CHAPTER TWENTY-FIVE

Harold walked back into the office, smiling at no one in particular. He put his feet up on his desk and waited. He knew Simon Kohl so well. He knew he was dying to know what had happened. This time Harold would make Simon come to him.

It didn't take long for him to get his wish. He heard the heavy footsteps on the thick oak flooring seconds before he heard Simon's voice. He braced himself and waited.

"Well, is she coming home?"

"I don't think so."

"Why the hell not?"

"She didn't like your offer."

"How does she plan to pay the hotel bill?"

"She isn't. I took care of the bill and I told them to charge whatever she needs to me."

Simon's mouth dropped open. "Why did you do that? Are you crazy?"

"I'm not crazy, which is exactly why I did it. Your wife is six months pregnant and I will not see her on the street. If that is your choice, it isn't mine. Besides, you told me to protect her."

He watched while Simon paced angrily around the room, tearing his finger through his hair. "What did she say?"

"She said she loves you."

"Why are those words so easy for her to say now? I waited forever to hear her tell me and now she says it to anyone. I don't get it."

"Maybe you don't have to get it. Maybe you just have to accept it, maybe you should just ask for her forgiveness and forgive her for whatever you think she may have done."

"I can't forgive her. She slept with Tommy."

"She didn't, Simon. She told me she didn't. It was just as I thought. Janice dropped her bracelet there and Tommy brought it to you to bait you."

"I don't believe her. She always loved Tommy. I forced her to love me."

"God, man, wake up! You can't force anyone to love you. You forced her to acknowledge her feelings for you, but you didn't force her to love you. You have to get over that. If you're trying to repeat your parents' life you're doing a damn good job of it."

"Well, my father never had to compete with another man for my mother's love. She slept around strictly for the sex. He never had to worry whether he was my father. He told me she didn't start until way after I was born. So as you can see, Harold, there's a lot of difference between my father and me."

Harold pulled his feet from his desk, closed his eyes, and thought of his conversation with Janice. Simon had no idea how closely his life paralleled his parents'. He hoped Janice would find a way to make him believe in her love. Hell, he hoped when the two of them were done with their mud fight that she still loved him. Simon needed her in his life more than he was willing to admit. He was being a stubborn child, so afraid that he couldn't have the one thing that would make his life complete that he was ruining things himself to ensure that no one else would.

Janice took a deep breath. She remembered a couple of movies where the woman had framed the man for abuse. But in both movies the woman had injured herself. Janice wasn't into inflicting physical pain on herself. How was she going to frame Simon?

She pushed in the number that would connect her with her husband. She hadn't called him in over two weeks. What if she were wrong? Maybe he wouldn't give a damn. Maybe he wouldn't even come. She held her breath and waited and at the sound of his voice the tears came and they weren't fake. Must be her hormones. Thank God for them, she needed them right now.

"Hello," Simon bellowed.

"Simon, there's something wrong. I don't know what. I'm scared," Janice whispered and began to cry in earnest.

"I'll call your doctor."

"No, Simon, I just need you."

"Hold on, baby, I'm coming."

She hung up the phone. He did give a damn and she'd put her plan into motion. She wondered for a moment if she could just let it go when he got there, just go into his arms and tell him she was sorry. But that wasn't the way war was waged. War was waged to win. She had to win her husband's respect to save the two of them.

"Something's wrong with Janice or the baby," Simon said to Harold as he ran out of Harold's office. "I'll call you later and tell you what's going on."

Harold watched his godson run from the room, then crossed to the window and watched Simon climb into his waiting limo, glad that he wasn't driving himself. Harold didn't want him having an accident.

At least Janice had gotten her stubborn husband to do something that Harold had been unable to do. She'd made him come to her. That was proof that he loved her still. God help both of them. No one else could ever put up with them.

Janice lay on the bed waiting, wondering if she was making a mistake, wondering if it would backfire on her. Her hands were sweaty and her pulse was racing. When her phone rang she knew without a doubt it would be her husband.

"Baby, are you sure you don't want me to call an ambulance?"

It was Simon's worried voice and it made fresh tears come. "No," she answered. "I only want you; I'll be okay until you get here." Janice sobbed in earnest. Her words to her husband were true, she did want him, but just admitting that to him was not the way to go. She had to play this out.

"Don't try to talk. Keep your phone open so I can hear you, okay?"

"Okay," she whispered and lay on the bed sobbing, knowing her husband could hear her, knowing she was crying for them.

It was killing Simon to listen to Janice cry. He'd not expected tears from her. She always fought back. He was surprised that she hadn't. He was feeling like a heel, a foolish heel, a foolish, jealous, suspicious heel.

It seemed to take forever for the chauffeur to get him to the hotel and finally when he arrived, he burst out of the car and raced toward the elevator, praying that his wife and child would be safe. "Open the door," he said into the cell phone. "Baby, open the door, I'm here."

Janice heard him and got up and opened the door. Then she locked it behind him, ignoring the curious look in Simon's eyes.

"What's wrong?" he said coming to her, holding her close to his heart. His heart was beating so fast. It had been way too long since he'd held his wife, since he'd touched her. "Baby, I'm so sorry, I've been such a fool." He forced himself to gently push her away in order to examine her. He turned her this way and that. She looked up at him, smiled and moved a step away and his heart melted from her smile.

She stared at her husband thinking how good it had felt to be in his arms. She missed him, but if she went home now it would be on his terms. She had to even the playing field before she returned home. Suddenly, Janice screamed as loud as she could and Simon fell back alarmed

With more speed than she knew she had, Janice begin flinging crystals bowls and vases across the room, breaking glass after glass. She picked up the phone, dialed the front desk and screamed for help while throwing more glass to the floor.

Simon stood back, stunned, as his wife seemed to be going through some kind of fit. He watched as she tore at her hair, her clothes, and then it hit him. He was being set up. He laughed. So she was fighting back.

He sat in a chair to watch, ducking the flying glass and admiring what she was doing, surprised that she'd not thought of it sooner.

In a matter of minutes keys were being shoved in the lock. Janice looked at him, smiled, and slid to the floor a millisecond before the manager rushed in, saw her there, and reached for the phone to call the police.

Simon didn't protest. Why would he? There was a pregnant woman lying on the floor, the room was destroyed, and he was the only other person in the room.

Several more employees rushed into the room, grabbing wet towels to revive an acting Janice. By the time the police arrived, the place was pure pandemonium and she was crying for all she was worth, her eyes red and bloodshot, her wild mane of hair even wilder because of her tearing her hands through it. She wore torn clothing and there were even red marks on her face, though he knew he sure as hell hadn't touched her.

Without asking him a question, the officer roughly pushed his hands behind his back and handcuffed him a little too tightly, probably anxious to make a big arrest, happy to have bagged a billionaire.

Paramedics arrived and he watched while the men gently lifted his wife, his unhurt wife, from the floor and placed her on the stretcher to take her to the hospital for observation.

Simon was ready for the hordes of cameras that greeted them when they came out the door. He saw his chauffeur coming toward him and shook his head. There was no reason to get his employee involved. He saw Janice crying as the cameras were aimed in her face. "He didn't do anything," he heard her moan. "It was all a misunderstanding."

She was very good Simon had to admit, very thorough. She wasn't filing false charges. It didn't matter that she was going to the hospital and he was going to jail. They would both be released in a matter of hours.

Simon accepted the rough shove of the officer pushing him into the car. Hell, if he had really hit his wife he would deserve the rough treatment. He glanced out of the window of the squad car toward his wife. He'd gotten to hold her and she'd held him in return and he'd felt her tremble against him. She was safe and their baby was safe. That was all that was important, nothing else mattered.

Janice could only pray that what she was doing would not boomerang. Simon knew what she was doing. She'd seen the gleam of respect in his eyes as he became aware of her plan. And he'd made no move to protest, offering only, "No comment," to the paparazzi.

She'd have to admit that it felt good fighting with him again. And it felt good that he was getting a taste of his own medicine. Let him see how all that bad press, true or not, hurt you. Janice wasn't foolish enough to think that with the money he had they would keep him for long, and she wasn't going to be foolish enough to file false charges.

When she had been meticulously checked out and it was determined that neither she nor her baby was at risk, she was released. When the officer who had remained at the hospital with her asked if she wanted him to drive her back to the hotel, she said yes.

The penthouse had been cleansed of all broken glass. The manager was so apologetic that she actually thought he was going to cry. The room was filled with fresh fruit and flowers and she was told that the next week the bill would be comped. She argued that it wouldn't be necessary, feeling guilty for the lie she'd told. But the manager wouldn't hear of it. "Thank you," she murmured. "I don't think I'll be here too much longer. And she didn't think she would be.

Simon stayed in jail several hours longer than he thought he would. His wife being pregnant was one of the reasons. The hatred policemen held for wife beaters even filtered to the prisoners. Simon could hear the murmuring. When he was finally released, he said a silent thank you.

When he returned home, Harold was waiting. "Is she home?" he asked.

"No, she went back to the hotel."

Simon looked away. He'd thought Janice would at least move back home and get a restraining order and make him have to be the one to stay in the hotel. He was a little disappointed. "I thought she was going to have me kicked out."

"So did I," Harold agreed. "Looks like she only wants to take your war so far. I guess she loves you too much to take you down to the mat."

"Have you ever thought that she set this up to look like I abused her not because she loves me but because she's angry, that she's just pissed?"

"She has a right to be pissed." Harold narrowed his eyes. "I thought this was your thing, the fighting. The two of you have always seemed to get off on that."

"Then why isn't she home?"

"Maybe because you haven't asked her to come home."

For a moment Simon stared at Harold as though he had two heads and then he called his wife. "I want you home. It's time to end all of this childish nonsense. You're not going to win so you may as well admit it and come home."

"Go to hell, Simon," Janice answered and slammed the phone in his ear.

"What did she say?"

"She told me to go to hell," Simon said. "Now we know why she fought back. She did it because she was pissed. I gave her a chance to end this."

"You did not, you ordered her." Now Harold was shouting, appalled. "You are out of your mind! Did you really think she was going to come home because you ordered her?"

"Do you want more proof that she did nothing out of her love for me?" Simon shook his head sadly, looking at Harold and wishing he could believe as Harold believed, but he didn't, he couldn't. He dialed again.

"If you're not downstairs in an hour, your friend Tommy's bookstore will be history. Do I make myself clear?"

"Simon, stop this," Janice said. "You don't want to do that."

"I'm serious. Don't push me."

"You have no idea what you're doing, do you?"

"Oh yes, I have an idea. Now I suggest you pack your bag and get your ass downstairs. I'm coming for you."

"What are you looking at?" Simon asked Harold, who had a horrified look on his face.

"Do you really believe that this is the way to get your wife back?"

"Let's see if she's there. I'll bet you a million dollars that she will be there waiting for me."

"Why?"

"Because of Tommy."

"You think she'll come because she wants to save Tommy Strong's bookstore?"

"Yes. That will bring her home, not her love for me."

"How do you know? You haven't given her a chance."

"I gave her a chance, I told her to get her ass home."

Harold shook his head. *Unbelievable*, he thought. "Simon, why the hell do you fight so hard to make your life a mess? For God's sake, man, if she's waiting for you, tell her you love her."

"No. If she's waiting for me, it won't be because she loves me, but because she wants to protect another man."

"Could it be she doesn't want any more innocent people getting involved in your war?"

"I think she'd move so fast only for one man."

"So we're back to where this all began. We've come full circle. Your obsession with her past has led you to this moment. You weren't content until you dug him up. Now you're not going to be content until she actually sleeps with the man. Will that make you happy, when you finally see that you're right? When you drive her into another man's arms, who will you blame? Her or yourself?"

Harold turned and left the mansion, shaking his head in sadness as he watched Simon climb into his limo and drive away to collect his wife. A part of him prayed that she wasn't downstairs. But he knew she would be, and it wasn't because of her love for Tommy, but her love for Simon. She wouldn't want anyone hating him any more than they already did. The only thing wrong with that was that Simon wouldn't see it that way.

Janice threw the last of her belongings in her bag and wheeled it to the elevator. "I'm checking out," she said to the manager when she stopped at the front desk.

"You don't have to, Mrs. Kohl. Where are you going?"

"I'm going home," she said softly. "My husband will be here for me soon."

"Are you sure?" he asked.

"I'm sure. Don't worry, I'll be alright."

"Mrs. Kohl...."

"Don't worry." She smiled. "I know what I'm doing."

But she didn't. Truth be told, she had no idea what she was doing and now more than ever she wished that she did. Simon had taken their war too far and he'd pushed her farther than she cared to be pushed. Janice was truly angry now and as she saw the limo pull to a stop rage filled her. Perhaps if Simon had gotten out of the car some of her rage would have dissipated, but he didn't. It was his chauffeur who got out, opened the door and took the bag from her. She stepped into the limo, glared at Simon and waited.

Simon smiled, though it didn't reach his eyes. "Tonight we resume being man and wife. We will not have a marriage in name only, you can make odds on that."

Janice moved to the other side of the limo as far from her husband as she could get, anger at him and herself making her shake. They were making a real mess of this.

"I hate you," she hissed.

"Tell me something I don't know," he answered.

When they reached the mansion, Janice jumped out before either the chauffeur or Simon could open the door.

She burst through the doors of the mansion and ran up the stairs as fast as a six months pregnant woman could. She ran to her room and attempted to close the door in Simon's face but he'd taken the stairs two at a time and had his foot and hand in the door she was trying desperately to close.

"Move away from the door," he said quietly. "I have no plans on hurting you but you're not locking me out of my own bedroom."

"Then I'll sleep elsewhere," she muttered and turned away.

Simon came in and closed the door firmly and turned to her with measured precision. "No one's changing rooms. We're married." Then he sat on the divan and stared at her.

He brought her bracelet from his pocket and held it up. "Your Mr. Strong brought me this."

Janice remained silent.

"He brought me something else. He brought me your panties, with your scent," he whispered raggedly.

"Did the two of you have a panties sniffing contest?"

He was waiting for her to deny it, to do anything but mock him. For the first time since he'd fallen in love with her he wished he'd followed the original rules, that he had remained uninvolved, kept their relationship uncomplicated. He stared at her. Now it was too late. It was as if he'd been dealt a hand and now he had to play it out. He loved his wife and he was killing any love she'd ever had for him. But he seemed unable to stop himself.

"How many times have you slept with him?"

"I didn't keep count."

Pain so intense filled his chest that for a moment all he could do was close his eyes. When it passed he came to her. "Do you think this is a joke? Do you think you can stay away for two weeks screwing him and just come back and play the wounded little woman?"

"Don't you listen to anything that I tell you? I didn't sleep with Tommy, Simon. I haven't slept with anyone for," she counted, "for the last four years but you. What am I going to have to do to make you get over this? Maybe if I actually sleep with Tommy this ghost that has been riding your shoulders can vanish. Maybe then you'll know that it's not the end of the world."

"It would be the end of us."

"And you think this isn't? Do you really think this is what a marriage is supposed to be?"

"I wasn't the one who left home."

"I was coming back."

"Then why didn't you?" He ignored the look in her eyes. "I know why you came home, because I threatened to take your lover's store. And because you ran out of funds. Tell me something, if you'd had the money to pay the bills, would you have bought him another store?"

Janice was trying to find a way back but she was slowly losing her patience. Her husband was pushing her toward being downright bitchy and she didn't want to go there.

She glared at him, thinking how true the saying was that there's a thin line between love and hate. She now found herself tottering on the line. "Simon, I'm going to tell you this once more. I have never cheated on you."

"Not even when you kissed him?"

"Why don't you get the firing squad ready for that one? Ooh, I kissed another man. Maybe you should have that printed up in the paper." At the look on Simon's face she scooted back on the bed. He hated her too.

"Do you want a divorce?" he asked.

Her mouth felt suddenly dry. *Oh God*, she thought and moaned silently. "Simon, stop," she said. "You're making a mistake."

He'd already made the mistake. He looked down at his wife, knowing that his dream was still a dream. "After the baby is born if you want to go to him you can. I'll make sure you have all of your money; everything that I took I will give back. Just leave me with the baby and you can have whatever you want."

Fear filled Janice's heart and laced her voice. She couldn't believe what Simon was purposing. She had to make him say the words. "What are you saying, Simon?"

"I'm saying that if you leave the baby with me, you can start over and I'll make sure you're taken care of. I won't try and stop you from seeing the baby. You can have visiting privileges."

"You expect me to leave my baby?"

"If you want your freedom you have no other choice."

"You're going to give me back all my money?" she asked, not wanting to admit how much this was killing her, "Every dime?" she asked.

"Every dime."

"And my royalties?"

"Those too," he said, looking at her.

"What about the advance that Davis wants back? Will you repay him?"

"You won't have to worry about that." *Why wasn't she saying no, that she didn't want a divorce?* Simon swallowed. "I'll have the papers drawn up," he started but she interrupted.

"Are you going to put in there that you're buying the baby?"

"I'm not. . . ." She was glaring at him with such hatred that it froze him. "I just want to keep the baby." He wanted to tell her that he wanted to keep a part of her, but her hatred stopped him. "That wasn't what I said. I said I wanted custody."

"You're asking me to sell you a child."

The muscle in his jaw twitched. "I asked as your husband for you to give me custody of my child."

"And you're willing to give me my freedom. I can buy that from you with the birth of a child." Janice stood to face him and tried to stop the trembling but she couldn't. It ran from the top of her body to the bottom. "The apple really doesn't fall far from the tree, does it, Simon? Once a slave master always one." She watched as the color drained from his face and his eyes filled with pain.

"You've made my decision for me, Simon. I want out of this marriage and I don't want you hurting anyone that I choose to be with. Tommy was right when he said you tried to buy him. Now you're buying our child."

"Janice, that wasn't what I meant and you damn well know it."

"Yes, it is, Simon. You're an important and intelligent man. You're well educated. Suppose you tell me the meaning of slavery. You won't give me my freedom unless I sell you someone to replace me, a child." She smirked as she saw the pain intensify on his face, distorting his features. He closed his eyes and she watched.

"I love you," Simon said over the lump in his throat, knowing that it was too little too late. Once again Harold had been right. He should have told her he loved her the moment she was in the limo. Hell, he should never have done any of the things he'd done in the last year, including finding Tommy Strong. He bit his lip. "I do love you."

"No, you want to possess me. You want to own me and since you can't own me without a fight, you want a child, another possession. You're a real bastard, Simon but I'm a bitch because I'm going to take you up on your offer."

"Why are you making this so hard? You know that's not what I meant."

"You keep telling me that I know what you mean. I only know what I see, what I hear. You had this fixation on who I slept with, even before we got married. Why is that so damn important to you? It's my body, Simon. You don't own it or me."

Janice was angry now and saying things just to hurt him. She'd not expected him to ask for a divorce and the thought of leaving him was killing her. She glared at him. "I think I've figured it out: The slave master doesn't want his property sleeping with the other slaves. That has to be the reason you're so damn worried about me sleeping with Tommy."

She watched as he blanched even more. Janice opened her mouth to spew out more vile things and stopped as she looked at Simon. Her words had hit his heart. His pain became so palpable she could feel it. She'd gone too far. "I'm sorry, Simon, I didn't mean that," Janice said, wishing she could pull the ugly words back, wishing her plan had worked. It had only made things worse.

"Yes, you did," he said sadly. "Yes, you did."

"I didn't. I was just trying to hurt you. I don't hold your family's past against you. I don't think of you that way. Please listen," she said softly, not wanting it to end this way, not with all of the vileness between them.

"Simon, I just wanted to hurt you and I knew that would. Hurting you is an old habit with me. You hurt me and I struck back. I want to stop the need to see you in pain. It's killing you and it's killing me. Maybe I do need to leave," she said, crying and not bothering to wipe away the tears.

She knew he hadn't heard her but her baby kicked in her belly and she rubbed it, comforting her unborn child.

"I'm tired of fighting," Simon said softly. "It's not doing the baby any good and it's not helping us. You're pregnant, you don't need this." He sighed and took a deep breath. "I never started out to hurt you." He stopped speaking and stared at her for a moment, then smiled, a sad little smile.

"That's a lie, isn't it; I did want to hurt you. I wanted to force you to love me. You're right. I am what I am. Don't worry," he said, and walked toward the door. "How could I expect you to truly love me with my past between us?"

"But I do love you, Simon," she said without hesitating. "I do love you. As much as I hate you right now, I still love you."

"Then why would you agree to divorce me? You could have said no," he said, preparing to leave the room.

"Simon, I didn't sleep with Tommy." Janice wanted to try at least once more to make her husband look past his doubts.

"After everything that's happened do you expect me to believe that?"

"Believe what you want to. When have I had the time to have an affair with anyone? Simon, with the exception of the time I spent at the hotel I've been swamped with work. I stayed locked up here for over a month getting that damn book done and then we went to Italy. Please tell me when I slept with Tommy or anyone else other than you? Can't we please stop fighting about this?"

Simon looked down at her, a great sadness filling his chest. "I agree we shouldn't keep fighting, but I can't get the picture of you making love with him out of my mind."

"The picture should have never been there to begin with. It never happened." Janice fell silent. "Maybe your wanting a divorce is the right thing," she whispered and closed her eyes, hoping God would give her the inspiration to know what it would take in order for her husband to let go of his delusions.

Simon stared down at his sleeping wife. Her hair was wild and loose and covering her pillow. He couldn't stop himself from wanting to touch her. His eyes dropped to her rounded belly. He'd screwed everything up, he thought as he allowed his hand to touch her. He ran the tips of his fingers around the outline of her belly., felt the baby kick inside her, and his resolve vanished. He pulled his sleeping wife into his arms and pressed his body against her, holding her close to him. He shook with his emotions and tears ran down his cheeks.

"Simon."

"Shh, just let me hold you," he whispered. "I just need to hold you."

Janice was awake now. She started to move, to not give him the comfort that he sought but she hesitated a second and she felt the heat of his tears as they spilled on her shoulders.

They'd spent so much time hurting each other. Her throat closed up with her own pain and tears seeped beneath her lashes. Instead of pushing her husband away, she lay where she was, trembling in his arms, feeling his pain with every fiber of her being.

It swirled around and through her and she recognized it. For the first time in over twelve years, Janice became Mary Jo Adams again in spirit. She allowed herself to go back to the day that she'd changed her life. If she had not made a decision to have an abortion twelve years before, Tommy wouldn't have hated her, she wouldn't have hated him. And there would have been no need for Simon to root around in her past. He would not have worried about her carrying a torch for an old flame. The secret she'd kept buried for so long was part of the reason she couldn't convince her husband that she loved him. If she had not worked so hard to keep Tommy buried, Simon would not have worked so hard to find him. If he had not thought she loved Tommy he could believe she loved him. Her hidden secret was in part responsible for the shambles her marriage was in. She and Simon had made a mess of loving each other.

She cried in her husband's arms as she hadn't allowed herself to cry then. She cried over the pain of the procedure. And she cried over what she knew in her soul had been so very wrong for her. She cried for Tommy, admitting for the first time that he had a right to his anger. She'd cheated him out of his right to have a say. At last with this baby kicking in her belly, she cried for the baby whom she'd aborted, only it was years too late and there wasn't a damn thing she could do about it.

But she could do something about Simon. She was determined to find a way to make him believe, to erase the damage their years of fighting had done. She loved her husband and their baby and there was no way on earth she was giving either of them up. Maybe it would take Simon believing the worst thing he feared had happened to make him see that she and he were not his parents, they could be happy. It had taken a lifetime to understand that she didn't have to continue reliving her pain. Now she had to find a way to make her husband join her.

She didn't know how long she lay in her husband's arms sobbing, only that when she woke the next morning she no longer hated her husband. She felt cleansed, as though a great weight had been lifted off her shoulder.

"I don't want to fight any more, Simon," she said into the quietness, knowing he was still awake.

"Neither do I."

"You know, they say babies can feel the emotions of their parents and they react to it. I want our baby to hear something other than the two of us snipping at each other. We still have to take the Lamaze classes and I'd rather we not fight while we're taking them." She was holding out an olive branch and praying her husband would take it.

He looked down, not answering.

"Simon."

"Are you sure you want me with you?"

"I need you with me."

His eyes met her. "If you need me I'll be there. I'll always be there when you need me even if—"

Seeing doubt cloud Simon's eyes, Janice's hand moved across her belly as she attempted to soothe the movements of her baby. "Simon, if I told you this was Tommy's baby, would it make you feel better? Should I tell you that I have been carrying on an affair with him since the moment you forced him back into my life?" She pulled away from him and stared at her husband as the sadness of what they'd done to each other filled her anew.

"I love you, baby. I also know love isn't always enough and I wish that it was. I know I've made a mess of our lives and we have nothing left. I had such hope for us, for the family we'd have together." Simon sighed, and shook his head. "I wish I didn't know about my family. Maybe then it would be easier. But I do love you."

Janice remained silent. For weeks she would have given anything just to hear her husband tell her that he loved her. But this seemed to be love based on some unfounded guilt. That she didn't want.

"I don't want you loving me because you want to make up for what your ancestors did. I've told you honestly that there is no need. I was being a bitch when I used that against you. But I can't be the salve that soothes your conscience."

"So you're going to go to Tommy after you have the baby?"

Janice sighed again before deciding to answer. "How did you ever get so far in business without listening?" Then she went down to her office to write. It would never be published but the writing was cathartic.

For the next few months Janice and Simon called a sort of truce. Together they went to the Lamaze classes and Simon was with her for all doctor visits. They even shopped together for the baby. On several occasions they found themselves having fun until one of them would stare at the other and an invisible veil would fall. But in bed together, when the lights were out, they behaved as man and wife, making love as they lay next to each other. Whether out of need or out of love they didn't know.

Janice woke and lay on her side of the bed for awhile with her back to Simon. She could feel his eyes boring a hole in her back. She faced him, thinking he would at least speak but he didn't. He just continued to stare until she could take it no longer. He'd been staring at her for twenty minutes, not speaking, just staring, and it was driving her crazy. "Simon, why are you staring at me?" Janice finally asked. "Is there something on your mind?"

"I want to ask you something. And I was hoping I could ask without your biting my head off."

She'd have to admit that this was progress. "Sure, go ahead and ask me. I promise I won't bite your head off."

"When you met me, what were you looking for? What was missing from your life?"

"I was looking for a needle."

"Come again?"

"I was looking for a needle in a haystack."

"Excuse me?"

Janice laughed softly. "Simon, I was looking for the impossible. I'd allowed too many things to get in the way of my living. I was looking for something to make me feel, to make me bleed. Maybe even someone who would bleed for me." She sat there watching as Simon got up from the bed, marched out and came back in a few seconds.

"You should have told me what you wanted." He held a needle in front of her face before bringing it down to prick his finger. "I bleed red blood, Janice," he whispered, and then he pricked her finger. "And so do you." He pressed his finger to hers and looked down into her eyes. "We don't have to keep trying to hurt each other. We both know we can and do hurt. We both have baggage."

"Can you let go of yours?" Janice asked.

"I've been trying," Simon said, looking her in the eye, "and it's hard. I'll admit that much. I do love you. I never knew that I was obsessively jealous but I am. I hate the fact that I allow Tommy to get to me. I hate knowing that you have more of a history with him than you do with me. And I hate thinking that you might be remembering him now and the baby you aborted." He stared at her for a nanosecond seeing the pain in her eyes but wanting to continue. "I hate thinking that you might be having my baby out of guilt for what you'd done in the past."

"Are you insane? I'm having our baby because I love you, Simon, because I trusted that you loved me, that you wouldn't hurt me. I trusted you enough to tell you a secret that had torn me apart for twelve years. I told you of my pain because I trusted that you wouldn't use it against me." She pulled in a breath. "If you believe what you've just said…that you could even say it…makes me think I was wrong to have trusted you."

❧

"Mrs. Kohl, there's someone here to see you. He says it's urgent."

Janice looked up from her computer and blinked. No one ever interrupted her while she was writing. "Who is it?"

"Mr. Strong. He said it's imperative that he see you. He's waiting in the den."

Janice wondered what Tommy wanted. What would be so important that he would come to the mansion? She glanced at the clock, hoping whatever it was wouldn't take long. All she needed was for Simon to come home and find Tommy there.

A contraction hit her on the way to the den and took her almost to her knees. She'd been in labor now for the past three hours. She believed her water had broken but she wasn't sure. She just knew that she'd found herself wet and fluid running down her legs. Embarrassed, she'd cleaned up the floor, showered and put on a pad and sat down to wait.

She'd heard how long first babies took to come and she was determined to not sit in a hospital room for hours doing nothing. So she'd started writing again on the book Simon had thought was autobiographical. And now in a way it was.

Janice had begun printing up her work each day and leaving it out so that Simon could read it. He never said that he had and she never asked but she knew that he was reading it and believing it. And with it she believed she'd found the way to mend her husband's heart. They would both have to go through the fire and come out on the other end. Halfway measures would not be enough. He needed to believe, truly believe, that there was nothing left. She had to do this to save them.

Janice bit into her balled fist to keep from screaming out with the pain. She wiped the perspiration from her face and walked toward the den. "Tommy, what's going on?" she asked in as calm a voice as she could with the pain still riding her spine.

"I brought you proof."

"Proof of what?" she asked, reaching for the paper he was holding out to her.

"Proof that your husband engineered the bad press against you, that he was behind the entire thing. I even have proof that he was involved with closing up the bookstores."

"Tommy, I know that already." She laughed harshly. "Do you really think I'm that naïve?"

"Then why are you still here?"

Janice looked down at her belly, wondering if all men were dense.

"I can take care of you and the baby. You can divorce him. I'll be the father."

"Only if it's yours." Simon said and both Janice and Tommy turned around.

"There is that possibility," Tommy muttered angrily and Janice glared at him.

"Leave, Tommy," she said moving between him and Simon. "No more fighting. You two have done enough."

She pushed Tommy toward the door with one hand and placed her body in front of Simon. When Tommy was out of the door she looked at her husband. His eyes were filled with pain, so much pain, and it was happening too often. There was no need for such pain but he wouldn't see beyond anything that he believed to be true.

"Simon."

"Will you at least have the decency to wait until after the divorce?"

"You jackass," Janice screamed. "You stupid, stupid jackass. Do you really think sex is on my mind right now? If I want to screw Tommy, it's my body. You can't give me permission." She stopped screaming as the pain gathered momentum in the small of her back.

Simon ignored her and glanced at the scattered papers on the floor that Janice had dropped while trying to keep him and Tommy separated. "What is all of that?" he asked, seeing his name scrawled on one of the papers.

"That's Tommy's proof of the things you've done."

"So this is what you're going to use to divorce me."

Janice opened her mouth and screamed as loud as she could. "God, you make me so angry, Simon, that I could easily hate you. If that's what you're after, keep talking and you'll get your wish." She glared at her husband, wanting to slug him and wanting to hug him to take away the sting of her vicious remark. But that wouldn't undo the damage. Besides, she was pissed. She leaned over, trying to hold on until she gave her stubborn and foolish husband a piece of her mind.

"Every time I think there's hope for you, you do something even crazier. I'm in the middle of labor, you jackass! Do you really think I've been thinking about screwing Tommy? Get over it. The moment that I push this baby out I'm going to do what you've been afraid of. I'll sleep with Tommy since you seem to think I'm doing it anyway."

She dropped to her knees and screamed out, feeling the contractions coming stronger and faster, hoping her plan to wait wasn't another wrong choice. She wanted to deliver the baby in a hospital with doctors. She wanted numbing drugs, mind-numbing drugs.

Simon was by her side but she pushed him away with one hand while she clung to the chair with the other.

"Baby, we need to get you to the hospital," he said as he reached for her.

"Leave me alone," Janice screamed. "I don't want you with me. I don't want you anywhere near me." She moaned aloud with the pain and dropped even lower as another contraction ripped through her body, making her spine feel as though it was on fire. She felt Simon's arms going around her and in spite of the pain she dug her nails into his arms. "Don't touch me," she moaned, her voice filled with pain.

"Shut up," Simon answered as he lifted her into his arms and yelled for the staff to bring the limo around. He carried her to the car, sat with her in his lap and cradled her against his chest, ignoring her protests, soothing her. His heart was pounding in his chest. He felt guilty for making her upset, guilty for her pain.

"Stop fighting me, it's not good for the baby."

"I don't want this baby," Janice screamed. "And I don't want you," she hissed between contractions.

He was trying to ignore her and her evil words, knowing that she wanted to hurt him. Well, she was doing it. And damn it, she had every right. He'd done everything to make her hate him. And now he had what he'd sowed. His wife was about to give birth and she was screaming that she didn't want him or the baby. He'd heard that a woman's hormones made her say horrible things to her husband during this time, but he didn't recall anyone ever saying that women said it with the intensity that his wife was.

It seemed to Simon that it was taking forever to get to the hospital. Maybe it was due in part to his wife trying her best to move away, not allow him to touch her, while he was trying like hell to hold her on his lap. He was determined that she wouldn't shut him out of this experience. Still, he was relieved when at last they made it to the hospital and the chauffeur ran inside and came back with a nurse and a wheelchair for Janice.

Within a few minutes the nurse was wheeling her to the birthing room, Simon's presence having cut through all of the paperwork. Simon walked beside his wife, stroking her arm and attempting to offer words of comfort.

"I don't want you in there," Janice hissed, pushing his hand off her.

He stepped in front of the wheelchair, narrowed his eyes, and gave the nurse a cold stare. "Give me a moment with my wife," he instructed. Then he turned to Janice, who was still glaring at him with brown fire in her eyes.

"Why don't you want me with you?" he asked. "We took Lamaze classes together. I'm your coach, you need me."

"I don't need you, Simon, and I don't want you."

"I'm coming in."

"No," she hissed. "I'll tell the doctor to keep you out."

"You can't do that and neither can your doctor. I have rights."

Janice looked at her husband and remembered Tommy telling her he had rights. She hadn't liked it much then either. "You don't have rights if I don't want you in there, and I don't."

"The father has a right to be there," Simon said, trying to reason with her.

"Then maybe you should call Tommy. He's the father, not you." She watched as the blood drained from his face for the second time that night and he staggered back. She saw the pain that moved through him, crowded in on him and she saw the tears fill his eyes. Then the nurse returned and whisked her away. For that Janice was grateful. Once again she'd gone too far. She was wrong. She knew it but then a horrible contraction hit her more intensely than any of the others and her regret was lost in her screams. She hadn't expected this. She'd gone through an abortion without a sound. This, she had thought, was going to be a breeze; it wasn't.

She felt her tears running down her face. This pain was different. She wanted Simon with her as much as she didn't want him there. She didn't want to go alone through this a second time.

Ten minutes later the room filled with people and preparations began in earnest. Then Simon came into the room and she saw his face. His eyes were still pain-filled and she winced inwardly that she'd been the one to put the pain there. Still, some residual anger filled her and she glared at him, wishing she could stop

It made her angry that he had believed her. He came to the head of the bed and she hissed, "What the hell are you doing here? I told you to leave; I told you it's not yours." She saw her doctor's head poke up but Janice ignored her.

Simon leaned down and whispered in her ear so no one could hear. "You know, I finally agree with Tommy about one thing. You can be a real bitch when you want to." Then he sighed. "I'm here because I love you and I don't want you to go through this alone. Like I told you before, I'm not Tommy, and regardless of whose baby it is, I will be here for you. I'm not leaving, so get that through your pretty stubborn head. I'm here to stay."

"Leave, Simon," Janice screamed, pummeling him with her fists. "I don't want you with me."

"Mr. Kohl, you're upsetting her. Maybe it would be best if you—"

"I am not going anyplace." Simon looked at the doctor. "You worry about delivering the baby, I'll worry about my wife." He turned back to Janice. "You're not going to win this. You need me and I'm going to be here for you. I will always be there when you need me no matter where you are. Remember that." His heart constricted with pain. He'd messed things up for them, but for this he could be there. He would not leave no matter what vile things she had to say.

Janice looked at him, attempting to glare, but the pain of another contraction hit and she grabbed for Simon's hand and squeezed, screaming out. In the mist of the pain she heard his voice, soft, reassuring and strong. She forced herself to listen to his words of encouragement. She gained strength from hearing him tell her over and over that he loved her, that he wasn't going anywhere.

And she squeezed his hand harder for all the pain they'd caused each other, for she knew it wasn't over.

Something terrible had happened between them. The trust had not just been broken, but destroyed and it would take something equally as drastic to repair the damage.

She traveled backwards in time, remembering her fear and abject loneliness years earlier and her total emptiness when the procedure was over. As pain pushed her farther, she begged for forgiveness for what she'd done twelve years before and what she was doing to Simon. This should be a time of joy for them in spite of the pain. She wanted that memory for the both of them.

Janice opened her eyes and looked at Simon through her tears and saw the tears that were coursing down her husband's cheeks. She reached up to wipe the tears and he gripped her hand, kissed it and held on. And when the next contraction hit, and the next, they were not nearly as bad as they had been. And she knew the reason why. Simon was there for her. He was attempting to take her pain into his body, to shield her with his love and for that she was grateful.

One final push and she knew it was the last.

"You have a son," the doctor said excitedly. Simon looked down at her and smiled. "Thank you," he said, "thank you." And he placed a soft kiss on her lips. He clung to her hand and she smiled for the first time in hours.

"Go see your son, Simon," Janice urged. "You've waited a long time for this."

"You don't mind?"

"I don't mind," she said, squeezing his hand and releasing it so he could go and see the miracle they had created despite their fights. She listened to the squalling of the baby and thanked God. Her heart was full. And she prayed for one more thing as Simon brought their son to her. Janice prayed for God to show her a way to banish all of the ghosts.

She needed something permanent, something that would prove to Simon that she loved him. She needed to make him understand that it wasn't Tommy that she wanted. She needed him to know that they could both let go of their past. But first she had to get him to acknowledge his fears. Her words alone had failed to carry the power, at least her spoken words. She was praying that her written words would have more of an impact.

For the past several hours Janice had been happy. She had been watching Simon hold their baby. He'd barely let her hold him for a moment. But when she had, she had breathed in his newborn scent, touched his hair and looked into his silver blue eyes, eyes that she knew were the duplicate of his daddy's. Simon had smiled at both of them while her heart melted with love for him.

"What are we going to name him?" she asked.

"I like Mack if you don't mind."

"Is that a family name?" Janice bit her lip at the look that came into Simon's eyes. *No*, he wouldn't give their baby a family name.

"No, but I'm thinking if anyone ever says to him, 'Hey Mack,' that will actually be his name. What do you think?"

"I like it."

A soft knock sounded and a nurse came and instead of going to Janice or the baby she went to Simon. Simon opened his mouth without being asked, his eyes focused on her, and she pulled her lips into her mouth, biting down softly, knowing the pain in their relationship wasn't over. She held Simon's gaze as he opened the mouth of their son for the nurse to swipe. The nurse headed for her and she opened her mouth, not saying a word. No one spoke until the nurse left the room.

"You're not going to use the baby as a weapon against me. I'm not waiting twelve years to find out if he's mine or not. This will be one thing we will not fight about. I don't plan on playing this out in my head. I'm going to know. I'm going to have proof."

Janice still didn't answer. What could she say to a man who was holding the spitting image of himself in his arms? *Maybe it was for the best,* she thought. She'd done enough to give him room for doubt. She should be grateful that he'd know the truth but what she felt was hurt that he thought he needed to do it. Then she thought of his parentage and knew it was the right thing.

"Congratulations, Simon, that's a beautiful baby you have there. He looks exactly like you."

"I'm not going on looks," Simon said. "I'm waiting for DNA results."

Harold rubbed his eyes. "When will the two of you end this?"

"She wants a divorce."

"What the hell are you talking about? Did Janice ask you for a divorce?"

"No, I asked her if she wanted one and she told me yes." Simon sighed and looked down at the baby in his arms. "She's going back to Tommy."

"Simon, did she tell you that?"

"She didn't have to. Why else would she leave me?"

"Because you asked her if she wanted a divorce, man. What was she supposed to do?" Simon stared at his son. Janice had made him soft and Baby Mack had turned him into mush. He couldn't run a business being mush. He sighed. "This was my destiny." He smiled sadly at Harold. "I tried to break a curse that couldn't be broken."

"Bull," Harold retorted. "An unhappy marriage is not a curse; a marriage is what the two people involved make of it. You love her, why are you letting her leave?"

"It takes two people to make a marriage work."

"And you think she doesn't want to make it work?"

Simon shook his head slightly, smiling down at his son when he held his finger. "We've made so many mistakes. We've hurt each other so much. The last few months, all we've done is fight."

"What the hell do you mean, the last few months? That's all you've done throughout your entire relationship."

"It's different now. Since Mack was born we haven't fought, but before, even our fighting had changed. It wasn't the same. She wouldn't look at me. She'd fight back but it...it just wasn't...it wasn't us. There was no making up after, no touching and I can't live with her and not touch her. I can't lie in the same bed with her and not make love to her."

"Then damn it, sleep in another room until you can repair your marriage."

"I would repair it if I knew how. Maybe it's best this way," he said and smiled again at his son. At least he would have Mack. He thought of the DNA test, wondering what he would do if they said Mack wasn't his. His heart lurched in his chest for a moment and his son's ice blue eyes stared back at him. Mack was his son and it didn't matter what a test said. He wasn't giving him up.

Janice stood outside Simon's study listening to him talk to Harold. She hadn't intended to eavesdrop but there she was. So Simon still thought she was leaving. She almost smiled to herself. The man was nuts if he truly thought she was leaving him. And he was downright insane if he thought she was leaving her son.

She wondered if he thought she didn't miss his touch. At least before she gave birth to Mack, they'd fulfilled their needs. Now they didn't have that. She had to wait for six weeks.

She walked backwards a few paces, then retraced her steps, making noise so the men would know she was coming. She went inside the room and stared for a moment at Simon holding his son. There was something else she had to do. She had to apologize to Tommy.

For a dozen years she'd truly thought she'd had the right to make the decision all on her own to have an abortion, that it was her body, her call. Now she knew it wasn't all on her. She'd robbed Tommy of this joy that Simon was experiencing. It had been only on seeing Simon at the birth of his son that she had realized it. And as each day passed she realized it more. She'd always thought she was the only person with a reason to be angry. Tommy had a reason.

"Hi, Harold," Janice said. She turned her gaze toward Simon and smiled at him. Her heart ached for them. She saw him blink and then she walked toward him. "I need to feed Mack," she said, taking the baby from him. She held Simon's gaze allowing him to see the hunger in her eyes. The feel of his fingers on her skin caused a tightening in her womb as the electricity shot through her.

For a moment she couldn't breathe and then Mack gurgled and she averted her attention from her husband and looked at the baby. She brought Mack upwards with one fluid motion, loving the soft baby feel of him. She sighed deeply. "I'll see you both later," she murmured. and walked away.

"If a woman who doesn't love you looks at you that way, I wonder what would happen when a woman who loves you looks at you. I felt the heat from over here."

Simon felt the hunger in his body. His loins tightened and he looked toward the door. "It's been weeks. She has needs same as I do."

"Simon, are you serious? Do you really think the way your wife was looking at you has more to do with the physical and not her trying to tell you that she loves you?"

Simon didn't answer; he just kept staring at the door. He thought of all the things he'd done in…it was four years. In a couple of weeks they would be celebrating their first anniversary as man and wife, only he didn't know if celebrating was the right word. He licked his lips. He really did believe his wife was his soul mate. He didn't blame her for wanting to leave him. He'd done too many things for her to continue loving him. One day she would stop. Maybe it would be better for the two of them to end it while they loved each other. He'd hate to put Mack through the same things he'd gone through as a child.

At the sound of voices Simon and Harold turned toward the open door and Simon groaned aloud, then sighed, blowing the aftermath of his frustration out through his mouth.

"What's wrong?" Harold asked. "I thought you liked your in-laws."

"I do. But I haven't seen them since…since I was arrested for spousal abuse."

"Haven't you talked with them?"

"Talk wouldn't be the word I'd use. I've listened as I've been scolded, questioned and given unsolicited advice." Simon glanced at Harold, giving him a wry smile. "I think I might have even received a thinly veiled threat or two from her brothers."

Suppressing a grin Harold asked, "Didn't any of them ask for your side of the story?"

"What the hell was I going to say?"

"Maybe that you didn't do it."

Simon rolled his eyes. "But I did everything else. Besides, if my wife hates me..." He paused again. "Let's go, old man. I'm not hiding out in my own house."

Harold laughed as Simon glared at him and walked out the door to greet his in-laws. "Hello," he said first to Joe, holding his hand out for the man to shake, relieved when he did. There was a frosty politeness but at least Joe was being civil. "Joe, you remember Harold. He's my only family and surrogate father."

Simon turned toward Harold and caught a funny gleam in the old man's eyes, surprise and something else. It occurred to Simon that he hadn't done enough lately to show Harold that he appreciated him. He was glad to have Harold in his life to be the father to him that his own father had not been.

He looked toward Janice, saw her watching Harold and wondered but didn't linger on the thought as his eyes gazed on his son in his mother's arms. He would never allow Mack to feel unloved. He would always be there for him. Mack was wanted. A lump formed in his throat as he watched Janice place the baby in her mother's arms. For the second time that day she looked at him and smiled softly, making his heart catch, making him wonder if they could be saved.

"Mrs. Adams, how are you?" he said, not going up to her. He tensed as he saw the woman studying him, her head tilted to the side.

"Why are you standing over there, Simon?" She raised Mack, sniffled under one arm and then the other and Simon laughed.

The tension was broken. Simon kissed his mother-in-law, hugged her and placed a kiss on Mack's forehead.

Simon looked with confusion at his wife when he noticed her eyes filling with tears. She would be leaving him soon and he knew if it were he he couldn't do it. He wanted to tell Janice not to worry, that she didn't have to leave but he didn't want her to stay just for Mack. He wanted her to stay for both of them.

Simon felt slight pressure on his arm and looked down at Carol Adams trying to push him toward the open archway. "I'm really thirsty," she said. "Do you think we could get me a drink?"

"Pardon me for not having asked. I can have someone bring you something."

"I think we're capable of doing it together. You do know where your own kitchen is, don't you?"

Simon laughed, knowing she wanted to talk. This was what he'd wanted for Mack, grandparents. Now…now who knew what would happen?

"Simon, why are you looking so unhappy?"

"I guess I'm not very good at hiding my feelings." He opened the fridge, pointing at several things until Carol made a choice. He handed the cola to Carol and took Mack from her. "We're going to get a divorce," he said sadly.

"I'm so sorry to hear that."

"There are too many things that went wrong." He looked directly at his mother-in-law. "I know that you're aware of all the things I've done. When we fight we make it public," he said, not looking at her but at his son.

"Simon, if you're talking about that mess that Tommy's dug up, yes, I know about it. We all have skeletons in our closet, things we wish we could change, including Tommy. There are some things you can't change, no matter what. You can only live this life to the best of your ability."

"You don't hate me?"

"Of course I don't hate you. That would be foolish."

"What about my being arrested for…for hitting Mary Jo?"

"Please, do you really think either Joe or I believed that nonsense?"

"But…"

"I know you'd never hit my daughter," Carol replied firmly.

"How do you know that? How can you sound so sure? There are people who've known me for years and they believe that I did it."

"Then they don't really know you. Just because you may have gone to the same school or social function doesn't mean that a person knows your heart or your soul, for that matter. You're a good man and you love my daughter. I knew that nonsense was a lie when I first heard it.

"Besides, Mary Jo would have got her licks in. And you, well, when they showed your picture on television you looked shell-shocked in the beginning, then later amused. As for Mary Jo, I could always tell when that child was lying. She never came right out and said it was true, that you did it. She cried those fake tears for the camera."

Simon laughed and looked at her. "You knew?" he asked, surprised.

"Of course I knew. I'm her mother. I knew she was denying it and giving those fake tears just to give the impression that you were guilty. Her father...wants to have a little private talk with you though."

"Oh."

"Don't worry, he just wants to talk."

"Janice told me she'd talked to him."

"Janice?"

"Sorry, Mary Jo."

"Joe talked to Mary Jo," Carol laughed. "Now he wants to talk to you. I made him wait until we came here so he could talk to you face to face."

"What about you? What did Mary Jo tell you?"

"I never even bothered asking her about that."

"You haven't talked to her?"

"Not about that nonsense. No need to."

"If you didn't ask her if any of it's true I'm surprised you're talking to me." Simon stared at her for a second or two, then smiled. "Why are you talking to me?"

"Because I don't want you thinking we have bad feelings about you. Both you and Mary Jo have the habit of hiding your feelings and assuming things. I don't want you assuming how we feel about you."

"Thanks," Simon answered softly.

"Now I'm not saying that I approve of what you've done, either of you. But you're a member of this family and we love you."

"Will I still be a member after she leaves me?"

"You'll always be a member but this is another thing I think you could stop if one of you would just be honest. I know the two of you like fighting but maybe you should stop for a minute and listen to each other without the fighting. I know you still love her and she loves you."

Simon looked hopeful, then doubtful. "Sometimes love is not enough. The way we've been living has got to stop. It isn't any good for any of us, and I can't live with her the way we've been doing."

"Then change things."

"I can't, she's going back to Tommy."

"Did she tell you that?" Carol asked, coming closer to him and placing a hand on the baby as she held his gaze. "What are you going to do, Simon?"

"What I promised. I'm going to let her go. She wants her freedom and I'm going to give it to her. She's not going to fight me over Mack," Simon almost whispered, looking at the baby.

"Mary Jo agreed to give you custody of Mack?"

"She wants out. There's something she wants more than the two of us," he said, stroking the baby's soft skin.

"It's not true, Simon."

"You could have fooled me." Simon swallowed. He shouldn't be having this conversation with his mother-in-law. He should be having it with his wife. And he would. "Come on, let's go back," he said, putting an arm around the woman's shoulder as he wrapped the other more securely around his son.

"Simon, I'd like to talk to you in private," Joe said the moment Carol and Simon returned from the kitchen.

While Simon ushered his father-in-law toward his office he glanced over his shoulder and saw Carol with her head bowed talking to Janice. His gaze quickly swept the room for Harold and he spotted him studying a portrait of Simon with his parents. Harold glanced at him, raising a brow as if to say, "You wanted family involvement, now you have it."

An hour later Simon emerged from his office thoroughly chastised. Joe had not been quite as forgiving as Carol. He'd wasted no time in telling Simon what he would have done had the rumors been true.

When they left a week later Simon finally breathed a sigh of relief. Fences had been mended but just barely. The news that Simon was taking custody of the baby had made Joe and Carol a bit tense. Hopefully they'd work through that. He still wanted Mack to know his grandparents. He wanted his son to have a family.

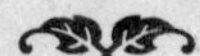

Simon stood for a moment in the doorway. Janice had been watching him all through breakfast as though she wanted to tell him something and was afraid. "I'll see you this evening," he said, giving her a chance to tell him what was on her mind.

"I'm going out for a little while today."

He watched as she licked her lips and refused to look at him. "Where are you going?" he asked, knowing the answer in his heart.

"I'm going to call Tommy and ask him to meet me for lunch. I have to talk to him." She hesitated. "I wanted you to know. I didn't want you to find out later and think I was trying to hide it."

Simon narrowed his eyes as he stared at her. His palm twisted the handle of the door and he held on as the onslaught of arrows pierced him. Before one volley would end another would begin. So this was how his marriage would end, not with a bang but with a whimper, with his wife telling him calmly as she walked out the door that she was calling another man to take his place.

"Fine," he answered at last. "I hope you find what you're looking for in his arms." Then he closed the door and walked away.

Janice went to the window and watched as Simon got in the limo and it drove away.

"This had better work," she said to the baby in her arms. "If it doesn't, your mommy and daddy are going to be in a battle to end all battles, because there is no way that I ever plan to leave you." She gave the baby her finger. "Or your daddy."

The stubborn jackass, she thought, but she wouldn't say those words aloud to her son. "I'm going to do my best to keep us a family." She smiled at the baby.

Tommy was waiting for her when she entered the restaurant. He had a sort of smirk on his face, making her wonder at her choice for a meeting place. She'd chosen the place because it was quiet, but of course since it was quiet, it had a lot of ambiance, which had apparently given Tommy the wrong impression.

"Hello," he said, rising to kiss her. Janice turned slightly, ensuring that his kiss landed on her cheek and not on her lips as he intended. "I wanted to tell you I'm sorry," she said, sitting down.

"What, you found out finally that I'm right?"

She ignored him. "I wanted to ask for your forgiveness for not asking you what you thought about my getting an abortion, for not giving you a chance to be involved. All of these years I've blamed you and it was wrong. I was wrong. I want you to forgive me, Tommy."

Tommy sighed and took her hands. "Do you mean that?"

"I mean it. It took me a long time to realize that you did have rights. When Simon held his son in the delivery room I realized what I had taken from you. And I knew I had to tell you how sorry I am for that."

For minutes she sat in silence while Tommy sat with his eyes closed. When he opened them he looked at her for a long time. "Thank you," he said. "I've waited a long time to hear you say that. I know you hated me, Mary Jo. You had a right to hate me. I hated myself. I always wanted the chance to make it up to you. I think that's why I've been so angry with you, maybe why I…"

"Tried to ruin things with me and Simon?"

"I think so, but I also wanted to see if maybe there was something left." He squeezed her hand in his. "There isn't, is there? I could tell it from the moment you sat down. You really do love the guy, don't you?"

"I do."

"Does he know that you're here with me?"

"He knows I'm with you, but I'm sure he thinks we're in bed together having wild sex." Janice smiled. "He had a little help from you in that department."

"I'm sorry but it just pissed me off that you would want him and not me. Then you married him. And when you got pregnant it was like a slap in the face to me."

"Maybe I should have told you this sooner. Then Simon would not have had to be a part of our war. But then again, in a way it took all of this, the past eighteen months, to let me know just how much I do love him."

Janice looked away for a second before deciding whether to go on. "I'm not saying this to hurt your feelings, Tommy, but I would have thought that after all the things Simon and I have done to each other that I wouldn't want him, that I would stop loving him. But I haven't."

"He's hurt you much more than I ever have."

"No, he hasn't. No matter what we do to each other, all the fights, everything, when I need him I can depend on him, he's always there for me. He may not go about things in the right way to help me but it's my happiness he's thinking of. Even right now, Tommy, if I called and told my husband that I needed him, even if he thought I was here sleeping with you, he would come. He loves me."

She saw Tommy wince and she gave the hand she was holding a squeeze. "I'm not saying this to hurt you. I'm just telling you Simon isn't the monster that you want him to be." She smiled slightly. "When I was in labor I tried to push him away. I told him the baby wasn't his, that it was yours. I told him I didn't want him with me."

"What did he do?"

"He stayed there anyway. I needed him and he knew it." Janice closed her eyes, feeling overcome with emotions. "He would never leave me, no matter what the reason, but he will allow me to walk away from him."

"Why are you still having problems?"

"He thinks the worst thing that could happen in a relationship is infidelity. I know that it isn't and I have to prove that to him. I don't want him always thinking that you're a threat to us. I want to prove to him that we belong together."

"You're behaving a hell of a lot differently than you were when I first saw the two of you together. Maybe if I had seen this then...Oh hell, I would have still gone after you," Tommy grinned.

"It took me an awfully long time to thaw. I was afraid that we would end up where we are right now. I know now that this isn't my worst nightmare. Losing my husband is. Now that I've gotten rid of the wall around my heart I have no plans on rebuilding it. I couldn't if I tried. I love Simon, flaws and all. I'm going to let him believe his worst fears."

"That you slept with me?"

"Yes. In fact," Janice paused, then decided to say it anyway, "I thought of going through with it, of going to bed with you. Afterwards I was going to tell you I didn't want you. I was going to do it to make you feel like a fool, to hurt you. But that was before I knew I owed you an apology. I wanted to use you for hurting Simon. I don't want that anymore. Besides…"

"Besides, you can't stand the thought of another man's hands on your body."

She smiled. "How did you know?"

"I know you."

"Wish me luck. Now come on, let's order lunch, my treat."

"It really is over isn't it?"

"Yes, it is. How do you feel?"

"I'm okay with that." He smiled at her. "You have no idea what your coming here means to me. Thanks."

Janice smiled. She did know what it meant. She had a son now and she knew what it meant.

There was one more thing Janice needed to do and that was to ensure a quiet place for Simon to blow his stack. The mansion was always filled with staff but tonight she intended for there to be only her family. She smiled as she thought it. Mack, Simon and she really were a family. And she was going to do everything in her power to make sure they remained one.

Janice's next stop was the Edwardian. She secured six rooms for two nights for the staff and paid cash, making sure to include more than enough for any expenses. She wanted the management to know that it didn't have to worry about payment. She wasn't doing this with Simon's funds but with her own restored accounts.

When she reached home, she called the staff together and held out the keys. "I have rooms for each of you at the Edwardian for two nights." She looked at the chauffeur. "I want you all to pack an overnight bag, take the limo and go. I want to be alone with the baby and Mr. Kohl."

"How soon do you want us to leave?" Marcus asked.

"In the next half hour."

"I haven't prepared dinner," Elizabeth muttered.

"I can cook. Please don't worry about us. Have a good time." She held out the keys and one by one the staff took them. "Whatever you want, charge it to the room and it will be taken care of. I've already made sure of that. This is my treat," she said, hoping that would stop them from calling to check with Simon. In less than half the time she'd asked them to leave, the staff was heading out to the limo.

Marcus came back. "Mrs. Kohl, are you going to be all right?"

In all of this time none of the staff had ever asked her if it were true that Simon had hit her. Now it was time to set that story straight.

"I'm going to be fine. Simon never hit me, he never would," she said, smiling. "Don't worry about me, but thank you. We're going to be fine."

"Will you still be here when we return?"

"That's my plan." Janice said. "Say a prayer for us."

"I will, Mrs. Kohl," Marcus answered and walked out the door and to the waiting limo.

So the man knew a hell of a lot more than he let on. Why shouldn't he? The entire world had been made privy to their fight. She intended to make sure they would be soon be privy to their love.

❧

Running his hand over his face Simon hung up the phone and heaved a sigh of relief before turning toward Harold. He shook his head, deciding to suck it up, to tell Harold that at least one of his evil deeds had been reversed.

"Was that that bastard Eric?" Harold asked.

Simon smiled at Harold's open dislike of Eric. "Yes, that was him. I finally got him to sell me the leases."

"How?"

"I told him the truth. When he learned the stores weren't a part of any big project I'm working on but a part of my insanity, he relented and allowed me to buy them as was the original plan."

"And?"

"And I'm going to deed them to the people who were leasing them. I'm going to give them the stores, lock, stock and barrel." Simon grinned and shook his head at his usage of the old cliché.

"How much?" Harold asked.

"You don't want to know."

"Last time it was for ten times more than what he'd paid. Is that what you had to pay to get them back?"

"A bit more," Simon admitted. His eyes met Harold's and he shrugged. "Penance for my arrogant and evil ways."

"You're not evil, Simon."

Simon smiled but didn't answer.

"You're not. You were just going about everything the wrong way, being a bit stubborn, hotheaded and a bastard, but you weren't evil."

Simon grinned at the look of pride on Harold's face. That alone was worth the price he'd paid for the stores. Having his godfather's respect back was priceless. "I'm glad to know you think so highly of me." He rose and walked toward Harold, holding out his hand, clasping Harold's hand in his own and patting him on the shoulder. "I have to go home and play with my son and spend some time with my wife while she's still my wife."

"You can change that, Simon. Just ask her to stay, tell her that you've undone one wrong."

"I didn't buy the leases to gain points with my wife. That was one act I never should have initiated. I didn't need you to tell me that."

"When is she planning to leave?"

"I won't know until I read about it," Simon said, not bothering to explain to Harold that he'd taken to reading Janice's book about the two of them. He glanced at his watch. "I really have to go. Janice keeps Mack up until I get home and it's getting pretty late for him."

Simon closed his eyes and smiled as he pictured his son's sweet face. "I never knew I could love so much," he said. "If I tried to undo my wrongs you might say it's because I never want Mack to be ashamed of me."

Simon walked toward the door, then turned back. "I've never told you thank you for all that you've done for me, for being like a father to me. I love you, old man."

CHAPTER TWENTY-SIX

Janice looked over the words she'd typed. This was the last chapter. She was praying that her plan would work. For the past few weeks she'd been aware that Simon was reading the manuscript and she'd also been aware that he thought it was true. Hopefully her plan wouldn't ricochet. Hopefully this would be the vehicle that would enable them to repair their marriage and make it stronger.

She looked over the words again, wishing a less drastic approach would be enough but she knew it wouldn't be. Sooner or later Simon's jealousy would rear its ugly head again and she would spout off things that she didn't mean. No, it would be better for them to have the mother of all fights and get it over with. Win or lose, she was going out in the only manner she knew how, swinging. They'd begun their relationship fighting and if it were to be saved, it would be saved by fighting.

"Why are you here," he asked me. "Have you finally realized that we belong together?"

"Yes, I realize that we have unfinished business."

"What about your husband?"

"He has what he wants," I answered, "He has a son. "

"Tell me why you're here. If you want me to touch you you're going to have to tell me to do it."

I looked at the man from my past. "I want you to touch me. I came for you to make love to me. Please," I begged, moaning, "make love to me."

He pulled me to his hard body and I felt the steel of his embrace as he held me tightly and shoved his tongue into my mouth. I waited for the sweetness, the wanting, the lust, the need, but it didn't come. What came instead was a picture of my husband standing in the doorway of the mansion looking at me with our baby son cradled in his arms. His pain was etched so clearly on his face that I almost cried. I closed my eyes to the images. This was my destiny.

It was over quickly. He rolled over to his side. "It's over, isn't it? You're not in love with me."

"I haven't been in love with you in twelve years."

"Then why did you sleep with me?"

He looked at me and I knew he had his answer. Still, confusion clouded his eyes. I shrugged my shoulder and stared at him. A mixture of pity and compassion filled me.

"You used me," he said. "How is that going to help you? Are you planning on going back to your husband?"

"I am. You used me to hurt my husband and I used you to save my marriage. You thought the information you gave me would destroy us but it didn't. I've tried to think of a way to prove to both of you that I'm no longer in love with you. I haven't been in love with you for a long time."

"What if he doesn't forgive you? What will you do?"

"I don't know," I answered honestly. "I'm just hoping that this works. I love him and I don't know how else to prove it. Now that I've done the thing that he's feared the most it won't have the power to hurt him any more." With that I walked

away. I had no idea how it would go but at least I'd done something. The next move would be up to my husband and God willing, we'll be able to put the infidelity behind us and start again. What more do I have to lose?

The End

Janice typed the words at the bottom of the page of her manuscript and printed it out. Simon would read what she'd written and he would believe it. She needed him to believe it in order for them to let it go. She had to prove to him that he had been right in the beginning. Then they could forgive each other anything and get stronger from the experience.

Janice placed the pages haphazardly on her desk, turned out the light and closed the door. She knew Simon wouldn't go into her computer for the information but he would read the typewritten pages.

She heard Simon come in the door, heard him downstairs calling out to the staff. She kissed Mack and laid him in his crib, turned on the baby monitor, and marched downstairs.

"What's going on?" Simon asked. "I thought you were going to Tommy."

"I did."

"Then why are you back? He didn't want you?"

She ignored him. "I gave the staff the evening off. I'm making dinner." Janice saw his mouth open quickly in surprise and saw when he made a quick recovery.

"What's going on? Should I hire a food taster?"

"We need to talk tonight. What do you want for dinner?"

"It doesn't matter." Simon couldn't begin to figure out what was going on. "I need to take a shower so whatever you want to make will be fine. Where's Mack?"

"He's sleeping."

Simon glanced at his watch. Usually Janice kept the baby up until he came home.

"Why?"

"Go check on your son and shower. We'll talk later." She walked toward the kitchen, a slight tremble evident in her hands but she knew Simon hadn't seen it.

Simon walked slowly up the stairs to check on his son. In four years Janice had never cooked once for him or even offered to. And she had never offered or given any instructions to the staff without first checking with him. Something was definitely up. He checked on Mack, making sure he was breathing. He checked the monitor and decided to go back downstairs. The shower could wait. He peeked in the kitchen, saw Janice busy at the stove, and decided to see if she'd written any more.

Janice was aware that Simon was watching her and she did her best to not turn around. This had to go the way she'd planned. She could barely keep still as she listened to the sound of him walking toward her study. Then she heard the door open. She knew he was going to read it. She had been planting little tidbits for him for the last couple of weeks. He wouldn't have been able to stop himself from reading it if he'd wanted to. All she had to do now was wait.

Simon read the last line of Janice's book several times. And each time the anger inside him increased. This was the reason she had sent the staff away, the reason Mack was asleep. *Well, good*, he thought. If she was preparing for a fight, she sure as hell was going to get one.

"Why the hell did you come home?" he asked as he stood angrily in the door frame of the kitchen.

"A son needs two parents," Janice said, turning slowly and deliberately.

"He has two parents; you can see him anytime that you want. Why the hell did you come back?"

"I'm not in love with Tommy."

"You couldn't find that out until you slept with him?"

"I knew before I went to see him that I no longer loved him," she said, evading his question and trying to answer as truthfully as possible. She turned away from the anger in his face, knowing that if she didn't take a moment to gather her strength she might not be able to go through with it.

Simon spun her around to face him. "Then why the hell did you sleep with him? Tell me why you're here, why you even bothered to come back," he yelled.

"I came back because I can't share the things with Tommy that I can share with you."

"What did you want to share with Tommy, your blackness?" he growled.

"I wanted to share my pain with him but it didn't work. You and I, Simon, we've shared our pain."

"And you're back with me because we know how to make each other hurt? God, that's sick." Simon shook his head, his instincts telling him not to go closer to her.

"Did you really think it was going to be that easy? That all you had to do was decide that you now want me. It's going to take a hell of a lot more than that. You sleep with another man, then come back to me, and I'm supposed to just forgive you and welcome you back with open arms? No, baby, it's not going to happen like that this time. Get the hell out. Now!" he screamed.

Janice sucked in her breath. This was it, she was about to lose her husband. The knowledge ripped through her and she knew what she had to do. For once she knew what to do. "No. I'm not going anyplace." She tuned the stove off, checked the pans, and marched past Simon with him screaming behind her. "I love you," she said calmly, walking up the stairs to the bedroom. "We're going to talk and for once you're going to listen."

"What the hell are you talking about?" Simon shouted.

"Could you please keep your voice to a mild roar? Your son is trying to sleep," Janice said, dropping her voice.

"What I mean is, you're going to listen to me. I've been telling you for over a year and you haven't heard a word I said. It seems you heard me pretty good before I told you that I loved you. You said you knew it and you kept after me. I told you this would happen if I said the words but you didn't want to listen. I finally admitted that I love you and since then you've done everything in your power to try to make me stop. Maybe you should ask yourself why."

"You're crazy."

"I was but I'm not anymore. Simon, I love you," she said as tears rolled down her cheeks. "I love you."

"Then why the hell did you go to Tommy? Why did you sleep with him?"

"Didn't you think that's what I've been doing all along? You've accused me of it a million times. Why are you so worried about that? Do you think that's all that's in a marriage?"

"Are you telling me that you don't think fidelity is important?"

"I think trust is more so."

"How the hell can you have trust and still screw around?" He tore his hand through his hair. He growled, ran downstairs and in a few minutes was back with bags, taking her things from the closet and throwing them into the luggage.

Janice sat calmly watching him. "I'm not leaving so you're going to have to put all of my clothes back."

"What do you want?" he said, coming to face her, dropping to the floor on his knees and locking his arms around her. "Do you really want to make those abuse charges come true?"

"You would never hurt me."

He closed his eyes and shook his head. "You have no idea how badly I want to change our past. I have hurt you over and over. I know why you went to Tommy. You're trying to repay me. You were trying to get even with me for hurting you, weren't you? Admit it," he said, reaching out and holding her chin in his firm grasp. "Admit the truth. You wanted to make me crazy, just like when you left without telling me where you were going. For days I didn't know where the hell you really were. When you left me, you wanted me to believe you were in Tommy's arms."

Simon looked at her calm demeanor. "You wanted me to find what you'd written; you set this up. Why? Do you hate me that much? I knew you hated me but this..."

"Tell me something, Simon," Janice interrupted him. "Right now at this moment, which are you more worried about, that I hate you or that you hate me?"

He stopped for a moment, startled, and stared at her. Then he continued. Two hours later he was still yelling as loud as he dared with Mack sleeping. Then to his amazement, he realized his wife had fallen asleep. He couldn't believe it. "I'll be damned," he murmured softly and walked over to Janice, shook her shoulders and waited for her to open her eyes.

"Am I boring you?"

"A little." Janice smiled. "I know you need to get this out of your system but I don't particularly need to hear it all. I'm not going to stop loving you, Simon, so if you're done, maybe we can talk."

Maybe having a baby had made her insane. Or all the fighting they'd done through the years. He didn't know what it was but it was evident his wife was insane. And he was almost as insane as she was, he thought as he moved backwards, because he was ready to listen to her. He plopped into a chair and sighed.

"What can you say? I told you a thousand times what would happen if you ever slept with anyone else. My feeling on the subject comes as no surprise to you."

"I have something I want to ask you." She pushed her body forward and allowed her legs to dangle from the bed. "Is this the worst thing that you could imagine to happen? I mean, is this what you've been so afraid of? Now that you feel you've relived your parents' life, are you ready to let it go?"

"What the hell are you talking about?"

"I know about your parents. You even told me some of it. It's as though you've written a script that has to parallel their lives. You've sworn you didn't want it but you've done everything in your power to recreate it."

"Who told you that?"

"It doesn't matter, Simon. I need to know and please, for once don't be so hot tempered. Think about the answer before you give it. Your worst fears have been realized and I know that you're hurt. I think the entire block knows that you're hurt. Are you going to be able to forgive me for betraying you?"

Janice watched the tortured expression on her husband's face and knew she had to go all the way. She had to shove the blade into his heart and make him bleed. "I love you, Simon. I don't want to leave you. I want our marriage to work. Can you forgive me for the things that you've read, for the things that I've done and allow us to continue as a family?"

"Say it. Can I forgive you for sleeping with Tommy?" Simon fell to his knees and pain filled sobs tore through him, making his entire body heave with his suffering.

Janice fell to her knees also and moved toward her husband, putting her arms around him as he sobbed, replacing them as he continually pushed her away. "I love you, Simon," she crooned through her own tears. "Forgive me, baby, for making you hurt this way."

"Why?" he moaned.

"I wanted to take away the pain that was in your mind, the constant thought that I might cheat on you. Look where I am, Simon. I'm on my knees, in your arms. It's you I want, Simon, it's you that I love."

"You didn't have to write it…for me…to read it…" A shudder ripped through his body and he clutched her to him. "You didn't have to do it." His voice broke and he held her even tighter. "Why?"

"I told you, baby, I wanted to stop you from hurting."

"You didn't do a very good job of that."

We'll see, she thought, but to Simon she said, "I'm sorry, baby, so very sorry to have to take you though this but I do love you. I'll always love you."

They stayed like that until they'd both cried themselves out and they'd dropped from their knees to sit on their butts still locked in each other's arms. Janice continued crooning to Simon as though he were Mack, running her fingers through his hair, wiping his tears and her own, telling him over and over how much she loved him. When he took a deep breath at last and brought his head up from hers she knew it was time. She saw the resignation in his eyes. He was now ready to listen.

"So tell me, Simon, is this pain the worst pain? Is there anything that would hurt you more?"

Simon looked at his wife for more than a moment, his suspicions confirmed. She was insane. What could be worse than this? He closed his eyes, breathing deeply. Then he sighed and opened them and looked at his wife.

And in that moment Simon knew what she meant. He didn't believe it. He'd always imagined enduring the infidelity his parents put up with to be the worst thing he could conjure. It wasn't. As much as he hurt, no, it wasn't the worst pain he could imagine. Finding out his son wasn't his would be a much worse pain. Losing his wife, he realized as he looked at her, would destroy him.

"There are worse pains," he finally admitted.

"Tell me," Janice said, getting up from the floor and holding her hand out to him. "Tell me, Simon."

"Losing you," he growled as the pain of that reality burned through him. "I don't want to lose you."

"You don't have to, Simon. I don't want to leave."

"I just can't forgive you for what you've done. It's not going to be that easy."

"Are you willing to try?" she asked as tears streamed down her face.

"God help me, what choice do I have?" He pulled his wife into his arms, crushing her to him, lifting her tear-streaked face to kiss her. "I'm willing to try." Tears fell from his eyes also and mixed with those of his wife.

"Simon, can you forgive me for one more thing?"

"What?" he whispered raggedly. "What else?" He held her closer, praying she wouldn't tell him that Mack wasn't his.

"I never slept with Tommy, not once."

"But your book?"

"I told you that was fiction. As usual, you didn't listen to me."

"I was right. You did set me up."

"I had to. You've been so worried that you were going to repeat your parents' lives that it became the main thing in your life. You've threatened me so many times that I thought about doing it just to piss you off. Later I thought maybe if I did it, it would help you to get over Tommy. I would have done almost anything to save our marriage, but I couldn't sleep with Tommy. I couldn't allow anyone other than you to touch me. I love you, Simon."

"Then why did you go to see Tommy today? Why did you make me believe that you were leaving me for him?"

"I never said those things. You thought them and I'll admit I wanted you to. I went to Tommy to apologize. I've known since Mack was born that I had to. I took something from Tommy that I didn't have a right to take. I had to tell him that finally I knew that. Until Mack, until you held your son, I hadn't really understood what I'd taken from Tommy."

Janice stopped and held her husband's gaze. "And Mack is your son, Simon. What I did to Tommy was the catalyst for what he did to you. It wasn't you he hated, it was me and what I'd done. I had to tell him that I understood, that I was sorry that I'd thought he had no right in the decision. I believe we've both finally let go of the anger. There will always be pain but he knows that there is nothing between us."

Simon wanted to be angry that she had even gone to see Tommy. Then he heard Mack gurgling over the intercom and his chest constricted. *If Mack weren't here, if Janice had made the same decision to abort their son...*He breathed deeply, closing his eyes against his thoughts.

"You're right," he said. "As much as I hate Tommy I can understand how he must have felt all of these years."

"Simon, you can hate Tommy, but don't hate him because you think I love him. I don't. He's my past and your fears should be also."

She opened her mouth to say something more but her husband cut off her words with his lips. He took possession of her lips and her body and she could feel his need. She saw the passion in his eyes, felt the fire in his touch and felt his flesh pulse. He pushed her back toward the bed.

"No, baby," Janice moaned. "We have forever. First, I want you to tell me about your parents. Talk to me."

"Now?" Simon groaned, his erection growing with each breath. "Feel me, it's been so long. You sure you want to talk now?"

"We need to talk now," she said, moving to sit on the bed, making room for her husband, going into his arms.

And they talked.

And then they made love.

In the morning they awoke in each other's arms. Mack had slept through the night. Simon went for his son, changed him, and brought him to the bed so that Janice could feed him. He watched her breast feeding Mack and thanked God that she'd gone to the lengths that she had to show him how much she loved him.

"Baby, I'm sorry about all the things I did to hurt you. Thank God I came to my senses before I did any real damage to your career. I'll make sure you're bigger than ever before."

"No, Simon. From here on out I don't want you butting into my career. No matter what happens to the two of us I want my career to be just that. *Mine.* If I make it or not, I want it to be me, Simon, not you, not my wondering if you pushed my book to the number one slot. I don't want it that way, Simon. In truth I never did. So promise me that you will stay out of that area of my life. And, Simon, I want you to mean it."

"I promise, baby."

"Another thing: I'm going to start writing under Mary Jo Adams. I'm glad now you insisted on following my parents' wishes and married me under my real name. I don't need to be Janice anymore. I'm not running away from anything anymore. I've found everything that I was looking for."

Mary Jo looked at the baby in her arms, then at her husband's face. "This is my dream, you and Mack. No more manipulating"

"I'm sorry, honey. Aren't you going to miss being Janice Lace?"

"Yes, but it's not the thing in my life that I would miss most."

"Will you forgive me for that?"

"Today is the beginning of our lives, Simon. There are no more demons chasing either of us. The slate is clean and everything is forgiven and forgotten." She got up and placed a sleeping Mack into the cradle they kept in their room. Then she came back to the bed and pulled Simon to her, determined to make love to him until he was too tired to think.

A few hours later Mack forced them from the bed with his needs. Smiling, they carried the baby downstairs, both grateful for the second chance to be a family. The moment they stepped on the last stair the doorbell rang.

"Good timing, Mack." Simon smiled at the baby and went to answer the door. "Harold," Simon said, moving for him to come inside.

Harold held the mail out to him with the telltale envelope on the top of the pile. It contained the information Simon had been waiting for. He looked at the envelope and held it out to Mary Jo. "I don't need this; we can shred it. Mack is my son."

Simon looked over at Harold, knowing that Mary Jo didn't mind his being there. They were both staring at him and at the envelope in his hand. He looked at them and knew his wife and surrogate father shared a secret. But that thought was best left for another time. Besides, he already knew it was Harold who'd filled Mary Jo in on his parents and their lives. And for that he was grateful. His gaze landed on Mack nestled in Harold's arms. He was Mack's godfather, the same as he was for Simon.

Simon, looked into the ice blue eyes of his son, knowing they would one day turn gray. Like his. This was his son, his flesh and blood his soul cried out. He didn't need a paper to tell him that.

"Simon," Mary Jo said softly.

He looked to his wife. "I know you know," she said, "but every man deserves to have that certainty."

He saw her gaze slip to Harold and again he wondered.

Mary Jo took the envelope from her husband's hand, opened it and handed him the paper. "I want you to have your proof, Simon."

"I don't need to see it," he whispered softly not looking at the paper, keeping his eyes on her.

"Look at it, Simon," Harold said, adding his voice to that of Mary Jo.

"Yes, darling, you need to see it."

For a moment Simon grappled with the thought of whether it would make his wife wonder if he trusted her. They'd been through so much together. They didn't need even a hint of mistrust to cloud their marriage. His eyes flew back to hers and she was smiling at him, urging him to read the paper.

At last he lowered his eyes to the numbers on the page. Ninety nine, point ninety nine percent positive. You couldn't get surer than that.

Mary Joe watched as her husband read the results, saw his face, the light in his eyes and the love reflected there as he wrapped her in a bear hug.

"What about that book," he asked, "the one you wrote about us. Is this how it ends?"

"That book was just for you, to show that nothing is all black or white. There are many shades of gray, even in love," she said and slid her arms around her husband and son. "Even in love. The real ending wasn't written until this moment. Now we can be happy. Now I can write, THE END."

ABOUT THE AUTHOR

Award winning author **Dyanne Davis** lives in a Chicago suburb with her husband Bill and their son Bill, Jr. She retired from nursing several years ago to pursue her life-long dream of becoming a published author. An avid reader, Dyanne began reading at the age of four. Her love of the written word turned into a desire to write. Her first novel, *The Color of Trouble,* was released in July of 2003.

Dyanne has been a presenter of numerous workshops. She has a local cable show in her hometown to give writing tips to aspiring writers. The show will soon be part of the streaming videos and will be able to be seen by anyone with internet connection.

When not writing, you can find Dyanne with a book in her hands, her greatest passion next to spending time with her husband Bill and Bill, Jr. Whenever possible, she loves getting together with friends and family.

A member of Romance Writers of America, Dyanne is now serving her second term as Chapter President for Windy City. Dyanne loves to hear feedback from her readers. You can reach her at her website, www.dyannedavid.com You can also find her on http://Myspace.com/dyannedavis.

MANY SHADES OF GRAY

2007 Publication Schedule

January

Corporate Seduction
A.C. Arthur
ISBN-13: 978-1-58571-238-0
ISBN-10: 1-58571-238-8
$9.95

A Taste of Temptation
Reneé Alexis
ISBN-13: 978-1-58571-207-6
ISBN-10: 1-58571-207-8
$9.95

February

The Perfect Frame
Beverly Clark
ISBN-13: 978-1-58571-240-3
ISBN-10: 1-58571-240-X
$9.95

Ebony Angel
Deatri King-Bey
ISBN-13: 978-1-58571-239-7
ISBN-10: 1-58571-239-6
$9.95

March

Sweet Sensations
Gwendolyn Bolton
ISBN-13: 978-1-58571-206-9
ISBN-10: 1-58571-206-X
$9.95

Crush
Crystal Hubbard
ISBN-13: 978-1-58571-243-4
ISBN-10: 1-58571-243-4
$9.95

April

Secret Thunder
Annetta P. Lee
ISBN-13: 978-1-58571-204-5
ISBN-10: 1-58571-204-3
$9.95

Blood Seduction
J.M. Jeffries
ISBN-13: 978-1-58571-237-3
ISBN-10: 1-58571-237-X
$9.95

May

Lies Too Long
Pamela Ridley
ISBN-13: 978-1-58571-246-5
ISBN-10: 1-58571-246-9
$13.95

Two Sides to Every Story
Dyanne Davis
ISBN-13: 978-1-58571-248-9
ISBN-10: 1-58571-248-5
$9.95

June

One of These Days
Michele Sudler
ISBN-13: 978-1-58571-249-6
ISBN-10: 1-58571-249-3
$9.95

Who's That Lady?
Andrea Jackson
ISBN-13: 978-1-58571-190-1
ISBN-10: 1-58571-190-X
$9.95

2007 Publication Schedule (continued)

July

Heart of the Phoenix
A.C. Arthur
ISBN-13: 978-1-58571-242-7
ISBN-10: 1-58571-242-6
$9.95

Do Over
Celya Bowers
ISBN-13: 978-1-58571-241-0
ISBN-10: 1-58571-241-8
$9.95

It's Not Over Yet
J.J. Michael
ISBN-13: 978-1-58571-245-8
ISBN-10: 1-58571-245-0
$9.95

August

The Fires Within
Beverly Clark
ISBN-13: 978-1-58571-244-1
ISBN-10: 1-58571-244-2
$9.95

Stolen Kisses
Dominiqua Douglas
ISBN-13: 978-1-58571-247-2
ISBN-10: 1-58571-247-7
$9.95

September

Small Whispers
Annetta P. Lee
ISBN-13: 978-158571-251-9
ISBN-10: 1-58571-251-5
$6.99

Always You
Crystal Hubbard
ISBN-13: 978-158571-252-6
ISBN-10: 1-58571-252-3
$6.99

October

Not His Type
Chamein Canton
ISBN-13: 978-158571-253-3
ISBN-10: 1-58571-253-1
$6.99

Many Shades of Gray
Dyanne Davis
ISBN-13: 978-158571-254-0
ISBN-10: 1-58571-254-X
$6.99

November

When I'm With You
LaConnie Taylor-Jones
ISBN-13: 978-158571-250-2
ISBN-10: 1-58571-250-7
$6.99

The Mission
Pamela Leigh Starr
ISBN-13: 978-158571-255-7
ISBN-10: 1-58571-255-8
$6.99

December

One in A Million
Barbara Keaton
ISBN-13: 978-158571-257-1
ISBN-10: 1-58571-257-4
$6.99

The Foursome
Celya Bowers
ISBN-13: 978-158571-256-4
ISBN-10: 1-58571-256-6
$6.99

Other Genesis Press, Inc. Titles

A Dangerous Deception	J.M. Jeffries	$8.95
A Dangerous Love	J.M. Jeffries	$8.95
A Dangerous Obsession	J.M. Jeffries	$8.95
A Drummer's Beat to Mend	Kei Swanson	$9.95
A Happy Life	Charlotte Harris	$9.95
A Heart's Awakening	Veronica Parker	$9.95
A Lark on the Wing	Phyliss Hamilton	$9.95
A Love of Her Own	Cheris F. Hodges	$9.95
A Love to Cherish	Beverly Clark	$8.95
A Risk of Rain	Dar Tomlinson	$8.95
A Twist of Fate	Beverly Clark	$8.95
A Will to Love	Angie Daniels	$9.95
Acquisitions	Kimberley White	$8.95
Across	Carol Payne	$12.95
After the Vows	Leslie Esdaile	$10.95
(Summer Anthology)	T.T. Henderson	
	Jacqueline Thomas	
Again My Love	Kayla Perrin	$10.95
Against the Wind	Gwynne Forster	$8.95
All I Ask	Barbara Keaton	$8.95
Ambrosia	T.T. Henderson	$8.95
An Unfinished Love Affair	Barbara Keaton	$8.95
And Then Came You	Dorothy Elizabeth Love	$8.95
Angel's Paradise	Janice Angelique	$9.95
At Last	Lisa G. Riley	$8.95
Best of Friends	Natalie Dunbar	$8.95
Beyond the Rapture	Beverly Clark	$9.95
Blaze	Barbara Keaton	$9.95

Other Genesis Press, Inc. Titles (continued)

Blood Lust	J. M. Jeffries	$9.95
Bodyguard	Andrea Jackson	$9.95
Boss of Me	Diana Nyad	$8.95
Bound by Love	Beverly Clark	$8.95
Breeze	Robin Hampton Allen	$10.95
Broken	Dar Tomlinson	$24.95
By Design	Barbara Keaton	$8.95
Cajun Heat	Charlene Berry	$8.95
Careless Whispers	Rochelle Alers	$8.95
Cats & Other Tales	Marilyn Wagner	$8.95
Caught in a Trap	Andre Michelle	$8.95
Caught Up In the Rapture	Lisa G. Riley	$9.95
Cautious Heart	Cheris F Hodges	$8.95
Chances	Pamela Leigh Starr	$8.95
Cherish the Flame	Beverly Clark	$8.95
Class Reunion	Irma Jenkins/ John Brown	$12.95
Code Name: Diva	J.M. Jeffries	$9.95
Conquering Dr. Wexler's Heart	Kimberley White	$9.95
Crossing Paths, Tempting Memories	Dorothy Elizabeth Love	$9.95
Cypress Whisperings	Phyllis Hamilton	$8.95
Dark Embrace	Crystal Wilson Harris	$8.95
Dark Storm Rising	Chinelu Moore	$10.95
Daughter of the Wind	Joan Xian	$8.95
Deadly Sacrifice	Jack Kean	$22.95
Designer Passion	Dar Tomlinson	$8.95
Dreamtective	Liz Swados	$5.95

Other Genesis Press, Inc. Titles (continued)

Ebony Butterfly II	Delilah Dawson	$14.95
Echoes of Yesterday	Beverly Clark	$9.95
Eden's Garden	Elizabeth Rose	$8.95
Everlastin' Love	Gay G. Gunn	$8.95
Everlasting Moments	Dorothy Elizabeth Love	$8.95
Everything and More	Sinclair Lebeau	$8.95
Everything but Love	Natalie Dunbar	$8.95
Eve's Prescription	Edwina Martin Arnold	$8.95
Falling	Natalie Dunbar	$9.95
Fate	Pamela Leigh Starr	$8.95
Finding Isabella	A.J. Garrotto	$8.95
Forbidden Quest	Dar Tomlinson	$10.95
Forever Love	Wanda Y. Thomas	$8.95
From the Ashes	Kathleen Suzanne Jeanne Sumerix	$8.95
Gentle Yearning	Rochelle Alers	$10.95
Glory of Love	Sinclair LeBeau	$10.95
Go Gentle into that Good Night	Malcom Boyd	$12.95
Goldengroove	Mary Beth Craft	$16.95
Groove, Bang, and Jive	Steve Cannon	$8.99
Hand in Glove	Andrea Jackson	$9.95
Hard to Love	Kimberley White	$9.95
Hart & Soul	Angie Daniels	$8.95
Heartbeat	Stephanie Bedwell-Grime	$8.95
Hearts Remember	M. Loui Quezada	$8.95
Hidden Memories	Robin Allen	$10.95
Higher Ground	Leah Latimer	$19.95
Hitler, the War, and the Pope	Ronald Rychiak	$26.95

Other Genesis Press, Inc. Titles (continued)

How to Write a Romance	Kathryn Falk	$18.95
I Married a Reclining Chair	Lisa M. Fuhs	$8.95
Indigo After Dark Vol. I	Nia Dixon/Angelique	$10.95
Indigo After Dark Vol. II	Dolores Bundy/ Cole Riley	$10.95
Indigo After Dark Vol. III	Montana Blue/ Coco Morena	$10.95
Indigo After Dark Vol. IV	Cassandra Colt/ Diana Richeaux	$14.95
Indigo After Dark Vol. V	Delilah Dawson	$14.95
Icie	Pamela Leigh Starr	$8.95
I'll Be Your Shelter	Giselle Carmichael	$8.95
I'll Paint a Sun	A.J. Garrotto	$9.95
Illusions	Pamela Leigh Starr	$8.95
Indiscretions	Donna Hill	$8.95
Intentional Mistakes	Michele Sudler	$9.95
Interlude	Donna Hill	$8.95
Intimate Intentions	Angie Daniels	$8.95
Jolie's Surrender	Edwina Martin-Arnold	$8.95
Kiss or Keep	Debra Phillips	$8.95
Lace	Giselle Carmichael	$9.95
Last Train to Memphis	Elsa Cook	$12.95
Lasting Valor	Ken Olsen	$24.95
Let Us Prey	Hunter Lundy	$25.95
Life Is Never As It Seems	J.J. Michael	$12.95
Lighter Shade of Brown	Vicki Andrews	$8.95
Love Always	Mildred E. Riley	$10.95
Love Doesn't Come Easy	Charlyne Dickerson	$8.95

Other Genesis Press, Inc. Titles (continued)

Love Unveiled	Gloria Greene	$10.95
Love's Deception	Charlene Berry	$10.95
Love's Destiny	M. Loui Quezada	$8.95
Mae's Promise	Melody Walcott	$8.95
Magnolia Sunset	Giselle Carmichael	$8.95
Matters of Life and Death	Lesego Malepe, Ph.D.	$15.95
Meant to Be	Jeanne Sumerix	$8.95
Midnight Clear	Leslie Esdaile	$10.95
(Anthology)	Gwynne Forster	
	Carmen Green	
	Monica Jackson	
Midnight Magic	Gwynne Forster	$8.95
Midnight Peril	Vicki Andrews	$10.95
Misconceptions	Pamela Leigh Starr	$9.95
Montgomery's Children	Richard Perry	$14.95
My Buffalo Soldier	Barbara B. K. Reeves	$8.95
Naked Soul	Gwynne Forster	$8.95
Next to Last Chance	Louisa Dixon	$24.95
No Apologies	Seressia Glass	$8.95
No Commitment Required	Seressia Glass	$8.95
No Regrets	Mildred E. Riley	$8.95
Nowhere to Run	Gay G. Gunn	$10.95
O Bed! O Breakfast!	Rob Kuehnle	$14.95
Object of His Desire	A. C. Arthur	$8.95
Office Policy	A. C. Arthur	$9.95
Once in a Blue Moon	Dorianne Cole	$9.95
One Day at a Time	Bella McFarland	$8.95
Outside Chance	Louisa Dixon	$24.95
Passion	T.T. Henderson	$10.95

Other Genesis Press, Inc. Titles (continued)

Passion's Blood	Cherif Fortin	$22.95
Passion's Journey	Wanda Y. Thomas	$8.95
Past Promises	Jahmel West	$8.95
Path of Fire	T.T. Henderson	$8.95
Path of Thorns	Annetta P. Lee	$9.95
Peace Be Still	Colette Haywood	$12.95
Picture Perfect	Reon Carter	$8.95
Playing for Keeps	Stephanie Salinas	$8.95
Pride & Joi	Gay G. Gunn	$15.95
Pride & Joi	Gay G. Gunn	$8.95
Promises to Keep	Alicia Wiggins	$8.95
Quiet Storm	Donna Hill	$10.95
Reckless Surrender	Rochelle Alers	$6.95
Red Polka Dot in a World of Plaid	Varian Johnson	$12.95
Reluctant Captive	Joyce Jackson	$8.95
Rendezvous with Fate	Jeanne Sumerix	$8.95
Revelations	Cheris F. Hodges	$8.95
Rivers of the Soul	Leslie Esdaile	$8.95
Rocky Mountain Romance	Kathleen Suzanne	$8.95
Rooms of the Heart	Donna Hill	$8.95
Rough on Rats and Tough on Cats	Chris Parker	$12.95
Secret Library Vol. 1	Nina Sheridan	$18.95
Secret Library Vol. 2	Cassandra Colt	$8.95
Shades of Brown	Denise Becker	$8.95
Shades of Desire	Monica White	$8.95
Shadows in the Moonlight	Jeanne Sumerix	$8.95
Sin	Crystal Rhodes	$8.95

Other Genesis Press, Inc. Titles (continued)

So Amazing	Sinclair LeBeau	$8.95
Somebody's Someone	Sinclair LeBeau	$8.95
Someone to Love	Alicia Wiggins	$8.95
Song in the Park	Martin Brant	$15.95
Soul Eyes	Wayne L. Wilson	$12.95
Soul to Soul	Donna Hill	$8.95
Southern Comfort	J.M. Jeffries	$8.95
Still the Storm	Sharon Robinson	$8.95
Still Waters Run Deep	Leslie Esdaile	$8.95
Stories to Excite You	Anna Forrest/Divine	$14.95
Subtle Secrets	Wanda Y. Thomas	$8.95
Suddenly You	Crystal Hubbard	$9.95
Sweet Repercussions	Kimberley White	$9.95
Sweet Tomorrows	Kimberly White	$8.95
Taken by You	Dorothy Elizabeth Love	$9.95
Tattooed Tears	T. T. Henderson	$8.95
The Color Line	Lizzette Grayson Carter	$9.95
The Color of Trouble	Dyanne Davis	$8.95
The Disappearance of Allison Jones	Kayla Perrin	$5.95
The Honey Dipper's Legacy	Pannell-Allen	$14.95
The Joker's Love Tune	Sidney Rickman	$15.95
The Little Pretender	Barbara Cartland	$10.95
The Love We Had	Natalie Dunbar	$8.95
The Man Who Could Fly	Bob & Milana Beamon	$18.95
The Missing Link	Charlyne Dickerson	$8.95
The Price of Love	Sinclair LeBeau	$8.95
The Smoking Life	Ilene Barth	$29.95

Other Genesis Press, Inc. Titles (continued)

The Words of the Pitcher	Kei Swanson	$8.95
Three Wishes	Seressia Glass	$8.95
Ties That Bind	Kathleen Suzanne	$8.95
Tiger Woods	Libby Hughes	$5.95
Time is of the Essence	Angie Daniels	$9.95
Timeless Devotion	Bella McFarland	$9.95
Tomorrow's Promise	Leslie Esdaile	$8.95
Truly Inseparable	Wanda Y. Thomas	$8.95
Unbreak My Heart	Dar Tomlinson	$8.95
Uncommon Prayer	Kenneth Swanson	$9.95
Unconditional	A.C. Arthur	$9.95
Unconditional Love	Alicia Wiggins	$8.95
Until Death Do Us Part	Susan Paul	$8.95
Vows of Passion	Bella McFarland	$9.95
Wedding Gown	Dyanne Davis	$8.95
What's Under Benjamin's Bed	Sandra Schaffer	$8.95
When Dreams Float	Dorothy Elizabeth Love	$8.95
Whispers in the Night	Dorothy Elizabeth Love	$8.95
Whispers in the Sand	LaFlorya Gauthier	$10.95
Wild Ravens	Altonya Washington	$9.95
Yesterday Is Gone	Beverly Clark	$10.95
Yesterday's Dreams, Tomorrow's Promises	Reon Laudat	$8.95
Your Precious Love	Sinclair LeBeau	$8.95

Running for Jesus

Order Form

Mail to: Genesis Press, Inc.
P.O. Box 101
Columbus, MS 39703

Name ______________________________
Address ______________________________
City/State ______________ Zip ______________
Telephone ______________

Ship to (if different from above)
Name ______________________________
Address ______________________________
City/State ______________ Zip ______________
Telephone ______________

Credit Card Information
Credit Card # ______________ ☐Visa ☐Mastercard
Expiration Date (mm/yy) ______________ ☐AmEx ☐Discover

Qty.	Author	Title	Price	Total

Use this order form, or call 1-888-INDIGO-1

Total for books ______________
Shipping and handling:
$5 first two books,
$1 each additional book ______________
Total S & H ______________
Total amount enclosed ______________

Mississippi residents add 7% sales tax

Visit www.genesis-press.com for latest releases and excerpts.